Here Are My

A colllection of short stories for the imagination of

Dara J. Carr

Here Are My

A colllection of short stories for the imagination of

Dara J. Carr

San Antonio, Texas

Acknowledgements

I would like to acknowledge gratitude and thanks to Jeff L. Carr, Linda S. Carr, and Betty Powell for their assistance in making this happen.

Table of Contents

FORWARD

When you read through the story you may find several places where the laws of the land do not jive with what is being said. When I look at other stories, be it in movie, a book or television, I have found that some authors will use "Poetic License" to change things to fit their plot. If you watch the movie, "Liar, Liar," there is a glaring discrepancy where the law does not fit the outcome of the court case. If the proper legal decision were used in the movie it would ruin the plot (plus it might give a lot of minors an idea of how to try to get away with something). In "Star Trek" and "Quantum Leap" they constantly misused the laws of physics. A Certain US Senator said that he was being fired upon by the Khmer Rouge, while he was in Viet-Nam, even though that political group did not appear on any political scene until after the USA was out of Viet-Nam. If other authors of fiction and science fiction can use it - so can I. If a United States Senator can boldly get up and be some kind of historical revisionist then who are you or anyone else to say that I cannot. If you try to say that I cannot improvise, revise or use poetic license, then all I have for you is a very loud, sloppy raspberry.

BEING SERVED

Triyeetha rode into the town wondering what she could find here to obtain. The guards at the gate had not paid very much attention to her. It looked like a nice town, full of nice people. She hoped that they were nicer than the last town she had been in. Hopefully not so quick to judge and condemn…especially since, in the last town, she had not been anywhere near that snotty little woman who cried "thief." 'Of course, I'm a thief,' she thought. 'But I didn't steal *her* broach. The one that I had, I stole from that drunken prostitute.' Either way, she had to escape that town, quickly…and on a stolen equine.

She also hoped that these people did not judge her, because she was an Elf. There were so many places that did not like any Elf because of certain nasty races of Elf like the Galsino. The Galsino were easily identifiable by their bone-white skin, bulging red eyes and the fact that they had talons instead of hands. Triyeetha, on the other hand was a Dawm-Or Elf. She had the same normal features as humans, except the skin of her race was dark maroon and they had very dark hair and eyes.

She opened her pouch and counted her meager coins. Hopefully there was enough to get some kind of porridge or even just a loaf of fresh bread. Right now, she did not care what she could get her hands on, to shove down her throat.

She dismounted and just let the equine go. As it was with most of those animals, they knew where home was, and if she let it go, it

1

would...probably go home...maybe. If not, then who cares? The silly thing was well past it's prime.

She walked down the street, looking over the different taverns. Too expensive, too dirty, too loud...that one just had someone thrown out. 'Someone who was dressed better than me, and has a fatter pouch, on his side.'

The tossed customer got up and spewed several curses at the bouncer. The bouncer ignored it, until the curses mentioned the bouncer's mother. The bouncer stopped, shook his head, threw his arms out, turned and grabbed the loudmouth. He then, brutally, removed four or five of the loudmouth's teeth, with his fists.

As the loudmouth stumbled away, Triyeetha followed discretely. Maybe a good mark for a few more coins. Then she noticed that she was not the only one who was following the man. 'Too much competition,' she thought.

She walked on. She found an old woman, selling some kind of fruit she was not familiar with. The old woman did not want very much, so Triyeetha bought one. It had a very strange, however nice, flavor to it. She ate it all and sucked on it's rather large pit, for a while. She licked the sticky nectar off her fingers and then washed her hands off in a watering trough.

While washing her hands, she heard something that she thought she had left far behind her, in Eang or...somewhere else.

"Well, bless my soul," said the voice. "If it isn't that little purple-skinned twit, Triyeetha."

She turned and looked as disgusted as she possibly could. Yes, it was that big smart-mouthed Bertheelan warrior woman - Jantay. Jantay stood just eight and a half taja tall. She was strong as a bear and nothing but a bully from top to bottom. Her scraggly blonde hair formed an unkempt, tangled mane around her head. Her dark eyes seemed a little too small for her head. She did seem to be dressed a little better than what Triyeetha had ever seen before, in clean leather pants, a brown cotton shirt and high leather boots. She still looked just as strong and mean as Triyeetha remembered, and she still had that haughty grin on her face.

Seeing as how Triyeetha, just a little over six taja tall, had to stand a little distance from Jantay in order to keep from looking at the Bertheelan without hurting her neck. "Well, well…here you are again…just like one of those nasty diseases that you catch from a sailor."

Jantay gave one of those silly insincere laughs. "Just as witless as ever, purple-skin. I wonder, would you like to try and get some of your money back? I haven't seen a good sucker, like you, in some time. I enjoy taking your money and making a fool of you. Of course, when you do most of the work, making a fool of you is not a challenge."

"You haven't changed a bit." Triyeetha said, with a half-smile. "You're still even uglier than I am and you have the charm of a rabid dog. My skin is maroon, not purple."

Again, an insincere laugh. "Oh, that's right. What are you again? What do your people call themselves? Isn't it a dumb whore Elf?"

Triyeetha could feel her anger rising. "That's Dawm-Or, you

stupid fungus," she said slowly through clenched teeth.

Again the laugh. "Well, would you like to try getting some of the fortune that I have taken from you, back? This place is full of all kinds of people, who have more money than sense."

"I'll just do what I want to do and be where I want to be, thank you."

She started walking away as fast as she could. The problem there, of course, was that Jantay was almost two and a half taja taller. Her stride was much longer and she did come from a very hardy breed of strong soldiers. Triyeetha still tried to ignore her.

"What's the matter, little woman? Is your courage as small as your size? Why not try again? I'm always game for a good wager. Come on, one more time. What could it hurt?"

She realized that she would not be able to get rid of the arrogant Bertheelan until she gave in to one of the stupid wagers. Maybe getting rid of the equine was a mistake.

Triyeetha turned and glared at Jantay. "Every time I have been pulled into one of your wagers, it has always been rigged. You have always found some way of setting me up, to where I can't possibly win. You cheat! You are a cheat! You are a cheap cheat! All I want is to get by. You want to degrade and demolish. I won't stoop to your type of game. So no! The answer is no. Now, go away."

"Oh come on! You call it rigged, because you lost. You're just a poor loser. Come on now - I'll let you pick the place and set the rules."

Again she realized that the only way to get rid of Jantay was to attempt to set something up and then disappear. She looked at the tavern, where she had stopped. "This one! This one here. When the sun goes down, I leave. It's just before noon, so you can't go in before then. Tomorrow, you hit it. I'll bet that I have more money from the suckers, than you do. That's the bet."

Jantay looked slightly worried for a moment. Then she shrugged. "Okay. It's a bet." She looked a little upset for a moment. Then she cocked her head. "That's fair."

"Until then, leave me alone."

Jantay laughed and walked away. Triyeetha hung her head, looked back at the tavern and walked in. It was not as bad as it looked from the front. The place was…clean. Off to the right, a very old woman was selling porridge to customers. She thought for a moment and headed to the line. If she was going to sit down for a while, she had to have a good reason. Getting something to eat was a perfect way to be able to sit and look the place over. She did a little scoping, while in line.

She got up to the front of the line and pulled out her money. The old woman took what was required (which was most of what she had) and then used a big oversized ladle to fill a bowl. She then placed a wooden spoon in the bowl. Triyeetha took her porridge and walked to the nearest table. It was a long table, with equally long benches on each side. She sat down at one end, where she had a good view of the entire room. She counted her coins - now she was going to need to do a little pick pocketing if she was going to be able to afford her next meal.

A dwarf, dressed in rags, walked up and seated himself on the opposite side of Triyeetha's table, and at the opposite end. Triyeetha and the dwarf's eyes met in a quick glance. The dwarf then went to the task of attacking his bowl of porridge. Triyeetha did not pay the fellow any more attention. He looked as if he were in a worse position, financially, than she.

She took a mouthful of the porridge. It had mainly potatoes and carrots in it. There were some kind of other lumps, but she was not sure what they were. It tasted rather bland, but it was food.

She started scanning the other patrons of the tavern. None of them looked impressive. There were two men at a table near Triyeetha, who looked angry and started raising their voices.

'Oh no,' thought Triyeetha. 'Not now. Wait a few minutes, until I have some more of this muck in my stomach.' She quickly wolfed down a few mouthfuls, without chewing.

The two men who were arguing stood up. Triyeetha pulled the bowl up to her mouth and started slurping it down. They were getting louder.

One of the men was tall and skinny, with very greasy looking, long brown hair. The other was short and stocky. He was bald, had a thick, dirty looking black beard and no teeth. The small bearded man slapped the tall one. Triyeetha now took her spoon and started shoveling the stuff into her mouth. The dwarf turned and had a very worried look on his face. He turned back and started shoveling porridge into his mouth as well. The dirty beard took a bowl and threw it at the tall one, who side stepped the bowl. The bowl skipped off of Triyeetha's table. The dwarf took his bowl and quickly ducked under the table.

The tall one picked up one of the bench seats and tried to swing it at Dirty Beard. The bench was a little too cumbersome for that task and Tall Greasy started looking around for another weapon. Dirty Beard punched Tall Greasy in the stomach.

Triyeetha dropped her bowl and got up to escape. There was no way to get to the exit without getting uncomfortably close to the combatants. She looked around and took the only avenue she could see. She vaulted over the counter, where the old serving woman was, and ducked down, low enough to see what was going on, hopefully low enough that she would not get hit with anything.

Tall Greasy reached down under the table, where Triyeetha had been seated. He pulled the dwarf out from under the table, by the poor man's feet, and then swung the unfortunate man, like a club, at Dirty Beard. The dwarf's scream was cut off when he had head-to-head contact with Dirty Beard.

Triyeetha heard the old woman behind her shouting. She turned back and looked at the woman. Triyeetha was the object of the old woman's concern. She was ordering Triyeetha to get out of her area. Ignoring the old woman, she looked back at the fight. The old woman seemed to be the least of Triyeetha's worries.

Tall Greasy took at least three more swings with the unconscious dwarf. Dirty Beard was able to duck the swings and punch Tall Greasy in the stomach and chest several times. Tall Greasy threw the ill-fated dwarf off to the side and started wrestling with Dirty Beard.

Triyeetha felt a horrible sting in the back of her head. She put both of her hands on the pained area and felt a wetness. She pulled her hands out in front of her face to see if it was blood - it was gravy

(?). She looked back at the old woman. The woman had the big ladle raised up to strike again, the ladle had a big dent on the underside of it's bowl. She swung at Triyeetha. She saw this one coming and was able to catch the ladle in her hands. She yanked it out of the old woman's grasp and threw it off to the side. She did not need an attack on some gray-haired old lady on her record. She turned to try and get back over the counter, feeling very groggy. She tried to pull herself up onto the counter and felt another painful sting on the back of her head. As she lost consciousness, all she could think of was the old biddy had clubbed her again…with a lousy long-handled serving spoon.

She woke up, face down, on a bed of foul smelling hay. There was light coming in through a small window, that was high up, but she could not tell whether it was still the same day or not. She pushed herself up a little and looked around. She groaned as she realized that she was in some kind of prison cell…along with a couple of passed out drunks, who had obviously vomited all over themselves. She sat up and felt the back of her head. She could feel two large knots, along with some congealed gravy and a couple of unidentifiable lumps. She pulled the lumps out of her hair and looked at them - a piece of a potato and two pieces of a carrot. She sighed and popped them into her mouth. No telling when she would be able to get something to eat.

She had to urinate and was not sure whether she should call a guard and request the use of an outhouse or just let it flow in here. The smell in the cell left no doubt, that some other people had used this place as a "facility." She looked at the two drunks, sitting side-by-side. She got up, opened her pants and relieved herself, on the floor, between the two cell-mates. Neither one of them moved.

8

After closing her pants up, she turned and went to the bars of the cell. The hallway was what would be expected. Other cells on the other side, with other prisoners sitting there looking totally despondent. She sank to her knees and joined them in their melancholy silence.

Two guards came in. They went to one of the other cells and pulled a man out. His hands were shackled to a belly band and chains were on his ankles as well. He tried to fight them, but had little success.

One of the guards laughed and said: "Time for the gallows for you, whore-killer."

They dragged him out and it was quiet again.

Eight more guards walked in, stretching and scratching as if they had just awakened. Each one walked over to two buckets that were near the end of the hallway. Each one urinated in the buckets. Triyeetha, again, looked around her cell to see if there was any form of a chamber pot in here…nope!

One big guard stopped by Triyeetha's cell and looked at the two drunks. He gave an evil laugh and looked back at his colleagues. He shrugged and said: "Why not?" Several of the others laughed as well. Two of them went and picked up the urine buckets, while another unlocked the cell door. They walked in with the buckets.

'Oh no,' thought Triyeetha. 'They wouldn't…"

Yes, they would! They did! The two drunks were splashed with the contents of the buckets. Both men sat there sputtering. When they realized what they had been splashed with, they both gave a cry of surprise and tried to wipe the "liquid" off their faces as the guards guffawed and giggled.

"Get up you two," growled one of the guards. "This is not an inn."

The two men got up slowly, giving the guards a nasty look. They both stumbled out of the cell, still trying to wipe any "moisture" off of themselves.

A new man walked into the corridor. He was dressed better than any of the guards and was carrying some papers with him. The demeanor of all of the guards changed as soon as he walked in. The two drunks stopped and looked at him expectantly. The new man sniffed the air and looked at the two drunks in total disgust.

"Oh, you useless slobs! Get out of here and go…clean yourselves up." He looked around at assembled guards. "The execution went well. I don't know how you got that fool to keep his mouth shut, but there are those who do, really appreciate it."

"We cut out his tongue, two days ago," said one of the guards.

"What? That wasn't part of his punishment."

"No, milord, but we were getting a little tired of all of his disobedient yelling at us."

The head guard contemplated for a few moments and shrugged. "Where is the stranger who assaulted the old woman?"

Four of the guards pointed at Triyeetha.

Triyeetha could do nothing but sit there shocked. She stood up. "Who assaulted who? I'm the one with the lumps on my head. I didn't have time to attack anybody. Those two fools started a fight and

I tried to get out of the way. I didn't hit anybody."

The chief guard walked up to her. "That is for his Lordship, the Magistrate, to decide." He turned back to the guards. "Clean this fool up a little…before you take her in for judgment. The Magistrate does not like the smell of some of the prisoners that are brought before him."

Two of the guards grabbed Triyeetha and roughly hauled her out of the cell. She was virtually carried outside, where they walked over to a very dirty looking stream and hurled her in. The water was only thigh deep, so standing up, after the soaking, was not hard.

"Come on back, this way," said the bigger guard. "We don't want to have to chase you. That would make things worse for you… and more fun for us."

Triyeetha had seen enough of their fun, so she grudgingly obeyed. As she got out of the water, she did not think that she smelled any better. The stream looked as if it was even dirtier than she.

The two guards, with swords drawn, escorted her to the hall of justice. They had to wait outside for a while because of some other things going on inside.

When she was finally allowed to go in, she saw Jantay sitting in the spectator area of the courtroom. Usually, when dragged up in front of a Judge, she would give a false name. With Jantay here, that could only serve to hurt. That vindictive crud would, in all probability, let the court know what Triyeetha's real name was. She could do nothing but wait until she heard what was going on.

A very fancily dressed man pointed at Triyeetha. The two

guards prodded her with their swords and she headed up to see the Judge. The Judge was one of those self-righteous looking prudes with that stupidly long, fancy wig and frilly looking, multi-colored silk outfits. After reading a document, the Judge looked down his nose at Triyeetha.

"Your name?" snapped the Judge.

She sighed. "Triyeetha."

The Judge raised his eyebrows and cocked his head to the right as if he were expecting more. After hearing nothing, the Judge looked off to the side and huffed: "Of?"

Triyeetha rolled her eyes. 'So that's what the silly old coot wants.' She took in a deep breath. "Of the Dawm-Or Elven race. Most recently of the cargo ship, *Ranifar*, out of some port in Chogine."

The Judge looked a little surprised. "What…did you jump ship?"

Triyeetha felt her hackles rise a little. "No, Milord." She tried to control her breathing. "I was shanghaied, in some port, in Chogine. They forced me to sign on the ship for three years of servitude. The three years was up a few days ago. They wanted me to sign on again but I ran as fast as I could from that ship…I am not a sailor, Milord. I owe it no more allegiance."

"We can check on that story, to find out whether or not you are telling the truth."

Triyeetha smiled. "You have my permission to do so."

"Impertinence will only make things worse for you," snapped the Judge. "I suggest you keep the sarcasm out of here."

Triyeetha rolled her eyes again. 'How could it get worse?' she thought.

"So…Triyeetha, why did you assault the old serving wench at the Fork Road Tavern?"

Triyeetha clenched her teeth. "I didn't assault anybody. There was a fight that broke out and I tried to avoid it. Somehow, I got my head busted and woke up in that smelly cell. I didn't have time to attack anybody because I was too busy trying to avoid being in the fight."

The Judge raised his eyebrows. "We have witnesses who saw and say differently."

Before Triyeetha could argue the point, another fancy dressed man brought two men in: Tall Greasy and Dirty Beard. The two started telling some yarn about how Triyeetha had been the main instigator of the fight and that they had just been peacefully sitting there eating, when the whole thing started. They also spun a yarn about the injured dwarf, being attacked by her.

She had never killed intentionally. Now, she was seriously contemplating the thought of changing that thought process, for these two pieces of trash.

Now, they got to the old woman. She, like the dwarf, was not in attendance. She, like the dwarf, was too badly injured to show up, at today's proceedings.

Triyeetha gave up any idea of getting out of here without incarceration. Those two liars were local. Triyeetha was an outsider. What was the norm for a situation like that was definitely looking like it was going to happen.

To add insult to injury, Tall Greasy and Dirty Beard also put in an addendum to their story - Triyeetha had intentionally dented the old woman's serving spoon after the fight. Now, she was absolutely planning two counts of first degree murder.

The Magistrate looked sternly at Triyeetha. "You caused injury to two people, you could have caused injury to these two men…and just to be vindictive, you damaged that old woman's serving ladle." He closed his eyes and shook his head a little. "Causing the fight was bad enough…but injuring the old woman…stupid. Damaging her spoon, just for evil fun…really stupid. Before I pass sentence, do you have anything to say for yourself?"

"You mean…like the truth? I've already given you the truth and you've ignored it. What difference would it make what I say?"

He shook his head sadly. "No remorse, whatsoever. Where does trash, like you, come from?"

She thought of saying: "Same place as you came from." She thought of it, but…better not.

"I can pass a sentence of financial reparation - do you have any money?"

Her shoulders sagged. "The guards, in that jail, picked me clean of everything. Where would I have been able to keep any money?"

"Then, unless someone will pay the money, for you, you will have to spend some time in prison. So…"

"Milord, Judge!" shouted Jantay. "I have need of a servant. I seem to be having a tough time finding anyone who will work for me. Would I be able to take her…as an indentured servant?"

Triyeetha looked back and saw Jantay standing in the back of the room. At eight and half taja tall, she was hard to miss - when standing.

The Judge stared at her for a few moments. He cleared his throat. "Are you prepared to take care of the financial reparations… for her?"

Jantay was taken aback. "Well…yes, but…I thought I could have her as a servant…why would I have to pay?"

"If you pay her fine, then she is definitely, financially beholden to you. Then, you will be able to claim her, as an indentured servant, working off the financial burden that has been inflicted on you."

"All right, Milord. I can live with that."

"Very well. Come forward. The scribe has all of the necessary notes on all of the finances. Once you have paid the money, she is your indentured servant for the next seven years."

Triyeetha's shoulders sagged even lower. Seven flaming years as an indentured servant to that hag. 'Why didn't I just run?' she thought.

Jantay came up and looked the document over. She shrugged and pulled her fat money pouch off of her belt. She counted out several large coins and handed them to the scribe. He counted them and nodded to the Judge.

"This court is content. You now have a servant for seven years. You are accountable and responsible for her activities in this area. If she gets into any more mischief, you will have to answer for all such occurrences."

Jantay smiled. "Of course, Milord. Don't worry. I'll keep her on a very short leash."

Triyeetha was taken from the courtroom to a blacksmith. There, they put slave bracelets on her wrists. There were rings on the bracelets so a chain could be hooked in, if necessary. The bracelets did not trouble her, much. She had been 'decorated' like this before and had found a way to get them off. The escape was what was bothering her. She was going to have to bide her time until she could figure some way of getting away...clean.

Jantay grabbed hold of the back of Triyeetha's shirt and dragged her off to her new home...for the next seven years...maybe.

They arrived at a small house, that unlike most of the houses in this area, did not share a wall with any other house and it had a fence that completely encompassed the yard. Triyeetha could see that there was a vegetable garden in the front and on each side.

'Oh great,' she thought. 'Now I'm going to be a gardener. I hate digging in the dirt.'

Jantay went up to the door. She pulled on two strings that were hanging from the top of the door and heard two thumps. Then she opened the door. Hanging, just inside the door, were two rather large rocks.

Triyeetha wondered how many more booby traps were strategically located throughout the house.

Jantay looked up at the sun and grunted in disgust. "I think that you will start in the basement. Yes, cleaning the basement is first."

"A pigsty with a basement? Well, I never," Triyeetha said sarcastically.

Jantay gave a look of disgust and then dragged Triyeetha to a ring on the floor. The ring was pulled and a trapdoor opened the way to the basement. Triyeetha was then dragged down the stairs. There was a window on each of the four sides of the basement and it let in a somewhat dim light.

"Now, slave, you are going to clean this place up and arrange everything."

Triyeetha looked around incredulously. "Clean what? There's nothing here but junk. Broken crates, broken casks, broken barrels… nothing is down here but firewood. I don't see anything in the broken crates, there is nothing leaking out of the casks or barrels…clean what? Arrange what?"

"Just do what you're told to do." With that Jantay headed back up the stairs.

Triyeetha wandered around the piles of junk for a few moments. Then threw her arms out in disgust. "How does that idiot want this stuff arranged?" She walked back up the stairs to ask the question. Jantay was not in the house. There was no place for someone that big to hide inside this place, so she went to a front window and looked out.

She immediately ducked down and hissed in anger. She slowly got back up and peeked out the window. Standing in the front garden, with Jantay, was Tall Greasy and Dirty Beard. Jantay was counting out some money as she dropped it into their cupped hands. When she finished, the two of them looked at each other, looking just a little upset. Triyeetha perked her ears up to try to get any information, she could.

"That's not enough," said Dirty Beard.

"You promised more," said Tall Greasy.

"I also told you, that if you broke the place up, the damages would come out of your pay. You broke three benches, two tables and two people got hurt, not to mention something of a big ladle." Jantay looked at both of them impatiently. "Now, get out of here…before the fool finds out about you two."

"But, we need enough money…to get passage back to Kipat," said Dirty Beard. "This is barely enough for one…in steerage!"

"Maybe we should tell that fool," said Tall Greasy. "Maybe she'll help us get back at you and get us some more money."

Jantay slapped Tall Greasy on the side of his head. He went down hard. "Don't you even think of doing that! If the Magistrate finds out about that, then he'll put you in jail for telling lies in court."

Tall greasy picked up several coins that he had dropped.

Dirty Beard looked at her angrily. "How do we get more money? We need more, to get passage, and then we have to have something when we get there."

Jantay looked up disgusted. "Come back, in two days…after lunch time. I'll see what I can do. Until then, stay out of sight."

Triyeetha turned and in a quick crawl headed back to and down the stairs. She wanted to break something. Everything down here was already broken so that just added to her frustration. She knew that she was not strong enough to out-muscle Jantay but she had to figure out some way of getting out of this mess. Until then, she had to arrange *this* mess.

She decided to arrange the junk by name: Broken crates, over there - broken casks, over there and broken barrels, over there. Any other junk that turned up would be in the last corner.

Jantay came down the stairs. "Come on back up, it's time for you to fix some lunch. You get to cook it."

She dropped the cask she was holding. "You missed *my* cooking?"

"No, stupid, I missed having someone else cook it, while I'm relaxing. Now get up here and start making some lunch."

She slowly went back up the stairs. On the table, she found a few potatoes, carrots and some kind of tuber (that she was not familiar with). She took the big knife on the table and started cutting them up, wishing that the knife were going through Jantay's throat, instead. She then took the diced vegetables to the fireplace. There was a large kettle hanging there and it already had some old stew, still in it. She dumped the new stuff in and swung the kettle over the fire.

When she turned back, she saw that Jantay had taken the big knife off of the table and was cleaning it. She then snickered at Triyeetha as she put the knife in her belt. She then went to a chest and opened it. She dropped the knife in the chest and then took several moments, fiddling with something, before closing the chest.

'How rude,' Triyeetha thought. 'She doesn't trust me. Of course, I wouldn't trust me either…but she's just…rude.'

Jantay pulled a chair up to the table and sat down with her back to the fireplace. "There's a spoon over in that cabinet. Get it and stir the stew."

Triyeetha silently scowled at Jantay. She opened the cabinet and found the stirring spoon. It looked very much like the spoon, from the tavern, except it was a little shorter. She pulled the spoon and two bowls out and went back to the fireplace. She put the bowls down, away from the fire. She stirred the new vegetables into the stuff that was already there. She looked down in the kettle in disgust. There was no telling how old the other stuff was and whether or not it was fit to eat.

"How old is this other muck in the kettle?"

Jantay laughed. "Don't worry, I don't like the idea of poisoning myself. That stew is only two days old."

"Oh? Is that the last time you were making some nasty brew, using the dark arts?"

"Oh, aren't we funny. Stop trying to be funny. You have no talent for it."

She continued stirring the stuff while Jantay sat at the table guzzling some kind of wine. Triyeetha wondered where the wine had come from, seeing as how she had not noticed Jantay getting it from anywhere.

"Hey fool! I saw that you had two bowls. Were you planning on eating something now…with me? If you are, forget it. You eat when I decide you eat. Put the other bowl away."

She grudgingly took one of the bowls back to the cabinet. Then she returned to the kettle. The contents were now bubbling and there was a somewhat pleasant aroma coming out of the kettle.

"Serve it up, fool! I'm hungry, now! Use the big serving ladle. Only don't ding my ladle up, the way you did the one at the tavern. Honestly, I don't know why you had to damage her spoon. What did she ever do to you?"

She froze in shock. She looked to the left of the hearth, then to the right. She got a huge evil grin on her face when she saw the big long-handled serving spoon hanging to the right of the hearth.

She swung the kettle out and picked up the bowl. She took the big ladle and scooped some of the stew out of the pot. She slowly poured the stew in the bowl. She then lovingly cleaned the ladle, as she felt the weight of it in her hands. The whole time, she still had the big grin on her face.

"Where's the food, fool?"

She cleared her throat, and snarled: "It's coming."

"When?"

"Now."

She walked over to Jantay with the bowl in her left hand. She held the ladle in her right hand, slightly hidden. She came up to Jantay's right and placed the bowl down in front of the big woman. She turned to her right, took two steps, then turned and swung the big ladle as hard as possible. It made a strange hollow sound when it hit Jantay's head. Her head snapped forward on contact. Triyeetha stepped back to watch the Bertheelan fall…she didn't. She sat back up shakily. She had her hands out as if trying to grab something to steady herself. Triyeetha brought the ladle up again and did a full round house swing at the other side of Jantay's head. Again that hollow "thwock" sound. This time, Jantay fell off of the chair and went face down on the floor. She slowly put her hands on the floor and tried to push herself up. Triyeetha took the ladle in a high, arcing swing and clubbed Jantay in the back of the head. Now, she lay still.

Triyeetha listened for breathing. It was easy and regular. Finally, that big headache was out cold. Triyeetha had heard that the Bertheelan warrior women were hard-headed but she thought that people were talking figuratively, not literally.

She sat down and quickly ate the stew in the bowl. She looked down at Jantay several times, to make sure she was not faking. "I'll eat, when *I'm* ready," she said sarcastically.

After her hunger had abated, she went to check this chest where the knife had been placed. She examined it closely and saw what Jantay had been fiddling with - a booby trap. It was not very sophisticated, however, if you were not looking for one, it could cause considerable pain. She snickered as she "deactivated" the trap, so as not to get injured by it. She then opened the chest.

There was a lot of junk associated with the status of a Bertheelan warrior. Worthless to anyone else, but almost sacred to Bertheelans.

She found the carving knife and…money (!). There were several big pouches of coins. Some of the coins were foreign currency - some of which, Triyeetha was unfamiliar with, but most of it, she knew. She took all of the money, in the chest, she could find and put the pouches on the table.

She then went back to close the chest - and had a very nasty idea. She found a few little goodies in the chest and a few outside of it and she rigged her own little trap, for Jantay. She then reset the original trap and closed the chest.

Jantay groaned and started stirring. Triyeetha grabbed the ladle and went over to the big woman. As she was trying to get up, Triyeetha swung hard again and belted Jantay in the head again. This time she flipped over on her back. She once again, lay there motionless.

Triyeetha got another vicious idea. She quickly knelt down and opened Jantay's pants. Triyeetha then opened her pants and peed down into Jantay's crotch. After finishing, Triyeetha closed Jantay's pants. She stood up, closing her pants, feeling deliciously naughty.

She looked down at Jantay: "If the puddle had been on the outside of your pants, you would have known what happened. This way, you'll never really know, that it wasn't you who wet yourself."

She went to the door and peered out. She went to each side of the house and looked around at the area. She went to look out the back door. She saw a large shed of some type, behind the house. It was inside the fence so it had to be a part of the property. She opened the door and walked out to the shed, as if nobody had a better right.

She walked in the shed and found that it was a very small barn, complete with a big roan stallion, saddle, saddlebags and a few other interesting items.

She went back into the house, belted Jantay in the head again, and then headed back to the barn with the money pouches and the big ladle. She saddled the equine and headed out.

There was no telling how long Jantay would be out. Triyeetha hoped that it would be long enough. If not that, then hopefully she would be too groggy to do anything for a while.

She did not want to head out of the town, the same way she had come in. She might end up going past that same tavern and that could be disastrous to her escape.

She came up to a different gate and got another evil idea. "Ho, guardsman! Your attention, please!"

One of the guards looked up, rather bored. "What is it, citizen?"

"Do you know of that big Bertheelan woman, Jantay?"

The guard rolled his eyes. "Who doesn't know of that trouble maker?"

"Well, she was entrusted, with a law-breaker, as an indentured servant."

"So?"

"So…she was supposed to keep the law-breaker as a servant for seven years. She let her go!"

The guard perked up and three others were now giving Triyeetha their undivided attention.

"Well that's just…criminal! If she was supposed to keep the law-breaker, she shouldn't let a criminal go."

"Well, she did. I suggest that you say something to his Lordship, the Magistrate."

"Oh, yes we will investigate it. Thank you, citizen."

She headed through the gate as one runner was sent off to inform the garrison commander and another to check on Jantay.

She chuckled as he left.

A short distance out of town, she saw Tall Greasy sitting against a tree by the side of the road, asleep. She dismounted from the equine and slowly walked over to Tall Greasy. The smell told her that she was looking at a man, who was passed out drunk.

She then heard a noise off to her left. She quickly slouched down and headed towards the noise. Dirty Beard was leaning against a tree, relieving his bladder.

She ran back to the equine. She untied a long-handled serving ladle off of the saddlebags. She ran back to Dirty Beard. Before the man could do anything, she smacked him in the back of the head… with the ladle. Dirty Beard fell forward…into his own puddle. She then relieved Dirty Beard of his money pouch.

She walked back over to Tall Greasy. The man was still sound asleep. She figured that this man should have a knot on his head just like the other two conspirators. Tall Greasy never knew what hit him or why.

She then took Tall Greasy's money pouch as well.

She snickered as she left the two unconscious men. "It will be even longer before you ever get to Kipat now."

She then headed off, hoping that she would never come in contact with Jantay again.

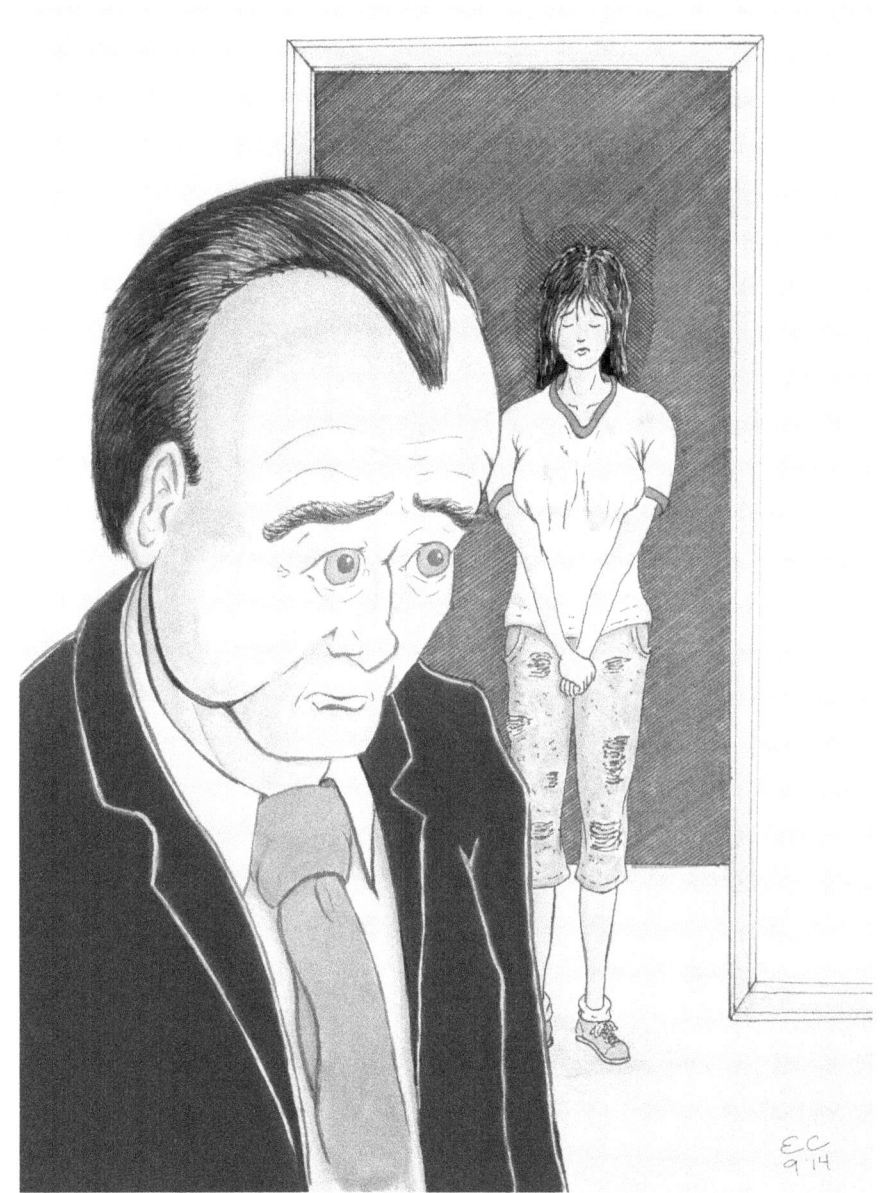

BAD...DREAM?

The two men sat on opposite sides of the desk, rechecking their figures. All of the money from the offering plates, had been counted and recounted in order to make sure that they were in agreement on the final figure. On one side of the desk was a short, thin man who had just wisps of brown hair left on his head and a bit of a smile showing in his eyes. He had come up with the same figure all three times.

The man on the other side of the desk, a man who was also thin and just a little taller, with dark, thick hair was adding the figures on a calculator, for the fifth time, trying to come up with the correct amount, or at least the same amount twice. He was trying not to show any consternation, but was a little unsuccessful at hiding it. His counterpart worked at a bank, and was, irritatingly, always correct in his final figure. His tally finally agreed with what his colleague had come up with, so he decided that it was best to leave it at that.

The smaller man had already finished annotating all of the checks on the deposit slip and was waiting for what would be the final decision on the cash. "Did Pastor Fontenot say how much needed to go into the 'cash on hand' fund?"

"Yeah, he said that we needed to replace about six hundred dollars."

The smaller man looked shocked. "Six hundred? Why so much?"

"That windstorm played havoc on our outside storage shed, and the Winslow family had that fire. Both situations were taken care of from the fund."

The smaller man nodded. "Okay, yeah, I forgot about the fire. How is that family doing, after the fire?"

"It wasn't that bad. The fire was isolated to that one room and we nailed some plywood planks up, in order to keep people out of that room as well as hoodlums from sneaking into the house."

"Wasn't there supposed to be a little set aside for that special women's meeting on Thursday?"

"Yeah, though I'm not sure how much Mrs. Davenport needs."

"Well that's all right. I know how much is in there and you'll be getting the deposit slip to me tomorrow anyway. Just annotate how much you give her on a slip of paper and stick it in the pouch."

"If anything else comes up, I'll make an annotation of that, as well."

"What else could possibly come up?"

"You know full well that there's always someone who need something. Why don't you take the checks and coins and finalize that deposit slip and I'll take care of the paper on a separate one?"

"Sound's good." He leaned back and stretched. "Been a long day."

The taller man just chuckled.

The shorter man finalized the checks, placed them in a pouch along with the coins and headed out with a friendly wave.

The taller man dropped the six hundred dollars through the one-way slot in the top of the safe. He then took a look at what he had left. All of the currency was in neat stacks, according to denomination. He quickly figured what he had left, minus the six hundred. He needed to get in touch with Mrs. Davenport and a couple of other people in order to find out if any other emergencies had arisen. He stacked up the cash and placed it in another pouch.

"Excuse me," came a woman's voice.

He looked up a little startled from not expecting anyone and then he stared in shock at what he saw. Standing in the doorway was a very unkempt, thin woman who was either in her late teens or early twenties. Her stringy hair was hanging down in a matted mess. Her threadbare T-shirt showed that she was wearing nothing underneath it. The rips and holes in her ratty blue jeans gave the impression that there was no underwear under the pants either. She looked (and smelled) as if she had not taken a bath in weeks.

"Can I help you…" he stammered nervously.

She smiled. I understand that you're the one to talk to about possibly getting some money…for what I need it for."

"I am one of the deacons for this church, so yes, I can help with certain…financial things…if needed."

She smiled again. "There's a family who needs some help… right now. They both lost their jobs, some time ago, and they have some children. They've run out of money and they're not sure what to do. They're getting kinda desperate."

"Uh, well, I'm…not sure…what I could do right now."

"If you could just give me some money…then I could give it to them."

He felt a little troubled at the request. "We don't just hand out cash. If they need help, then I can buy some food and take it to them."

"How much food?"

"How many children are there?"

"Four or five…I'm not sure."

He felt that the request was getting really suspicious. "I can't give you cash, I can buy some food and take it to them."

She had a nervous smile. "Okay."

"I have to do something, and then I'll be right with you. You can wait out there on the couch."

She looked a little troubled. She glanced off to her right at the couch in the other room. She shrugged, looked slightly upset and then headed for the couch.

He was relieved to get her out of the office. He scooped up the cash quickly and shoved most of it through the slot into the safe. He quickly counted two hundred dollars in twenties and then put the rest of the twenties into the safe. He figured that two hundred should get a family of six something that would get them through a few days. He scribbled a quick note and shoved it into the safe. He then headed into the other room while pocketing the money.

She saw him and stood up. "Ready?"

He nearly gagged. Where she had been sitting on the couch, she had left a body print of grime. He wondered just what it would take to get that couch cleaned…or if it was worth trying to clean that mess off of it.

She looked at him a little confused. "You…okay?"

He fought off his disgust. "Yes," he said weakly. "Uh…let's go."

They headed out to his car. He was polite and opened the passenger door for her. When she sat down, he thought of the filth that had been left behind on the couch. He fought off another wave of nausea. "Well go to the supermarket first," he said, trying to not think of the grunge.

"Sounds good," she said with a mysterious looking smile.

As he drove to the store, he wondered if his interior would ever be clean again. He was going to have to scrub it…hard. He could not remember his children ever making a mess this bad…in the car. He rolled his window down in order to blow her smell away from him.

Upon arrival at the store, she got out of the car quickly. He looked at the passenger seat and shook his head sadly. What had possessed him to get a white interior? He decided that it would never be clean again.

Once inside, he began to wonder if she was telling the truth. The things that she was putting in the cart did not make sense. Chips, beer, jerky, soda pop, dips…she looked as if she were preparing for a party. She seemed a bit upset when he put all those things back and replaced them with soups, canned vegetables, bread, cold cuts, cereal, orange juice and milk. She seemed reluctant to surrender to his shopping list instead of hers, but gave in without too much complaint.

He spent almost all of the two hundred. He made it a point to keep track of the receipt.

When she put some of the bags in the trunk, she left just as much grime on the bags as she had everywhere else. Her filth trail seemed to be unending.

He sighed. "Okay, where do we go from here?"

She gave him some strange directions. He did not argue, he just followed her instructions while still fighting off his gag reflex. They headed completely out of town. They were in a rural area that he was completely unfamiliar with. They left the paved road. On and on he drove. He checked his watch…almost two hours of driving. He was baffled. How had she originally been able to get to the church?

He was driving along the face of a cliff when she told him to turn left. At first he thought she had gone completely mad, when he saw an opening in the cliff.

He was shocked again. "Are you serious? You want me to drive inside that cave?"

"There's enough room," she said cheerfully.

'No wonder, she's so dirty,' he thought. When he had first seen her, he had humorously wondered if she was living in a cave…she did.

He turned on his headlights and slowly turned into the cave. Moving along carefully, he noticed that there did seem to be sufficient space on either side. He was still not ready to speed up…in here.

She cheerfully steered him through a few twists and turns in the cave. They came into a large underground room. Finally, she told him that they had arrived.

He looked around incredulously. He saw no humans in the cave. There seemed to be a strange green glow, coming from some kind of moss on the walls of the cave. He looked around for... something. He opened his door and his nose was assaulted by a smell that would make a cesspool seem pleasant.

She got out and had an evil grin on her face. "We're here!" she shouted. "I brought him!"

He looked around confused. 'Who is she talking too?'

Her voice had echoed throughout the huge space.

Something in the middle of the room started moving. It... stood up...? Rose up...? Changed shape...?

A portion of it rose up at the top of the...whatever it is. It seemed to have a face...maybe. It looked as if someone had tried to make a face by throwing the different parts at the face and had had very bad aim. It started talking. The voice sounded like stone and metal grating against each other. "What did you bring, slave?"

"I brought a new one. One that will take my place. You promised that if I brought one, you would let me go."

The thing seemed to look around. "What did he do, that he should replace you?"

"He stole money from his church," she said triumphantly.

"Stole?" it said. "Did he take it for himself? Did he use it for pleasures of the flesh? Did he take it for illegal personal gain? No, he used it for that which it was intended! Charity!"

The girl looked terrified. "But, he...the money...he wasn't supposed to...what charity?"

"Purchasing food for a needy family. That is a charity. He has a receipt that he is going to give back to the church. He has left a note, letting his counterparts know what he did with that money. Now, what sin has he committed, that makes him worse than you, that he should replace you?"

She swallowed hard and looked around desperately. She opened her mouth trying to say something, but could not think of anything to say.

Suddenly the ground opened up under her and she screamed as she disappeared into the hole.

The thing turned its' attention to the man. "Go!" it said angrily. "Leave my presence!" Some kind of smoke flew out of the thing towards the man. The smoke hit the man and knocked him back.

He stood up screaming and waving his hands in shock and horror. He looked around him and was startled to see that he was back in the counting room. He looked down at the desk and saw the cash sitting there still laying there in their neat stacks. The tally sheet was next to the stacks, with the pen, waiting for him to annotate how much Mrs. Davenport was going to need.

He laughed nervously. "It was a dream," he said in a shaking voice. "It was just a...strange, silly dream."

He sat down. He chuckled again, trying to calm himself down. Perspiration was pouring down off his face and his heart was pounding. He was breathing as if he had just finished running a very long sprint. He tried to dry the sweat off his forehead, with his sleeve and found that the shirt was just as wet as his brow. He shook his head.

He headed to the water dispenser to get some cold water. His body was covered with sweat but his throat was parched. He pulled one of the flimsy little paper cups out of its' dispenser and attempted to fill it with water. His hands were shaking so badly that the innocent little cup was totally mutilated. He dropped the damaged cup and tried another one. This one received the same deformation without him getting any water in his mouth.

With his eyes, teeth and fists clenched, he spoke to no one in particular: "It was only a dream." He repeated it over and over, trying to calm himself.

After several moments of controlled breathing and hand wringing he finally calmed down…a little.

"Excuse me," came a woman's voice.

He looked up a little startled and his heart nearly skipped a beat. Standing in the doorway was a very unkempt, thin woman who was either in her late teens or early twenties. Her stringy hair was hanging down in a matted mess. Her threadbare T-shirt showed that she was wearing nothing underneath it. The rips and holes in her ratty blue jeans gave the impression that there was no underwear under the pants either. She looked (and smelled) as if she had not taken a bath in weeks…

FIGHT FOR WHAT IS RIGHTFULLY YOURS

The Healer stroked his chin slowly. "I really don't' know. I've been doing this for almost sixty years…and I have never seen anything like this disease."

Princess Hanooya clenched her fists. She scanned the faces of the five Healers. She saw fatigue, frustration, anger, confusion and sadness. "Is there anything, in your collection of smelly potions and noisy spells that will do something, to cure him?"

Munkron, the oldest spoke up: "We have found nothing, in our books of history, that describe this malady. All we can do is slow the effects, and prolong his life…for a short while…but…no permanent cure or…" He trailed off. He shut his dark brown eyes. "Your Majesty, I have never felt so helpless in my life. I will consult the Sibilitak, in prayer."

Hanooya was enraged. "Sibilitak! Who is that? What is that? I'm tired of hearing the names of all the supposed omnipotent beings that do nothing for us. First, I see my brother Chontayn, come down with this disease - you pray - he dies, and no god helped. Then Perimon and Soltearn fall sick. Again the prayers. They are both dead. All three of the princes of the realm die of this disease. Now the king is rotting away, and what do you do? Pray? Why? What good has that done anyone, so far?" She stormed out of the room, muttering a few more blasphemies about the gods.

She flicked her long brown hair off of her face in frustration. All the sorrow that she had seen over the past few months were beginning to really take a toll on her.

She remembered all three of her brothers. They had been strong proud men. Like her, they had all three inherited the thick brown hair of their father. She had her mother's vibrant green eyes, while her brothers were all brown-eyed, like their father. Her brothers had been tall and big boned. She was like her mother - short, but full figured, and did not really have any of the toughness of her brothers. Of course not! She was a princess, she was never trained to be tough... gracious and tender, but not tough.

Princess Hanooya looked at the huntsman. "Pelroosh, I would like an elven maidservant. One of those of the Shan-Karoot tribe.

His eyes widened and his mouth fell open in shock. "A... what?"

"You heard me."

"Yes, I did...but...why?"

She gave him a polite smile. "Just do as I say."

He tried several times to say something.

Hanooya put her hand on his shoulder. "I want this new maidservant here, as soon as possible."

His face went blank. His shoulders sagged. "If you insist..."

"I do."

"Yes, your highness. As soon…as I can; I will return with… the uh…your request."

As he left, he shook his head several times. He ran it over in his mind, but could not make sense of it. 'A Shan-Karoot? Why? Doesn't she know how dangerous they are? Maybe it's the grief she's going through.'

Princess Hanooya walked silently into her father's private chambers. The only sounds were his ragged breathing, and the crackling from the fireplace. She readied herself, and walked up to his bed. The smell of his disease was horrible. The skin on his face had turned dark brown, mottled with gray and green spots. A black furry fungus was where his right eye had once been.

She closed her eyes and swallowed hard.

"Yes, it is a frightful sight," he said calmly.

She gasped, and moved back a step. She looked at his face again.

"Yes, I'm awake." He smiled. "I'm not dead yet, neither are my senses. You're wearing that lovely perfume, that I like so much."

She gave him the kindest smile that she could muster.

"Last night, I had what I thought was a dream." The smile was replaced by anger. "It was a visitation. That animal that I married, after your mother died. It was her." He closed his eye and sighed. "*She* is doing this. *She* is the one who killed my sons."

"But how could she...why would she?" Hanooya was confused.

"She is a master of one of those magical arts. She planned this years ago. She is the one that gave your mother, that deadly sickness." He looked up at her. "She comforted me, in my grief, when your mother died. She trapped my affections. I married her, and took her to my bed."

"I know that - what about this...visitation?"

"She has a son - my son. She has been training him for the last seventeen years. Training him to take my throne and rule this kingdom, as she sees fit."

"But, I'm eighteen...how could he become king? I'm older than her son, and I'm from your first wife."

"I know, my sweet, but you're a woman." He sighed miserably. "The only way that you could become the reigning sovereign, is if I had no sons, and no wife."

"But you could deny that he is your son. Deny him and I'll be named, your only remaining child. I'll inherit the throne that way."

"It won't work. She registered his birth, and I endorsed it. You were too young to remember."

She clenched her teeth. The system was not fair. She was next in line in age. Why should she be skipped, because of sex?

He continued: "She had it all planned, so long ago. She would deliver a child, and kill all the other, of my sons, so that her whelp would sit on my throne. She is going to renounce her right as Queen, and give it to him. She would be able to control the country. She will have all the authority, but none of the responsibility."

"But, why?"

"She will have the freedom to do whatever she pleases, she will be able to control everyone and everything, in my country." He stared up. His face became stern. "Hanooya, she does not look upon you as a threat. Please…prove her wrong. Don't let that thing sit on my throne. Don't let that woman do this to us."

Two days later - the King died.

There was a loud knock on the door. Dinmar, the old nurse, walked over and opened it. A teenaged boy stood there, somewhat winded. His eyes were wide with horror. He glanced around the room, and then rested his gaze on Hanooya. He bowed his head. "Your Majesty, the General has requested that you come to the wall."

Hanooya gritted her teeth slightly and then said: "Very well. Tell him I will be there directly. You can go now."

The youth bowed a little lower, and then took off running. She followed at a calm pace. No hurry in her steps. Dinmar walked behind Hanooya. The old woman was wringing her hands and sobbing slightly.

Hanooya was a turmoil inside. She did everything she could to maintain her regal composure, as she slowly walked through the hall, down the stairs and out of the main part of the palace.

A large contingency of the army, was on the north wall. They were glancing about nervously. Some of them paced, some were on their knees - praying to whatever deity they felt was the most powerful.

47

Most of them were looking over the battlements in stoic silence.

She felt perspiration in the middle of her back. Another trickle of sweat on her forehead, went down the side of her face. She tried to ignore it.

The chief of the archers, met her at the bottom of the stairs. "The General awaits you, in the north central tower, Your Majesty."

She smiled politely, and took his arm as they ascended the wide staircase. When she got to the top, she went to the battlements, to see what this spectacle was, that made them all so nervous. She visibly lost a little of her dignity, from what she saw. At least twenty divisions of Oroban's army could be seen spread out in the distance. Sixteen ominous siege towers were rocking back and forth as they were dragged across uneven terrain. She had to strain her eyes a little to make out the numerous catapults, battering rams and assault ladders.

She looked around at the faces of the soldiers that were on the wall. She saw fear, anger, desperation, determination, awe, and hatred. Each showed his feelings and emotions in silence, as they watched the approaching horde.

The walk to the tower was slow. She could not take her eyes away from the enemy. It was unbelievable that they could have raised such an army in such a short time. Short time? Who was she kidding? That rotten woman had been planning this for years.

In the tower, General Korotan was sitting at a table. He had a map in front of him, but his mind was somewhere else.

"You requested my presence?"

He looked up at her, surprised. Then he stood up, "Yes, Majesty, I did. I wanted you to see the size of his army."

"I saw it. Have you something in mind?"

His expression turned grim. "We have no hope whatsoever, of holding off, that large a force."

They stared at each other in silence for several moments.

"What do you suggest, General?"

"Our choices are simple: Surrender, or be massacred in battle…or be starved out."

"Is that all?"

"Well, the last choice doesn't seem likely. Considering the size of the force, we could probably hold out longer than they could. The supply problems for them, would be incredible."

She stared at the floor, pondering his words. Looking back up at him, she said: "I will give you my choice…later."

She got back to her private chambers. She was about ready to fall on her bed and just cry herself out, when there was another knock on the door. 'Oh, what now?" she thought.

Pelroosh stood there looking a little haggard. "Your request has been filled, Majesty."

Hanooya looked at his prisoner. A very angry woman was tied up with chains, behind him.

Hanooya was a little confused. "Why is she chained?"

"Because she can chew through any rope, with very little problem.

The elven woman opened her mouth, and showed her very sharp pointed teeth. Though her lips appeared to be normal, when she opened her mouth, she was able to stretch her lips in an abnormally large manner, where she showed, even all of her back teeth. Her skin was an unusual shade of light brown - not tanned, but still light brown. Her hair was rather short and a very dark brown. Her eyes were the same color of brown as her skin and would probably look very pretty, if it were not for the fact that she was so angry. Her clothing, that was different shades of green, had the appearance of something that would camouflage her in the woodland area, where her people lived.

Hanooya took in a deep breathe. "I am sorry for the inconvenience. My father wanted to meet someone of your race." She looked at Pelroosh. "Please take her to the King's chambers, in the *north* wing. My father will try to attend her, and explain why she is here."

Pelroosh looked confused. He closed his eyes and stood frozen for a few seconds. He opened his eyes frowning. "You want me to take her to the *north* wing."

"Yes, those are my father's orders. When you get her there, get her something to eat, and get those nasty chains off of her. Make her as comfortable as you can." She looked back at the Elf. "What is your name, my dear?"

The Elf looked indignant.

Pelroosh cleared his throat. "Uh…Your Majesty, the Shan-Karoot do not talk. Those teeth have a tendency to destroy the tongue, when they are young, so they use a sign language." He looked at the chains. "Right now, it would be a little difficult for her to communicate anything."

"Oh! I see. Well, take her to the north chambers, and make her as comfortable as you can." She looked back at the Elf. "It may be some time before my father can attend you. We are a little busy... with an invasion."

The Elf now looked a little surprised. She sighed and looked off to the side, brooding.

As Pelroosh and his assistants headed away, Hanooya called him back. He signaled his men to continue and came back. Hanooya got close to him, and whispered: "Whatever it is, that her people value, I want plenty of it in the shed, near the kitchen gate...as soon as you can gather it."

Pelroosh again looked a little surprised. He shrugged and smiled. "Consider it done, Majesty." He then departed.

She turned back to Dinmar. "I need to change. I cannot move about, very well, in this huge hoop dress. I need something...a little smaller. Something where I do not have to have both doors opened, in order to fit through."

Dinmar looked towards the closet. "The only thing that you would have like that, would be the things that you wear, when you are watching the hunt...or participating in the hunt."

"Yes. That will do. I think I want that shimmering blue outfit."

Dinmar hit a small gong. Several women appeared from a side room. "Her Majesty wishes to change her attire. She wishes to wear the blue silk, hunting dress."

The women all responded to their duties.

Hanooya went back to visit the General.

He sat there looking at the approaching enemy. "Have you made a decision, Your Majesty?"

"Yes, I have," she said dejectedly. "I cannot allow…thirty or forty thousand troops to be…slaughtered…for nothing. You say that we can't stand against that multitude. Fighting back will only cause…unnecessary carnage." She sat down and cleared her throat. She was again trying to keep her composure and not cry. "According to what my father said, this man, Oroban, does have a legitimate claim to the throne." She looked the General directly in the eyes. "Hear his claim! If it is…legal…then don't let thousands die…to…fight against a legality."

General Korotan closed his eyes and clenched his teeth. He cleared his throat and looked at the ceiling. "Do we strike your banner?"

She placed her fingers on her temples. "No. You show my banner and welcome him…as you would welcome any…visiting Monarch. Again, you hear his claim. If it is legitimate, then there is nothing I can do…"

"Is this truly, what you want, Your Majesty?"

"I do *not* want a blood bath. We will hear his claim and act accordingly."

"Do you have something in mind, to stop or combat him?"

She hung her head. "I have very little that I can do, legally. According to you, I have very little that I can do militarily. If I have something planned, then I will have to observe and learn before I can execute it, with any certainty of success. Whatever happens… as I said…I don't want the palace grounds, littered with hacked up corpses."

The General sighed and looked at the members of his staff. "You have heard the orders. Go! Take care of the arrangements."

The guard on the walls was reduced to the normal contingency. All of the rest of the palace garrison, was ordered to the streets, to line the way through the city, to the palace. Most of them seemed dejected and reluctant over the decision, but they obeyed.

The citizens were all made aware of the situation. Many of them were as shocked and confused as the military personnel, but took it with a modicum of dignity and went about their normal daily routine.

Hanooya was still up on the wall, watching the advancing army. She could hear their drums as they got nearer. She swallowed hard and continued watching what the enemy was doing.

When the advancing army got closer, they were just as confused by what they saw. They figured that all the gates would be closed and the only people they would see would be the archers and soldiers at the ramparts. Instead, the three gates of the northwestern wall were wide open and the citizens were milling about doing their marketing, bartering and other chores.

The entire group halted. They all stared in silence and confusion. A man in fancy armor, kicked his equine to a gallop and headed closer to the city. He was followed by four others in formation behind him.

He arrived in the market area, and looked confused over the fact that no one ran in fear. He slowed his equine to a walk and headed through the market. All five men looked around in silence and confusion, but still alert, looking for any kind of surprise attack.

After going more than half way through the market, the head man stopped. He got off his equine and walked to a stand, where an old woman was selling fruit.

From where she was watching, Hanooya could not tell what was being said, but it appeared that the head man bought a piece of fruit. He took several bites from it, as he continued his reconnaissance.

He got back up on his equine and continued, at a walk, towards the big central gate. When his group arrived there, the four guards on duty, saluted him. He returned the salute. There seemed to be a few words exchanged between the leader and the guards. He sat back in his saddle, looked up at the top of the wall and took another bite of the fruit. After looking both directions at the men on the wall, he turned around and looked at his followers. He shrugged, threw his arms out and shook his head.

He threw the remainder of the fruit to a small child, sitting by the roadside, spurred his equine and headed back to the army, with his followers in tow.

Hanooya sighed. "I will head back to the palace now," she told the General.

After an hour of people just standing around, while Prince Oroban made a decision, a group came from the back of the army and headed for the central gate. It was Prince Oroban, Queen Tyma, their personal guard and a group of soldiers, leading and following.

As they made their way through the market, the people calmly got out of the way and bowed as the Prince went by.

Prince Oroban kept looking for some kind of surprise attack. He looked suspicious and somewhat angry.

No attack occurred. The group rode through the streets, getting saluted by all of the military that lined the route. They rode on in silence up to the main gate of the palace. The palace guard saluted the Prince and opened the gate for him.

The Prince went through, followed by the Queen's carriage. They still all looked around confused, just waiting for some kind of attack…or something.

Prince Oroban and Queen Tyma, surrounded by their personal guard, entered the palace. The heralds sounded the trumpets as they walked in. Oroban still looked around in angered confusion.

They arrived at the throne room. Princess Hanooya stood, with her hands clasped in front of her, waiting for them as they approached. She tried to show absolutely no emotion. She did not want to give them any satisfaction of seeing fear on her face, nor did she want to make them think that she was happy to see them.

When they got close, the personal guard parted around Hanooya. She gave a slight curtsy. Oroban, still frowning, bowed slightly. Tyma just stood there glaring at Hanooya.

"Welcome, Queen Tyma and Prince Oroban. You are too late to greet my father. He has passed away, due to a strange illness."

"You will address me!" Oroban looked at her indignantly. "My mother has abdicated, due to grief at the death of her husband the King. As a result of that, *I* am *now* the King."

"I have heard that there are those who question the legitimacy of your claim to the throne. First of all, I have not seen any document, where the Queen has abdicated. Second, I have not seen any documentation that appropriately states that you are the heir."

Oroban gave her a wide eyed look and giggled. "Legitimate? Appropriate? You would like to hear my claim? You know, full well that *I* am now, the one and only rightful heir to the throne. Who are *you* to question it?"

"I am the Princess Hanooya of the Kingdom of Festrema. The people here, know me and are waiting for what I say to them. It is possible that there are some who may question your claim. If I approve it, then they will not question it, anymore."

He giggled again. He turned to a small man that was standing directly behind him. He held out his hand and the little man pulled a document out of a rather ornate box that he was holding. Oroban took the document and almost threw it in Hanooya's face. "This is proof of my birth, and the fact that you and I have the same father."

Hanooya read it carefully. She knew before she touched it,

that it was legitimate. "Yes, this is in order." She looked up from the document. "I still have not seen anything that gives any intention of Queen Tyma abdicating."

"You don't need to see it, you little brat," said Tyma. "I can say it out loud, in front of witnesses, and that is sufficient. I cannot rule, because I am so grief stricken at the loss of my husband. I abdicate, in favor of my son."

Hanooya had a hard time hiding her disgust. This woman was talking about the grief over the King's death. A man that she had not been anywhere near, for almost fifteen years.

Oroban giggled again. "You see, dear sister? I am now the ruler of this kingdom. I don't like the way that you have insulted me, so I must think of what to do with you as a result of that insult."

"I do only that which is according to protocol," said Hanooya flatly.

"Well, since you have insulted my person, and my claim, you can contemplate your idiotic protocol, from the dungeon." He turned to one of his personal guard. "Pulgrim, you do remember your way around here?"

The man turned to Oroban and gave a sinister grin. "Oh yes, Your Majesty. I certainly do."

"Excellent," giggled Oroban. "I want this useless whelp taken to the deepest, darkest cell in the dungeon."

The door slammed shut. She listened as they had their conversation, just outside the door.

"Pulgrim, you are certain that this *is* the deepest section of the dungeon?"

"Yes, Your Majesty. This particular section, is three levels lower than any other part of the dungeon."

"Why did they dig, only this section, so deep?"

"Because, Your Majesty, every other place they tried to dig, this deep, they found water."

Oroban giggled again. "Water? They were stopped, because of water?"

"That is the reason, Your Majesty."

Now she listened as the three braces were put in place. Then the footsteps of the men slowly retreated from the cell. She could hear that bothersome giggling, long after the noise of the booted footsteps subsided.

She waited until the silence was as absolute as the darkness. Her hand followed the chain, up to where it was connected to the peg in the wall. Push the peg in, until you hear a click, then a quarter turn to the right, and pull the peg out of the wall. Do the same on the other side.

After releasing the chains from the wall, she got down on her hands and knees and felt her way to the door. Once at the door, she started feeling her way, along the wall to the right. There was one brick that was pushed in. She found it and pushed hard on it until she heard a grating sound. Then the entire wall swung away from her.

A small ledge immediately to her left, had a key and a tinderbox. Directly below the ledge, was a bucket with three torches, soaking in oil.

She pulled a torch and the tinderbox. Laying the torch on the ground, she struck a spark to the head of it, with the tinderbox. The flare, as it ignited was blinding. Her eyes stung a little, until she became used to the light.

After unlocking the manacles, she pulled an extra torch out of the bucket. She turned to the stairs and sighed. It was a long, long way up.

About three quarters of the way up, the first torch started giving out. She held the second torch, up to the dwindling flame and it immediately ignited. She held the first one down and let it burn out, while she continued the weary climb.

Finally, mercifully, she reached the landing that she had been looking for. Her legs were causing her no end of grief, but she could not take the time to wait. She had to get to the place that overlooked the throne room.

She walked through the narrow corridor. The torch was too bright at this point. She could not afford to give herself away. She found a candle and lit it from the torch. The burning torch was placed on the floor, away from her destination. The other torch was placed in a bucket, with four others, in order to replenish it.

She found the place she was looking for. She placed the candle behind a small barrier and pulled a tab, out of the wall. She peered through the hole into the throne room.

She was surprised to find out that she was somewhat early.

The nobles were still coming in. The ceremonial necessities would not start, until all of them were there.

Oroban was standing in front of the throne. He was twirling the crown on his left hand. In his right hand, he had a ceremonial golden sword. He looked around in a condescending manner as people continued to fill the room.

Standing in the middle of the room, she saw all of the high ranking military officers. They all stood patiently, showing the discipline, that was their pride.

When Oroban was satisfied that all were there, who needed to be there, he raised the sword high. "Who will proclaim their obedience to the new King?"

None of the military officers moved. It was as if the question had fallen on deaf ears.

General Korotan took a step forward. "By what right, do you claim this title?"

Anger crossed Oroban's face. He showed his clenched teeth a moment, then switched to a smile. Again that stupid giggle. "King Halkain was my father. I am the only remaining male heir to the throne. My scribe has a copy of the official registration of my birth."

A murmur went through the ranks. The General raised his hand. "I understand, your mother, Queen Tyma, is still alive, and is present. If that is true, then she is still the reigning Queen."

Oroban raised his eyebrows and giggled. "My mother - Queen Tyma, has renounced her title and all claim to the throne." His smile broadened. "She is too grief stricken, over the death of my dear father, to lead this kingdom. My scribe, has in his hands, her official abdication. I declare this day, that she has permanently renounced the throne, forever."

The General looked back at the other officers. Hanooya noticed a large bruise on his left cheek. He looked around through the group and sighed. He turned back to Oroban. "I would hear it read aloud to all those gathered here."

Again the giggle. He flipped the crown over onto the throne. He then turned and gave a long slow gesture to the scribe. The short man opened the ornate box, pulled out a document, cleared his throat and started reading. It was a long boring lecture, full of legalistic mumbo-jumbo and jargon. It had a real load of garbage, about Tyma's ardent love and tremendous grief over the King's death.

Hanooya heard what was needed - a complete and permanent renouncement, by Queen Tyma, in writing.

Oroban looked around and shrieked. "Well? You have heard it. Do you swear your allegiance, to King and country?"

Slowly the entire group dropped to one knee. Oroban flipped the sword over to the throne. He clapped his hands together, then covered his mouth, stifling another giggle.

She replaced the tab in the hole, feeling a little smug. She took the candle, pulled a fresh torch out and lit it. After blowing out the candle, she headed off to the north chambers.

Hanooya reached the secret entrance to the King's chambers. She pressed her ear to the door, and waited until she heard that irritating giggle. She heard a woman crying. The cry turned to a yelp, as someone was slapped. More giggling - more tormented crying - another slap - another yelp - more giggling. An anguished scream, and some furniture being knocked over. More of that wretched giggling.

Then there was a new scream. High pitched, but not from the woman, who had been crying before. It changed to a strange choking scream, and then was suddenly cut off. A sputtering, ragged coughing - then nothing.

Hanooya reached up to the lever and pulled down. The lever clicked and the secret panel swung open.

She thought that she would be prepared for the sight in the room - she was wrong!

Oroban was sprawled on the floor on his back. The majority of his throat had been torn away. Several spurts of blood shot out of the gaping wound - each one a little weaker than the last. His right hand started twitching in an uncontrollable manner.

The Shan-Karoot woman was kneeling over the body. She stared at Hanooya in surprise. Her clothing had been partially ripped away. Her right eye was swollen and dark. A large amount of blood was dripping from her mouth. Her cheeks were puffed out, due to the fact that her mouth was overstuffed with…!

Hanooya clenched her eyes shut, and swallowed hard, fighting off a wave of nausea. She took a deep breath and opened her eyes.

The Elf took a deep breath and, reared her head back, and spat a huge glob of bloody flesh at Hanooya. It hit the wall next to her… and stuck. The mess slid slowly down to the floor. The Princess barely had enough time to turn her face, back into the secret corridor, before vomiting. She could not afford to leave any evidence, of her being in the King's chambers.

The Elf snarled, revealing those nasty shark-like teeth. She slowly rose up and started advancing, with a wicked grin on her face.

Hanooya held her hands up, and swallowed hard. "Please... stop! My father never intended for any harm to come to you. He merely wanted to meet someone of your race."

The Elf stopped. Her eyes narrowed. Confusion crossed her face. The grin subsided.

Hanooya did not really want to lie to the Elf, but found little choice, at this time. "My father died, before he could make proper acquaintance. It was his wish to meet you...and then send you home." She prayed that the Elf would buy her story. "I am here...now...to help you...get out."

The Elf looked back at Oroban's body, then turned back to Hanooya with a suspicious look on her face.

"If he hurt you, then you have made him pay. As I said, my father only wanted to meet you. There are those who will be very angry about that man's death...but that can be taken care of. Come with me now, and I will help you depart...quietly and safely."

Again the suspicious look. The Elf looked around in contemplation. After a few moments, she snarled, clenched her wicked teeth, then sighed and shrugged in resignation.

"Before you leave, I suggest you get something to cover yourself."

The Elf froze. She looked down at her partially exposed body. She looked around the room, walked over to the bed, yanked a sheet off of it, and wrapped it around herself. She headed towards Hanooya, looking somewhat disgusted.

Hanooya led the way. She was nervous about this Elf behind her. Those horrible teeth that could rip chunks off of your body, like that made her shudder. Another thing that set her on edge, was how absolutely silent the Elf was. Several times, Hanooya had to look back and make sure that the Elf was still following. Each time she was met by a look of mild bewilderment and suspicion.

They finally arrived at the destination, in the secret corridors. Hanooya handed the torch back to the Elf. "Here, hold this, please."

The Elf's brows went up in a questioning manner. She took the torch and changed to a look that gave an accusation of extreme stupidity. Hanooya was amazed at how much the non-talking Elf could say, with mere facial expressions.

Hanooya placed her hand on the brick that marked the entrance and pushed. A loud thump from the opposite wall made the Elf gasp. A crack in the wall became larger, as the door swung open. Hanooya pushed it open, and turned back to see a face showing astonishment.

"This is your way out, my dear."

Pelroosh was sitting at a table, nodding off. He looked up at Hanooya and shook his head. He looked almost as astonished as the Elf, when he realized that Hanooya was coming out of a secret panel, with the Elf in tow.

He stood up and bowed. "Your...Majesty! I have...uh...what you asked for. It took a little doing, but...mission accomplished."

Hanooya looked in horror, where Pelroosh was pointing. She almost gasped, herself. A large two-wheeled cart was sitting there, full of animal pelts. Hanooya looked at Pelroosh, who looked at the pelts himself. He looked back at Hanooya and nodded.

Hanooya looked at the Elf, to see if there was any reaction. The Elf was looking at the pelts, but did not seem in any way fascinated.

Hanooya bit her lip and hoped that Pelroosh was right. She put a hand to her forehead as she prepared herself, for another line of nonsense. "My dear, this servant of mine, has brought some gifts for you...as an apology, for how you were treated...by that horrible little giggling man. The...furs on the cart...you may take...have...all that you wish to have..."

The Elf woman's jaw fell open. Her eyes were wide with shock. Her shoulders sagged, she dropped the torch and the sheet. She slowly walked over to the cart, looking in amazement at the pile of pelts. She looked back at Hanooya and made a few gestures with her hands.

"Yes," said Pelroosh. "My Princess has said that you may take all that you wish, to take."

The Elf got a huge greedy grin on her face and started rummaging through the furs.

Pelroosh went to the front of the cart and pulled two large pouches out. He took one of the pelts, flattened it out and then dumped the contents of the pouch, onto the pelt.

Hanooya was shocked, to see a large pile of animal teeth. She looked to see the Elf's reaction. When the Elf looked at the teeth, her eyes seemed to get even wider.

Pelroosh then opened up the other pouch and dumped out a pile of animal claws.

The Elf put both hands over her mouth and stared at the two piles in amazement. The Elf looked back at Hanooya. The Princess gave her as friendly a smile as she could muster, and nodded.

Hanooya looked at Pelroosh, while the Elf was scooping the claws and teeth, back into the pouches. Pelroosh shrugged and smiled. Hanooya had been thinking of questioning the items, but when she saw the reaction, by the Elf, her questions were already answered.

The Elf was now looking through the furs, trying to find something. Pelroosh walked over to her confused. "What is it that you are looking for?"

She made more hand gestures.

Pelroosh looked back at Hanooya, helplessly. "She is trying to figure out, how much, she can carry."

Hanooya felt badly over that. "You can have the cart, if you wish, my dear. As I said, you can have all that you want of this… fine treasure. If you need the cart to take it all, then you may have the cart."

The Elf's jaw again went slack. She stared at Hanooya, dumbfounded. She then looked back at the cart. She then placed her index fingers on her temples and gave a slight bending of the knees. She made this gesture several times.

"You are quite welcome," said Pelroosh. He turned to Hanooya. "That's the way, they say 'thank you'."

Hanooya smiled at the Elf. "Yes…as he said, you are welcome."

The Elf started pawing at the pelts randomly, overwhelmed at her new, abundant wealth.

Hanooya suddenly had a thought: "My dear, may I know your name?"

The Elf looked at her and snickered. She made a few gestures.

Pelroosh watched her. "Bright Sky…"

The Elf stopped her gestures and glared at him angrily. Then she started making the gestures again.

He again tried to translate. Again she stopped gesturing and glared at him angrily, only this time she snarled. She made a few more rapid gestures, stamped her feet and then held her hands down at her side with her fists clenched.

Pelroosh cleared his throat. "My apologies, to you, my lady," he said weakly. He turned to Hanooya: "The custom of her people, is that…names are not spoken aloud. Her name is signed."

"Oh, really," said Hanooya. "Would you teach me your name?"

The first sign was that both hands were on each side of the face, palms out and fingers fully spread. The next one, both arms were held out, with the fingers still fully spread out. She then cocked her head to the right, placed her left hand under her right cheek, palm down, the right arm then was held out, palm up. Hanooya practiced these movements several times, and then did what the Elf had done to say 'thank you'.

The Elf returned a very cheerful smile.

"As I said..." Hanooya made the gestures for the Elf's name. "...you may take the cart, as well. I will also have some of the huntsmen, escort you back to your...home, so that you get there safely. Again, I apologize to you, for the wicked way, that my half-brother treated you."

The Elf walked up to Hanooya. She kissed the index finger on her right hand and then touched the finger to Hanooya's forehead.

Pelroosh was standing behind the Elf and mouthed the words: "Do the same."

Hanooya quickly kissed her right index finger and touched the finger to the Elf's forehead.

The Elf smiled and went back to ogle her treasures.

Hanooya and Pelroosh watched as the Elf and her temporary escort headed out.

"If I may, Your Highness...what just happened?" Pelroosh looked at Hanooya helplessly. "You had me drag her in here, and then, for no reason, whatsoever, you give her a pile of booty, that just made her, one of, if not *the*, wealthiest member of her tribe. Why?"

Hanooya sighed and looked down at the ground, feeling rather guilty. "I used her." She sighed again. "I used her, to get myself on the throne."

"But...Oroban! He just got here...and...what?"

"They may try to delay announcing it, but Oroban is dead."

Pelroosh looked stupefied for a moment. "Huh?"

Hanooya looked at him reassuringly. "Yes, Oroban is dead. Most of his lackeys don't know it yet, but he is most definitely dead."

Pelroosh stood there with his eyes clenched, his mouth open and his arms open wide, in total confusion. "Does the blood on her face have something to do with...that?"

"Don't ask," said Hanooya. "Just accept my word, and don't tell anyone. Don't ever speak of this incident, with anyone but me."

He sighed helplessly, and shook his head. "As Your Majesty wishes," he said helplessly.

"By the way, she didn't want her name, spoken aloud...I would like to hear it now."

He smiled: "Bright Sky in the Morning."

"Lovely. I shall have to remember that. I would like you to remind me, every now and then, the proper gestures for her name."

"I can do that...no problem, Your Majesty."

"Remember, you don't know anything of Oroban's death, until you hear it, officially from the palace. What ever they say, is the cause of death, you accept it."

"As you wish, Your Majesty."

Hanooya frowned and looked at Pelroosh: "Furs, teeth and claws?"

He chuckled. "You said to obtain, that which is valuable to *her* people."

"Furs, teeth and claws!"

"Yes, Your Majesty."

Hanooya returned back to the cell in the dungeon. She had some candles with her, to keep her company, while she waited for the official announcement of Oroban's death and the fact that she was now, the only legitimate heir to the throne of Festrema. It was a boring wait, however, it did not take as long as she thought it would.

At first she was worried about the smell of the candle being detected, when they arrived at the cell - the smell of the torches, quickly erased the smell of the candle.

Now she stood in front of the throne, holding the crown and the golden sword. The former Queen Tyma, was standing off to the side looking totally confused and dejected. Hanooya wondered if there was some other, nasty plot, cooking behind those evil eyes.

B. U. S.

Matthew sat there waiting for the late evening news to start. After (what seemed like) twenty boring commercials, the New York Lottery bi-weekly drawing came on. He picked up his handy pad and pen from the coffee table and watched as the numbered balls came out. 49, 6, 23, 35, 11, 17. He listened as the announcer repeated the numbers. He stared at them. He covertly checked to see if his wife, Jeannie was still busy in the kitchen. He went to the bedroom, reached up on top of the armoire and pulled his lottery envelope down. He checked the numbers on the pad and one of the ticket several times as blood pounded in his ears. 6, 11, 17, 23, 35, 49. Perfect match on one of his tickets - six for six. He stood there with his full 6 foot 5 inch frame spread out, arms nearly touching the ceiling. He let his Texas background come through as he let out a "Yeehaw" at the top of his lungs.

Jeannie came in from the kitchen. She stood there with her fists on her hips trying to make her 5 foot 3 inch frame appear taller. As usual, at this time of the evening, she was wearing almost nothing other than one of his T-shirts. "What is your problem? You know how these stupid New Yorkers don't like to hear that kind of thing. It's bad enough that we gotta hide our Texas accents, cause these bigots automatically think that we're dumb, just cause we're from Texas... now you go and let off with a big 'yeehaw' and..." She huffed and shook her head.

He stood there with a huge grin on his face the entire time

she was venting. He covertly put the lottery ticket up on top of the armoire, acting as if he were just resting his hand on top of it. "Hey Honey, do you want to go back to Texas?"

She snorted. "Course, I do. But how? You got yourself established here and…after all that stuff back home…well how?"

"We won't have to worry about that now, lover. We'll just go back home and snub our noses back at them."

"Right! We're living from paycheck to paycheck in this heavily over tax infested, high-priced state, and you just want to up and move back. I just found out that we're now expecting our second child. Where would we go? All the jobs are taken. You'd have to be some half-salaried substitute for…who knows how long? We couldn't afford to live."

"We can now, Baby Doll."

She huffed again. "Oh, don't 'Baby Doll' me, babies don't get pregnant…grown women who're married do. Now, what are you talking about?"

He thought for a moment. All he had was the numbers that he had jotted down on the pad. She would not accept that. He decided to wait until he could show her the "official numbers" in the newspaper - tomorrow. "Well, let me put it this way: I've got something that I'm working on right now, and once I get all the stuff together…we can give this godforsaken state the boot and go back home. If anyone wants to say anything back there, then we can just laugh at them."

"Every one of them have been laughing at you, ever since the accident. They've been laughing at me, because I married you. What in tarnation, do you have that could possibly stop all that?"

He chuckled. "It may not stop them, but it will definitely give me something to laugh back at them...harder than they have been laughing at me."

Her shoulders sagged and she sighed. "There you go, talking in circles and riddles again. Make some sense!"

"Tomorrow," he said with a huge grin.

She walked up to him snarling with anger in her big brown eyes. "Tomorrow, my foot! You're gonna explain something to me *right now*! I hate it when you talk in circles and riddles."

He reached down, put his arms on her sides, just below her arms. He picked her up and brought her face to face with him. "You also don't like it when I say something when I have no proof. Tomorrow, I will have proof - then you'll understand."

She squirmed in his grasp. "Put me down, you big ape! If I weren't pregnant, I wouldn't mind. Now, when you do this, you just might hurt the baby."

He pulled her close. She snickered a little. She put her arms around his neck and her legs around his waist. He switched his hands to cradling her derriere, holding her up.

"I love you, my cute little darling, and I would never do anything to hurt you or the baby."

"Then tell me your happy secret," she snarled.

"Tomorrow," he said with a big smile.

She grabbed hold of his curly brown hair on the back of his

head. She started shaking her head back and forth several times. She used her long brown hair to whip the sides of his face. When she stopped, she felt a little dizzy, but was still trying to maintain her snarl. "I wanna know, NOW!"

He swatted her on her right hip. "Tomorrow," he said with a chuckle. "You know that you always get upset about things that I say that I can't prove - right now! So, tomorrow, I will be able to prove what I'm saying."

She sighed dejectedly. "Put me down."

He walked over to the bed and sat down. She unwrapped her arms and legs, crawled off of him and to her side of the bed and pulled the heavy quilt up to her neck while still scowling at him.

He chuckled a little bit more as he took his clothes off. He came out of the bathroom after doing his evening constitutionals. As usual, on a cold January night in New York City, she was laying there shivering. He climbed into bed and she snuggled close to him.

"There's times that I thought of getting rid of you," she said. "But then I'd freeze. You make a real warm bed."

He chuckled. "It's you that warms me up, Baby Doll."

"I wish," she huffed. "What's that stuff you're always saying?"

He snickered. "Body heat is directly proportional to body mass. The more body mass you have, the more body heat that you create."

"Is that what you teach that bunch of rich, snob brats at that rich, snob school you teach at?"

"Yes, that is part of the science of biology. That is my specialty."

She raised up a little. "When you gonna finish doin' that doctoring stuff?"

"Doctorate!" He shook his head. "PhD, Doctor in the Science of Biology."

"Okay, okay," she snapped impatiently. "When you gonna finish? I mean, as soon as you do, then you can leave that rich snob, high school and start teaching at a college - a good college."

"With the Masters degree that I have now, I could teach at a college - now. The problem, like I told you before, is that I have to establish tenure. I already have myself established at the high school. Reestablishing at a college could take some time. With another little one on the way…well, after you see what I'm going to show you - tomorrow - all of that may be moot."

She raised up a little. "You're not gonna tell me anything right now, are you?"

He stroked the back of her neck. "I love you," he said softly.

She huffed, kissed him and raised up again. "I love you." She then went back to snuggling close and the two of them fell asleep together.

The next morning, when the alarm went off, he awoke and saw that she was already up and around. He stretched, working out the kinks and smiled. "Today is the first day of the rest of your life," he said quietly. He sighed in satisfaction. "A new era starts…for me and little Jeannie, our son Robert, and the new little youngun that's on the way." He inhaled deeply and smelled the coffee brewing. He got up, put his robe on and headed out to the kitchen.

Jeannie was standing next to the front door, looking up at him. She had a somewhat disgusted look on her face and had her arms folded across her chest.

He felt a little self conscious. "What?"

She huffed. "The thieving little brat, from across the hall, stole our newspaper...again!"

His shoulders sagged and his chin hit his chest. She opened the door and he sighed. He walked across the hall and banged on the door. When the door came open, a short balding fat man in a green plaid robe stood there looking up at Matthew.

"Can I help you, Mr. Tate?"

"Can I have my newspaper back, Mr. Gokey?"

Gokey looked down at a portion of the newspaper in his hand. He closed his eyes and exhaled sharply with his teeth clenched. He looked back into his apartment. "Solomon! Where did you get this newspaper?"

There was some mumbling from inside the apartment.

"Don't tell me that...now that I think about it, you weren't gone long enough to have gone down to Pete's newsstand."

"And I saw him pick it up and head into your place," snapped Jeannie.

A teenage boy with shoulder length black hair came up behind

Mr. Gokey. "It's cold outside!"

"That don't give you the right to steal Mr. Tate's newspaper. Besides that, that means that you still have the money that I gave you *for* the paper. What were you intending on buying with that?"

The boy scowled.

"Now, go get a paper for Mr. Tate," scolded Gokey.

The angry youth pulled his coat down from a rack just inside the door. He put it on slowly as he headed for the stairs.

"…and make sure that Mr. Tate gets the whole newspaper intact, or you're going back down there again…for one that is complete."

The boy's shoulders sagged as he trudged on.

Gokey looked as if he was going to say something to Matthew, then turned back to his son: "…and make sure that it's *today's* paper!"

The boy's shoulders seemed to sag even further.

Gokey cleared his throat. He inhaled deeply and shook his head. "I'm sorry, Mr. Tate. I don't know what I'm going to do with him."

Jeannie stood there with a sweet smile. "A two-by-four might help."

Both men chuckled.

"I'll make sure that you get your paper," said Gokey.

"Thank you, sir," said Matthew. He went back to his apartment.

After closing the door, Jeannie looked up at him expectantly.

"Okay, Darlin', it's tomorrow…what's the news?"

He gave her a half-hearted smile. "It's in the newspaper."

She looked back at him shocked. "What kind of stupid shenanigan did you pull to get in the newspaper?"

"It's good news, Baby Doll…*good news!*"

She growled, bared her teeth and held her hands up as if they were talons that she was going to rip him apart with. "Why didn't you tell me that? If I'd a known that, I'd a beat that punk to the newspaper."

"Not to worry," he said calmly. "The little punk will be back soon."

"At least gimme a hint!"

He yawned. "Where's the coffee?"

She grunted in disgust and headed to the kitchen with her arms held firmly against her sides and her fists clenched.

He stood there waiting. He heard Jeannie mumbling to herself in the kitchen. He heard eggs and bacon start sizzling in the skillet while the mumbling continued. He heard a knock on the door. He opened the door up. There stood Solomon Gokey shivering, with a newspaper in his hand. Matthew was not sure if the shivering was real or not.

"I'm sorry about your newspaper," said Solomon, with absolutely no sincerity in his voice at all.

Matthew took the newspaper and said: "Thank you," with equal disingenuousness.

He walked into the kitchen and started looking for the Lottery information.

Jeannie walked over to him. She watched him digging through the pages. "Okay, what's the *good news*?"

"I'm looking. Don't let the eggs burn."

"Huh?" She looked back at the stove and sniffed. "Oh, fooey!" She went back and pulled the skillet off of the stove.

He found the page and hugged it close to his chest. He was waiting until the eggs and bacon were on a plate…and she did not have an *iron skillet* in her hand.

She put the skillet in the sink, walked back to the table and sat down. She noticed his strange pose and looked in his eyes, thoroughly confused. He gave her a guilty smile. Her expression changed to impatience and irritation.

"I have the part of the newspaper that this event applies to." He then gave her a warm smile.

She put her fists on the table. "…and?!"

He set the paper down on the table with the words, Lottery Results, showing clearly.

Her expression changed to fury. She stood up with her entire body shaking with anger. "YOU IDIOT!" Her face turned red and she bared her teeth. "I told you I didn't ever want you playing that stupid lottery! We got one youngun just about out of the house and now in about seven months we'll have another one, just coming in! We'll have one in college and one in diapers…and…and…and… you're playing that stinkin' lottery!"

He closed his eyes against the tirade. He put his hands up slightly in order to try to calm her.

Then - the loud pop as she did a giant round-house slap with her right hand to the left side of his face.

He calmly sat there as she was now dancing in a circle, with a grimace of immense pain on her face, holding onto her right hand with the left, trying to will away the throbbing, agonizing pain in her right hand, as she spewed a string of curses in several different languages.

He shook his head and spoke calmly. "Baby Doll, when are you going to learn? Every time you do that you hurt yourself. You have never hurt me doing *that*." He walked over to the refrigerator, whistling *How Great Thou Art,* opened up the freezer and pulled the ice trays out. He went to the sink, pulled a small bucket out from under the sink, deposited all of the ice cubes into the bucket and filled it with cold water. He walked back to the table and sat down pushing the bucket towards his ranting wife.

Since coming to New York, she had learned all kinds of curses from the many different nationalities that they met in this international city. He had always wondered why she wanted to learn the cuss words first. Why not the "please", and "thank you", or "hello", and "good-bye"? No, she learned all of the "colorful" words first.

She finally ran out of her long list of foreign and domestic profanity. She was holding her right hand up against her chest, rocking back and forth at the waist. Her breath was going quickly, in and out through clenched teeth. Finally the pain subsided enough to where she opened her eyes and glared at him again. She held up her right hand as if she were going to do something with it as she scolded him. She looked confused as she noticed that her right hand was just hanging limp off of the wrist and stopped whatever she had been planning on saying. She saw the bucket of ice water on the table and huffed. She plunged her hand into the water and gasped. After she got used to the chill on her hand she now started wagging the index finger of her left hand at him. "I told you…I told you, time and again…that…that stupid lottery is a waste of money. You have to think of me and your son Robert and this little one that's growin' insida me."

"But, I…"

"Shuttup, I'm not finished!"

He shrugged his shoulders and leaned back in the chair, clasping his hands behind his head.

"All that money that people put in the lottery and they never get nuthin' back out. Now, you tell me that you've been wasting money on that silly gambling for…" She stopped and collected her thoughts with a confused look on her face. "How long have you been doing it?"

"Long enough to…"

"THERE YOU GO AGAIN! You're talking in circles and riddles!"

"Baby Doll, if you don't stop shouting and raving, Mrs. Goldberg is going to call the police again."

"I DON'T CARE!!!" She sat down and momentarily took her hand out of the ice water. She shook her hand a few times, grimaced in pain again and put her hand back in the water. "That silly old busy-body doesn't have anything better to do anyway and I doubt if the police will answer...again."

"Mm-hm," he said quietly. He picked up his fork and started eating the scrambled eggs.

"What are you doing?"

He looked up confused. "Eating."

"Well, I'm not finished talking! What are you eating for, in the middle of getting chewed out?"

"Do you want me to waste the food?"

She pulled her hand out of the water and waved it at him, splattering some of the ice water on his face. She immediately realized that she had made a mistake doing that as a new wave of pain shot up her arm. She clenched her eyes and teeth...again. She then put her hand back in the water. She took several deep breaths. "No, don't waste it. I just want you to listen."

"I can't help but listen. The whole neighborhood can't help hearing you."

She snarled at him.

"Do you mind if I eat the bacon?"

"Eat it," she growled through clenched teeth. "Enjoy it! How much more could we have had, though, if you had not been wasting money on...?"

"That stupid lottery, yeah, I heard you. The whole neighborhood can hear you." He looked at her with a dull stare. "Mrs. Goldberg can hear you."

"Someone needs to tell that stupid hag, to mind her own business."

At that moment, there was a knock on the door, and someone on the other side of the door saying that they were the police.

Matthew sighed and went to the door. He opened it up and gave a friendly smile. "Hey, Ski, how's it going?"

The policeman stood there scratching his chin. "Don't tell me...let me guess. She smack you again?"

"Yup!"

The policeman shook his head and sighed. "Is she ever gonna learn?"

"I doubt it," said Matthew shaking his head.

A woman behind the policeman spoke up: "Hey Sgt. Koski, what are you doing? His wife could be dying in a pool of blood! You're standing here talking like it's a friendly reunion!"

Koski closed his eyes, looking a little disgusted. He cleared his throat and smiled. "Uh, Matt? Meet my new partner." He stepped a little to his side and turned. "This here is my new partner - Connie Odem." He turned to Connie: "This is a call that Delaney and I came to...several times. If I thought that Jeannie was in any danger, I would have busted the door down and had Matt cuffed already."

Odem calmed down a little, but looked very confused. "What's going on then?"

Koski sighed. "Where's Jeannie? You know...we need to talk to her."

"Oh yeah, yeah, yeah, I know," said Matthew. "She's soaking her hand in ice water in the kitchen."

"Okay," said Koski calmly. He walked in.

Odem stood there looking even more confused.

Koski turned around: "Are you coming?"

"Huh? Oh…yeah." Odem walked past Matthew, still bewildered.

They all walked into the kitchen.

Jeannie looked up and then hung her head. "G'Mornin', Ivan," she said quietly as her face flushed.

"Jeannie," Koski said cordially. He looked around the room. "So, what brought this little tirade on?"

She wagged her left index finger at Matthew. "It's his fault! If he hadn't been doing that…if he…" She huffed and put her left hand over her face. She looked up at Odem a little confused. "Where's Frank?"

Koski looked at Matthew. "Did what? What shameless thing did you do?"

Matthew shrugged nonchalantly. "I played the lottery."

"I told him…I told him years ago…do NOT waste any money on that stupid lottery. Now, he comes up to me and tells me he has been…playing." Jeannie looked up at Matthew and snarled. She looked back at Koski: "Where's Frank?"

Koski chuckled. "In all the times that I have had to come

here, this one…at least has some kind of logic to it. Most of the other times…you got real mad over…"

While Koski was trying to think of the right word, Matthew spoke up: "Trivialities?"

Koski smiled and nodded.

Odem was looking around at the people in the room partially baffled and partially horrified. "Are we going to arrest somebody here? She's hurt and you people act like it's nothing!"

Koski closed his eyes and shook his head. "Hey Matt, how many times does this make that I've been here…fourteen…fifteen?"

Matthew pulled a magic marker out of a drawer. He opened a cabinet and added a mark to several others that were on the inside of the door. He then counted. "Eighteen," he said nonchalantly.

Jeannie let out a squawk. "You been keeping score?!"

Matthew sighed. "Just for grins and giggles."

"Eighteen," said Koski as he chuckled. "Hey, little lady, you need to keep your temper in check. Each time you hit him…you're the one who gets hurt. Glass fist versus iron jaw just ain't no fair contest."

Matthew picked up the coffee pot. "Would either of you like some coffee?"

"Sure," said Koski.

Odem huffed. "What is this? Coffee? Now?"

Koski looked at her and sighed. "Are you planning on arresting somebody?"

"Well…I mean…there was a fight…she's hurt…and…I don't know." She shook her hands at her side with her eyes closed. She then put her fingers against her forehead. "What's going on?"

Koski accepted a cup of steaming coffee from Matthew. He blew on it a little and took a sip. He sighed. "Jeannie Tate has a temper. Every now and then she gets really, really upset and takes a poke at her husband. The main problem for her is that she can't give a hard punch, without hurting herself. Matthew Tate is a big man who can take a punch…especially if the punch is coming from little Jeannie Tate. After hitting her husband, she has this thing about screaming her head off in pain and one of the neighbors has to call the police because they think that the punch is the other way around. This has happened - according to the hash marks on that cabinet door - eighteen times." He looked at Matthew. "Did I leave anything out?"

Matthew pondered for a few moments. "Only the fact that on two occasions, she actually broke her hand when she hit me."

"She broke her hand…" Odem got nods from both men. "Twice…" Again two nods. "Did she do it again?"

This time both men looked questioningly at each other. They then looked at Jeannie.

"I didn't bust any bones," snarled Jeannie. "At least I don't think I did," she added. She pulled her hand out of the ice water and slowly clenched and unclenched her fist. "No, I didn't bust any bones…but it's sure tender." She put her hand back in the ice water. "Hey, where's Frank?"

Odem looked around confused. "Are we going to arrest her?"

Koski was ready to take another sip of coffee. He gave Odem a disgusted glare. "For what?!"

"She hit him…I mean isn't that assault?"

"If you want to push it, yes."

"So we use the authority we have and arrest her for assault!"

"We also have to use common sense," scolded Koski in a whiny voice. "Why should we arrest her? Right now, she's suffering more embarrassment - because she was the one who was hurt - than we could ever put against her in a court of law. The victim - her husband - hasn't pressed charges, the previous seventeen times, so why would he do it now?"

"I'm going out to the living room," whined Jeannie. "The chairs out there are a lot more comfortable." She picked up the bucket with her left hand while keeping her right hand in the water. She headed to the living room, with the other three people following behind her. She sat down cross-legged, in an overstuffed chair, placed the bucket on her right knee and held the bucket in place with the injured hand inside the bucket. "Hey, Ivan, where's Frank?"

Koski sat down on the couch. "Now, my rookie partner, are you really wanting to make an arrest that badly?"

Odem gave a few pouting scoffs as she tried to think. "What did you say caused the problem to begin with? Didn't you say that it had something to do with the lottery?"

"I told him, over and over and over and over and over, don't play that lottery. Don't waste our money on the lottery. Now, he tells me that he has been playing it. Now, he's probably trying to tell me that he won a few bucks in order to make me say it's okay to keep playing it."

Koski looked at Matthew. "So, you won a few bucks?"

Matthew gave a warm smile. "Yup."

Jeannie snarled. "What'd you do, match three numbers? That's worth what…a whole three dollars?"

Matthew looked at the ceiling. "I did not match three."

"Oh," said Jeannie mockingly. "You got four? So what's that worth…eighty dollars?"

Koski snickered. "Matching four on this drawing is worth four hundred seventeen dollars."

Jeannie scowled at Koski. "How would you know that?"

"Because I checked the numbers, first thing this morning. I play the lotto too and I don't have a wife snarling at me about it."

Jeannie wrinkled her nose and looked off to the side, shaking her head.

Matthew still stared at the ceiling. "I did not match four."

"Oh, my," said Jeannie with mock awe. "So, it's five numbers. What's that worth a thousand?"

Koski snickered. "Matching five on this drawing is worth one hundred fifty-five thousand two hundred and six dollars."

Jeannie now was staring at Koski with a blank expression on her face. "Well, a hundred fifty-five grand ain't nothing to scoff at, but it still don't solve all of our problems. That would hold us for two years…then what?"

Matthew still stared at the ceiling. "I did not match five."

The silence in the room was deafening. All eyes turned to Matthew.

Finally Jeannie broke the silence with a near whisper: "What?"

Matthew still stared at the ceiling. "I did match six."

Koski looked stunned. "You hit the jackpot!"

Matthew still stared at the ceiling. "I did match six."

"Oh, my…uh…wow." Jeannie was not mocking anymore. "That's usually a few million dollars, ain't it?"

They all looked at her as if she were an idiot.

She inventoried the faces around the room. "Well…ain't it?!"

Matthew smiled at her. "Yes, Baby Doll…a few."

Now her interest was piqued. "Well…how much?"

He slowly moved closer to her. He moved his face closer to her. He spoke slowly: "Three…hundred…forty…three…million… dollars."

She sat there staring dull eyed and open mouthed. Her eyes started brightening and widening with realization. Her shoulders sagged a little as the reality hit her, she lost control of the bucket, the contents spilled into her lap and when the ice cold water soaked in, through her pants, and started freezing "certain tender areas", she let loose with a loud pained gasp. She pushed the - now empty - bucket off of her lap with her left hand and stood up. She then started a very awkward, bow-legged waddle to the bathroom, making all kinds of pained sounds as she went. After disappearing into the bathroom, they heard several more quick moans of pain and then a loud splat, as the wet pants were thrown into the tub. A few moments later, she hollered: "Matt, come in here and help me. I can't tie this robe with one hand."

Matthew shrugged, gave a small chuckle and headed to the bathroom. "Excuse me," he said softly.

Koski and Odem both stood there slack-jawed as they watched him walk away. After he turned into the bathroom, their stunned gazes met. Odem now sat down on the couch with Koski. "Even if I did want to arrest someone…with that much money…" She shook her head. "…they could hire a real expensive mouthpiece and it would all be for nuthin'."

Matthew came back into the living room.

Koski looked up, still a little slack-jawed. "Congratulations," he said in a somewhat stunned way.

"Thank you," said Matthew warmly.

Jeannie came out of the bathroom with an angry look on her face. "Why didn't you start, by telling me that you won the jackpot? A HUGE jackpot!"

"Well…you never gave me a chance." He looked up at the ceiling. "You just went and WHAM! You jumped to a conclusion and, up until now, I've had difficulty getting a word in edgewise."

"I wanna see it! I wanna see this winning ticket!"

He smiled and went back to the bedroom. She followed closely, still holding her injured hand up to her chest. He reached up and pulled the envelope down from the top, back of the armoire.

She growled at him. "So that's why you're always reaching up there! You weren't doing any kind of stretching…you were checking your…oh you rat!"

With a few more strange sounds coming out of her mouth she reared her right hand back as if to slap him again. She stopped and looked at her right hand, closed her eyes and then hugged her hand back up against her chest. She gave him an angry look and stuck her tongue out at him.

"I love you too, Baby Doll." He put his hand on the back of her neck and pulled her close. "I love you with all my heart."

She gave him a look of disgust and then put her arms around him. "So…where's this magic ticket?"

"Let's go out where there's more light."

They walked out to the living room. She never took her eyes off of the envelope that he had in his hand. They found Koski and Odem still sitting there with blank looks on their faces.

Matthew put his hand on Jeannie's shoulder. "Have a seat and I'll go get the newspaper."

She gave him a dirty look. "That seat is wet and what do you need the newspaper for?"

"Then sit on the other chair and I need the paper, so I can show you the official winning numbers."

"Oh." She went over to the other chair and sat down. She started to sit cross-legged again and then realized that she had nothing on under the robe. She flushed, pulled the robe together, as best she could with only one hand and crossed her ankles.

He came back with the newspaper and handed it to her. He pointed to the winning numbers. "That's the numbers...right there." He reached into the envelope and pulled out several tickets.

She snarled at him. "How long you been playing this?"

"Long enough," he said cheerfully.

She snarled again.

"Here's the good one." He looked at it with great pride. "Oh what a feeling. I don't have to lick any more boots at that snob school anymore."

"Lemme see the ticket," snapped Jeannie. He handed her the ticket. She carefully looked over the numbers in the paper and on the ticket. She shook her head. "Well, I never would've figured on winning the lottery - especially one this big."

"It's all ours, Baby Doll. From now on, everything is coming up roses."

"Don't ever say that," said Jeannie fearfully.

"Why not, Baby Doll?"

"Cause roses got thorns!"

Matthew chuckled. "Well, let's do everything we can to strip those nasty thorns off." He looked at Koski: "Say, do you have any idea where we go in order to collect the winnings?"

"Sure," said Koski. He snickered. "Albany."

"What?!" Matthew stood there shocked. "Aren't we in one of the largest cities in the world? Don't they have some office for the lottery commission, somewhere in this vast expanse of concrete?"

"Oh, sure, they got an office. As a matter of fact, they have an office in each one of the boroughs. One in Queens, one in the Bronx, one in Brooklyn, one…"

"So, why do I have to go to Albany?"

"Hey, the state capital has to have something. I mean the offices here can give out the lesser prizes. Anything below five hundred grand. If you want to collect on a big one, or the *really* big one… well…you gotta go to Albany. Don't you think that three hundred forty-three mil is worth a trip to Albany?"

Matthew snorted. "It would be worth the trip for five million."

Jeannie handed him the ticket. "So…when do we go?"

He let out an evil chuckle. "I think that I'll give the school my two weeks' notice and then…" He chuckled again. "…we can shake the dust off of our shoes, and leave this town for good."

Jeannie looked at Koski. "HEY! Where's Frank?"

Koski sighed. "Do you really want to know?"

"I wouldn't ask if I didn't want to know!"

He sighed, hung his head low and shook it. "My 'ex-partner', is now an ex-cop."

Jeannie and Matthew both stared at Koski in shock. Jeannie

was the one who spoke: "Really?"

"Did you see, in the news, about two weeks ago, that big hubbub about police brutality?"

"I vaguely remember something about that," said Matthew. "It seems to happen so often, coming from that one specific channel, where all of the journalists are wild-eyed, radical, anti-cop, that I really don't pay that much attention to it."

"Well, this time..." Koski shrugged. "...they were justified. It seems that we got an 'All Points', about a robbery that had just occurred. The thief was...uh...white guy...about 6 foot 4 or 5...blonde hair...dressed in black...carrying a gun and a brown satchel full of money. So, me and Delaney, we start checking the sidewalks on both sides as we're cruising, because we're about three blocks from the scene of the crime. All of a sudden, Delaney shouts that he sees the perp, he doesn't even wait for me to stop the car, he's out and running. I pull to the side, start the lights, get out and try to find him. He's gone around a corner. When I get there, he's clubbin' the crap out of someone on the ground. I gotta stop him. Whoever it is, ain't movin'. Then I see who he's hittin'. White guy? No! Japanese woman. 6 foot 4? No! She's maybe 5 foot 2. Blonde hair? No! She's Japanese so, she got black hair. She's wearing some bright yellow scarf around her head. Dressed in black? No! She's wearing light green silk. Brown satchel full of money? No! A big white bundle, full of laundry. Gun? No!"

Jeannie looked horrified. "And you say that I go off half-cocked."

Koski looked at her and grunted. "Yeah, well, anyway, there's this pharmacy across the street that has a security camera, outside. We collect the film from them and…wow! Delaney came up behind that broad and gave her no warning at all. He just clubbed her and she goes down like a rag doll. He then keeps hittin' her. Boom! Boom! Boom! Boom! He don't stop…until I grab him and make him stop. When the higher ups have him checked…turns up that he's drunk. I hadn't been able to notice it, cause he been chewin' a lot of peppermint gum lately. Anyway…he's no longer a cop, and that broad's family is gonna end up getting a lotta money from the city. Delaney will be lucky if he don't end up in jail."

Matthew closed his eyes and shook his head, a little confused. "Aren't you supposed to wait until the investigation is completed before talking about it?"

Koski finished the last sip of coffee in the cup. "What investigation? After seeing the security tape - Delaney, on the advice of his lawyer, gave up any defense. Films don't lie."

Jeannie still sat there horrified. She looked off to the side. "Uh, let's talk about something a little more…I don't know…happy!"

"Okay," said Matthew. "After a little trip to Albany, we're going to have a *real* happy time."

She stood up with a big smile on her face. "Hey, baby, I guess I'm gonna have to forgive you for playing that lottery." She put her hands in the air as she walked towards him. "I can hardly wait to see a *real* bluebonnet and hear a *real* mockingbird again. The pictures just don't cut it."

He walked toward her with his hands raised a little. "We'll go all the way from El Paso to Beaumont and Brownsville to Amarillo.

We'll see *all* of Texas and find out what we missed from home. We'll…"

He took hold of her hands to swing her around in celebration. As soon as he grabbed her right hand, she looked at it in anguish and screamed. She pulled her right hand up by her neck, with a pained grimace on her face, and cradled her right hand in her left.

He hugged her close, with a pained look on his face. "I'm sorry, Baby Doll, I'm sorry. I forgot! I'm sorry!"

When the pain subsided a little she looked up at him, still in pain. "When we get to Albany, there's probably someone there who'll want to shake my hand. What do I do?"

Odem snickered. "Why don't you put your whole right arm in a sling? Tell them that during your celebration, you hit something hard with your hand or arm and it's still a little tender."

Jeannie sighed. "Yeah, I did hit something…hard." She gave Matthew a nasty look. She sighed again. "I guess I'll find a towel or something that I can use as a sling."

Matthew and Jeannie went to Albany. Matthew called in to work and said that something important had come up and he would not be able to make it in today. The trip to Albany was impeded, at first, by traffic in New York City. Trying to get out of the city was slow and tedious. After getting out onto the highway, it was smooth sailing all the way to the state capitol. It took an hour or so before they found the correct address. Once inside, they identified themselves, showed the winning ticket and then, were treated like royalty.

Matthew had chosen the payment option on the jackpot. Instead of receiving a lump sum *now,* he would get $1/26^{th}$ of the winnings today and another $1/26^{th}$ of the winnings each year on the anniversary of the jackpot drawing for 25 years. $13,192,307.00 (before taxes) ($8,311,154 after taxes) was a nice tidy sum. Matthew told Jeannie that even if they screwed up and squandered this first payment, they would have another thirteen million next year. Both were very happy with that arrangement.

They decided to spend the night in Albany. After all they had to go through, with the lottery commission, they were pretty well exhausted. Drive back tomorrow and start getting a new life going for themselves.

Their son Robert had not really wanted to go to a city college in New York, however, they could not afford anything else - at that time. Now, if he wanted to switch to some other college - they definitely could afford it now. They sat there in a hotel room, discussing what they knew about the different major colleges that he had mentioned. Sometime during that conversation, they both gave in to the fatigue from the activities of the day.

After a very refreshing sleep, they drove back to New York City and went straight to their bank. The check was going to be deposited, because that was just way too much to be carrying around…even if it was a check and not cash.

Of course, Matthew missed another day of school. He did not really care. He remembered that there was some kind of fine that the school had for a teacher missing a day of school - without a valid reason. The fine, if he remembered correctly, was around $500.00. Big deal! He had just deposited over eight million dollars into his account. He figured that he could afford one or two of their penalties... with a great big yawn.

The next day was Sunday. Matthew contemplated what he was going to do at the school on Monday. They had seen that the news of their winning was all over every news station and newspaper. The fact that it was one of the largest amounts ever won, made it such a big deal.

Their phone was ringing constantly. Both of them were tired of answering it. When he was able to (between all of the scam artists, money-grubbers and 'so called' financial mangers), Matthew made an outbound call to Robert. Robert (and all of his friends) had heard of the big win and he was being pestered at school as well. He was getting tired of all the "brand new" friends. They were coming up with very inventive ideas as to why he should be giving them some money. He was wanting to quit here, help them move to Texas and start all over again at some major college...next year. Matthew and Jeannie both decided to go along with that plan. Then the phone was unplugged.

No good! Since the phone was unplugged, all of the scam artists, money-grubbers and 'so called' financial managers were now coming to the door. Matthew promised young Solomon Gokey $200 if he would run interference. At first Solomon wanted to get greedy and demand more - until he found out that there were a few other teenagers in this apartment building who would do it for $200. Faced with $200 or nothing...$200 was fine.

Even when they had been in Albany, Matthew and Jeannie were getting tired of answering the question: "What are you going to do with the money?" The couple decided on a mocking pat answer that they would give to everyone: "We are going to go on a six month alcohol binge and if there is anything left over afterwards, we are going to donate it to a rest home for retired exotic dancers." They included Robert in on this little conspiracy.

On Monday, Matthew waded through all of the reporters and other morons. He almost had to fight to get to the subway. Some of the morons followed him down the stairs. Most stayed up on the street. Once he got into the subway car, he was (for the most part) left alone by the morons. It was the morning rush and trying to carry on an interview in a sardine-packed subway car was impossible.

When he got out at his stop, the parasitic morons were, once again, on his tail. He ignored them completely on his quest to get to the school. When he arrived at the school, he groaned in misery when he saw that there was a new entourage of morons at the school. Several of the teachers were doing everything they could to keep the morons out. Fortunately, they had a few police officers there to help.

Matthew fought his way through the morons and into the school. Once inside he breathed a sigh of relief and then looked around him. All eyes - students and teachers that were close by - were on him. He grunted in disgust and headed for the teachers lounge.

Once in the lounge he met more stares. Some of them snickered a little, others whispered. Some smiled and a few stared in contempt.

Mr. Stanley Waterman, the calculus teacher, walked up to him with a look of disdain. Waterman was very tall and lanky. When Matthew had met the man, over twenty years ago, he had looked as if he were in his seventies. He still looked that old. He always wore dark, three piece suits. He always had a dull look of disdain in those bloodshot gray eyes, and he kept his thin gray hair very short. "Well, the *wealthy* prodigal son, hath returned." He sniffed derisively. "Since you now have all that money, do you think you could put something into the coffee fund?"

Matthew had prepared for this. He was expecting someone else to mention the coffee, but was not surprised at Waterman being the one. He pulled two-one pound cans of coffee out of the big pockets of his parka. One pound of regular and one decaf. "Do you think that this is enough to stop you from belly-aching for at least three minutes?"

Waterman looked down his nose at the cans. "I suppose that there's enough there to last us the day. What *shall* we do tomorrow?"

"We may have to suffer," said a cheery voice behind Matthew. Matthew turned around and saw the head of the history department: Cecil Ressler. Mr. Ressler was more congenial then any of the other teachers in the school. He was about five and one half feet tall, had a little paunch in the middle, a very bad comb-over with what was left of his dark brown hair and a very thick mustache that completely hid his upper lip. "Congratulations, sir," he said very cordially as he stuck out his hand for a shake. Matthew believed that this was the one man who was really sincere in what he was saying.

"Thank you, sir," said Matthew with an equal amount of sincerity.

The girls physical education teacher sat there shaking her head. Her blonde ponytail wagging back and forth. "Why couldn't it have been me? Oh well, congratulations on your win."

Several others congratulated him and a minority of them were exactly like Waterman.

The principal came up to him: Mr. Lionel Youngkin. This man was of average height, light brown hair, graying at the temples, and one of the people who (like Waterman) always wore a three piece suit. "Congratulations on your new fortune. I wonder! How long are we going to have to put up with running a gauntlet of journalists in order to get into our school?"

"Only about two weeks," said Matthew calmly. "I am giving you my two weeks notice today. I plan on being back home in Texas soon enough to where I can see bluebonnets blooming again."

There were several different protests from virtually all of the teachers in the lounge.

Youngkin flapped his hands at all of them to quiet down. He then looked back at Matthew, with irritation on his face. "You can't quit now…not in the middle of a school year. You have to stay and maintain till the end of the year, and then you can go…where ever you want to go. Quitting now would hurt the students. Where would we possibly find a biology teacher with your qualifications, especially at such a short notice? You would be upsetting the entire curriculum."

Matthew looked at Waterman. "I'm sure that Stan could find someone very quickly. He never wanted me here to begin with and he has constantly stated that 'any idiot' could replace me."

"We could try one of those prostitutes that patrol Broadway," said Waterman as rudely as he could muster. "They could teach biology with the similar results as any heathen from Texas."

Youngkin snarled at Waterman. "That's enough of that!"

Waterman just grunted.

Youngkin looked back at Matthew. "The top three candidates for valedictorian are in your class. I mean..."

"Two," said Matthew emphatically.

Youngkin looked as if he had been slapped. "What do you mean, two? There are three who are up there with the 4.0 GPA dating back to their freshman year."

Matthew thought for a moment. "Who is the third?"

Youngkin huffed impatiently. "Bartlett, Cunningham and Zamarippa!"

Matthew sighed. "Zamarippa and Bartlett - yes. Cunningham? Not a chance."

Youngkin almost looked scared. "What do you mean?"

Matthew looked around at the other teachers. "Lucy? Where are you?"

A cheery voice came from somewhere in the crowd. "Back here, in the back as usual." Several people parted to make a path as Lucy Crippin - the chemistry teacher came forward. "What is it that you want, dear?"

"What are the chances that Tyler Cunningham will pass

chemistry?"

The smile left Crippin's face and she made wide arcing thumbs down with both arms. "As far as chemistry is concerned, I could show him a pile of fools gold and convince him, *easily*, that it was a cheese fondue."

Youngkin looked horrified. "But...but...but he was doing so well...I mean, all of his classes so far...he has excelled, hasn't he?"

"With a lot of tutoring," said several of the teachers.

Matthew gave Youngkin a faint smile. "Again - Zamarippa and Bartlett - yes. Cunningham is bombing in chemistry and I don't think he'll make it through biology as well. The only interest that he has, biologically speaking, is to somehow get into the panties of those two Chinese girls. Other than that, he has not gained any knowledge in biology."

"We're getting off of the subject," said Youngkin. "You cannot leave! Not now! Not in the middle of the school year."

Matthew looked up and shook his head. "What is to stop me from just walking out the door and never coming back?"

"You are a professional teacher! You are supposed to care about your students!" Youngkin appeared to be getting flustered.

Matthew stared at the principal dull-eyed. "If I were in a school where the students cared - I might. This is not a special school for gifted students or over achievers. This is a snob institution for children of the filthy rich. It is not special academic achievements that get those students in here, it's their parents bank accounts."

Youngkin huffed in desperation. "Is that so wrong? Those

parents are paying a lot of money, so that we can give their children a good quality education. Okay, there are some dead-beats…but you're going to get that in any school. We should still care…for the students who care."

Matthew addressed the entire room. "How many of those students care? The vast majority of them are here just to use up time. Time while they are minors, waiting to become adults. When they become adults, then Mommy or Daddy will give them a, very undeserved, position in the firm or company that Mommy or Daddy built from scratch. Most of these punks will be getting a position, not a job. They will get a position that they do not deserve and have not worked for. Tell me folks, how many of them really care?"

Waterman snorted. "That's not for us to worry about. You're getting paid to educate these, what did you say, "punks". You are getting paid well…"

"Go ahead," teased Matthew. "Finish it! I'm getting paid - what?"

Waterman wrinkled a piece of paper in his hand in anger. He glanced down at the paper, got a pained look on his face and gasped. He then went over to a table and started smoothing the paper out.

"I deposited a check, into my bank account, for over eight point three million dollars. *What* - exactly do I *need* from this school… *now*?"

"Please," pleaded Youngkin. "I know that the money…I know that you won't need it…but…think of…" He broke off, looking around for some word or ideology that would turn the argument to his favor.

"I will talk it over with my wife," Matthew said flatly. "She has it in her heart to go frolicking in the bluebonnets in the Spring. *This* upcoming Spring…with me. I really don't want to disappoint her."

"Send her back to Texas," said Youngkin quickly. "You can join her after school lets out. It's only until June 4th or 5th that you'll be separated."

"I'm not breaking up my family, for your convenience," said Matthew through clenched teeth. "When we go back to Texas, we go together. We have always been together and I don't see any reason to change that now."

"One positive for the school," said Waterman. "We don't need to pay him anymore…not with 8.3 million dollars in the bank."

"Oh, no, no, no, no, no, no," said Matthew. "If you want me to stay - you will pay. If I get no pay - I am gone, NOW!"

"All right!" Youngkin looked even more desperate. "Please, talk to your wife. Please, reason with her."

From off to the side: "Oh, GAD!"

Both of them looked at the man who said had interjected. It was the big muscle-bound coach of the boys physical education, Roger Du Bois. He walked over to Youngkin, shaking his head. "Have you ever met his wife? Have you ever tried to, in any way, shape, or form try to get a point across to that little hard-headed wildcat?"

"Uh, no…I don't remember…talking to…her," said Youngkin defensively.

"Give it up! You've already lost the argument." Du Bois

walked away shaking his head.

Youngkin looked at Matthew with fear and confusion in his eyes.

"I will talk to her," said Matthew again.

Lionel Youngkin did not get very much accomplished during the rest of the school day.

Matthew Tate did not get very much accomplished either. His students (as usual) did not care very much about biology. They had all kinds of questions about his plans for the money. No matter how hard he tried to follow the lesson plan, they all persisted in questions about the money. He went home with a headache.

When he arrived home, he was hoping for a quiet night. Jeannie was sitting in the living room with a big smile and a pile of travel brochures. There was some big lump on the coffee table that she had covered up with a bath towel.

Their son Robert was also there. He was not quite as tall as his father, but he was over 6 feet. He had brown hair like both of his parents and had inherited his fathers curly hair as well as his facial features. "Well, Dad, when do we head to Texas?"

Matthew's shoulders sagged as he sighed. "I don't know," he said solemnly.

Jeannie lost the smile that had been on her face. "Whatcha

mean, Baby?"

"The other teachers at the school…they are saying that I should stay and finish the year. If I don't then they say that I will foul up their curriculum."

Jeannie was a little angry and confused. "How can you foul up that bunch of snobby brats? You've told me a bunch of times that most of them don't care."

He sighed. "There are some who care. They are asking me to finish the school year for those students."

Robert grunted. "So what am I supposed to do? You said that I could walk away from that local yokel college and start looking at a seriously good college."

"Don't change your plans, son. We can still afford to send you to whatever college you want to go to. Think of your future. Your real life is just beginning and I don't want that trampled." He walked over and sat next to Jeannie. He looked at the pile of brochures. "They simply want me to postpone the move until June. Once June comes along, then they will not and cannot have any argument to keep me here at all."

"So, what do I do? I got all ready to move and I got all these brochures so I can plan a vacation after the move." She sat there frowning at Matthew. "I'm really beginning to hate that school. We got something where we can control our lives and that snob school has to stand in the way."

He put his arm around her shoulder. "They suggested that you go ahead to Texas and I follow in June."

She stood up and put her fists on her hips. "NO! NO! I ain't going back without ya! Don't you know, that if I do that, then some old busy-body like Mrs. Goldberg will start rumors that you and me is havin' trouble in our marriage. I am not going through that."

He put his arm around her waist and pulled her close. She sat down straddling his left leg. He hugged her close with both arms behind her back. She put her arms around his neck and rested her head on his. "We have never been apart. I don't like the idea of doing that. Why don't we try to think of some…some positive in this situation?"

They all sat in silence for a while.

"It's easier to move during the Summer," said Robert. "No snow to worry about. Not here or anywhere along the way to Texas. There is a mountain range that we have to drive through to get there."

Matthew kissed her neck. "We will be together…as always."

She pulled her head back in order to look Matthew in the eyes. "Tell that bunch of stuck-up Yankees, that if they irritate you, then you'll leave anyway, in spite of those *needy* brats."

He stood up still holding on to her. She squawked in surprise and grabbed hold of his head. She wrapped her legs around his waist.

He snickered. "It will also give us plenty of time to pack. We can do it at a leisurely pace. We'll have plenty of time to get everything together."

"Okay. Okay, we'll stay," she said. "But come June…we go like scalded dogs, so we don't give them any chance to come up with another reason for us to stay."

"Agreed," said Matthew.

"Absolutely agreed," said Robert.

Matthew looked down at the towel covered lump on the coffee table. He sat down, looked up at Jeannie with his eyebrows raised. He reached over and pulled the towel away. He looked in stunned surprise. "What…?"

Jeannie kissed him several times and hugged his head closer. "I just wanted to see what a hundred thousand dollars in cash looked like. That's all." She pulled back a little and tilted his head back so that she could look closer into his eyes. "It's our money and…we can do things that we never done before. We can put it back in the bank…I just wanted to see what it felt like to hold that much cash in my hands at one time…knowing that it was *my* money."

He stood up again, still holding on to her. He growled and shook his head. He looked deep into her eyes. "Oh, you little scamp! Of course it's ours to do with as we please and…wait a minute…how did you get out of the building? And, how did you get back in with all that money?"

She giggled. "Them critters outside are looking for me…or you…or Robert. They are not looking for a fat old woman. I pulled out that silly white fright wig that you got last Halloween. I did a little styling on it, bundled up with several layers and then walked out of here a little hunched over. They never gave me a second glance."

"Well, you had to show your ID at the bank, didn't you?"

She giggled again. "When I got around the corner, I took the wig off. I went all the way to the bank, got the money out, came back, and before I came back around that last corner, I put the wig back on."

He looked up at the ceiling and huffed. He sat there just staring up and then started chuckling. "So…other than looking at the money, what are we going to do with it?"

"I don't know. Buy a new car maybe."

Robert chimed in. "Maybe you could buy a car for me?" He sat there with a big smile on his face.

"No," said Matthew flatly. "We are not wasting any more money on any New York jalopy. When June comes up, we will put all of our possessions in a moving van, we will sell that rust bucket that we have now, and then we will fly - *first class* - back home to Texas. Once in Texas, that's when we will buy a whole fleet of sedans, coupes, pickups or whatever."

They all laughed.

"Meanwhile, you find a good place to hide that cash."

Jeannie grabbed Matthew's ears. "How about on top of the armoire?" She gave him an angry look.

He laughed out loud. "I love you, Baby Doll."

The next few school days were not any easier. No matter how hard Matthew tried to stay with the lesson plan, someone always figured out a way to get nosy about the money.

One of the other tasks that Matthew had at the school was to be a student counselor. The purpose of the counseling was to try to get them on track with their academic goals, and plans for the future. Now, the only thing that most of the students wanted was to discuss the money, and how he went about picking the winning numbers. Others just wanted to complain about how "Daddy" had taken away or decreased how much they could charge at all of the different department stores.

The most vocal about losing her charge accounts was Olivia Siegelman. Olivia was a very cute, brown-eyed blonde. She had a figure that she was always willing to show off. She always had plenty of cleavage exposed and wore very short dresses. Matthew would try to ignore her monetary complaints and her obvious feminine attributes and shift the conversation around to her scholastics, so that she could work to obtain her own accounts, that no one could cut off. No, she mainly wanted to be able to buy anything she desired and have someone else pay for it. She wanted a rich "Sugar Daddy" who would worship and pamper her for the rest of her life. There were never any positive accomplishments in her counseling sessions.

A cohort in crime to Olivia was another little gorgeous knockout named Cynthia Augsburger. She had raven hair and no one was sure what color her eyes were because she wore a different set of colored contacts every time you saw her. Her charge accounts had been severely limited by Daddy as well. She did not care about her GPA, or school, she did not care whether $1 + x = 18$ or 99 or 4 to the 6th power. All she wanted was to get an unlimited charge account in any store in New York, Newark, Philadelphia and the surrounding area for at least 500 miles. Matthew was not sure she could really comprehend what 500 miles was.

A third headache of a greedy little gold digger was an overly friendly, very bubbly, highly attractive girl named Patricia Hamond. Most of the time she was distracting all of the boys, because she would go around braless. The school had somehow forced her into wearing shirts that were not too tight or transparent. Her flaxen hair was very long and always in a ponytail behind her back so that she was not covering her ample breasts. There always seemed to be some kind of look in those hazel eyes. She always looked as if she was scheming. She was one person that Matthew felt he could never trust, just from the look in her eyes.

Most of the time, Matthew wondered why he ever wasted any of his time counseling any of these students. He rarely walked out of one of the sessions with any positive feelings. His patience with all of these spoiled brats was getting very thin…especially now that he had enough money and really did not have to put up with any of it.

Two weeks after Matthew and Jeannie had picked up their first lottery check, the police were pounding on the door while the Tate family was having breakfast. The entire family was surprised because Jeannie had not had one of her loud tantrums. Matthew had not cut loose with any loud "Yeehaws" lately. Robert had decided to cooperate and not vibrate the entire building with his loud stereo. Why are the police here? Why are they being so noisy?

Jeannie answered the door. She had become somewhat accustomed to seeing Sgt. Ivan Koski. He was not with this group.

A large man wearing a suit and an overcoat, who had a large wart on the left side of his forehead, looked down at Jeannie with a great deal of anger in his eyes. "Where is Mr. Matthew Tate?"

She stammered a little. "He…he…uh…at the kitchen…table. What…what's going on?"

"We have a warrant for his arrest," the man said gruffly.

Jeannie stood there stunned. She could not think. She could not move. She watched as the policemen quickly moved into the apartment. She felt dizzy. She held onto the door for dear life. She stood there frozen.

The police walked into the kitchen. They saw Matthew and Robert sitting at the table.

Again, it was the suit that talked. "Which one of you is Matthew Tate?"

"I am," said Matthew. "What's going on?"

"Stand up!"

"What for?"

The suit leaned his head back and looked down his nose at Matthew. "You're under arrest."

"For what?" Matthew was ready to start swinging wild, just like Jeannie. "All I did was win the lottery. How is that a crime?"

The suit pulled his gun out and aimed it at Matthew. The look on his face was pure hatred. "You are under arrest for five counts of child molestation." He took hold of his gun with both hands and aimed it even more carefully. "I hate monsters like you. I hate child molesters. *Please*, do something stupid. Give me a *reason* to pull this trigger…a good reason, *please.*"

Matthew was just as stunned as Jeannie. He, however, did not have the luxury of a door to hold onto. He slowly stood up and put up with being frisked and shackled.

Without putting his gun away, the suit stared with even more hatred at Matthew. "Unfortunately, even walking phlegm like you has rights under the Constitution." The suit quoted the familiar lines of the Miranda rights.

Jeannie had finally come out of her daze and had come back into the kitchen. "What is goin' on?"

"We're taking this child molester in, to face judgment."

Jeannie looked at Matthew in shock.

"It's a big mistake," said Matthew. "They're making a *huge* mistake. I'll get it cleared up and have the moron with the wart on his forehead begging for mercy."

"Excuse me," said Robert. "I need…"

The suit cut him off. "Unless you have something pertinent to say - keep your trap shut!"

"This is pertinent!" snapped Robert.

"Oh yeah?" said the suit in a whiny voice. "What could you possibly have to say that has anything to do with what's going on here?"

Robert spat back with equal venom: "Where are you taking him?"

The suit closed his eyes. He sniffed, cleared his throat and swallowed. "Fourteenth precinct," he said quietly. "It's located…"

"I'll find it myself," said Robert. "I can't trust directions from a moron with a wart on his face."

The suit scowled at Robert. He looked back at Matthew. "Do

you understand your rights?"

"Not coming from you," said Matthew flatly. "I don't understand or speak wart moron. Someone with a lot more intelligence than you is going to have to quote them before they make any sense."

The suit got an evil smile on his face. "Oh, you are going to be a *lot* of fun."

After the police left with Matthew in tow, Jeannie stood there staring into space in shock. Robert put his arms around her and walked her to a chair. He sat her down carefully. "Mom?" He waved his hand in front of her face. She barely responded. "Mom!" She slowly turned her head and looked at him.

"What just happened?"

"The cops…took Dad away." He looked at the door. "Come on, get dressed. We gotta find out what this is all about."

"Yeah," she said softly. "Find out." She slowly wandered back to her bedroom to change. "Find out," she said still in shock.

The group arrived at their precinct. They hauled him into an interrogation room, sat him down and shackled him to the table. The suit with the wart sat down on the other side of the table. Another suit walked into the room and sat down next to wart. They said nothing. They just stared at Matthew. He shook his head and stared out the barred window. The three of them sat there, without moving, in total silence, for almost an hour.

Finally a third suit walked in. "Get the show on the road. We don't have time for this mind game."

Wart turned and gave a disgusted look at the third suit. He turned back to Matthew. "I'm Detective Lawson. My partner here is Detective Andrews. We work in a special unit that deals with perverts...like you. We like putting scum like you behind bars... for the rest of your worthless life. Why don't you make it easier on yourself and tell us what happened?"

Matthew, still staring out the window, grunted in disgust. "I don't know what you're talking about."

"Well," said Andrews. "What brought you here?"

"An idiot with a wart on his face," said Matthew bluntly.

Lawson looked slight miffed. "*You* are the idiot! *You* are the one who forces minors into sex acts and then thinks that you'll get away with it."

"The only woman, that I have ever had sex with is my wife, Jeannie. She was nineteen when we got married, so I can honestly say that I have never had sex with a minor."

"Oh come on!" Lawson chuckled and rolled his eyes. "You've been teaching at that school for years. All those good looking girls. Are you going to try to tell me that you never poked any of them?"

"That's your perversion. I'm not a pervert and I don't need anyone other than my wife."

Lawson stood up. "Then WHY, all of a sudden, did five of them come forward and claim that you've been forcing them to have sex with you for at least three years?"

'Five,' thought Matthew. 'What five?' He was the primary counselor for fifteen students. Only four of them were girls. He

120

inventoried the list in his mind. Olivia Siegelman: Conceited exhibitionist, gold digger, greedy, totally without conscience, only goal is to be pampered for the rest of her life. Patricia Hamond: Another exhibitionist, schemer, seemingly amoral, another one who wanted to be pampered. Cynthia Augsburger: Narcissistic, greedy, greedy, greedy, no concern for scholastics at all. Stacy Van Cleave: The only one of the four girls who cared about academics. A brilliant mind. Ugly as sin. Big enough to be a starting middle linebacker for any team in the National Football League. Hardcore lesbian. Olivia, Patricia and Cynthia might be three of the five that Lawson was talking about. Stacy - no way! Who could the other two be? He did say at least three years. That meant they had to be either juniors or seniors. All four of his female counselees were seniors. No help there.

Matthew's thoughts were broken by Andrews. "Well? What do you have to say for yourself?"

Matthew sighed. "Who are these…five? Since I haven't touched anyone, I have no idea who is doing this."

"Oh, I see," said Lawson. "You mean: *which* five. So you've molested so many girls that you don't have a clue who finally got tired of your illegal advances."

Matthew looked at Lawson doing everything he could to control his anger. "Hey Wartface! Unless you have something pertinent to say, why don't you keep that rancid vomit-hole of yours shut? Nobody's interested in your infantile stupidity. And *I* said what *I* meant. I said that I don't know who these five are, because I have *not* touched anybody."

Andrews raised his eyebrows. "You never touched any of the

girls that you counsel?"

"Never. I haven't touched them for several reasons. One of those reasons is that they *are* minors…and students. I don't touch either. Another good reason is that I am married. I am married, with a pre-nuptial agreement that would lead me to total ruin if I were to do anything…along the line of adultery. Third, most of those girls are so conceited that they would not bother themselves with someone like me. I'm too poor."

"Poor! Poor?" Lawson looked at Andrews and laughed. "Not any more! You got millions!"

"Not enough," said Matthew in a demeaning manner. "Most of the students at that school have parents that are on the 'Fortune 400' list, or darn close to being on it. Not one of them would consider fooling around with a piker like me. The amount of money that I have would not keep them in new shoes for a year."

"Well, why don't you run down the list of the girls that you…" Andrews looked sideways at Lawson and back at Matthew. "… counsel?"

Matthew did not like the game they were playing, however, he decided that it might be the best way to get any information out of his antagonists. "Patricia Hamond."

"Ooh, one for one," teased Lawson.

'Not surprising,' thought Matthew. "Cynthia Augsburger."

Andrews chuckled. "Two for two."

'Again, not surprising,' he pondered. "Olivia Siegelman."

"Still batting a thousand," chided Lawson.

"Stacy Van Cleave."

Both detectives were taken by surprise and were unable to hide it. They both sat there frozen with stupid smiles on their faces. The smiles faded and they both opened a file that was in front of them and checked several pages. They looked at each other confused.

"So," said Lawson. "Either she hasn't had the courage to come forward with the charges or this is one that you left alone."

"I kinda think it's the first one," said Andrews.

"Keep running down the list," said Lawson.

Matthew took in a deep breath. "Adolpho Zamarippa, Damon Maldanado, Daniel Cuniowski…"

"Just the girls," growled Andrews.

"…James Hartze, Alfred Sutherland, Donald Smith, Gilbert Young…"

Now Lawson chimed in. "Hey fathead! We said just the girls."

"…Manuel De La Garza, Jonathan Perkins, Justin Charles and Frank Seago."

Andrews looked very upset. "What? You don't hear so good? We said: Just the girls!"

"I just ran through all fifteen of *my* counselees. Four girls and eleven boys. That's why I don't know who the *five* are. I am only counseling *four* girls. And if you don't believe me as to who I counsel - why don't you get off of your lazy butts and go check with the school. They have records of who I am the primary counselor for." He leaned forward and gave Andrews an evil stare. "I dare you, to go to the school and check on *that*."

"Nice try," said Andrews smirking. "We have checked. The other teachers at the school already told us that from time to time, the students will seek the advice of someone other than their primary counselor."

"There would be a record of that. If I had counseled someone else, to the point where I got into their pants, they would have, in all probability, missed a class or would have been late to class. There would have to be a record of that somewhere. There is only a ten minute interval between classes. No one can diddle someone else, between classes. There just is *not* enough time."

Lawson looked thoughtful for a moment. "Isn't it mandatory that all students take your class? I mean, when I was in school, biology was a mandatory course."

"Not all schools have the same curriculum. In ours, you can take any one of the sciences as a mandatory course: Biology, chemistry, anthropology, sociology, botany, paleontology or oceanography."

Lawson looked at Andrews. "He has a nice way of hedging around the issue, doesn't he?"

Andrews nodded. "Not gonna help him at all though."

"I've had enough of you cavemen," said Matthew scornfully. "I want a lawyer right now. I'm sick of your childish attitudes."

Lawson chuckled. "It may be a while before we can find one for you. We'll have to put you in the holding cell. It would be a shame if any of those cons in there were to find out that you're a child molester. Why don't you just make it easier on yourself and confess to the whole thing?"

Matthew felt a chill go down his spine and his heart started hammering in his chest. He had heard about what happens to child molesters in prison. He had not done anything and he could not afford to be put in a cell with, who knows how many, hardened criminals that cannot stand a molester. "Are you telling me that you are willingly violating my civil rights? You are planning on using coercion in order to obtain a confession to a crime that *I did not* commit?"

"Oh no," said Lawson with a fake sympathetic attitude. "We just don't know how long it's going to take to find a lawyer for you. We wouldn't dream of violating anything." He then let loose a low evil chuckle.

The door came open and a high pitched male voice was heard: "Too bad. I was hoping that you would violate his rights and then that would make this case *so* much simpler." In walked a man who stood only about five feet tall. He was completely bald on the top of his head and the red, mixed with wisps of white, hair partially covered his ears and the back of his collar. He had a very pale complexion with a few freckles dotting his face. His high voice was a little irritating to the ears but whenever he spoke, he did so with an air of complete confidence. He looked at Matthew with his very small dark eyes. "Hello, I am Marcus Orsini. Your wife has retained my services as your lawyer."

Matthew's heart rate started slowing quickly. He did not want the two detectives to see any relief on his face so he did everything he could to maintain a complete "poker" face. 'Thank God, that little

Jeannie had come to the rescue,' he thought.

Orsini turned back to the two detectives. "I believe my client said that he wanted to talk to his lawyer. Time for you two threats to society and sanity to leave the room."

"Marcus, Marcus, Marcus," said Andrews in a demeaning tone. "I thought that you dealt with fraud cases. What are you doing, lowering yourself to helping a sex pervert?"

"This is a fraud case, you moron. Five snotty little bimbos are trying to defraud my client out of his lottery winnings."

"Oh come on! Those families have plenty of money," said Lawson. "Are you trying to tell me that they are so greedy that they want Tate's money as well?"

"Yes, they are very greedy," said Orsini impatiently. "Now, would you please get out of here? I need to talk to my client!"

Lawson and Andrews got up grudgingly. They both had distasteful looks on their faces.

Orsini followed them to the door. "Shut the microphone off."

"We always do," said Andrews.

"Excuse me," said Orsini in a demeaning tone. "But after that incident with those three Puerto Rican boys, I find it impossible to believe anything that comes out of your mouth. Your own department doesn't trust you either, do they?"

Matthew heard a snarl. He then heard Jeannie's voice - hollering: "I wanna be in there too!"

"Mrs. Tate, I need someone out here to make sure that they

don't turn the microphone back on."

"Robert, honey, you can do that for Momma, can't you?"

"No problem," said Robert flatly.

Jeannie came marching in, arms held tightly at her sides, with a stern look on her face. "Give me a reason!"

Orsini put his hand on Jeannie's shoulder. "Please, Mrs. Tate, let me do this. I know that you're upset, but I need everyone to keep a cool head right now."

Matthew was a little confused. "A reason…?" He shook his head and held his arms out wide in a questioning manner. "What do you mean?"

"A reason to trust you…a reason to believe you!"

Now Orsini was a little more firm. "Mrs. Tate! I am wondering the same thing. *Please,* my dear, have a seat and we'll work this out."

She took in a deep breath and blew it back out. Her gaze went back and forth from Orsini to Matthew several times. She clenched her jaws tight, sat down in a seat on the other side of the table from Matthew and folded her arms. The look in her eyes showed confusion, anger and hurt.

Matthew leaned over the table. He looked deep into her eyes. "You know… *You* know that I did not do anything like this. You *know.* After the accident…the aftermath…the pre-nuptial agreement… coming to New York…you know that I would not do anything to hurt you, or endanger our relationship in any way. You know."

Orsini cleared his throat. "Please, Mr. Tate, you need to talk to me."

Without moving his head, only his eyes, Matthew looked at Orsini: "One thing at a time." His eyes went back to Jeannie. "I love you, only you, I've never touched anyone but you."

Orsini sighed and started tapping his fingers on the table.

Matthew leaned back in the chair, looked over at Orsini and sighed. "Okay, what do you need?"

Orsini pursed his lips and stood there thinking for a moment. "I need what your wife asked for…a reason. I need a reason to trust you. I need some shred of evidence that will help me believe you." Orsini suddenly looked as if he had been hit by something. "Wait a minute," he mumbled. "Did you say something about a pre-nuptial agreement?"

"Yes," said Matthew calmly.

"Is there something in this document that could help your situation?"

Jeannie started to say something and Matthew held up his hand to silence her.

"Baby Doll, give him a copy of the agreement. Let him read it and let him decide if there is anything that he can use to help the situation."

Jeannie gave Matthew a dirty look. She glanced at Orsini and then said a small: "Okay." She hung her head and sighed.

"Let's get one thing straight," said Orsini. "I am *her* lawyer. *She* hired me. She is now asking me to help you. I haven't decided whether I am or not. I need something from you, to give me a reason to defend you."

Matthew's shoulders sagged and he hung his head. He sighed and looked up. "So you don't trust me? Well, the lack of trust goes both ways. You want something from me in order to give you a good reason to defend me? First, I need something from you."

Orsini was taken aback. He stuttered for a moment, clenched his eyes shut, opened them and looked incredulous. "What? What could I possibly have that would help you?"

"Names."

Orsini looked off to the side perplexed. He slightly shook his head. He looked at Matthew. "Need more information."

Matthew sighed. "Those two pinheads told me that there are *five* girls who filed a complaint. They said that all five were getting academic counseling, from me, at the school. Problem: I am currently the primary counselor for fifteen students - eleven of which are boys. Only four are girls. This causes a conundrum in the numbers. Now, you might initially say: Who is the fifth girl? That question is only partially correct. When I asked them who the *five* are, they decided to try a mind game, in order to try to trap me. I named my primary female counselees: Cynthia Augsburger, Olivia Siegelman, Patricia Hamond and Stacy Van Cleave. Now...the detectives confirmed that the first three, that I named, definitely are three of the five complainants. The other two complainants...I have no clue. Since I have not molested anybody, in or out of that school, I am drawing a complete blank, as to the names of the other two. I would be throwing a couple of darts in a dark room and I can't even guess which direction to throw the darts.

I need the names of the other two."

Orsini digested the information. "This information about you only counseling four girls...can this be confirmed through school records?"

"Absolutely."

He licked his lips. He set his briefcase down on the table, opened it, pulled out a file and started thumbing through the papers in the file. "All right, I'll give you a clue."

"Anything, please!"

He looked back down at the paper. "The first names of the other two girls are Teresa and Laura." He looked up at Matthew expectantly.

Matthew gave him nothing but a blank stare. "Nothing," he said flatly.

Orsini sighed. "Teresa Maltby...Laura O'Reilly."

Matthew contemplated for a few moments. "Nothing...I've heard that name."

"Which one?"

"O'Reilly. I've heard it...but...I don't know. Neither one of them are students in any of my classes."

"Are you telling me that biology is *not* a mandatory course?"

"Science is mandatory. Which science you go to is optional."

"What options?"

"Chemistry, Oceanography, Botany…"

"Okay, okay, okay, I get the picture - any science. So obviously these other two girls are in one of the other science classes."

"If they're students at that school, then yes."

Orsini dropped his papers and looked stunned. "Wait a minute! You said: Stacy Van Cleave? The Van Cleave family…from…?"

"Uh…yeah…why?"

"Stacy? That big tall…uh…lesbian…?"

"Yes…why?"

Orsini cleared his throat. "Well, if she ever does become one of the complainants, then…my being here would be a conflict of interest."

Matthew could do nothing but close his eyes and groan.

"So you say that you do not know these other two girls and that you are not the primary academic counselor for them. How does that give me anything?"

"If they are saying that I am their primary counselor…that is the first part of their mendacity that can punch holes in the whole situation."

Jeannie broke in: "Huh? Men-what?"

Matthew smiled at Jeannie. "Mendacity…mendacious…look it up in the dictionary. It's another word for fibbing."

"Then why didn't you say fib?"

Dara J. Carr

"Because we are going to be going into a courtroom. They like big words."

"Okay, I'll look it up," she said while contemplating.

"Please, folks," said Orsini. "We need to focus on the case - not vocabulary...or vernacular."

"Okay," said Jeannie helplessly.

"I need to get into my office at the school and check on a few things, in order to prove that I do not have any contact with those other two girls."

"You can't do that, sir, the school has already barred you from the premises."

Matthew felt his temper rise a little. He calmed it back down quickly. "Isn't there something in the legal system, that says something about 'full disclosure'? Is there also, something in the system, that says that if evidence is withheld, then I am being denied my rights?"

"Yes, there most certainly is. But, we will have to fight the school in order to get anything out of there."

"What if there is some kind of escort, or I am allowed to go in - after school hours, when no one else is there - and get what I need then?"

Orsini smiled. He pointed a finger at Matthew. "Now *that* can be arranged."

"How about arranging to get me out of here?"

Orsini gathered up his papers, put everything back in his briefcase, picked it up and went to the door. He opened it and looked at whoever was on the other side of the wall. "Excuse me, Robert is it?"

"Yeah."

"Was the microphone off, the whole time?"

"Yeah."

"Good, thank you." He looked in a different direction. "Hey, Lawson, either do the arraignment…NOW…or let him go."

Lawson came up and looked down his nose at Orsini. "It may be quite some time, before we can get him arraigned. We may have to put him in the holding cell for a few…days."

"If my client ends up in the holding cell, and by some strange event, a rumor is started in that cell about 'child molesting', and my client receives any injury, then I will make sure that you and your idiot partner are both charged with attempted first degree murder."

The two detectives grudgingly took Matthew to the courtroom.

When his docket came up, Jeannie nearly gagged when she heard a quarter million dollar bond. After assurances that they would get the vast majority of the money back, as long as Matthew did not flee the jurisdiction, she calmed down.

"You better be worth it," she scolded while glaring at Matthew.

Orsini looked at Matthew. "They are talking a date of February 15 for the pre-trial hearing. I don't see a problem with that."

"I do," said Matthew bluntly. "We still don't have certain information that we need. Put it off."

"Till when?"

"Right now, I don't know. As soon as I get the information from the school, I will let you know."

"I have to give the District Attorney's office something. I have to give them a reason as to why I'm putting it off."

Matthew closed his eyes and mentally counted to ten. He opened his eyes and took several deep breaths. "What did we talk about before? Full disclosure? No withholding of evidence? Until I can get into my office at the school, I will not be able to answer that question. Maybe, just maybe that will get the ball rolling a little faster. Let me get in there, find out what I need and then I can give you a firm answer."

Matthew and Orsini stared at each other for a few moments. "Okay. Okay. If that will get *something* moving, I will get you into the school."

On the following Monday, Matthew was allowed in the school...with an escort of Marcus Orsini, two policemen, principal Youngkin...and Mr. Stanley Waterman.

Matthew brought a brand new 4 gigabyte flash drive with him. He sat down at his desk, turned the computer on, let it boot up and then plugged in the flash drive.

Waterman saw the flash drive. "Wait a minute! You're not going to put any information on that thing."

"I am here to get relevant information. Nothing more."

"How do we know what is relevant?" Waterman looked at Youngkin. "He could be pulling all kinds of confidential information..."

Orsini interrupted: "Excuse me, sir, but, are you an expert on constitutional law, and the judicial system?"

Waterman looked at Orsini as if he were some kind of insect. "No," he said indignantly.

"Are you a member of, or in any way, associated with the District Attorney's office?"

Waterman rolled his eyes. "No."

"Are you a member of Mr. Tate's defense team?"

Waterman stared straight ahead with a disgusted look on his face. "No."

"Then don't tell me, or Mr. Tate, what he can or cannot do. The police are here for that endeavor."

Waterman looked at Orsini with even more disgust. "You are a horrible, *little* man."

"As to which one of us is *really* little...that is a matter of perspective. Now please keep your inappropriate opinions to yourself."

Matthew kept on looking up information on the five girls. He pulled up anything that he could find and saved it on the drive. There was only one piece of information that he was really searching for... now. Once he found it, he simply pulled up other things that might come in handy, and saved them without reading them. Since no one was looking at what he was putting on the drive, as soon as he finished, he erased all of the historical cookies in his computer. He then shut it down and pulled the flash drive.

Orsini looked expectant. "Are we finished here?"

"For the moment," said Matthew flatly.

Orsini looked at Youngkin. "Now, these two officers are going to seal this office. No one, I repeat *no one,* from the school is allowed in, until the investigation is completed. The only ones who are allowed in here are members of the DA's office, the forensic personnel or myself. Is that clear?"

Youngkin looked a little troubled. "How long will that be?"

"At this time - I don't have a clue."

Waterman, of course, had to get his complaint in: "Just exactly where, is our new Biology teacher supposed to have his office?"

Orsini walked away from Waterman and simply spoke out. "Not my problem."

Matthew followed Orsini quickly. They saw the police pulling out their yellow tape and heard Waterman belly-aching to Youngkin. When they got outside the building, they beat a hasty retreat to Orsini's car. They could see some reporters running down the sidewalk towards them. Even if Orsini had allowed Matthew to talk to reporters - he had nothing he wanted to say to them. They got into the car and quickly pulled out.

Orsini checked his mirrors several times, to make sure they were not being followed. "Did you find anything useful?"

"Yes and maybe."

Orsini grunted. "Do we have a date, that I can give to the DA or the Judge?"

"Yes, you can tell them that we will be ready on March 19, 2010."

Orsini gave an irritated huff. "March...what? That's more than a full month after what Judge Vance originally suggested."

"You wanted a date...that's the date you give them."

"But...but...why? Why wait all that time? Is there that much information on that flash drive?"

"You talked about trust. You said that you don't trust me. Well, back at yah! If you refuse to trust me...I can reciprocate. The earliest that we will be ready is March 19!"

Orsini pulled over to the side of the street and parked. He shut off the engine. He pulled a quarter out of the ashtray. "Here, put that in the parking meter. That will give us a few minutes to sit here and get...something accomplished."

Matthew got out stuck the quarter in the meter and then got back in the car.

Orsini had pulled a laptop out and was watching it boot up. When it was ready, he hit a few keys. The screen changed to a calendar. After perusing the screen for a few moments, Orsini looked over at Matthew with a bit of helplessness on his face. "That's a Friday."

"So?"

"No Judge likes to start any hearing, even a preliminary, on a Friday."

"And?"

"They prefer to start any trial on a Monday or Tuesday."

"Okay!"

"Can we back date it to Monday the 15th or Tuesday the 16th?"

Matthew growled. "No! I said that the 19th is *the very earliest* day, that we will be ready."

Orsini hung his head. He looked up and sniffed. "Okay, how about…Monday the 22nd of March?"

"Perfect," said Matthew with a smile.

Orsini grunted and started rapidly hitting keys as he shook his head. He stopped and waited while looking at the screen. A "ding" was heard and Orsini hit a few more keys. He read what was on his screen. "Mr. Coopersmith, the DA, wants to know."

"Know what?"

"Why are we waiting so long?"

Matthew cleared his throat. "Because we will not be ready until then."

"He needs a better answer than that."

"Is he handling the defense?"

Orsini scoffed impatiently. "Of course not!"

"Tell him that if he wants to handle the defense then he can negotiate the starting date…from the defense's perspective. If he is *not* handling the defense, then he cannot dictate defensive terms. *We* will not be ready until March 22nd."

"Do you teach biology as vaguely as this conversation is going?"

Matthew just chuckled.

Orsini shook his head and sent another message. He waited a few moments for another "ding". "Mr. Coopersmith doesn't like it but will accept it." A few moments later - another "ding". "Judge Vance has accepted it as well." He looked at Matthew. "May I know, what is on the flash drive?"

Matthew pulled it out of his pocket. "I found that Teresa Maltby and Laura O'Reilly. They *are* students at my school. As far as the science classes go, Teresa is wasting her time in oceanography and Laura is wasting her time in paleontology."

"What do you mean - wasting?"

"They're both *just* barely passing. Which means that their grades are probably being upped to 70 because of Daddy's money."

"Are your three girls in your biology class?"

"They are *in* my class. That's about all they are doing."

"Is there a class that all five are attending?"

Matthew swallowed. "Yes."

"And?"

"It's the only class, that all five, are excelling - acting and drama."

Orsini's jaw dropped and he looked forward. "Acting," he

said helplessly. He closed his eyes and thought for a few moments. "Are any of the girls...attractive?"

Matthew looked over at Orsini despondently. "The three that are in my class..." He cleared his throat. "...very!"

"The other two...?"

"Again, I am not acquainted with them. I have no idea what they look like. I would have to consult last year's yearbook. If they are in there then we can find out."

Orsini scratched his chin. "Got a copy of that yearbook?"

"Of course."

Orsini grunted. "Let's go take a look."

Matthew grunted back.

With a sigh, Orsini started the car and headed for the Tate residence.

When they arrived, they had to run through a gauntlet of microphones, cameras and idiots (also called journalists) who were all shouting out a bunch of inane questions.

Once they were inside, Orsini was clenching his teeth. "And I thought that the paparazzi were bad."

They walked into the apartment. Jeannie was sitting in the living room on the couch, staring off into space. Robert was watching some documentary on whales. Robert acknowledged their presence with a nod. Jeannie did not look up.

Matthew found the yearbook and looked up the two

"unknowns". "I *can* say that I have seen these girls…around, in the school. I can also say that I have never counseled either one."

"Let me have a look." Orsini accepted the book and started looking for all five of the girls. After flipping through and looking at each girl he put the book down with a somewhat scared look on his face. "I thought you said that the girls were *very* attractive."

Matthew was surprised. "Uh…they are!"

"No, they're not…attractive…they're drop-dead gorgeous. I would estimate that there is probably over a million dollars worth of plastic surgery between those five. I'd like to see pictures of them when they were much younger."

"Bad, huh?"

"Horrible. Five pretty little girls, who will all get up on that stand and shed all kinds of tears…about what some mean, nasty forty-three-year old man did to them. I need something…anything…to break them."

Matthew got up and went to Jeannie. She was sitting there very quietly with a worried look on her face. "Hey, Baby Doll, did you get the pre-nup agreement out?"

She did not move a muscle. "Yeah, why?"

"Well, let Mr. Orsini have it so that he can see that any form of adultery would be very detrimental to me."

"It's over on the coffee table," she said with a sigh.

Matthew retrieved the agreement from the coffee table and gave it to Orsini. "You'll find a part in here, where if I were stupid enough to commit any infidelity…I'm out on my butt. Getting those rich, spoiled bimbos in bed…just would not be worth my time."

Orsini took the envelope. "You seem very confident about all of this, even though everything is against you. Do you have something that…could be used…in our favor?"

"Absolutely," said Matthew with a great big smile. "The truth!"

"Do you mind letting me in, on what this special truth is?"

Matthew got very serious. "You said that you don't trust me. Quid Pro Quo! You said that if Stacy Van Cleave gets involved - against me - in this mess, that there would be a conflict of interest. For that, I am holding back. When we go to court - on the 22nd of March - if Stacy has not become part of this fiasco, then I will let you in on a lot more."

Orsini rolled his eyes. "We should not be the ones battling each other."

"All right. Let's take a look at what is on my flash drive. Maybe there is something there that I can divulge to you…even though there is no trust."

Orsini did not find anything that interested him.

Matthew read all of the files, several times, looking to see if there was anything that he had missed. Was there anything that he could use to totally destroy any one of the five? That would help in bringing the other four down. He did not really want to go to trial, but it looked as if there was little choice.

Orsini escorted Jeannie into the kitchen, in order to talk to her privately. "Ma'am, I really don't understand why you don't just dump him and get out of this. What kind of hold does he have on you?"

Jeannie gave Orsini a dirty look. "He's my husband. So far, I ain't heard anything that says them bimbos are telling the truth."

"Can you tell me why you believe him instead of them?"

Jeannie sat there thinking about it. She got up and went to Matthew. "Matt, why ain't you telling him about the sessions that I walked in on? Why don't you tell...?"

"He doesn't trust me," snapped Matthew. "He has said, several times, that he does not believe me totally and now, he's probably telling you some kind of horror story of what could happen. Until he believes me and believes *in me,* then the mistrust goes both ways."

"So what do we do?"

"We wait until it's time to "lower the boom". When it's time, then we have fun. Until then, as long as he does not trust me...I give him the same."

She looked up and contemplated. She sighed. "Okay." She went back to the kitchen.

Orsini sat there at the table with several files in front of him. "Look, here I have the statements of the five girls. I want you to read them and see if you can find any flaws in them. I want you to convince me that I should keep fighting, for your husband, in this case." He pushed one of the files over in front of Jeannie.

She sat down giving him a suspicious stare. She picked up the file and started reading. Most of the time, she sat there with no emotion on her face at all. Twice she tightened her jaw. Once she

143

looked surprised. Another time her breathing showed some kind of agitation. She bit her lip several times. She finished reading it, set it down and looked at Orsini.

"I saw the looks on your face," he said expectantly. "Did you find something?"

"You said that you don't trust Matt. If you don't trust him, why should I trust you?"

He huffed impatiently. "He has given me virtually nothing. Why should I trust a man who gives me nothing?"

"Why should he trust you, when you don't trust him?"

He pursed his lips. "Is there anything in that statement, that you can point out, that gives me a reason to trust him?"

"Didn't you want me to read all five statements?"

He closed his eyes and cleared his throat. "Yes. Yes, I did." With that he took the first file back and pushed a second one in front of her.

She showed less emotions while reading the second one. Even less during the third. She showed no emotions at all while she read the fourth and fifth. She pushed the last one back and sat there giving him a blank stare.

He stared back for a few moments. "Can you *please* give me something...one little shred of information that gives me a reason to fight on?"

"He's innocent," she said flatly.

"That's not a shred...that's an ideology."

She closed her eyes, sighed, leaned back in the chair and folded her arms. She opened her eyes and looked at him. "My husband has been teaching at that school for eighteen years now. Any time he has had to stay late, in order to counsel one of them snobby little rich brats, he has always called...always! I'll admit that in the first few years, I was suspicious. All that money, just dripping off of those brats, I thought he might be tempted. So, that first year, after about the eighth or ninth time he called, I decided to go check. I made a couple of sandwiches, as a bit of a cover, left my little boy with a neighbor and headed to the school. The only time he was surprised to see me, was the very first time. He asked me, why I had come and I told him, because every time in the past, when he'd come home, he'd been really hungry. So, I brought him something to eat, here. After that, any time that I showed up, he was never surprised. There was a lot of times that he was counseling a girl. Matt was on one side of the desk, the girl was on the other side. Nobody was hugging. Nobody was kissing. Nobody had to scramble to get their clothes back on..." She threw her arms up. "Nothing that I could call suspicious."

"Did you ever listen to what was being said?"

"Sure! It took quite a few times, but I'm convinced that the whole reason Matt was in there was to give them some kind of advice on their schooling. A lot of them wanted to talk about other things, but Matt never commented on it, he always went back to what they should be doing in school."

He perked up a little. "So...you never, in any way, ever announced when you were going to show up?"

"Nope!" She smiled. "Never. I just walked in."

He smiled a little. "Well, I am suddenly beginning to trust him."

"Good," she said with a big smile.

He put his hands on the files. "Now, these statements - is there anything that you saw in them that...well, it just doesn't hold water?"

She leaned forward with her eyes wide open. "They are fibbing!"

"What are they being mendacious about?"

She huffed. "There's that word again...I'm getting a dictionary." She got up and headed to the living room, leaving him there with a sour look on his face. She came back in with the dictionary and looked the word up. She said it several times and gave a nod of approval.

After she closed the dictionary, he gave her a friendly smile. "What are they being mendacious about?"

"Everything."

"What? Is there some habit...?"

She flushed and looked off to the side rather upset. She folded her arms tightly across her chest.

"There is something," he said triumphantly. "What?"

She breathed in and out, hard, several times. When the redness left her face, she gave him a stern look. "He said that he doesn't trust you, because you don't trust him. Until my Matthew says that he trusts you, because you trust him...that's all you get."

"I am your lawyer…"

She leaned forward. "Until you trust my Matthew, you are nothing more than a paid employee. He *is* innocent. I believe him. The only thing that he told me to give you was that pre-nuptial thing. Go home and read it. When you can say that you trust my man - *and mean it* - then you'll get something from me and him. Understand?!"

The look on her face told him many things. He had been wrong in not trusting either one of them. Matthew and Jeannie Tate were holding back because of what Marcus Orsini had said. He was not sure whether it was the original statement of mistrust of the possible conflict with the Van Cleave family. Either way he regretted it. He looked down at the big envelope with the pre-nup in it. He gathered up all of the papers and placed them in his briefcase. "I understand," he said with a warm smile. "I will take this and read it. When I come back, I have a strong feeling that I will believe and trust both of you, a lot more." He got up and headed for the front door. Jeannie followed closely behind. He put his hand out to shake hers. "Will you say the goodbyes to your husband for me?"

She smiled and shook with her left hand.

He left after she closed the door. He remembered that there was a possibility of snow flurries tonight and he wanted to get home before the roads were impossible. He got home just as the snow started really collecting on the streets. He let himself in and was greeted cordially by his housekeeper, Carlita. He headed for his study.

He was greeted at the door to the study by his wife, Dahlia. As usual, she had a Bloody Mary in her hand and a glazed look in her eyes. Her black hair (with the gray roots) was very unkempt. Her green silk robe looked as if she had spilled some of her drink down her front - as usual. She staggered a little as she walked towards him. She sniffed. "Another important client?" As she got closer he could see that she had tried to use too much makeup to cover her red nose - as usual.

"This one is very important. With this one, I won't have to wait four or five years to collect my fee."

She brightened up a little. "You mean you finally got someone who's rich? Maybe we can get rid of some of our debt."

"We would be able to afford a lot of things, if you weren't constantly blowing all of our money on vodka," he scolded.

She snarled at him and staggered away. She started screaming: "Carlita! Where are you, you little wetback? I need a fresh drink!"

He let out a disgusted huff, went into the study and slammed the door. He went to his desk, placed the briefcase on his desk and sighed. He opened it pulled out the Tate's pre-nuptial agreement and got ready to read.

There was a knock on the door.

He looked up a little surprised. "Yes?"

Carlita opened the door and came in. She looked fearful. "Sir," she said in a small voice. "Your wife has passed out in the hallway."

"Leave her there. Maybe if she wakes up, face down on the floor a few times, she'll get the message. Nothing that I've said has phased her."

"But…if she throws up?"

He let out an aggravated grunt. Then he thought of something. "There's that large thing of plastic paper rolled up in the kitchen."

"Yes, Sir."

"Bring it up, lay it out and roll her over on it…face down. That way you won't have to clean the carpet…again."

"But…if she throws up…"

"What?"

"She will be…"

"Yes, she will! Again, maybe that will convince her. Waking up, face down on the floor, swimming in her own mess. Oh - Carlita, would you be kind enough to bring me a glass of ice water?"

Carlita looked around a little confused. She contemplated for a moment. She got a helpless smile on her face. "Yes, Sir." She left.

He started reading. At first he was bored to tears with things that he had seen dozens of times in many other pre-nups.

Carlita knocked on the door again.

"Yes?"

She opened the door. "Your water, Sir."

"Thank you, just put it on the desk."

She brought it over and stood there, wringing her hands a little.

"Was there something else?"

"Uh…your wife…I can't get her on the plastic…by myself."

He shrugged. He went with Carlita to where Dahlia was snoring on the carpet. He rolled her onto the plastic and then headed back to his office.

"Are you sure this is okay?"

He stopped and without turning around, he said: "Can you think of anything else that might teach her a lesson?"

"Uh…no, Sir."

He grunted and went back into the study. Back to his desk and back to reading. He got to one passage and stopped - shocked. He stuck his fingers into the ice water and cleaned his eyes out with it. He re-read the passage. He sniggered. He re-read the passage again and did everything he could to stifle himself from laughing out loud. 'I wish that I had had a clause like this in my pre-nuptial agreement,' he thought. 'If I had, I could have dumped that drunken pain-in-the-neck a *long* time ago.' He sat back and chuckled. "No matter what…," he said out loud. "No matter what those girls do…Jeannie Tate doesn't lose a dime. Even if her trust is misplaced…and he is guilty…those girls get nothing."

The next Monday, Orsini got a phone call from Jeannie. She was ranting incoherently at first. He had to tell her several times to calm down and speak slowly. Finally he heard just breathing over the phone.

"Are you calm yet?"

"I'm trying," she snapped.

"Did something new happen?"

She huffed. "I just had some people knockin' on my door. They each wanted to talk to Matt. When he come to the door, they each handed him a piece of paper and said: You been served - git a lawyer. What's it mean?"

"What was on those paper?"

"I'll have to get Matt…MATT, PICK UP THE EXTENSION!"

Orsini nearly lost an eardrum as Jeannie hollered, without taking her mouth away from the speaker on her phone. He sat there rubbing his left ear, trying to get the ringing to stop.

"Okay, I'm on…who are we talking to?"

"The lawyer," said Jeannie. "Mr. Marcus."

"I thought his name was, Orsini," said Matthew.

Orsini switched to speakerphone. "My full name is Marcus Orsini, Mr. Tate."

"Oh," said Matthew. "What can I do for you, Mr. Marcus?"

"Your wife said something about being served some papers?"

"Stupid term," said Matthew. "They should say: Smacked in the face."

"Whatever! What did you get ser…smacked with?"

"I got five summons. The girls have filed lawsuits against me. A bunch of crap about defiling their innocence, sexual abuse, misuse of my authority position…and a few other silly terms. Each one of the little tramps is suing me for sixty-eight million dollars. Gee, what an odd figure."

"Why is it odd?"

Matthew chuckled. "68 x 5 = 340. They are being kind enough to leave me three million out of the original three hundred forty-three million from the jackpot."

"Yes, and they are generously making sure that they don't tread on each other's toes."

Jeannie sounded a little panicked. "So what happens with this?"

"Well, my dear," said Orsini. "If you are so sure that they are fibbers and your husband is innocent - nothing. The criminal case has to be proven before any civil case can be brought forward. If you destroy the criminal case then the civil case, in many instances, will be a lot harder to prove."

"Oh," said Jeannie merrily. "So, once we prove that them mendacious little bimbos is nothing more than fibbers, these things go away."

"If we can prove that they are fibbers," said Orsini.

"I wanna do something here," said Jeannie. "I wanna go smack them silly mendacious bimbos."

"I would highly advise against that," said Orsini. "They would charge you with assault."

"No, they wouldn't, I'd smack em too hard."

Matthew growled. "And probably break your hand in the process."

"Okay," said Jeannie. "Why don't you give me one of those little baseball bats that the cops carry."

"NO," shouted Orsini. "That would be assault with a deadly weapon! Matthew, talk to her!"

Matthew scoffed. "I've been trying for almost twenty-four years. She hasn't listened yet."

'That sounds familiar,' thought Orsini. "Well, let's do everything that we can to keep her separated from...the silly mendacious bimbos."

"I'll try," said Matthew.

"Matthew, Can you send those summons, to me?"

"How, I can't get out of the apartment, without being swarmed by newsmen, paparazzi and a few vigilante types."

"Vigilantes?"

Matthew huffed. "Sex crimes..."

"Oh, okay. I'll send a courier."

"Thank you."

Orsini was sitting in his office going over a contract. His intercom buzzed. He got a little irritated as he lost his train of thought. He angrily hit the button. "Yes?!"

"Sorry, Sir, but that Mrs. Tate is on the line and she's *very* upset."

Orsini rolled his eyes. "Which line?"

"Number four."

"Thank you." He remembered the last time Jeannie had screamed through the phone. He was having a few headaches and he attributed them to that scream…or his wife's drinking…or the press badgering him about the Tate case…or… He sighed, and put line four on speaker. "Yes, Mrs. Tate, can I help you?"

She started babbling at 100 miles per hour. He listened for a few moments and then hollered at the phone himself. "STOP! Slow down! I can't understand a single thing that you're saying." There was silence on the phone. He listened to the quiet for a few moments and then: "Mrs. Tate? Are you there?"

"Yeah," came a sheepish voice. "Can I talk now?"

"Slowly and clearly, yes, please."

"The bank just called and told me that someone froze our money. We can't get anything out of the bank. Why'd they do that? I mean, they can't do that to me, can they? I didn't do anything. And we got bills that we gotta pay. We got the rent and the electric and water."

"Are you going to need to get to some money…now? Do you have any cash, on hand, at your home?"

"Well…yeah. When we put that big check in our account, we…er…I took some cash out, so's I could just sit n look at it. Then Matt got some for himself and then we got some for Robert."

"How much cash do you have on hand?"

She cleared her throat. "Oh, about three hundred thousand."

Orsini felt a little like banging his head on his desk. He bit his lip, trying to hold back a sarcastic comment. "Can't you take that money and pay your bills?"

"Well, that means that I gotta go out and get some money orders from somewheres. Usually I can just write checks here, but now…"

"Mrs. Tate, until this thing is resolved, you're going to have to make a few sacrifices. Now, three hundred thousand should keep anyone from financial insolvency…unless you owe your life to a loan shark. Let me make a couple of phone calls and then I will call you back. Hopefully, I can get something resolved quickly. If not then the three hundred thousand will have to tide you over, until further notice."

She sighed. "Okay."

After they hung up, he checked the summons. These people were outrageous. They had jumped the gun. It was a well-known fact among all lawyers that the criminal case takes precedent over any civil suit. Freezing the assets would be part of a civil suit…or an IRS action. The IRS could not have anything to do with this because when they picked up the first check, the taxes were taken out before the Tate's got the money. Someone was going to be in big trouble.

Four of the summons had been signed by one judge…one by another. That simplified things. He only had to check with two judges. He made the phone calls. The single case judge had been the one who froze the assets. When he found out that the criminal case had not even gone to a preliminary hearing, he nearly blew a gasket.

After he hung up from talking to the judge, he looked at the summons and chuckled. "Mr. Jacob Forester…you are about to get a phone call that you will definitely not like."

He then called Jeannie and let her know that the account was now going to be unfrozen.

Matthew had a few things that he needed to get done prior to the trial. His main problem was getting out of the building and being able to get where he wanted to go, without an entourage of idiots, following along, asking stupid questions, snapping pictures and making vicious threats.

He found that getting a taxi and tipping the driver, at least one hundred dollars, got him into and out of some of the strangest places. A taxi gave you a little anonymity and gave the followers a big pain trying to keep up.

After several of these - very roundabout - taxi quests, he finally had all of the documentation that he needed…he hoped.

Finally the day arrived. Monday. March 22, 2010. The preliminary hearing. Matthew and Jeannie waded through another gauntlet of idiots, blinding lights, flashing camera lights, inane questions, protesters against sex crimes and openly hostile threats, with Orsini spearheading the maneuver. He knew where they were going, Matthew had to follow, almost dragging Jeannie while keeping a firm grip on her arm. When they got into the courtroom, they were again assaulted by more photographers and journalists with idiotic questions. Fortunately, in here, there were eight bailiffs who would not allow the journalists to impede any of the people involved in the case. They headed up to the front of the room. Jeannie was just a little miffed when she found out that she had to sit *behind* the "funny wooden wall" (as she put it). Only Matthew, Orsini and Orsini's secretary were allowed through the gate.

Once they sat down, Orsini looked at Matthew and then both of them looked back at Jeannie. She leaned forward expectantly. Orsini spoke to her, almost in a pleading manner. "Mrs. Tate, during the last month, I have talked to you several times...today...for heaven's sake...today, *please* control your temper. If you do *anything*, you could hurt your husband's case...and they *will* throw you out of here."

Matthew added: "They'll throw you out and you'll have to face all those people out there...alone."

She got an angry look on her face. She glared back and forth at both men. She sat back and folded her arms pouting.

The two of them started whispering between them.

"I must tell you," said Orsini in a friendly manner, "that I definitely do trust you a lot more than I thought I would."

"Oh really. How is that?"

"I went to the Van Cleave home and talked to Stacy."

"Really."

"Yes. I had to ask her...you understand, it was painfully necessary...I asked her if you had made any advances to her...just like the charges against you right now."

"I think that she has a lot more integrity then these snobbish broads. So I can't find a reason to be afraid of what she had to say."

Orsini chuckled. "She said that you had not. She also said that she would believe anything you said - without proof, before she could ever believe anything that those girls said - with proof."

"She is absolutely more level-headed than these girls."

"Can we both trust each other some more?"

"Yes, we can," said Matthew as he gave Orsini a sly look. "I have some information here that you might be interested in." He pulled an envelope out of his pocket and handed it to Orsini.

Orsini pulled the papers out of the envelope, unfolded them and started reading the first page. His look of interest changed to shock. "Are you crazy? I can't use this."

"Why not?"

"You got into her medical records in order to get this. Without a search warrant, it...it's totally inadmissible. I mean, she's not the one on trial. They'll never let me use this."

"I didn't find, look at or get into any medical records."

"Then how did you get this information?"

"Look at the next two pages."

Orsini cleared his throat and quickly looked over the next two pages. "This is real! I am beginning to see the strategy of this."

"Right. She is saying how she was so pure, until I got a hold of her. How pure can you convince anyone that you are when something like this happens?"

"Well, it does help a little, but what I need…"

"Before you say anymore, look at the *next* two pages."

Orsini's eyes got wide. He checked the next two and read them quickly. "Oh…my…word. This will devastate her. Wow! Unfortunately it will only devastate one of them. Can you give me anything that will hurt the others?"

"I've got two words for you: Distinguishing characteristics."

Orsini licked his lips as if he were about to receive a hearty meal. His eyebrows went up and he had a huge grin on his face. "Do you have any?"

"That is a question that should be put to all five…in front of my dear wife…and they have only one chance to get it right."

"Another question that is usually helpful, especially against a pack of liars, is sexual habits or quirks."

"Let's hold off on that one."

"But, it could…"

Matthew glared at Orsini with his teeth bared. "I said: HOLD OFF! Hold off on that one…for now. We'll use it *only* if we have to."

Orsini shrugged and nodded. "Okay. Okay, we'll do it that way…for now. One thing, though, could you tell me *why* we had to wait until the 22nd?"

"It was the 19th, and I'll save that surprise for later."

Orsini looked up at the ceiling and growled in frustration.

"One other thing," said Matthew. "I think that you should ask them about their personal financial situation."

"   W   h   y   ?   "

"There is a recession going on. The fathers of these girls realize it - the girls don't. The girls think that because "Daddy" is rich that the problems of the world don't exist."

"Do you really think that will help us?"

"Try it with the first girl and see what happens."

Orsini gave a shrug of approval.

Matthew looked back at the circus behind him. The journalists had taken up all seven of the back rows, on both sides. The front two rows, on each side, were empty, with a bailiff on each side standing guard. He quickly saw why they were standing guard. The door came open again and in walked Principal Lionel Youngkin and Stanley Waterman. The two of them showed the summons that brought them here and a bailiff (acting as an usher) motioned them to the front two rows. When they got up there, they showed their summons again and were allowed to sit in the un-crowded front rows. They chose to sit on the right side of the room.

Orsini leaned close to Matthew. "Who are those two men?"

"The short one is the principal at the school. The tall one is the enemy."

"Enemy?"

"He teaches calculus and snobbery at the school. He can't stand me, because I'm not from the northeast. Anything west of Pennsylvania and south of Maryland is heathen country to him."

"Are they possibly here to…damage your character?"

"Lionel…I don't know. Waterman…he will absolutely give it his best shot! Of course, with Waterman, in order to say anything about character - you have to have some."

There was some more noise as the doors came open again. In walked a man wearing an expensive business suit, and a rather disgusted look on his face. He had very thick, dark curly hair and a ruddy complexion. He was carrying a briefcase and leading a small contingency of his own.

"I recognize him," said Orsini. "He's a lawyer. His name is Myron Shapiro. Very big on family stuff. Who's that with him?"

"Uh…I'm not sure…oh wait - that's Olivia Siegelman. The other two must be her parents."

"What? She's a student of yours and you didn't recognize her?"

Matthew was a little confused as to why he had not known her right off. Then he glanced over and saw Waterman. That man was looking at Olivia and looked rather surprised as well. He spent quite a bit of time sizing up the new quartet. He turned, leaned over and whispered something to Youngkin. Youngkin looked back and his expression changed to confusion and then astonishment. Matthew took another close look - specifically at Olivia. "Oh," he said as he chuckled.

Orsini was getting impatient. "What?"

"I don't think that any one of us have ever seen Olivia dressed that modestly."

She was not showing any cleavage. Her outfit was a plain, neutral gray. The skirt went down, just below the knees. She had on a gray, V-neck sweater with a white shirt, buttoned at the collar. She was wearing very plain black loafers - not her usual opened-toed high heels.

The father: Christopher, was wearing a very expensive looking, dark pin-striped suit. His light brown hair was immaculately combed - every strand in it's place. The mother: Lucielle, was dressed to match her daughter. She was a very attractive blonde woman who was obviously down-playing her appearance for the situation.

"I've never seen her parents before," said Matthew. "She doesn't look like either one of them."

Orsini sized up the parents. He chuckled. "She was probably born, looking as homely as her father. I told you: Lots of plastic surgery."

Another brouhaha at the back of the room. In walked another man, carrying a briefcase and wearing an expensive three piece suit. Orsini immediately identified him as another lawyer - Alexi Markowitz.

Matthew identified the family of Cynthia Augsburger. That perfect raven hair and...what color are her eyes today? She was dressed in almost the same way as Olivia.

The father: Dieter, was a somewhat tall man with a total head of gray hair and a stern face that showed his German ancestry. He was wearing an expensive pin stripe suit as well. The mother: Carmine, was dressed as if she were attending a funeral. Her face was completely hidden behind a very dark veil attached to a rather gaudy black hat. The dress did not hide a very shapely figure and she walked like a professional model.

Again, Matthew noticed a look of surprise on Waterman's face when he noticed how Cynthia was dressed. He knew that Waterman was looking directly at the girls because he followed the man's gaze carefully.

A third time the doors came open, and another pin-striped suit came in using a briefcase to push reporters away. This man had brown hair that looked a little unruly and sideburns that went straight down to the bottom of his jaw.

"That one is James Douglas," said Orsini. "Who's the family?"

Matthew had to check the pictures of the girls. He looked back and forth a few times. "This one appears to be Teresa Maltby. In this picture, she's wearing a lot of makeup. That girl is not." Then he noticed that the other two girls were not wearing their usual makeup either.

Matthew looked at Waterman. When Waterman saw Teresa, he rolled his eyes and looked off into a high corner of the room shaking his head.

Teresa was a very petite, cute girl with long, thick brown hair and huge cheerful looking blue eyes. She was dressed almost like the other two girls, except her gray dress was darker. The father: Bernard, was a towering man over six and a half feet, with a waistband that equaled his height. The mother: Bobbi, was not much bigger than the daughter, it appeared that there had been some plastic surgery changes here as well.

Jeannie leaned forward and tapped Orsini on the shoulder. "Do you think that all of them are gonna come in - one at a time?"

"Oh of course, they each have to make their *special* entrance. After all, they all five are excelling in acting and drama."

She leaned back and muttered. "Hams!"

Another dramatic entrance with a brown suit leading the way. This not-so-tall man had a shock of red hair and dark sinister looking eyes.

"That one is Paddy O'Toole," said Orsini.

"Then that must be Laura O'Reilly," said Matthew. "Gee, why don't we go ethnic?"

Laura had a head of thick red hair that rivaled the color of her lawyers' hair. She had sad looking brown eyes and was dressed in a very light gray, very modest outfit.

Waterman again sat there shaking his head.

The father: Michael, was almost totally bald and had a look on his face as if he wanted to kill someone - like Matthew. The mother: Adriana was also a redhead, who was wearing a very garish turquoise outfit and showing off for the cameras.

"Now all we're waiting for is the Hamond family," said Orsini in a rather bored fashion. "Do you think that she's going to be as overly-modest as her counterparts?"

"If she's wearing underwear, then she's already dressed even more modestly than the others...comparatively speaking," said Matthew in a disgusted manner.

The door came open and this time only two people came in. A very skinny man carrying a briefcase and wearing a rather low-grade brown suit (compared to the other outfits in the room) came in with a woman by his side. She was a short Hispanic woman, with a totally green outfit and more makeup on her face than all four of the girls combined. It was not too much makeup, but it seemed that way considering how the girls were trying to downplay themselves.

"Those are our opponents. Mr. Jordan Coopersmith and Cristal Ayala. He's *very* good at questions that can kill you, and she usually goes straight for the jugular. Don't let her calm demeanor fool you."

The last player came in with a lawyer leading the way. He was another rather tall, skinny man with a very expensive looking, dark gray pin-stripe, three piece suit. He got a rather sour look on his face, when he spotted Orsini. He quickly looked away and brushed his dark hair back.

"That's the one, that I got in trouble. He tried to start the ball rolling for a civil suit, *way* ahead of schedule. I don't think that Mr. Jacob Forester likes me very much right now. I know that the judge that he suckered into freezing your assets doesn't like him much either."

"That has to be Patricia Hamond behind him," said Matthew. "That's the one that *is* the least modest of all. I wonder if they were able to make her wear underwear for this venue."

It became obvious that they had made her wear underwear. She spent the entire time in the courtroom, pulling at her bra with a very uncomfortable look on her face. Her mother had a hard time keeping the girl from fidgeting. Of course, she was dressed entirely in gray as well.

The father: Derrick was a man of average height who looked as if he had never missed a meal in his entire life. He had to use two canes in order to carry his ampleness and he was perspiring heavily. The suit he was wearing had enough fabric to make two suits for anyone else. The mother: Anita had hair that was a little lighter than her daughter. She was dressed in an identical manner as her daughter.

Again, Matthew watched Waterman's reaction. The man was not impressed with the costume party that the girls were putting on.

Orsini leaned over to Matthew. "I wonder if they arrived last, on purpose or because of Mr. Hamond."

Matthew shrugged. "It could be either reason. I just wonder how many of those people outside got plastered against the wall when he waddled through."

Orsini giggled. "Stop that. We have to get serious."

Jeannie noticed that she was sitting *very* alone. All of the people that had come in after her arrival had gone to the right side of the room. She was alone - in two empty rows - on the left side of the room. She tried not to get too self-conscious. She leaned forward. "Are they gonna let them reporters take up the empty area here?"

Orsini looked back at her. "No, my dear, those seats will be - very noticeably - empty for the duration."

Jeannie slouched back again, scrunched down a little and looked away from the rest of the people in the room.

Another bailiff brought six people in and had them sit in the jury box.

Matthew looked at the sextet and then to Orsini. "What happened to a jury pool and jury selection?"

"This is a preliminary hearing. In a lot of these cases, the judge picks a minor jury. This jury is not going to decide guilt or innocence. The only reason that they are here is to determine if we should go to a full trial."

Matthew huffed. "No wonder this crap takes so long!"

The bailiff, that had escorted the jury in, walked over to a door and opened it. He looked in. A few moments later, he started the "Hear Ye, Hear Ye!" He announced the entrance of Judge Eli Vance and told everyone to rise.

Matthew got up and looked back. Jeannie had not moved. He glared at her and silently lipped the words: "Get up!"

She gave him a sour look and stood. She stood there with her arms crossed looking into the top left corner of the room.

Judge Eli Vance walked in. He was an elderly man who walked a little hunched over. He had thick gray and black hair that was slightly unkempt. He had thick round glasses that sat low on his nose. He walked up to his bench and looked around the room with a lot of distaste showing on his face. He picked up his gavel and sat down. "This court is now in session. You may be seated." He banged his gavel.

Jeannie's posterior was the first to hit her seat…with a bit of a bang.

Coopersmith started to stand up but froze when the judge signaled with a simple motion of the hand for him to stop. Coopersmith sat back down, frowning in confusion. "Before this begins, I have something to say. You journalists finagled your way into being in this courtroom during the proceedings. This already puts all of you on my bad list. If *any* of you make any peep or snap a picture or anything else that disrupts these proceedings, even to the slightest extent…you will be thrown out, immediately. I obtained the services of several more bailiffs, just for the purpose of throwing out troublemakers." He leaned forward a little. "Do I make myself *quite* clear?" He glared around at all the reporters. He leaned back in his chair, looked at Coopersmith and raised his eyebrows questioningly.

Coopersmith stood up with a slight smile on his face. "Jordan Coopersmith and Cristal Ayala for the prosecution, Your Honor, we are ready to begin." He sat down.

The judge switched his gaze to Orsini.

He stood up. "Marcus Orsini, for the defense, Your Honor. I am quite ready."

"Good!" The judge looked around. "Where's Chet?"

The bailiff directly left of the judge spoke up: "Here, Your Honor."

"Huh?" Vance looked off to his left. "Oh. Okay. Well, read off the charges so we can refresh everybody. Of course, with this crowd of journalistic gawkers, I don't know if it's really necessary."

Chet started reading. Matthew blocked it out, because he was tired of hearing it. He had *not* molested anyone, and he absolutely had *not* had any desire to touch those five little snobby gold-diggers.

Vance looked at his jury. "I'm sure that a lot of you have seen trials and such on television and movies. Most of that is the actual trial. This is a preliminary, and during this part, you, the jury, may ask questions. Now please keep your questions to a minimum. The only *real* reason that you should be asking something is for clarification. Remember also, that in this preliminary, you are not trying to determine guilt or innocence. You are here to determine as to whether you think that there is enough evidence or information, to warrant the proceedings to continue to the next step. Any questions?" He sat there waiting for a few moments. "Nothing? All right." He looked around the courtroom, while scratching his left ear. "Mr. Coopersmith?" He held out his hands in a welcoming manner. "Proceed."

Coopersmith stood up. "Thank you, Your Honor."

The prosecution gave a great deal of data on what they had and what they intended to prove. Matthew did not like what he heard. He wanted to choke the arrogant fool and convince him that the whole thing was a scam.

Most of the information went over Jeannie's head. She thought that she knew a lot about courtrooms and trials from what she had seen on television. She found out that the only thing they showed in those TV shows, was the real meat. They did not show the boring repetitious procedures that courts had to follow.

After Coopersmith sat down, the judge looked at Orsini. "Okay, we've heard that side. What have you got to say Mr. Orsini?"

Orsini stood up and smiled. "Thank you, Your Honor." He looked at the jury. "I'm going to make this short. I nearly fell asleep while Mr. Coopersmith was boring us with his…nonsense. So, I will try not to bore you. Recently, my client, Mr. Tate, won a very large jackpot in the New York State lottery. The five complainants decided that they wanted that money. So, they fabricated a story of debauchery and now are going to try to convince you that their nonsense is actually the truth. One thing that the prosecution is going to tell you, is that there is only one person here that is on trial…my client. That is false! The fairy tales that those girls will be telling you are manufactured claptrap, and nothing more. They are on trial as well, because they are trying to sell gobbledygook as reality. I'm not going to try to defend my client as much as I am going to expose their deceptions." He looked at the five. All of them had a hurt look on their faces. He was able to hide his disgust. He turned back to the jury. "Thank you." He sat down.

"Well," said Vance with a smile. "The game is afoot." He looked at Coopersmith. "Hop to it! Let's not waste time."

He stood up and called Lionel Youngkin to the stand. Everybody watched with a modicum of boredom as the man walked to the witness stand and was sworn in. Coopersmith then walked up with a smile and started: "Mr. Youngkin, as the principal of your school, do you have access to the computers of the teachers?"

"Of course."

"Earlier last month, I asked you to check on Mr. Tate's computer. Did you?"

"Yes."

"Did you find anything out of the ordinary?"

"At first, I thought I did. After checking with some other teachers, I found out that there was nothing…untoward."

The DA was a little surprised by the answer. "What do you mean? I mean didn't you tell me that you had discovered some pornography in his computer at the school?"

Orsini leaned forward a little.

"Well, I thought it was porn…at first."

"What do you mean - it either is or it isn't! Now which is it?"

"The pictures are illustrations."

Again Coopersmith was surprised. "Of what?"

"Mr. Tate teaches biology. I found the illustrations in the middle of his lesson plan."

"So he uses porn, in his lesson plan, so that he can teach… what?"

Youngkin cleared his throat. "The human body is a biological specimen. When you are learning biology, anatomy is part of it. Biology is not just flowers and a few things about DNA."

"But, how can you justify…nude pictures in a lesson plan?"

"I checked with several schools around New York and Newark. I found that there are at least a dozen biology teachers, in other, highly credited schools, who use the exact same lesson plan. It seems that this lesson plan was written by a group of nine professors of biology. Those professors are the ones who put those illustrations in there. After I found that out, I read the captions under the pictures. It all fits within the parameter of the lesson plan."

The DA looked a little sick. "Did you find anything else?"

"No. We found nothing…untoward."

"Did you have the computer checked?"

"Oh yes, we have an excellent computer technician who went over the whole thing. He found absolutely nothing…that wouldn't be there on a normal basis."

A slight knocking sound was heard. Coopersmith turned around and saw his colleague, Ayala, glaring at him. She had rapped her knuckles on the underside of their desk. He turned back to the judge, again looking a little sick. "No more questions, Your Honor."

Vance looked at Orsini: "Any questions?"

He stood up. "No, Your Honor, I think that Mr. Coopersmith helped me enough with this one." He looked over at the prosecution desk. Ayala was glaring back with sheer hatred in her eyes. He sat down, coughing a little in order to disguise a laugh.

Vance looked over at Youngkin. "You may step down, Sir. Thank you for your time."

Youngkin gave the judge a friendly smile and a nod, got up and went back to his original seat.

Vance sat there with a little smile. "Who's next?"

Coopersmith gained back a little composure. "I call Mr. Stanley Waterman to the stand."

Waterman stood up, he adjusted his jacket a little and then walked to the stand. He went through the ceremonial swearing in and sat down. His face gave away nothing.

Coopersmith walked up to the stand. "Mr. Waterman, how

long have you been teaching?"

"Thirty-four years."

"How long has Mr. Tate been teaching at the school with you?"

"I believe that this is his eighteenth year."

"Have you ever seen any actions of his that seemed he was getting a little too close to any of the students?"

"No."

"But, you said…"

"What I told you Sir, is that I don't like him. I don't think that he came from a good place. To me, he doesn't belong here. *To me!"*

"Didn't you tell me that you have information in regards to unacceptable conduct towards the students?"

"Only rumors."

There were two more knocks. Coopersmith looked back at Ayala. She was glaring back with her teeth clenched.

"No more questions, Your Honor," he said flatly.

Vance shook his head. "Mr. Orsini?"

Orsini smiled. "Thank you, Your Honor." He did not get up, he simply leaned forward a little. "So, Mr. Waterman, this dislike that you have for my client…it's just of a personal nature?"

"Yes, he seems a little arrogant to me. He's not from around here."

"*Here,* Sir?"

Waterman got a sour look on his face. "He's not from anywhere in the northeast."

"So your dislike, refers only to the fact that he is from Texas."

"Isn't that enough?"

"For these proceedings - no sir. Have you compared any of the grades of your students?"

Waterman was momentarily surprised by the question. He contemplated for a moment. "Yes. Yes, I did."

"What did you find?"

"The students, that we have in common, have similar grades."

"Could you elaborate, Sir?"

"The ones who are getting A's in my class, are getting A's in his class. The ones who are failing mine - failing in his as well."

"Thank you. No more questions."

Vance looked at the prosecution with a little skepticism. "Thank you, Mr. Waterman. You may step down."

Waterman left the stand showing nothing on his face again.

Vance still looked a little puzzled. "Mr. Coopersmith, Mr. Orsini…a moment? Sidebar?"

Orsini, Coopersmith *and* Ayala went up to the side of the judge's bench.

Vance covered his microphone and leaned close to the trio, whispering. "Mr. Coopersmith, are you the prosecutor or defense?"

Coopersmith closed his eyes and flushed. "It...it's just...a little setback, Your Honor."

"Setback," the judge said dully. "Sir, you have had the rug pulled out from under you...twice. Isn't your back-side getting a little bruised up from the hard landings?"

"The information was...misleading. Once we get the complainants on the stand...this will change dramatically."

"You better. You're doing Mr. Orsini's job for him. Which means that you're wasting this courts time. Now get back to your place and let's see some prosecuting!"

The lawyers went back to their places. Coopersmith picked up a piece of paper. He looked up and cleared his throat. "I call Laura O'Reilly, to the stand."

Matthew leaned over to Orsini and whispered. "You definitely want to ask her about finances."

"Why?"

"Ask her and then sit back and watch the fun."

"But this is one that was not a student, or counselee of yours."

"She's putting on the same act as the three that I know. She can't possibly be any different than them."

Orsini sighed. He then pushed some papers in front of Matthew.

Matthew looked at the papers. They were forms that the teachers used, when counseling students. He felt his temper rise a little. "I never counseled her. I don't know where these came from."

"Shut up, and read them. See if you can find something that gives you a clue as to where they *did* come from." Orsini switched his attention to the proceedings.

Laura slowly walked up to the stand. She had her hands folded in front down by her waist. She kept her head down. When she raised her hand, she took the oath, still looking at the floor. When she responded to the oath, she did so almost inaudibly.

Vance turned an ear closer to her. "What was that?"

She looked up. There was a tear rolling down her right cheek. "Sir?"

"You're going to have to speak up, young lady. My court recorder needs to hear you clearly."

She swallowed. "Yes, Sir." She looked back at the bailiff. "I do," she said a little louder.

"That's better," said Vance. "Now, have a seat."

Coopersmith stood up and slowly walked up to the witness stand. In his mind, he was not thinking of what she would say, he was just hoping that she didn't blow him out of the water like Youngkin and Waterman had done. "Miss O'Reilly, I know that it's difficult to talk about...I know that it is embarrassing, however, we need you to be totally honest and tell us the complete story of what happened to you during those counseling sessions."

Her face turned red and she hung her head. She started wringing her hands a little. She sniffled. She looked up at Coopersmith with anguish on her face and tears flowing down both cheeks.

"Miss O'Reilly, please...I have read the counseling statements and we need to know…is this what was said and done in those counseling sessions?"

She sniffled a little more and wiped her nose on her sleeve. "No," she said in a small voice.

"What *did* happen?" Coopersmith was trying to ask the questions in as tender a voice as he could muster.

Her face turned red again. She took in a deep breath. She looked around at the prosecutor, at the judge, at the jury, at her mother… She sighed and started talking about getting undressed, being undressed, oral sex, fondling, sexual positions and other erotica.

Matthew leaned over to Orsini and whispered: "These counseling sheets were written by Lucy Crippin."

"Write the name down on one of the sheets. Who is she and how do you know that she wrote those sheets?"

After writing the name on the top page he leaned a little closer to Orsini. "Lucy is the chemistry teacher. Her vocabulary is all over these counseling sheets. She references molecules and chemicals most of the time she's talking. Here's a passage: The girl needs to get her electrons circling the correct protons. Here's another: She keeps trying to fire up her engines with helium instead of hydrogen. That stuff is absolutely Lucy Crippin."

"Okay." Orsini went back to listening to the "tale of woe" from Laura.

After Laura finished with a rather lengthy oration, Matthew looked back at Jeannie. He could almost see steam rising off the top of her head. He could see a few of the photographers and journalists wiping sweat off of their brows and making lewd gestures. Matthew also saw the jury glaring at him. So far - no good. The damage that had been done by Waterman and Youngkin was repaired in favor of the prosecution.

After Coopersmith sat down, Orsini stood up. He picked up the counseling sheets and walked slowly to the stand while browsing the papers. He smiled. "Who is your primary counselor at the school?"

Coopersmith was up in a flash. "Objection! That has nothing to do with the sexual escapades of the defendant."

"Your Honor," pleaded Orsini. "According to the witness, she was counseled by Mr. Tate. He claims that he did not author these counseling sheets. According to him, the vernacular used in these sheets is from another person. If Mr. Tate did not write these, then who did and why would they cover for someone else's..." He looked back at Coopersmith. "Sexual escapades." He looked back at Vance. "We need to find out: Who wrote these and why."

Coopersmith scoffed. "Do you actually think that that matters?"

"Yes, I am sure that it does. Mr. Tate has stated to me that this is not how he talks - or writes. This is the work of another teacher. Your Honor, we have two others from the faculty at the school... maybe we could have them take a look at these sheets and see if they agree with my client, as to who actually wrote these documents."

"We'll save that investigation for later...if we need it. I'll allow the question, for now," said the judge suspiciously.

Orsini turned back to Laura. "Well, who is your primary

counselor?"

She now looked more irritated then hurt. "It's that chemistry teacher...Crippin."

"So, you're saying that Mr. Tate counseled you, but Lucy Crippin wrote the sheets. Is that it?"

She looked off into the gallery with a frown. "I don't know why she did it. I know that that is not what happened at those... sessions."

"Your Honor, we may have to call this Lucy Crippin in, in order to find out why she wrote these counseling sheets."

Vance looked at the prosecution. "Yes, we might."

Orsini looked back at Matthew who glared back. Orsini licked his lips while contemplating. He turned back to the girl. "You claim that there was total nudity and fondling in these sessions?"

"Yes," she spat.

"Could you tell us of any distinguishing characteristics on Mr. Tate's body?"

She lost her composure. "Huh? What...? What's that?"

"Something that is unique to Mr. Tate. Are there any birthmarks, tattoos, moles, scars? The hair on his chest - lots of it - lack of it? Something that you could identify *him* while looking at his body and not the face. Something that you would know that it is definitely Mr. Tate."

She looked a little frightened. She swallowed and again looked into the gallery. She looked up at the judge. She stammered and stuttered a little. "I...I...uh...don't...I don't...remember anything...special." She looked back into the gallery at someone. "No...nothing special. I don't have anything to compare...him...with."

Orsini could not really follow her eyes but he knew that she was not looking in the direction of her mother, father or lawyer. He felt that he would need to watch the other girls *very* closely. He looked back at Matthew.

Matthew glared again and lipped the word: "Finances."

Orsini steeled himself and got ready for a class A battle with prosecution. "I understand that your father has cut your monthly allowance a little."

Her expression immediately changed to anger. She was ready to say something...but...

"Objection, Your Honor! That has no relevancy with this case."

Orsini quickly raised a finger: "Sidebar?"

Vance motioned them to come forward with a frown on his face.

The trio, once again huddled at the side of the bench.

"Your, Honor, I did say that this whole thing is a conspiracy hatched by these five girls. The financial situation *is* the motive for the conspiracy and I intend to prove it."

"Oh come on," said Ayala. "All you're trying to do is muddy the waters. Why would they do that?"

"Why, indeed," said Orsini. "Listen and learn."

"Step away," said Vance. After the three were back in their places, he looked at the jury. "I'll allow this for now," he looked at Orsini, "but be careful."

"Thank you, Your Honor." He turned back to the girl. "I believe you were going to tell us how your allowance has been cut."

The indignant look came across her face again and she burst into an angry oratory of how her cruel, vicious, evil, tight-fisted father had cut her *monthly* allowance from fifty thousand dollars to fifteen thousand dollars. She had no idea how she was going to survive on such a paltry amount. It was just inhumane what her father was doing.

Matthew, again, glanced around the room. Laura's lawyer, O'Toole was sitting there with an anguished expression. Over and over, he mouthed the words: "Shut up." Several of the people in the back of the gallery were looking at her very distastefully. One of the photographers was hiding his hand behind his camera (from the judge) and giving her a very nasty one-fingered-salute.

Juror number three was a heavy set man with very thin brown hair. He had on a very thread-bare shirt that might have been some plaid design…at one time…many years in the past. He looked as if he were about to throw up.

Juror number six was a young Afro-American wearing a black turtleneck that was losing it's stitching in the armpits. The elbows were in rather bad condition as well. He was looking at her with total hatred, clenched fists and teeth.

The other jurors all had looks of some kind of shock, hatred, disdain and disgust.

Jeannie had a look on her face like a hungry, angry wolf ready to pounce on a crippled rabbit.

Some momentum had definitely shifted back in favor of the defense.

After several minutes of her ranting, Vance told her to stop.

"But, Your Honor," protested Orsini. "She's not finished."

"She is giving off a bunch of repetitive babble. She has made her point. Are there any other questions for this witness…from either of you?"

Both sides shook their heads.

"Good! Young lady, you are excused," said Vance. He was doing his best to remain neutral, however, the look on his face showed that he was not very impressed with this witness as well.

She walked back to her seat the same way she had gone to the stand. She tried to give a very demure, hurt look. Now, it was not working. When she sat down she looked expectantly at her lawyer, O'Toole. He ignored her completely with his arms folded and a look of total defeat and disgust on his face.

Vance cleared his throat and shook his head. He looked at Coopersmith and clicked his tongue. "Okay, who is next?"

Coopersmith stood up, calmed himself and called Cynthia Augsberger to the stand.

"Oh joy," whispered Matthew as he pushed the special envelope towards Orsini.

"You're enjoying this *way* too much," said Orsini sarcastically.

Cynthia walked slowly to the witness stand. She did it in almost the exact same manner as O'Reilly had done it. When she took the oath, she also spoke in a very small voice. Three times the judge had to tell her to speak up.

Matthew leaned close to Orsini. "That's not the Cynthia Augsburger that I know."

Orsini smirked. "What if I told you that I'm not surprised?"

Coopersmith stood up and slowly walked up to the witness stand. He was hoping that this one would not turn out like the previous disaster. That girl had told a tale of woe and then blew it all with her greedy ranting. Miss Augsburger, I know that this is difficult to talk about. I know that this is embarrassing, however, we *need* you to be totally honest and tell us the complete story of what happened to you during those counseling sessions."

Her face turned red and she hung her head. She started wringing her hands a little. She sniffled. She looked up at Coopersmith with anguish on her face and tears flowing down both cheeks.

"Miss Augsburger, please…I have read the counseling statements and we need to know…is this what was said and done in those counseling sessions?"

She sniffled a little more and wiped her nose on her sleeve. "No," she said in a small voice.

"What *did* happen?" Coopersmith was hoping in his mind that this one would be much more genuine.

Her face turned red. She took in a deep breath. She looked around at the prosecutor, at the judge, at the jury, at her mother… She sighed and started talking about getting undressed, being undressed, oral sex, fondling, sexual positions and other erotica.

When she finished, Matthew leaned over to Orsini. "Is it déjà vu, or did I just hear that *exact* same story from Laura?"

"Precisely the same story!" Orsini sat there disgusted.

Vance got a little impatient. "Mr. Orsini…are you there? Any questions for this witness?"

"Oh, yes, Your Honor. Absolutely." He stood up and with a smile on his face and an envelope in his hand he walked over to the witness stand. "You claim that there was total nudity and fondling in these sessions?"

"Yes," she said and flushed.

"Could you tell us of any distinguishing characteristics on Mr. Tate's body?"

"I didn't notice anything." She sniffled and wiped a tear off her cheek. "I really wasn't looking for anything special or…what you might call different."

"How experienced are you in having sex?"

She jerked her head as if she had been slapped. She looked into the gallery. She looked up at the judge. "I'm not!"

"Really?"

"Yeah," she said indignantly.

"Then when and from whom did you catch herpes?"

Her eyes filled with rage. She stood up and screamed at Orsini.

"HOW DID YOU KNOW I GOT HERPES?" The expression on her face changed to shock and surprise. She clapped her hands tightly over her mouth and sat down quickly with her eyes clenched shut. She slowly opened her left eye and took a quick peek at her mother. She, of course, could not see anything through the thick veil that her mother was wearing. She lowered her head and buried her face in her hands.

Coopersmith stood up. "Sidebar!"

Vance was staring at the latest witness, with quite a bit of disgust. He was not really sure what to make of the current dilemma.

Coopersmith waited a few moments. "Your Honor?"

Vance looked at him. "Huh?"

"Sidebar, please."

"Oh, yes, okay." He motioned the trio forward. He looked back at Cynthia with disgust again.

"Your Honor, this is reprehensible." said Coopersmith. "This man has somehow obtained confidential information. The whole thing should be stricken from the record and all of these reporters put under a gag order."

"That all depends," said Vance.

"On what?"

Vance looked at Orsini. "Well, where *did* you get that information?"

"I received two affidavits from two boys who claimed that they contracted herpes, *from her*. When I asked the question, it may have sounded like an accusation, but it was still an inquiry. She has now confirmed that she does have herpes…so, who did she catch it from?"

Coopersmith looked at Orsini angrily. "Are you saying that she's promiscuous?"

"She had to catch it from somebody. These two boys both claim that they caught it from her. She claims that she had sex with my client. I have a medical affidavit from Mr. Tate's primary caregiver that he does not have any sexually transmitted diseases, nor does he have a history of having them. If she, in fact, did have sex with my client, then that is a minimum of four sex partners that she has been with. Even if she is telling a whopper of a lie and she did not have sex with my client, we're still talking about three sex partners. If that ain't sexually active then what is?"

"Mr. Orsini," said Vance. "You are telling me that you did *not* get into that girl's medical records. You did get the information from these two boys."

"Yes, Your Honor. I have the affidavits right here, and I plan on submitting them as evidence for the defense."

"Let me take a look," said Vance.

"Me too," said Coopersmith.

Orsini gave one to the judge and one to Coopersmith. They each read through the statements quickly and then traded papers. After they finished, both papers were handed back to Orsini.

Vance waved them off. Coopersmith and Ayala went back to their desk.

Orsini went back to have more fun with Cynthia. "Well, Miss Augsburger. According to these documents, these two classmates of yours both claim that you infected them with herpes." He brought the two pieces of paper up. He looked at the one in his left hand. "A Mr. James Hartze." He looked at the other one. "And Mr. Gilbert Young."

Orsini and everyone else in the room were startled as someone started screaming at the top of her lungs.

The screamer was Teresa Maltby. "WHAT? YOU WHORE! YOU'VE BEEN BANGING MY BOYFRIEND? YOU GAVE GILBERT HERPES? IS THAT WHY I HAVE THIS RASH ON MY...?" She stopped and had shock and despair on her face. The only portion of her body that moved was her eyes as her gaze darted around the room. She slowly turned her head to her right...to her mother. Bobbi Maltby was sitting there staring at her daughter with her eyes wide open in shock. Teresa's face slowly turned to anguish. She moved in slow motion as she sank back down to her seat. Her head went down between her knees and she covered her head with her hands. Both of her parents gazes followed her down and stayed glued to her as she tried to hide herself under her hands.

At the prosecution's desk, Ayala leaned over to Coopersmith. "I think we just lost another witness."

Coopersmith swallowed hard. "I'll take her off of my list. The only problem is that she's here...and Orsini can still call her up to the stand...and she can still create more havoc for our case."

Ayala stared at him with disdain. "Yuh *think*?!"

Vance looked down at the court reporter. "Melissa?"

She looked up, rather concerned. "Yes, Sir."

"That outburst...did you happen to get it?"

"Uh...yes...I did. I didn't stop. I just kept going on with the recording. Do you want me to erase it?"

"No! Usually I don't approve of interruptions like that... however, I think that this one might...just be relevant."

"Who is that specifically...for the record that is?"

"That's Teresa Maltby," said Coopersmith flatly.

"How do you spell it?"

"We'll worry about that later," said Vance. "Right now, let's get back to business." He looked back at Orsini. "Any more questions for this witness?" Orsini looked up. "Oh, yes...Your Honor. Absolutely." He turned back to Augsburger, opened his mouth and looked at his hands. He noticed that the two affidavits were not *in* his hands. He looked at the floor. Somehow during Teresa's outburst, he had dropped the papers and did not realize that they were no longer in his hands. He stooped to pick them up feeling a little self-conscious. Once he had them, he cleared his throat in order to get back some form of composure. "As I said, these two claim that you infected them with herpes, while having unprotected sex with them. Do you have any comment on this?"

She stared back looking sick or defeated or both. "No."

"Did you, in fact, infect them, with herpes, while having unprotected sexual relations?"

"I got nuthin' to say."

"Answer the question, young lady," said Vance.

She looked at the judge. "I think I'll use the Fifth Amendment."

Orsini stood there for a few moments looking accusingly at her. He remembered what Matthew had told him. "I understand that your father has drastically cut your monthly allowance."

Her face immediately changed from sick to indignant. She sat up and glared. "Yes, my *dear* Daddy has cut my allowance. I used to get about thirty thousand a month for my needs. Now, he has cut me down to *ten thousand.* Laura at least is getting fifteen thousand. My Daddy is getting really, really cheap. I don't know what I'm going to do. I mean…ten thousand is just not enough."

Matthew scanned the jury. The young man in the tattered turtleneck just leaned back rolled his eyes and looked at the ceiling, shaking his head. This was getting fun.

While she was venting her wrath, her lawyer, Markowitz was sitting there with his hands over his ears.

Cynthia ranted a little more until the judge stopped her for the same reason he had stopped O'Reilly - repetitious babbling.

"Have you any more questions?"

Orsini gave the judge a pleasant smile. "No, Your Honor, thank you." He turned and went back to his seat, stifling laughter.

When she was excused, Cynthia Augsburger went back to the act, in the same manner that Laura O'Reilly had done. She walked back to her seat in a very demure, non-flashy way. Matthew saw that

Waterman was getting more disgusted as the farcical show went on.

Vance looked at the prosecution. "Mr. Coopersmith - Next?"

Coopersmith looked utterly defeated. He took in a breath. "I call to the stand: Olivia Siegelman." He made the statement with no zeal at all.

Olivia Siegelman continued the "play". She walked up to the stand in the exact same manner that her two previous colleagues had done. She took the oath in the same manner.

While she was on her way to the stand, Coopersmith looked back at Myron Shapiro, her lawyer. "Did you tell her not to rant about the money...her allowance, in the same manner as the others?"

Shapiro nodded with a worried look on his face.

Coopersmith sat there dejected. His gaze went over the head of the new witness. "Miss Siegelman, we need to know, *truthfully*, what happened in the...so-called counseling sessions with Mr. Tate."

Her face turned red. She took in a deep breath. She looked around at the prosecutor, at the judge, at the jury, at her mother... She sighed and started talking about getting undressed, being undressed, oral sex, fondling, sexual positions and other erotica.

Matthew leaned towards Orsini. "Are they reading off of a script?"

Orsini turned to Matthew. "Sickening, isn't it?"

After she finished her part of the "act", Coopersmith tried to take some of the weaponry away from the defense. He asked the question on distinguishing characteristics. She repeated, almost verbatim, what she had heard the other two girls say.

Then he asked her about her allowance... Again, like the other two, she blew her stack. She said some rather uncomplimentary things about both of her parents, because they were trying to limit her finances.

Shapiro reached into his pocket, pulled out a bottle of aspirin, and popped three of them in his mouth.

Again, Judge Vance had to stop her, for the same reason as the other two - repetitious babbling.

Coopersmith flopped down into his seat. "No more questions, Your Honor."

Vance looked at Orsini. "Do you have any questions, for this witness?"

Orsini stood up and gave the judge a friendly smile. "No, Your Honor, I think that Mr. Coopersmith has damaged his own case enough with this one."

"Good!" Vance looked at his watch. "I think that we all need a lunch break." He looked up. "We will reconvene at 1:45 PM." He banged his gavel and stood up.

Chet snapped to attention. "All rise!"

Again, Jeannie was the last one to stand up.

Vance headed to his office shaking his head and muttering.

Orsini went to the prosecution's desk. He smiled at the two as he saw the glum look on their faces. "Well, folks. It looks as if you have me right where I want you."

Coopersmith looked at him and scowled. "Go away, you horrible little man."

Ayala stood up and glared. "You know full well that the judge will order that jury to concentrate on the sexual misconduct committed by your client. All that garbage about the money will have to be ignored."

Orsini gave her a mysterious smile. "Do you *really* believe that?"

She spat a few curses at him.

He walked away chuckling. "Such language from someone with her intelligence...my, my, my."

Matthew got up close to Orsini as he returned to the defense desk. "Are we going to have to get through those reporters again?"

"I'm afraid so. One good thing about this being a high profile case is that we can take two bailiffs along with us to run interference. We also have the use of a private conference room, where we can have lunch and discuss strategy."

"How are we going to discuss strategy with two bailiffs standing over us?"

"They will stand outside the door, making sure that no one breaks in on us. We will have some private time."

Two bailiffs did run interference and they were able to get to the special conference room. They walked in almost out of breath. They all sat down and Orsini's secretary started passing out some sandwiches and drinks that she pulled out of her very large purse.

Orsini look back at the door and then at the Tates. "There will be a bizarre, blustery, bone-chilling blizzard, blowing up Beelzebub's *BUTT*, before I would ever consider giving fifteen thousand dollars to a teenager for their monthly allowance." He looked around incredulously. "And she was cut *down* to fifteen thousand, *from* fifty thousand. That is *obscene*!"

Matthew held his arms out wide. "What can you say, about the super rich? Some of them always figure out a brand new way, of wasting money."

Orsini looked down at the sandwich in front of him. "I can't eat that thing right now…I couldn't possibly keep it down. I'm feeling a little sick over what I just heard."

"Well, I ain't one to waste food," said Jeannie as she dug in.

Orsini sighed. "Be that as it may, I still need something from you. If I didn't trust you before, I definitely do now."

Matthew perked up. "How's that?"

"Those girls were *absolutely* reading from a script. Even if you *had* committed some form of sexual misconduct with them, and even if you *had* done the *exact* same thing to all three, there would be *some* differences, somewhere in their testimony. No matter what happens, when you have three different witnesses to the same event, you get three different stories…unless someone has written a script and they are all following it to the nth degree."

"So…now…you trust me?"

"I have to."

"You have the pre-nuptial agreement to help you destroy

193

them."

"That will only work, in a civil case. This is a criminal case. I need something relevant to the criminal proceedings that will help blast holes in their stories. So far, all my ammunition is, for the most part, conjecture. I need cold, hard facts that I can use to demolish them."

Matthew smiled at Jeannie. "Hey, Baby Doll, why don't you give him a preview of your testimony?"

She gave him a "drop dead" look. Her mouth was crammed full. She chewed her food and then swallowed. "Why don't you tell him? You know what happened that day."

"No, I don't. I know what I was told. Most of that day, I was out of it. Partially from loss of blood and partially from the powerful painkiller drugs that the paramedics gave me. You were awake during the entire thing."

Orsini looked confused. "Loss of blood? Painkillers? So you were involved in some kind of accident where you got injured. What could that possibly have to do with what is going on here?"

Jeannie looked at Orsini and smiled. "After this is over, can I go over there and smack each one of those bimbos?"

"No! You may *not* smack anybody! They would be charging you with assault. Let's not hear about smacking anyone. Now, what is this information that he was talking about?"

Jeannie smiled while chewing on a mouthful of turkey salad. After chewing and swallowing, she started her story.

Orsini led his contingency back to the courtroom a little ahead of the scheduled time. He had a smile on his face and was using a toothpick after enjoying a large turkey sandwich.

They got back and found that they were first. Once again, they had to wait as each one of the other players made their entrances - one at a time.

After everyone was there and the ritual of standing for the judge was done, (where once again Jeannie was the last one to stand and the first one to sit) the judge banged his gavel and told the prosecution to call the next witness.

Coopersmith stood up. "I call Patricia Hamond to the stand."

Patricia walked up to the stand with more confidence than the other girls had shown. She was very relaxed and it almost appeared that she was smiling. She took the oath, showing more confidence. She even sat down showing more confidence.

Her face did not turn red. She started talking (with much greater confidence) about getting undressed, being undressed, oral sex, fondling, sexual positions and other erotica.

Orsini looked at Matthew. "I think that we found our ring leader."

"Why is that?"

"The way that she is reading the script...she wrote it. She probably changed it several times and sounded it out numerous times as she wrote it. This girl is definitely the prime suspect as the brainiac behind this misadventure."

Coopersmith tried to take a lead. He asked the question about distinguishing characteristics. She responded in exactly the same way as the other three girls.

Matthew was slightly miffed at the maneuver. "What's he doing?"

"He is trying to take some kind of control for the prosecution. We have kicked him in the head with his own witnesses so far. I guess that the bruises are getting pretty irritating."

Coopersmith then asked Patricia about her allowances.

Patricia shrugged. "There's a recession going on. We all have to understand that. I know that I am more fortunate than others so anything that I am getting is nice…however, I can't fault my father for trying to teach me a few things about finances. During a recession, we all have to be frugal and work with a little less."

Coopersmith sat down.

Vance looked over at Orsini. "Any questions, Mr. Orsini?"

Orsini stood up. "No, Your Honor, the prosecution has helped my case enough with this one."

Patricia, sitting in the witness stand, was the one taken by surprise. "What?!" She looked around indignantly and then stared forward poker-faced.

Vance looked at her slightly miffed. "Young lady, you are excused from the stand."

She got up and headed back to her seat. She gave Orsini and Matthew a very dirty look as she passed by.

Vance cleared his throat. "Who is next, Mr. Coopersmith?"

"At this time, Your Honor, we call Sgt. Ivan Koski."

Orsini started shuffling through his papers. He found a copy of a report that Koski had turned in. He read it and then looked at Matthew totally mystified. "The prosecution is trying to use him for…what?"

"I think that they may have their wires crossed," said Matthew.

"Well, let's listen."

"Try not to giggle too much."

Koski headed up to the stand. He gave Matthew a slight wave and a smile as he went by. Matthew returned the wave with a nod. Jeannie started to look a little worried. She turned red and scrunched down lower in the seat.

Koski was sworn in and he sat down looking slightly confused.

Coopersmith stood up and headed up to the stand. "Sgt. Koski, I understand that you have been called to the Tate home several times."

"Yes, Sir."

"Can you estimate how many times you have been called to that home?"

"No, I can tell you exactly how many times. I have been there eighteen times."

"Each time, was it a domestic violence case?"

"Yes, you could say that?"

"Wait a minute!" Vance looked at Orsini. "Aren't you going

to object to this?"

Orsini gave the judge a friendly smile. "No, Your Honor, I have nothing to object to."

Vance was baffled. "WHAT?!"

"No objections, Your Honor. I'm very interested as to how this is going to turn out."

Vance looked back and forth between the two lawyers. He leaned back in his chair and looked at Koski. He raised his eyebrows and looked at Orsini again. "Are you sure?"

"Yes, Your Honor, I'm sure."

Vance stared at Orsini now even more perplexed. He looked at Coopersmith. He threw his hands up in defeat. "Continue."

Coopersmith was a little suspicious himself. He was staring at Orsini as well. "Uh...thank you...Your Honor." He turned to Koski. "So you have been to their home on eighteen occasions but have never arrested anyone."

"Right."

"Why?"

"Because no one pressed any charges."

"Didn't Mrs. Tate suffer some broken bones, on at least two occasions?"

"Yes, she did."

"Mr. Tate broke some of his wife's bones and you didn't arrest anyone?"

"It's how her bones got broke as to why I didn't arrest anyone. She broke her fist when she hit her husband in the jaw."

Coopersmith went pale. He stuttered a little. "She…but he… what?"

"She has a temper and she's got this habit of smacking her husband. There was two times when she hit him so hard that she busted her own hand."

"She broke…she hit…"

"Yeah. It was Mrs. Tate who did all the hitting. Mr. Tate never filed any charges, so, who do I arrest and for what? Mrs. Tate hurt herself when she hit his iron jaw with her glass fist. He was never hurt - she was. How do you fill out that kind of arrest report?"

Coopersmith seemed to go even paler. "No more…questions." He slowly walked back to his seat seeing a venomous stare coming from Ayala.

Vance sat there trying to mentally digest the testimony that he had just heard. He kept on changing his puzzled stare from Coopersmith to Matthew to Koski. After several moments of trying to make sense of it, he finally just shrugged and looked at Orsini. "Do you have any questions?"

"No questions, Your Honor," said Orsini with a huge smile.

Vance, staring forward, said: "Sgt. Koski…you are… excused."

Koski again gave Matthew a friendly wave as he left. Matthew again nodded back.

Coopersmith stood up looking totally defeated. "At this time, Your Honor, the prosecution rests."

The courtroom heard another squawk of surprise. It was Teresa Maltby. She looked around surprised and then scrunched down in her seat.

Vance looked confused. "Are you sure?"

"Yes, Your Honor," he said without any emotion.

Vance shrugged. "Very well. Mr. Orsini, it looks as if it is your turn."

Orsini stood up. "Thank you, Your Honor." He got a very crafty look in his eye. He looked back to the gallery. "I call...Teresa Maltby to the stand."

This took almost everyone by surprise. The shoulders of Coopersmith and Ayala both sagged down a little. The other four girls all gave their cohort an evil look. Journalists all started writing furiously in their notebooks and laptops. All six jurors looked very surprised. Vance just sat there with both eyebrows raised.

"Mr. Orsini," said Vance. "Just what do you think you're doing?"

"Your Honor, she has never been given a chance to testify. I really don't like surprises. She was brought in here as a witness and I intend to hear her story - for the record - before this preliminary is over."

"Very well," said Vance. He looked at the bailiff, who again called Teresa Maltby to the stand.

Teresa headed for the witness stand. Her body language was the same as the first three girls. Her face, however, was a mass of confusion. She stared at the floor looking very distraught. When she took the oath, she tried to maintain the same demeanor as the first three girls. She tried but she was still visibly rattled. She sat down staring at Orsini with fear and suspicion in her eyes.

Orsini approached the stand with a big smile on his face. "Miss Maltby, who is your primary counselor at the high school?"

She clenched her eyes and hung her head. She sat there silently without moving.

"Miss Maltby," said Vance. "Answer the question!"

She looked up showing dread on her face. "Mr. Du Bois," she said in a slightly croaking voice.

"So, why do these counseling sheets show Mr. Tate's signature on them?"

She tried to look around and not have to look at anybody. She could not. To her left - the jury. Directly in front of her - prosecution desk and most of the people in the gallery. To her right front - Mr. Orsini. To the direct right - the judge.

"Miss Maltby," said Vance more sternly. "Answer the question!"

"I don't know," she said almost crying.

"I think that Mr. Du Bois wrote these. This vernacular sounds like a Physical Education teacher. Did you have something to do with fabricating these counseling sheets?"

She hung her head again. "I don't know," she said crying.

"What? You don't know, if you had something to do with falsifying these documents?"

She looked up with a tear trickling down her left cheek. "I want that government thing…the one where I don't have to say anything."

Vance spoke up: "Young lady, are you pleading the Fifth Amendment, in regards to the documents?"

She looked over at the judge and sniffed. "Yeah."

"You'll have to change the subject, Mr. Orsini," said Vance flatly.

Teresa sighed in relief.

Orsini gave the judge a sideways glance. "Miss Maltby, earlier you made a reference to a Mr. Gilbert Young being your boyfriend. Were you, at that time, saying that you think that you have contracted herpes from Mr. Young?"

Her face almost seemed like a bright red beacon. Her expression changed from relief to anguish. She hung her head and buried her face in her hands.

"Miss Maltby," said Vance. "Answer the question!"

She looked up at Orsini with pure hatred in her eyes. "Maybe." Her gaze of hatred moved to Cynthia Augsburger as she clenched her teeth.

"Miss Maltby," said Vance. "Answer the question!"

She looked at the judge. "I did," she said defensively.

"No, you did not. 'Maybe' doesn't tell us a thing. It's either yes or no."

She looked at Orsini. "I forgot the question."

"Do you think that you have contracted herpes?"

She huffed through clenched teeth. "Yes."

"From Mr. Young?"

Her expression did not change. "Yes."

"Miss Maltby, according to your statement, you have not had any sex with anyone other than Mr. Tate. Now, if you believe you contracted a sexually transmitted disease from Mr. Young, how can you say that you never had sex with anyone but Mr. Tate?"

She hung her head again. "I want another fifth of that government thing."

Every lawyer in the room showed different types and phases of disgust…especially Teresa's lawyer.

Vance covered his eyes with his right hand. He did not know whether to laugh out loud, puke or try to slap some sense into her. He looked at Orsini. "She wants another 'fifth'. Move on."

Orsini looked at the prosecutors. Coopersmith looked sick. Ayala glared back venomously. He turned back to Teresa. "What happened in those alleged counseling sessions with Mr. Tate?"

She got an angry look on her face. She took in a deep breath. She looked around at the prosecutor, at the judge, at the jury, at her mother… She started talking about getting undressed, being undressed, oral sex, fondling, sexual positions and other erotica.

Orsini looked back at Matthew.

Matthew mouthed the word "déjà vu."

Orsini smirked and turned back to Patricia. "Do you remember seeing any distinguishing characteristics on Mr. Tate's body…during these sessions?"

She appeared somewhat confused. Then she looked at someone in the gallery. She then looked at Orsini and confidently said: "No!"

"Nothing?"

"No, nothing."

"Did your father happen to cut back on your monthly allowance?"

Again her demeanor changed. She burst into her own angry oratory of how her cruel, vicious, evil, tight-fisted father had cut her *monthly* allowance down to ten thousand dollars. She was so embarrassed by this small amount. She just would *not* be able to survive the shame.

Orsini looked back at the prosecution. Coopersmith was sitting there dull-eyed and staring into space. Ayala was sitting there covering her eyes with her right hand.

"No more questions, Your Honor," said Orsini in a very congenial manner.

Ayala whispered at Coopersmith: "She's done enough damage."

Coopersmith stood up slowly. "No questions, Your Honor." He slowly sank back into his seat.

Vance looked at Teresa. "You may step down." He looked back to Orsini. "Anyone else?"

"Yes, Your Honor, I recall Mr. Waterman to the stand."

If Waterman was surprised he did not show it. He simply stood up and headed for the stand.

As Waterman sat down, Vance reminded him that he was still under oath. Waterman gave the judge a polite nod, sat back and crossed his legs. He looked at Orsini attentively.

"Mr. Waterman, when the students were first entering the room, you appeared to be a little confused at what you were seeing. What was so confusing to you, Sir?"

Without any emotion, Waterman simply said: "It is the way that they are dressed."

"What about the way they are dressed?"

"They are *dressed.*"

Orsini had to digest that one for a moment. "Uh…Sir…could you elaborate on that?"

"There have been many occasions where we have had to send some of the students back home, because of their lack of, or improper clothing."

"Have any of these five students been sent home for their dress?"

"Many, many times," said Waterman with a great deal of contempt.

"Was it for lack of, or improper?"

"Yes."

Orsini nearly laughed out loud. He coughed in order to cover… so did the judge. He cleared his throat in order to give himself more time to regain composure. He looked up. "Are you saying that some of them are a little immodest?"

Waterman came back immediately. "No, I would call it: Shameless exhibitionism."

"Do you have any documentation that shows the number of times any one of them was told to go home and…get dressed?"

"I don't, but Mr. Youngkin should."

"Thank you, Sir…no more questions of this witness, Your Honor."

Vance looked up expectantly. "Mr. Coopersmith?"

Coopersmith half-stood. "No, Your Honor."

"Thank you," said Vance. "You are excused."

Again a polite nod from Waterman and he went back to the gallery.

Vance looked at Orsini. "Next?"

Orsini thought for a moment. 'If I call Youngkin, all he could do at this time is confirm that some of them were sent home. He probably doesn't carry any documentation like that with him…forget it for now.' He faced the judge. "I call Mrs. Jeannie Tate to the stand."

Before the bailiff could repeat her name, Vance interjected:

"Sidebar!"

The trio headed up to the bench.

Vance frowned at Orsini. "I hope that this is not a character reference. This is just a preliminary and it just does not seem appropriate at this time. All I am interested in hearing is information that is evidentiary."

"Oh no, Your Honor," said Orsini with a smile. "This is evidence!"

Ayala huffed. "What possible evidence could she give? The police talked to everyone about this and she had nothing to say."

Orsini growled back. "No…the police did not. No one talked to Missus Tate. The only thing that they said to Mister Tate was confess or else. Anything that Mister Tate had to say, the police did not listen. I'm not even sure that the investigators could pick her out of a lineup."

Coopersmith got right in Orsini's face. "But you told your clients to keep their mouths shut. You told them not to say anything to the investigators."

"I told them not to say anything until the investigators were willing to listen. As I said, the investigators were not interested in listening to anything that Mister Tate had to say…unless it was a confession."

Vance studied Orsini's face for a few moments. "All right, let's get on with it."

As the trio headed back to their places, Vance nodded at the bailiff. He then called Jeannie Tate to the stand.

She sashayed up to the stand, giving each one of the five complainants a very dirty look, while mouthing the words: "Smack you." She took the oath and then sat down. Now she was glaring at the two prosecutors.

Orsini walked up to her doing his best not to giggle. "Missus Tate, during this entire ordeal, you have stood by your husband. Why?"

"Well, first of all, it's cause I can't lose nothing."

"What do you mean?"

She glared back at the gallery. "We already got these summons from each one of the lawyers for them slutty little mendacious bimbos."

Coopersmith was up immediately. "Objection! Please inform the witness not to state absolutes like that. We have no firm proof that there is any mendacity. Alleged mendacity, please. Plus, I object to her doing any name-calling."

Vance leaned forward. "Missus Tate, the prosecutor is quite correct. You must not call them mendacious, without proof, and the name calling is totally uncalled for."

"But, I can prove that them girls are fibbing."

Missus Tate," Vance said more sternly. "We don't have that proof and until we do have it, then calling them mendacious *is* just an allegation."

"Well, tell that *rude* man to keep his yap shut and I will give you the information."

"Missus Tate!" Vance was getting impatient.

"Oh…all right."

Melissa spoke up. "Your Honor, do you want me to change the statement in any way?"

"What was it?"

"We already got these summons from each one of the lawyers for them slutty little mendacious bimbos."

"Change, slutty little mendacious bimbos, to complainants."

"Yes, Sir."

Vance leaned back. "Now, you may continue, Missus Tate."

"As I was saying…we got these summons…" She closed her mouth tightly for a moment. She took a breath. "Those…*persons*… are wanting to sue us for most of the money that we won. Well, because of a pre-nuptial agreement, there is *no way* that they will ever get a dime, no matter what. There's a part of the agreement, where it says, that if one party commits adultery, then the injured party, can kick the offending party out of the house, with nothing but the clothes on their back."

Jacob Forester jumped up. "Your Honor, I demand to see a copy of this alleged pre-nuptial agreement."

Vance looked at Forester, shocked. "Who are you?"

"Your Honor, I am representing Patricia Hamond in the lawsuit."

"Sit down! You know full well, that before you can do anything with a civil suit, we have to finish all litigation in the criminal case. At this time you have no right to demand anything. So sit down and shut up before I hold you in contempt."

Forester turned red and looked around as if he was not sure what to do. He sat down and put his left fist up to his mouth.

Jeannie looked up at the judge. "Do I have to worry about what he said?"

"No, ma'am. Just forget what he said. Right now, it doesn't matter at all. Uh...please continue."

She looked back and gave the girls an evil grin. "So, if you... *people* somehow figure out a way to prove that he did commit adultery, then I kick him out. At that time...all the money is mine. Since I didn't do anything, you can't sue me. You'll have to sue him for whatever he's got. The five of you will have to fight over his dirty underwear, cause that's all he's gonna have...nuthin' else...and you're welcome to it."

All five complainants were staring at her with total horror on their faces. Each one started whispering to their lawyer, their father or mother. It took several moments for the five to be hushed.

"So, because of that clause in the pre-nup, you definitely can lose *nothing*. So, let's continue. Did you believe him, when he said that he had not done anything with the young ladies?"

"I kinda believed him. But now, I'm positive that he has been telling the truth all along and that he never done nuthin' with them..." She growled. Partially to stop herself from doing any name calling and partially from frustration. "...*persons*...cause of that thing you said...uh what was it...Distinguish something?"

"Distinguishing characteristics."

She looked at him somewhat awed. "Boy that's a mouthful, in just two words."

"So you're saying that he does have something unique."

"Yeah, and none of them said anything about it."

"Is it recent?"

"Does that make a difference?"

"Oh, yes, my dear. If it is something very recent then they could say that they missed it."

"Oh no! This happened a *long* time ago."

"All right, please tell us."

"It happened before, we got married. It was back on Fourth of July, in 1985. It was me and Matthew and a guy named Jimmy Braddock. Matthew and Jimmy was doin' their cock-a-doodle-doos, tryin' to vie for my affections. I was flattered, cause two big, good-looking men was fighting over me. Anyway, the three of us was in a boat on Canyon Lake, back there in Texas. We were just cruising around on the lake, having a good time. They was both trying to tell me why they was the better man…for me. Anyway, while we're out there, Jimmy was handling the motor on the boat and we ended up getting stuck on this log…"

Coopersmith stood up. "I'm sure this is a very interesting story, to be told at a dinner party, but what does it have to do with what we are trying to accomplish here?"

Jeannie stood up, teeth bared. "Hey stupid! If you'll keep your yap shut, maybe you'll find out!"

Vance banged his gavel several times. "Mrs. Tate, please! Let me do the admonishments!"

She looked back at the judge and sat down with a huff and crossed her arms, scowling at Coopersmith.

"Mr. Coopersmith, sit down and let her finish. So far, I haven't heard anything that is relevant, but then we haven't heard the whole thing. Wait until she is finished and then I will decide if it *is* relevant."

Coopersmith sat down.

Jeannie was still sitting there fuming.

Vance turned his attention to Jeannie. "Please continue, ma'am."

She looked at Vance and sniffled a little. "Thank you, judge." She sat up a little. "Anyway, as I was saying, we got stuck on a log. Matt straddled the side of the boat…so he could kick us off the log. Once we were clear, Jimmy gunned the engine. Matt didn't have time to get his leg back in and he ended up sliding down the edge of the boat. You know that little horseshoe shaped thingy that you put the oars in when you wanna row instead of using the motor? Well, Matt got tore open by that thing…"

Virtually everyone in the room winced or flinched when they heard (and imagined) the injury happening to each one of them. Matthew just turned his head away with a pained look.

Jeannie continued. "When Matt got torn open, he cut loose with a warhoop that scared every bird floatin' or flockin' anywhere near the lake. That was the day that I learned about a thing called the 'femoral artery'. I learned about it cause Matt's got torn open. I swear, I have never seen blood shoot out of anybody like that, before or since. Anyway, he fell down in the bottom of the boat and Jimmy gunned the engine again and headed for the middle of the lake. I was *screaming* at him to head for the pier. He just started laughin' and carryin' on like he was havin' a good old time."

Coopersmith stood up again. "Your Honor, from what I hear, the man has a scar between his legs. So what! Who's to say that any of the girls *really* saw the scar?"

Jeannie stood up and snapped at him. "Didn't your mamma ever tell you that it ain't right to interrupt? You are a *very* rude person!"

Vance banged his gavel. "Mrs. Tate! Remember me? I'm the judge! I'm the one who scolds people in this courtroom."

She snarled and sat down, folding her arms again and glaring at Coopersmith.

Vance held his gavel up, just in case he had to use it again. "Mrs. Tate, are you finished?"

She kept glaring at Coopersmith. "No."

Coopersmith glared back. "Again, Your Honor, this is pointless…"

"To whom," snapped Vance? "She said that she's not finished… and the story is just getting interesting. So…sit down and…shut your yap."

Coopersmith looked as if he had been slapped. He shrugged and sat down.

Vance leaned forward. "Please continue, ma'am."

She took two deep breaths. She sat up in the chair, still glaring at Coopersmith. "Anyway, there was a Sherriff's Water Patrol on the lake, lookin' for drunks or anyone who was causing problems. They heard Matt's warhoop and my screaming. They chased us down and made Jimmy stop the boat. When they saw all the blood and that Matt was hurt, they took all three of us onto their speedboat and took us to shore. One of them stayed behind in our boat to bring it in. While we were heading for the pier, one of them radioed for an ambulance, while the third one was asking questions. When I told them what happened, they arrested Jimmy for some kind of assault charge."

"The Sherriff people stuffed some things in between Matt's legs to try to stop the bleeding. When the ambulance got there, them people did some other things to that tear between his legs. They put me in the ambulance as well, cause I was covered with blood and they didn't know that all of the blood came from Matt. Anyway, once we got to the hospital, they took him off to one place and me to another. Once them nurses got me undressed and found out that none of that blood was mine, they let me take a shower and then they let me put on some of those surgical type clothes to wear."

"After I got dressed, one of the doctors came to me and asked me what had happened. I told them. That was when I found out that that little oar hook had torn open one of his sacks and ripped the left one off. They had to call out to the Sherriff Patrol and see if they could find a stray family jewel in the boat. They never did."

"Now, I heard all five of those...*persons* say that they had played with *two* family jewels. That ain't possible, cause as of July, fourth 1985, Matthew Tate only has *one* family jewel. Since that day, he got what I call his B, U, S."

Vance was confused. "Bus?"

Her shoulders sagged. "No! B, U, S. Big Ugly Scar!"

Coopersmith stood up. "That still does not mean that they saw it…the scar that is."

Jeannie lost her temper again. "If everybody was nekkid, and they was fondlin' his manhood, then they couldn't miss it."

"Be that as it may, Your Honor, I still think that we need a doctor to confirm this…B, U, S."

"Don't need no doctor!" She stood up and was ready to pounce on the DA. "Can you *count*?"

Coopersmith stood there stuttering.

Jeannie turned to the judge. "Can *you* count?"

Now it was Vance's turn to stutter. He cleared his throat and stared at her for a moment a little troubled. "Yes, I can count…"

"Well then, why don't you take him back to your office and check?"

Vance had to sit there and contemplate.

Orsini interjected. "Excuse me, Your Honor, but we don't really need a doctor's opinion. The question to answer is: Would someone who is not a doc…*could* someone who is not a doctor notice the scar?"

Vance stared at Orsini wide-eyed.

Coopersmith tried to say something and Vance banged his gavel. "Quiet! I'm thinking!" He leaned back in his chair. His expression changed a few times as he was mulling the matter over in his head. He looked over to his left. "Chet, get up here!"

The bailiff obeyed. The two of them got close and started whispering.

"I've just been cornered and I'm going to have to go look at this man's crotch."

"Yes, Sir…and?"

"I need you to make sure that no one leaves, while I am… indisposed in my chambers."

"That problem has already been taken care of, Sir."

"What?"

"The defense attorney told me that he was going to let loose a bomb. When it happened, he said that some of the complainants might try to beat a hasty retreat. So, I made a discrete call for a few more reinforcements…to come back and be ready for…anything."

"That's very good, Chet."

"Thank you, Sir."

"Okay, back off."

Chet went back to his post.

Vance sat up. He looked around the room. "Mister Orsini has asked the key question: Could someone, who is not a doctor, notice this…B, U, S? Mister Orsini, Mister Coopersmith…you will join me in my chambers."

Markowitz stood up. "Your Honor, if I may."

Vance looked at the man. "Who are you and what do you want?"

"Alexi Markowitz, attorney for the Augsburger family. Would it be possible for me to witness this as well?"

"Why?"

"Your Honor, this could make a big difference in the civil suits."

"You know that the civil suit can't happen until the criminal litigation is over."

"Yes, Your Honor, however, if what the witness is saying is true, then the civil suits could be nipped in the bud, right now."

"How many family lawyers are here?"

The other four stood up.

Vance threw his hands up. "Oh, good grief!" He put his right hand to his forehead. He looked up again, not sure what to do with his hands. "I will let two of you go in and witness it. The others will just have to take our word!"

Forester raised his hand. "Which two, Your Honor?"

Vance looked at Forester. "You're that guy that interrupted earlier aren't you? Well you are *not* one of the two."

Forester sat down dejectedly.

Vance pointed at one of them. "I remember seeing you before, who are you?"

"Myron Shapiro, attorney for the Siegelman family, Your

Honor."

"Okay, you and...what was your name again?"

"Markowitz, Your Honor."

"Okay, you two." Vance got up muttering: "These people should wear name tags."

"All rise," said Chet.

Jeannie started to leave the witness box.

Chet called to her: "Where are you going?"

"What's the problem?"

Chet pointed to the seat. "You stay right there until you are excused."

Jeannie squawked, sat back down and crossed her arms, sulking angrily.

After the group left the room, Jeannie pointed at Cynthia. Jeannie smiled and ran her right index finger across her throat. Jeannie then pointed at Patricia and did the same execution sign. She did the same to the other three girls as well.

The five girls all stared at Jeannie with hate in their eyes.

Less than five minutes later, the group came back into the courtroom. Vance flopped down in his chair with a somewhat stunned look on his face. He picked up his gavel and banged it halfheartedly. "Court is back in session." He looked at Coopersmith. "Mister Prosecutor, Do you have something to say, Sir?"

Coopersmith looked a little sick. "That was something that I wish I could *un*-see."

Vance drummed his fingers on his desk. "And…!"

Coopersmith came too. He looked up puzzled. "Huh? Oh! Yes…" He stood up and cleared his throat. "Your Honor, at this time, the State of New York is dropping all charges against Mister Matthew Tate…" He turned to face Matthew. "…with very humble apologies, Sir."

Vance looked at Matthew. "This court *absolutely* agrees with that."

"Your Honor…," said Markowitz.

"Oh, what now?" Vance said impatiently.

"Before the final gavel, in this case, I would like to have it on the record that I can no longer represent the Augsburger family - particularly Cynthia Augsburger. From what I saw, it is obvious to me that she committed perjury and as an officer of the court, I cannot condone perjury and therefore, on the official record, I remove myself from the services of the Augsburger family."

Vance looked down. "You got all that, Melissa?"

She smiled. "Yes, Sir."

Shapiro stood up. "Your Honor, I need to do the same - on the record."

Vance chuckled. "Of course, why not? Are there any other rats that want to abandon their sinking ships?"

Douglas, Forester and O'Toole all stood up.

Vance shrugged. "Of course. Well, all of you line up. Let's get this over with."

Each one in turn came up and "abandoned ship", and then left the room.

Vance waited until the last of the five lawyers left the courtroom. "Okay, Chet, you need to get your people to take the five slutty little mendacious bimbos into custody and start the processing of the paperwork."

"Yes, Your Honor," said Chet. He signaled to several other bailiffs who headed for the "bimbos" while pulling out their handcuffs.

At that moment Olivia stood up and pointed at Patricia. "She made me do it! It was her idea! I didn't want to do it!"

Cynthia, Teresa and Laura all stood up and pointed to Patricia and started in on a chorus of accusations.

Patricia closed her eyes, put her left elbow in her right hand and her left hand on her forehead, covering her eyes.

Vance looked at the prosecutors and shouted over the din being created by the girls. "Coopersmith and Ayala, you need to start the paperwork on the five bimbos for the crimes they committed."

Coopersmith stammered a little.

Vance was a little miffed at the hesitation. He slammed his gavel down. "QUIET!" The girls all stopped and stared at the judge fearfully. "Is there a problem?"

"A slight one, Your Honor. I don't know which ones are adults and which ones are minors."

"I can help with that," said Matthew merrily.

Coopersmith looked a little stunned. "You can? How?"

"I have a list of their birth dates, Your Honor. According to what I have here, the youngest of the five turned 18 years old on the 18th of March. So, while three of them - Siegelman, Hamond and Maltby - were minors at the time they filled out the police report, all five of them committed perjury as adults - today."

Orsini looked up at him and whispered. "You snake! That's why we were waiting for the 19th."

Matthew looked down and smiled.

As the five girls started receiving their new "bracelets", they all five started protesting, and begging, to Daddy, to stop this nonsense. The fathers were all sitting there with different stages of disinterest, disgust, loathing and revulsion on their faces as they listened to the protestations of their spoiled brats…and could do absolutely nothing about the situation.

After all five of the ranting girls were out of shouting range, Vance looked around the courtroom. "An interesting day, folks. Court is adjourned." He banged his gavel.

"All rise!" said Chet.

Vance got up and left, shaking his head.

The DA walked over to the defense desk. He held out his hand in friendship. Mister Tate, Jordan Coopersmith, District Attorney. You and I are now on the same side."

Matthew took his hand and gave him a firm shake. "What do

you need from me?"

"We may need a few more tidbits of information from you, to complete all of the paperwork."

Jeannie snarled. "Can I get out of this durn seat yet?"

Chet nearly laughed out loud. "Yes, ma'am," he said as he nearly choked from laughing. "The case is over, you are free to leave."

She got up with a huff and headed to Matthew. "Why are all them silly reporters still here?"

Coopersmith scoffed. "They have to finish their reports for their different...slander-rags. Since the case is over, this room is available." He leaned forward and whispered: "Plus, the cameras are still rolling, hoping to get some reaction from the parents of the five... bimbos."

Matthew looked down at Orsini and then back at Coopersmith. "Am I going to need my lawyer?"

"No, I don't think so. You don't need to be defended from anything anymore."

Matthew looked down at Orsini. "Then, Sir, I guess that you are off the clock."

"It's a shame," chuckled Orsini. "I was having a lot of fun with this case." He shook his head, gathered all his papers, closed his briefcase and then held out his hand to Matthew. "It's been fun, Sir." Matthew shook his hand. He then hugged Jeannie. "Madam, I have never enjoyed being in the presence of a temperamental wildcat before...until now."

Jeannie wrinkled her nose at him. "Thank you, for what you done."

"You won't be thanking me…when you get my bill."

Matthew looked puzzled. "Why, what do you charge?"

Orsini looked up and said - in a matter-of-fact manner: "A thousand dollars per hour."

Matthew looked at Jeannie, horrified. He opened his mouth but nothing came out.

"They told me to get a good lawyer," she whined. "I figured that he had to be good in order to be able to charge that much."

Matthew fell back down into his chair. He looked around in total dismay. He looked up at Jeannie. "Okay," he said weakly.

Coopersmith put his hand on Matthew's shoulder. "As soon as you get your legs back, we'll go to my office."

Meanwhile, Cristal Ayala headed out of the courtroom. She was swamped by numerous reporters.

One reporter got right in her face. "How does it feel to get hammered so badly in losing a case?"

She smiled sweetly. "When we come in here, it's not a situation where we worry about - me win, you lose - or vice versa. The main thing that we are trying to accomplish is to see that justice is done. If justice *is done,* then no one has lost - except the perpetrator. If justice does not prevail, *then* we have all lost. Today was not a loss." She then held her hands up and started forcing her way through the throng.

After Orsini had departed, Matthew finally got his legs back.

He stood up. "Let's get out of here."

As they headed out, someone grabbed Matthew's arm and spun him around. It was Adriana O'Reilly, the one with the ostentatious turquoise outfit. She screamed at him. "Where do you think you're going?" She pointed at Coopersmith. "You tell him the truth! You tell him that you lied! You tell him that you did do nasty things to my daughter, you…barbarian!"

Matthew quickly put one arm completely around Jeannie and the other hand over Jeannie's mouth, before Adriana O'Reilly got a face full of fist and an earful of cuss words (in at least eight colorful languages). Jeannie snarled and squirmed in his grip. "Look lady, I am not the one who committed any crime here. Your daughter and the others conspired against *ME*! I am the victim here, not your daughter."

"But you don't matter," screamed Adriana. "You're nothing! My daughter could go to jail because of you!"

Matthew was almost disgusted enough to unleash Jeannie. "Your daughter is going to jail because of her own greed and stupidity."

The news media people were holding up their microphones and taking numerous pictures of the confrontation.

Michael O'Reilly came up behind his wife and corralled her the same way Jeannie was being held. He looked up at Matthew with a bit of a strained smile. "Sorry, Sir, my wife is just a little bit too unwise in certain things."

'I understand,' thought Matthew.

They then proceeded to run the gauntlet in order to get to Coopersmith's office.

There were several women's rights activists who were carrying signs and protesting the abuse of women. They were screaming at Coopersmith and Matthew for exploitation of women and letting a pervert get away with unspeakable crimes.

Some gay rights activists were screaming at them as well… why, no one could figure out.

One of the bailiffs got on his radio and called for extra help. He also admonished someone over his radio for allowing these troublemakers inside the building.

As they got closer to the DA's office, more police, bailiffs and building security showed up and formed a barricade to stop everyone including journalists.

After they got into Coopersmith's office, they sat down to catch their breaths.

"I knew this was a high profile case…but…this…I don't know if they will ever believe what really happened in that courtroom. There'll probably be some wild-eyed radicals who will start screaming *cover up*."

"Maybe they should talk to the jurors," said Matthew. "I doubt that they'll think that those people are part of a conspiracy."

"You can never convince a bigot of the truth," sighed Coopersmith. "They don't like to have their bigoted ideology challenged."

"Let's get down to business here," said Matthew. "I want to get out of here as soon as I can. I want to get on with my *life*."

Ayala walked in. "That is one thing that I want to do too. I want to find out what really happened."

Matthew felt confused. "As far as what?"

"We were told," she continued, "that the investigators did a thorough job. We were told that they had talked to you, your wife, your son, neighbors and your co-workers. From what I heard in there...something is amiss."

"Nobody ever talked to me," said Jeannie. "The only time they asked me anything was when they first busted in and asked where Matt was."

Ayala closed her eyes trying to control her temper. "No questions, from anyone at any time from any law enforcement or legal group?"

Jeannie held out her hands. "Nuthin'."

Ayala turned her attention to Matthew. "What about you? The report I have...says that you were completely uncooperative and got very nervous when they were questioning you."

Matthew gritted his teeth. "They say uncooperative. The only thing that I was uncooperative about was admitting a lie. They didn't and wouldn't listen to anything that I had to say. They only wanted to hear me confess to all the charges that they were spinning in my face. The only time I got nervous is when they threatened to use coercion in order to obtain a confession."

Ayala contemplated. "Is there any witness to this...coercion?"

"You can ask Orsini. He came in just as they were attempting it."

Jeannie was tired of hanging around in this building. She had her own plans. "When do we get out of this place? I got other things that I want to do."

"First," said Coopersmith, "maybe you can satisfy some of my curiosities."

Jeannie looked at him suspiciously. "Like what?"

"You said that the guy…Braddock? Was that his name?"

"Yeah."

"He was arrested?"

"Yeah."

"For what?"

"At first they was debatin' between something called depraved indifference, reckless indifference or reckless endangerment. Then they decided on assault. They said that if he had headed for the pier to call an ambulance, then they wouldn't have charged him with anything. It would have been called an accident. Because he headed away from the pier and was laughing and wouldn't stop for the cops, they decided to upgrade it to assault."

"Did he serve time?"

"Oh, yeah. They gave him three to five. Unfortunately, he got out in three. After he got out, he was mad, cause I had married Matt. He wanted me to wait for him. So he started making it *real* public that Matt only had one family jewel. While Matt was trying to teach classes, all his students were more concerned with buggin' him about the *injury*."

Coopersmith asked: "So, why didn't you wait for him? Why did you marry Mr. Tate?"

Jeannie huffed. "When I saw Jimmy hurt Matt and then laugh about it, I said to myself that there was *no way* that I could hitch my wagon to someone that cruel. I mean, blood shootin' everywhere and Jimmy was laughing. No! That was not the man for me. Matt and me was married less than eight months after the incident."

"So, why are you in New York?"

Matthew snarled. "Like she said, Braddock kept on making sure that my students knew that I had lost *an organ.* He made sure that they *all* knew that this *organ* was missing. I couldn't teach anyone. I had obtained a Protection Order against him...but that didn't stop him from freely giving all kinds of information to my students. When I put applications out for 'other places', New York was the most compelling."

"Okay," said Coopersmith. "We are going to start our own investigation into this whole mess. It appears that we are going to have to go after a couple of negligent investigators and, thanks to you, we have five, open and shut cases, against those..." he looked at Jeannie, "...slutty little mendacious bimbos."

Ayala interjected. "One thing that will help immensely, is if you have anything else that we can know about, that those bimbos don't know about, other than...your distinguishing characteristic. A habit of some kind or...just about anything that is definitely unique."

Jeannie blushed. She sniffed, sucked her lips in and looked off to the side.

Coopersmith saw her reaction. "Is there something?"

Ayala stood up and went to Jeannie. "Maybe you and I should go into a different room and talk about it."

Jeannie got up and the two women went into a different room.

"So," said Ayala, "what is it?"

Jeannie blushed, closed her eyes and she looked down. "He got this thing…he just can't…perform…unless…"

"Perform? Perform what?"

"He can't do…husbandly things…in bed."

"So he has a sexual dysfunction?"

"That ain't what that head doctor called it."

"What did the doctor call it?"

"He said that it was…a…fetish." Even though she buried her face in her hands, Ayala could see the redness of her face showing through her fingers.

"Okay, he has a fetish. There are a lot of people who have fetishes. What is his…*different*…desire?"

Jeannie put her hands down. She had tears in her eyes. "I don't like talking about it. In the privacy of our bedroom, it ain't bad, but out here…I just…I don't…I don't want to talk about it."

"Does he hurt you?"

"NO," she scolded. "It's just…embarrassing…talking about it."

Ayala sighed. "Look, in all the time that I have been in the DA's office, I have heard all kinds of things. Just say it. Just tell me what it is. You will have to *really* come up with something strange to shock me."

Jeannie sighed. "Okay, he can't…do…anything…unless he…I let him…lick my…belly button. I love him, so…in the bedroom…in total privacy…I let him do it. After he…licks me…for a while…then he…he can do the deed. If he starts feeling frisky and I don't want to do it…all I have to do is keep my shirt on."

Ayala sat there dull-eyed. "A belly button fetish? A belly button fetish. Jeannie, honey, that is one of the tamest fetishes that I have ever heard of. I mean there are some fetishes where some people can't…*perform*, unless they draw blood, from their partner."

Jeannie's expression changed from anguished embarrassment to shock. "So, if he just…wants to…lick my…belly button…then that ain't, what you call…really kinky?"

"Mildly kinky. Definitely not destructive or life threatening."

Jeannie sighed in relief.

"Let's go back and join the men."

They went back in. Coopersmith looked up. "He talked about a non-injurious naval fetish."

"So did she," said Ayala.

Coopersmith shrugged. "None of the slutty little mendacious bimbos said anything about a fetish, so for the time being, we can keep that a secret…in case some other girls try to get froggy and take a jump of their own, now that they know about your…B, U, S."

230

"I believe that we have all that we need," said Ayala. "You can go. We would appreciate it if you would let us know where you are... just in case we need to contact you again."

With a big grin, Matthew said: "We are going to spend a month in the Bahamas."

Coopersmith smiled and nodded.

"First," said Jeannie, "I wanna go down where those bimbos are and smack em'!"

"You don't want to smack them," said Matthew.

She scowled. "Yes, I do! They tried to take our money. They lied about you. They made us go through a lot of crap, cause they're greedy. I wanna smack em'!"

"No, you don't," said Ayala. "If you do that, we'll have to arrest you for assault...plus, that will give them a reason for filing a lawsuit against you."

"I still wanna smack em'!"

Matthew picked her up under her armpits. He held her up against the wall about two feet off the floor. "You have a choice, Baby Doll: You are either going to the Bahamas with me, or you are going to jail for assault. Which is it?"

With a pouting look on her face, she said: "I wanna go with you to the Bahamas...after I smack them bimbos."

Without lowering her he hung his head and growled a sigh. He looked over at the two attorneys. "See what I have to put up with?"

Both attorneys stood there chuckling.

Matthew partially threw her over his shoulder. He gave her bottom three quick hard swats.

She had a look of total shock on her face. "OH! OH! Domestic violence! Spousal abuse!" She looked at the attorneys. "Do you see this?"

Ayala shook her head. "What I saw was a bulletin being delivered by way of the hindquarters in order to get a message across to the headquarters."

Jeannie growled in frustration.

Matthew cradled her bottom holding her on his shoulder. He turned to the attorneys. "I'm going to leave now. I'm headed to the Bahamas with this little wildcat. That's where you can get in touch with us, if you need us." He turned and headed for the door, still carrying Jeannie.

Jeannie wrapped her legs around his chest. She was resting her left elbow on top of his head. The doors of this building were rather high, so she did not have to duck when they went through any doorway. She saw the two attorneys standing there in the office and gave a half-hearted wave. "Bye-bye," she said with an equal half-heartedness.

The two attorneys returned her wave and gave her a friendly farewell.

"I like her," said Ayala. "She's got all kinds of spunk."

"She certainly has something," said Coopersmith while chuckling.

THE QUESTION OF SLAVERY...

1

The paper was dropped nonchalantly on the desk. Krezdon had been daydreaming, and had to stop for a moment in order to realize what was going on. He looked up at the old scribe.

"Here you are, Sir. This is the new yearly census for your perusal." said the old man.

'He sounds about as bored as I am,' thought Krezdon. "Any significant changes, anywhere?"

"It is all in the notes, at the bottom, Sir."

"All right." He glanced at the notes, not really reading anything. He gave the scribe a polite smile and said: "Thank you, Mr. Themeh."

Themeh returned the smile, turned and shuffled off.

Krezdon read all the figures and notes carefully. He had to make sure he knew what was on the report before presenting it to his superior. Besides, reading the report helped kill the boredom.

After the fifth reading of the report, he got bored with it and instead of daydreaming, he started reminiscing. Mainly thinking of how he had been catapulted into the current position that he now held. Krezdon Chashchy was the youngest individual to ever be promoted to the rank he now held: City Sector Commandant, Sector Four.

There were six other sectors, and all of their Commandants were at least nineteen years older than he was. Dumb luck and a few acts of bending, twisting, warping and fracturing the truth.

He had been a lowly member of the constabulary, in one of the precincts along the waterfront. After being relieved of duty for the day, he had wandered into one of the seedier brothels, and stumbled on his future. The City Governor had been assassinated, some three days prior, and without even knowing what the upper echelon was going through, he literally tripped over the information that exposed the entire plot.

The assassin had decided to blackmail all of the conspirators, in order to further his standing. Krezdon, though tipsy, had not been near as intoxicated as the killer. Krezdon had tripped over the man, scattering some papers. After having just been severely reprimanded by his Patrol Supervisor, he knew that he did not need another complaint registered against him. He decided to be helpful and gather up the stranger's papers. While picking them up, he read a few lines and noticed that it was a complete layout of the plot, including all of the names of those involved.

He looked around carefully to see if anyone was in any way paying attention to what he was doing. No one seemed to care. He rolled all the papers up, stuffed them into his belt, pulled the drunken assassin to his feet, threw the man over his shoulder and beat a hasty retreat to his home.

He had heard about how some of these professional assassins were very capable of killing in ways that you could not imagine, so he very securely tied the drunken man to a chair, using every piece of string, rope and twine that he could find, before any careful scrutinizing of the papers. It took some time to get the papers in the proper sequence, but once he had done that, he realized that the information had to be true. There had been a few details that had not been made public. They were well documented in this paperwork, leaving little doubt that this man knew quite a bit about what had transpired and why.

Krezdon kept the man tied up, for several days, smacked him a few times and then gagged him, while he copied the papers, in his own writing, in order to make it appear as if he had obtained a confession from this killer.

When he turned in his report, he bull-shot his supervisors into believing that he had actually obtained the information through careful meticulous procedures of questioning, along with a little torture.

His Supervisor had been somewhat enraged. "Why didn't you bring this information in sooner? Why did you wait so long before coming to me?"

"I had to make sure, Supervisor. When I first came across this man, I thought that he might just be spouting off, in order to impress…someone else. If I had brought him in then, with nothing but drunken mouthing off, then both you and I could have ended up being embarrassed if you were to take it to a higher level, and find out that it wasn't true. This way the information is a lot harder to argue with, because of the details that I got out of him."

After turning in the completed information, along with a very confused (and badly beaten) assassin, his rise in stature was astounding. The city executioner was kept very busy, swinging his axe at the necks of some 60% of the city government upper echelon.

The norm for any unsuccessful coup, is that there are, all of a sudden, many new openings and promotions in the aftermath. Krezdon had received one of them. He had been a Street Patroller - Grade 2. Now he had bypassed several hundred in the constabulary and judicial areas, to become one of the most influential in the city. At first he was terrified with this new set of responsibilities from this position. Then he found out that he was in Sector 4. This was the highest income and lowest crime rate part of the city. Rarely did anything reach his desk. When it did, it was because those of a lower office, were afraid to make a decision about any argument between the richest citizens of the city. Krezdon, who had the reputation of torturing information out of a professional assassin, had only to glare at the two in the argument, and they would decide to kiss and make up, rather than have "Krezdon the Vicious" make a decision for them. Usually it was some petty squabble that should never go to any court anyway.

Like today, the majority of his time was spent (unsuccessfully) in trying to kill boredom.

He looked back at the census report and took another few minutes memorizing some of the figures. Then he spent a few more moments reading the notes again.

He sighed and headed for the office of one of the two people in the city of Malantroi that outranked him. The City Governor, Angtozo Beremotz was one of those two. The other was on the military side, Supreme City Commander Jeltiynul Hremborn. During peace time, the Governor and the council are in charge. If the city was involved in a war then Hremborn and the Sector Commandants would be running things. Each helped advise others, at all times, so that relationships remained good.

Jeltiynul made Krezdon and a lot of other people feel very uncomfortable. He had a permanent scowl on his face and a very loud, piercing base voice. He was arrogant and did not take criticism very well at all. He was also a homosexual that had an irritating habit of trying to get any man he came in contact with, to participate in his sexual activities.

Krezdon had a hard time understanding the life style of Jeltiynul. The man was married and had fathered four children. The oldest of the children was 16, and the youngest 11. He had fulfilled his obligation of marrying according to the arrangements his parents had made. He had reproduced and was now living his life, as he saw fit.

Krezdon arrived at the office, looked in and nearly laughed out loud, when he noticed that Jeltiynul was probably leading a business life that was equally boring. The big man was currently tormenting a large black beetle, on his desk top.

Krezdon cleared his throat. "Excuse me, Supreme Commandant, but I have a report here."

Jeltiynul looked up. "A report on what?"

"The annual census report."

Jeltiynul rolled his eyes. "Oh how…thrilling," he said sarcastically. "Well bring it in. Maybe we can slow down some of the constant bellyaching from Sholloh."

"What is he complaining about now?"

Jeltiynul took careful aim at the beetle with his middle finger. He flicked it hard and it flew out the window from the force. He aimed his fist at the window and shouted: "Score!" Then he looked at Krezdon. "What is he always complaining about? He needs more people for the city guard, and for the precinct constable office."

Krezdon walked slowly to the desk. "Well...he does have control of the lousiest area of the city. 75% of the crime and criminals, and only 40% of the law enforcement."

"Well, what do the figures say about more people in law enforcement?"

"According to this, the new citizenry, and taxes can afford six more in the city guard and 3.4 in the constabulary."

Jeltiynul groaned. "Don't you love how those idiots come up with partial people, in their figures?"

"Oh yeah. I wonder just exactly which part they want for a constable and how they plan to divide him up."

"Well I suppose that I will have to be the one to make the grand decision. Do we make the other .6 a constable or a civilian? I know what Sholloh will say."

Krezdon sighed. "I wish that something exciting would happen. Stuff like this just bores me to tears. I almost wish that something big would happen, so that I could have something to do."

"Oof!" Jeltiynul gave him a pained look. "Don't ever ask for something to happen. Usually in a case like that - it does."

"And what's wrong with that?"

"Because, just as usual, it is something that you might not be able to handle."

Here Are My Shorts

"Maybe, whatever."

They discussed a few more things about the census, until Krezdon excused himself and returned to his office. He noticed a black beetle, similar to the one Jeltiynul had been torturing, wandering around the top of his desk. He walked up to his desk and smashed the bug. He sighed and decided that now was a good time to go home for the day.

On the way home, he decided he needed a woman for the night. After being in Jeltiynul's office and getting another proposition from him, there was a need to remind him of his masculinity. It was nice living in this section of the city. The young ladies of that persuasion, in this sector, were less exposed to certain diseases.

2

He was awakened somewhat rudely by…whatever her name is.

"What? What you want?"

She was only slightly awake. "Wake up! Someone…tryin' t' break down your door."

He perked up his ears. Someone was hammering, rather persistently, on his door. They were shouting something as well, but it was muffled by the thick door and walls.

He threw the blanket off, grabbed a robe and headed for the door. After donning the robe, and checking his appearance, he opened the door. One of the city guard was standing there looking a little flustered.

"Sorry to disturb you, Commandant, but we have a crisis."

"Oh! Do we?"

"Yes sir…Uh…Your presence is needed immediately. The Supreme Commandant, Lord Jeltiynul Hremborn, has been assassinated."

Krezdon closed his eyes, bit his lip and shook his head. "Please tell me, that you didn't just use the A word."

"Huh? But why, sir?"

"Never mind."

"I have a carriage here for you, sir. I was told to take you directly to the scene of the crime."

"Right. I'll be ready in a few minutes." He closed the door and went back to his bedroom, mumbling to himself. "Don't say that! It might happen...you might not be able to handle it. Crap! Now, can I handle it? Crap! Why me? Okay stupid, you bull-shot your way through a situation before...by fool luck. Now what? Crap!"

After shooing away, the good looking brunette with the big... brown eyes...and big soft...! After saying his reluctant goodbyes to her, he climbed into the carriage.

He then went through the most hair raising carriage ride of his life. He thought the streets were wider and the corners not quite so sharp. But then he had never ridden in a carriage, moving this fast. The equines were running like they had a hot branding iron in their tails. The constant cracking of the whip did not let them slow down. They arrived at the Hremborn residence in no time at all. Now came the hard part - prying his fingers loose from the armrests.

There were two men trying to tell him something, but all he could hear was the blood hammering through his ears. They gave up trying to communicate and stood there looking at Krezdon in a strange manner with their arms folded.

It took a few moments for his blood pressure and breathing to return to normal. He swallowed hard, gave the carriage driver a nasty look and headed for the front gate. "Who was first on the scene?"

"The man is inside, Milord," said one of the men.

"So, let's go inside and get this mess figured out."

Krezdon followed the two men. Both were wearing the uniform of the city guard. One was a Squad Leader. He was a large man with stringy dark brown hair sticking out from under his helmet. He had an incredibly thick moustache, which completely hid his lips when his mouth was closed. The other man was not quite as tall, but was bigger in the shoulders. His hair was a lighter shade of brown, and definitely neater. He was wearing the rank of Infantry Grade One.

'Apparently,' Krezdon thought, 'I am the first high ranking official here. Strange, seeing as how the City Governor lives directly across the street.'

The two guards parted, to allow Krezdon to enter the gate first. Like all gates in this upper class section of the city, it was an iron gate, with ugly looking points at the top. The entire house was surrounded by a stucco wall with iron points all the way around the top. This house was different in that the iron here was painted white instead of black. The walls of the two-story house were identical to the outer wall; stucco, and painted a rather tasteless shade of yellow. The thatched roof was almost to the stage where it needed replacing. There was a pleasant garden that filled the entire front yard. It was a splash of color that would drive a botanical expert crazy, trying to identify all the different flowers. They had all opened up to show their full glory in the morning sun. Almost as if to mock the malicious act that had taken place inside the house.

The shorter guard hurried ahead to open the front door. As the door came open, Krezdon could hear the sounds of crying women from inside. He readied himself for what he was going to face. He tried to remember the family - 'wife, two sons, two daughters…how many slaves?' That question would be answered once he was inside.

He walked into a very neat parlor. There was a total of fourteen people in the room. Great! Who is who?

The introductions started. The wife: Kamezee. She was in her early thirties and was a little wide in the hips - probably from giving birth to four children. She like everyone else had not had time to get dressed. Her eyes and nose were red and puffy, obviously from crying. As Krezdon walked in, she tried to do something about her appearance, but was not too successful. There were three slaves attending her. All three were very young and petite. They looked like they had to be sisters. They had very similar facial features, very dark brown hair and blue eyes.

The youngest of the four children was Breel. He like all four children had light brown hair and dark eyes. The younger daughter was named Tymay, the older daughter was Kendika. All three had a young slave girl sitting at their feet.

The oldest son - Dezond - was the only one of the family members that showed no signs of grief. He seemed more interested in the slave girl that was sitting in his lap. She was very young and could probably be called cute, if her teeth were not clenched so tightly. She was wearing a threadbare nightgown that hid nothing, including the fact that Dezond was openly fondling her.

The other two people in the room were more members of the city guard.

Krezdon noticed that none of the slaves showed any sign that they had been grieving and also showed no signs of sympathy.

He looked at the two guardsmen in the room: "Are you two really needed here?"

"The Squad Leader ordered us to stay, Milord."

Krezdon looked at the Squad Leader, who flushed and looked up at the ceiling. He looked back at the two in the room: "Which one of you was the first one here?"

"That man is upstairs, Milord."

"You two can go. I don't think your services are needed here."

They both gratefully acknowledged his order and left.

Krezdon went upstairs with the two ranking guardsmen trailing close behind. Another guardsman, who was standing near a closed door, snapped to attention. "Is there anybody on duty at the gates or on the wall?"

The Squad Leader sputtered a little, then said: "The day shift is there sir. All the people here are night shift."

"Oh really! Well where are the representatives from the precinct constable office?"

"Uh…constable?"

"Yes! You know! The people who investigate criminal activities. Criminal activities such as HOMICIDE!"

The Squad Leader cleared his throat. "To my knowledge, Milord, no one has notified them."

Krezdon looked at him in utter disbelief. "Your job, as a member of the city guard, is to protect the outer perimeter. The constables take care of the inner city. Go! Find a representative of the local precinct and inform them…NOW!"

The Squad Leader spun and ran.

Krezdon looked at the guard by the door. "Who are you?"

"Infantryman Grade Two Wincherok, Milord."

"You were first on the scene?"

"Most assuredly, Milord."

"You didn't touch anything did you?"

"Oh no, Milord. The people downstairs have also assured me that they didn't touch anything either."

"All right. Open the door and let me have a look."

Wincherok opened the door and stepped back.

The first thing that Krezdon noticed when he walked in was an odor. Something had burned in here, but he could not identify what. He had never smelled anything like it in his life. There was the remains of a candle on the end of a long dresser. Nothing unusual about it though. He started noticing other smells in the room. Perfume (?) and cosmetics. This looked more like a woman's dressing room than that of a man.

The big four poster bed was covered with white silk sheets. In the middle of the bed was the body of Jeltiynul Hremborn. He was lying on his back. His head was facing to the left. Buried in the right side of his head there was a very strange looking...knife (?)...dagger (?)...dirk (?). 'What is that thing?' thought Krezdon. The dead man's face looked calm. No sign of any shock or struggle. He had been asleep when it happened. The - whatever that thing is - was rammed into his skull, and death had to have been instantaneous.

He looked around the room. The window was lined with crisscrossing bars that would definitely keep burglars out. There were at least two dozen heavy bolts holding the bars in place. The only thing in the roof was the normal rings for holding up a mosquito net. There did not seem to be any trap doors - floor or ceiling. Only one window - barred. No other doors except the one Krezdon had just come through.

He walked out of the room. The two guardsmen were still standing there in the hall. "As soon as the people from the constabulary get here, you may go."

He looked through all the remaining rooms upstairs. All the windows were barred in the same manner. The only way to get to the second floor, was through the first floor.

The unfamiliar weapon could not have fit through the bars in the windows. The bars were way too close together for it to fit through.

Best to wait until the investigators arrived. They would have that smelly little truth box with them. No point in questioning anyone until then.

He went outside and looked around. Both side yards were much the same as the front. Floral glory and beauty everywhere. The back yard was a little different. There were several different fruit trees back there. The only reason he could identify what kind of trees they were was because most of them had ripening fruit, just about ready for picking.

He walked the entire perimeter of the back yard. None of the trees had any branches overhanging the wall. They were too far away from the wall, plus any branches anywhere near the wall were far too fragile for anyone to use it to get over the wall.

There was a small shed in the back yard for storing gardening tools. There was nothing unusual in there.

The only other thing in the back yard that got his attention, was a wrought iron door, in the back wall. There were no cracks between the door and its frame. It was securely locked. He kicked it out of frustration. It was very firmly in place.

He had looked at all of the points that lined the top of the wall. Other than a few bird droppings there was no sign that anyone, or anything, had touched any of them.

He had only been a minor entity in the constabulary when he was there, but anyone with any training at all could see that this was some kind of inside job.

A young girl wearing a slave bracelet on her arm, came running up to Krezdon, and dropped to her knees. "The people you asked for have arrived, Milord," she said breathlessly.

"Who are you? I don't remember seeing you before."

She looked up at him. "The mistress sent me to get the master's lawyer. I just got back with him, Milord."

'Lawyer,' he thought. 'Well, why not? Those legal freaks have their noses in everyone's life and business…why not their death as well?'

There were four new faces in the parlor. One was a short man with black hair, showing a little gray at the temples. He was looking at a document when Krezdon walked in. He glanced up at the newcomer to the room, then went back to his document. He had dressed hastily, and what he was wearing was a little too fine for anyone in the constables office. Obviously the lawyer.

Two of the others were dressed in the black uniform of the constabulary. They were watching the fourth man, who was preparing the truth box. The two constables were introduced as Lieutenant Ponodell Na and Detective Grade One Shojo Dooron. The Inquisitor with the box was Berber Jyktho.

The box was called something else by the people who knew how to use it. Krezdon had given up trying to pronounce it. He had seen it tested thoroughly and it worked. It had something to do with the emanations of a person's voice. If they were telling the truth - blue smoke would come out of the box. If they were lying - yellow smoke. The people who knew how to set them up seemed ecstatic about them. Krezdon could not stand the smell.

The box was lit. Krezdon called it: "The moment to rue." Everyone in the room held their noses, and involuntarily closed their stinging eyes.

When Krezdon had finally cleared the tears out of his eyes, he felt a strong desire for another murder to be committed - The one who had lit the foul thing was sitting there smiling.

The Inquisitor looked around the room smiling. "Who's first?"

They started with Breel's slave, Bantesha. She was just a child, and knew virtually nothing. Next was Vay. She was Tymay's slave. To call her a moron, was a compliment to her mental capacity. Kendika's slave Bentha was next. The only thing that she could tell them was that the place was locked up, when she woke up. The last of the children's slaves, the sad eyed Prenya came up. She confirmed that all the doors had been locked. She also brought up the fact that Fendina was missing.

Ponodell perked up at that remark. "Fendina? Who is she?"

"He," said Prenya flatly.

Shojo could not help his confusion. "He? Fendina is a woman's name. What do you mean, he?"

She shrugged. "That's his name."

"That's what my husband named him," Kamezee said sadly. "Jeltiynul bought him about ten years ago, and gave him that name. That was when I found out that my husband was not entirely masculine. Ever since he bought that boy, he has not spent one single night with me."

Krezdon joined in now: "Why didn't you tell us about him earlier? Has he been gone all along? When did you last see him?"

Dezond looked up. "You didn't ask. He's been gone all morning. The last time we saw him was last night when everyone went to bed."

The questions started getting very specific. They were directed at everybody, and answered accordingly. Certain questions were repeated, with answers that differed slightly, but not enough to make a difference. After nearly an hour of interrogating the household, they were told to search the house, to see if any valuables were missing. After a thorough search - the only thing missing was the slave Fendina.

Sometime during the inquiries and search, two more constables had arrived, and gone directly to Jeltiynul's bedroom.

Krezdon had to go outside. The smoke was giving him a headache. He went out back and sat under a fruit tree. His headache was subsiding slowly, when another headache showed up, in the form of Haneenda Jorsydo. She was the City Sector Commandant of Sector Six. She was one of the more influential of the upper echelon. She was dressed for battle. Why not? The Supreme City Commandant had just been assassinated. It could be a diversionary measure leading up to war for all anyone knew. She was in her mid-sixties and wore her gray hair loosely flowing to her shoulders. Her dark brown eyes that usually showed little or no emotion, now hid none of her anger.

"What are you doing here? Someone has just murdered the Supreme Commandant and here you sit…taking an inventory on… fruit?"

He smiled warmly. What he really wanted to do was kick her yellow teeth down her throat. "Ah yes. Charming to a fault as always, aren't we?" He closed his eyes and shook his head. "I have been inside with that wretched little truth box, stinking up the whole house. Why don't you go inside and sniff up all the stench so that nobody else has to put up with it?"

She stepped back looking indignant and sputtered.

"All the questions, that need to be asked, are being asked inside. I am waiting for the physician's report on what happened and the weapons specialist to tell me about that thing is that was used to murder him. As soon as we have that information, we can then move on from there."

She clenched her fists. "He is dead! He was stabbed! What more do you need?"

"He was stabbed in the head with some kind of weapon, that I have never seen the likes of before. I want to find out what it is and where it came from, and then follow up on the only suspect, that we really have in this case."

That took her by surprise. "You...have a suspect?"

"Yes," he sighed. "This might be just a simple case of a disgruntled slave. It definitely wouldn't be the first time that that has occurred."

She studied him for a few moments. He could tell by the look in her eyes that the wheels were turning, coming up with something nasty to say about him. "A slave who murdered his master...or a slave hired by someone ambitious, who needed Jeltiynul out of the way."

"That is possible."

"As I recall, the last time a government official was assassinated, you went from nowhere to somewhere, mighty fast. Another assassination? Maybe you are looking for another promotion?"

That did it. He had done his best to hold his temper, with the old bat, but no more. He jumped up and glared at her. "I am now going to kick holes in your theory, when I wish I was kicking holes in your hollow head. First of all, I am the youngest of any of the Sector Commandants, not to mention the least experienced. Second: It would take a majority vote, from the Council, the Governor and the Sector Commandant in order for me to be appointed to the now vacant office. Shall we take a roll call? Sector One Commandant, Kol Rebbed. His uncle was one of the people executed with the other conspirators. His favorite uncle. He acts as if I manipulated the assassin's confession, so that his uncle would get the axe. That is one against me. Sector One Council Representative, Premterol Jydo. When he is sober, he tells Rebbed to make the decision for him. When he is drunk, Rebbed usually makes the vote by proxy. That's two! Sector Two Commandant, Brakand Sholloh - he hates my guts, period! That's three! Sector Two Council Representative Brasothar Shorshkyn; he does exactly what Sholloh tells him to do. That's four! Sector Three Commandant Tamheta Dalay; her ambition is on the just vacated office, and no way is she going to vote for anyone else to be put in that position. I am now zero against five. Sector Three Council Representative Xuzo Poroby; he votes in favor of whoever can line his pockets with the most money. That is absolutely *not* me. Six against me. Sector Four Commandant - whoops, that's me - according to the law I cannot vote for myself. Seven votes gone. Sector Four Council Representative Tesha Telyil. She is totally gaga over Sholloh and will vote with him, just to please him. That's eight. Your attitude is obvious, so that makes nine against. Jeltiynul Hremborn is dead, so that vote won't happen. That leaves five votes that I have not gone over yet. At least one of those is Sector Seven Council Representative Grathgo Jop, who would definitely vote against me. With all that, I might get lucky and receive three votes in my favor. No, my dear colleague, unless I was to axe-murder you and all the others, I don't stand a chance at the office of Supreme City Commandant."

He had to stop and catch his breath. He could tell from his little speech, that as he had emptied the wind out of his lungs, he had taken a great deal of wind out of her sails.

She was not sure what to say about his tirade. She looked around while trying to think of some kind of retort. She normally could not stand anyone getting the last word, other than her. She was rescued by the appearance of two of the people involved in the investigation. She spat at them. "Who are you?"

Krezdon turned towards the pair that was approaching. A rather short, plump woman, with short brown hair, and a man that was only slightly taller than the woman. He was totally bald and had only two visible teeth.

The woman spoke first: "I am Lieutenant Sanmima Temo, weapons specialist in the constabulary, Milady."

The man bowed slightly. "Investigator Grajosh Dreedun. I work with the local constabulary as a physician and mortician."

Krezdon asked before Haneenda could draw a breath: "Have you finished your part of the investigation?"

"Oh, most assuredly, Milord." said Grajosh. "It is rather obvious, that Lord Hremborn died as a result of that rather wicked looking weapon being thrust through his brain. The only thing that I can add, is that he died shortly before sun up."

It was then that Krezdon noticed that the Lieutenant was holding the weapon, partially wrapped in a piece of cloth.

Before Krezdon could say anything, Haneenda spoke up: "What is that thing?"

Sanmima cleared her throat, and told them in a manner that sounded like she was very proud of her knowledge. "It is an antique weapon, believed to have been invented in Ciscaumen. Originally they meant for it to be used in close combat. As you can see the design was very bad for that. The blade is much too heavy to be handled in any kind of parrying contest. If you were to clash sword with this, there is a high probability that it would be knocked out of your hand.

This particular one is the newer type - if you could call an antique new. It has a ring on the end of the hilt. It was thought that if you tied a string through the ring, around your wrist, then if it got knocked out of your hand, a simple flip and you would be ready again. No good. As heavy and off balance as the silly thing is, that proves itself totally wrong. It is also totally off balance for throwing. You could do just as much damage, to your opponent, by throwing a rock. The only people who use it now are assassins. The only time they use it is for the final death blow, after the…victim is completely helpless. Just drop it on their head, point first and the weight of the thing does all the work."

Sanmima handed the weapon to Krezdon. He knew it was heavy, but was still not ready for the thing being balanced so badly. Now in his hands, he could not imagine anyone ever making any attempt to fight with the thing.

"Well, part of my theory is correct," said Haneenda.

Sanmima and Grajosh had matching confused looks over her comment.

Krezdon gave her an icy glare. "Which part?"

"A professional assassin did the job."

"Good possibility," he sighed. "However, who put the killer up to it and why? Another kick in the process is: Why did a professional assassin commit a murder and then steal a slave?"

Sanmima broke in: "Either an assassin got the slave to go along with it and aided in an escape, or the slave witnessed the killing and then was killed as well."

"Either one is possible. Let's go back inside and see if anyone in there has come up with anything that can prove or disprove any of the theories."

The three constables inside had reached basically the same conclusions. An assassin in league with a slave, or a slave killed as well as the master. The problem with the second one was that there was no body anywhere else on the grounds. All were in agreement that they needed to start an immediate search of the city for the missing slave.

Everyone was content with the conclusion - for a few moments. The family slaves had been in the kitchen preparing food for everyone. Now they came running - in a group - back into the parlor, virtually screaming that Fendina had just entered the back gate.

This was followed by a larger mass movement to the kitchen. Several comments of disbelief and confusion flew around, rhetorically, amazed, awed and baffled comments.

Krezdon arrived in the kitchen and had to push his way through the bodies in order to see out the window. Here is this Fendina - the sex slave of a homosexual, who a few moments ago was suspected of murder. He did not look anything close to what Krezdon could have imagined. He was just a little shorter than average. His short dark brown hair was plastered to his head, by a large amount of perspiration. His face was distorted by a scowl as he was fighting a push cart that obviously had a somewhat heavy load in it. There was no way of knowing what was under the tarp that covered the cart. He was wearing a light green silk outfit, which would normally be for a woman. It was plastered to his skin with perspiration as well.

"I wonder," said Shojo. "How does someone get that hot and

sweaty on such a cool morning?"

Ponodell looked baffled. "The thing that is more important, is what this does to our theory. We have a whole new set of questions and conclusions to work out, now."

"He doesn't look strong enough to properly handle the weapon," said Sanmima.

Ponodell looked at Berber. "Is there enough powder in your truth box?"

"There is enough for it to burn until noon time," said Berber. "If that isn't enough, I always have more."

Fendina had finally, successfully maneuvered the contrary cart up to the kitchen door. He leaned against if for a few moments, panting and wiping sweat on his sleeves. He reached back to a large pouch, hanging on the back of the cart, pulled it off, walked to the door and opened it. The crowd in the room shifted, for a better view of the "center of attention." The only individual who was not staring at Fendina was Berber. He had headed back to the parlor to retrieve his truth box.

As Fendina came through the door, a strong smell followed him. The mixture of fish and sweat chased a few people out of the room, holding their noses. He stood there for a moment staring back at the crowd, confused. He raised his eyebrows in a questioning manner. After receiving no response, he shrugged and said: "If you're here for dinner, it won't be ready for some time."

From what Krezdon had been told, Fendina was supposed to be in his early twenties. He looked more like mid-thirties.

Ponodell was the first to speak up. "Where have you been all morning?"

"You murdered my husband, you beast!" screamed Kamezee.

Fendina's mouth dropped open. All that came out was a sheepish little: "Huh?"

"Lady Hremborn, please! We will take care of the investigation," said Krezdon. "If there are any accusations to be made around here, we will make them, at the proper time."

Kamezee took a step back. There were tears in her eyes and she was shaking with rage. She looked over at Fendina, and screamed: "My husband is dead! You belong to me! On your knees, you animal."

Fendina clenched his teeth and slowly dropped to his knees. He looked up at Kamezee with nothing but total hatred in his eyes.

"It would be easier to question him if he were sitting at the table," said Ponodell.

"He is my slave," screamed Kamezee. "That filthy creature stays on it's knees, on the floor where it belongs."

There was a collective sigh from all of the constabulary representatives in the room. Yes, Fendina was now the slave of Kamezee. There was very little they could do about her ordering him to his knees.

Berber came back in the kitchen with his odiferous little box. Between the box and the sweat from Fendina, Krezdon felt his headache returning.

Haneenda came up with a perfumed handkerchief from

somewhere and held it under her nose.

"All right," said Ponodell. "Where have you been all morning?"

"Shopping," said Fendina.

"Shopping for what?"

"Last night, Master Jeltiynul, said he wanted a Melsoosta fish for dinner tonight. I left early this morning, to get a good one along with the spices."

Ponodell turned to Kamezee: "Can you confirm this, Lady Hremborn?"

She put her hands to her face, looking a little shocked. "Oh! That's right. He did say that. Oh my! I completely forgot about that."

Ponodell turned back to Fendina: "So, why did you leave, before everyone else got out of bed?"

Fendina shook his head in disgust. "The only time the fisherman can catch the Melsoosta, is at night. The time to get the best selection, is to be at the docks, when they come back in from their night fishing. It takes a while to get to the docks with that…cart. After I got the fish, I had to wait until the market opened in order to get the really fresh citrus fruits - as well as a few other spices that are needed - in order to properly prepare the Melsoosta. Then, I had to fight that cart, with that heavy fish, all the way back up the hill, to get here. Now, what in the name of the 666 punishments are you talking about?"

"Lord Hremborn was murdered, this morning," said Shojo. "Did you kill him?"

Fendina rolled his eyes. "Why would I *want* to kill him? Oh, yes, he owns me as a slave. However, Mistress Kamezee told me that she was going to whip me daily - if her husband died first. She said that she was going to give me one stripe for every day her husband had me in his bed instead of her. So, what would I have to look forward too, if I killed the Master: Death by execution if I did kill him, or a slow death by whipping from the Mistress, if I wasn't caught? Some choice!"

Everyone looked at Kamezee.

"Well, why shouldn't I beat him? I married Jeltiynul. I bore four children for him. I should have been the one in his bed, not that...that...slave."

"There goes that motive," said an exasperated Shojo.

"Perhaps not."

All eyes went to the new voice that had just broken in.

"Who are you?" asked Krezdon.

"I, Milord, am Haney Devotee. I am the late Lord Hremborn's private attorney."

"All right," said Ponodell. "What do you have to add, that might change our minds?"

"As his attorney, I made his will, and I have it right here."

Krezdon was losing patience. "So! What's in there, which might point the finger at somebody?"

Haney took his time looking over the document, before he finally answered. "Let me see. Paragraphs one through five, list what he leaves to his wife and children. Paragraph six, is the one we are concerned with, in this investigation. It states that at the moment of Lord Jeltiynul's death, the slave Fendina, is to be immediately declared a free man. It also states, that the three chests, beneath Lord Jeltiynul's bed, and their entire contents, are to be the property of Fendina."

Fendina was still kneeling on the floor. Now though, his shoulders were sagging and he had a look of total surprise on his face.

Ponodell looked at Fendina. "Well, that does change things, doesn't it?"

Fendina snapped out of his astonishment. "What do you mean? I knew nothing of that will!"

Krezdon took a quick glance at the truth box. The smoke was still blue.

Shojo had not looked at the smoke. He was looking at Fendina. "Do you mean to tell us that he named you as a beneficiary in his will and he never told you? Freedom and what ever wealth is in those chests, is a very good motive for murder."

Fendina stood up. "I knew nothing of the will, and I can prove it. You! Lawyer! When was that will written?"

Haney was taken by surprise by the question. He glanced at the document. "Uh...the date...uh...yes, here it is. This will was written about two and a half years ago. No changes to it, since that time."

Fendina stood there smiling and folded his arms, with a triumphant look on his face.

"Get back on your knees," shouted Kamezee.

Fendina looked back at her and his demeanor changed to that of disgust. "Oh, shut up, you useless old cow! Didn't you hear what's on that document? I'm a free man. I don't have to obey anything that you say, ever again."

The argument might have continued, if not for Shojo. He moved directly between the two combatants and used his loud voice to end their conversation. "IF YOU DON'T MIND!" He calmed himself. "That still does not tell us that you did not know about the will, or that you did not kill Lord Jeltiynul."

Fendina smiled menacingly. He got right in Shojo's face. "According to what that lawyer said, that will is over two years old. IF I had known about the freedom stipulation, at his death, in that document, then I would have happily killed him, before the ink was dry. I hate him, I hate that stupid wife of his and I hate what he did to me. As I said, if I had known that will gave me any chance at freedom, I would not have had any hesitation in exterminating that monster."

Krezdon looked back at the smoke again. He was not sure, but it seemed to turn a darker blue. He looked at Berber. The Inquisitor gave a shrug and silently mouthed the word: "Truth."

"Well...we are back to a lone assassin," said Ponodell.

Fendina started barking orders. "You! Lawyer! Do your job and give me the paperwork that proves that I'm free, so I can get out of here and get this atrocity off my arm."

"Not so fast," said Ponodell. "We still have some questions to ask you."

Fendina closed his eyes and huffed. "Like what?"

"When you got up, did you hear anything unusual? Did you hear, or see, anything or anyone unusual as you left? Did you see any stranger in the house? Maybe a few more questions as I think of them."

Kamezee walked up to Ponodell. "Are you insane? You're just going to let him go?"

Ponodell tried to answer as calmly as he could. "I am satisfied with what he has said, Lady Hremborn. Unless you have some other information to prove a motive for him, or anyone else, we can only go on the assumption of a hired assassin."

Kamezee wagged her finger at Fendina. "He could have hired the assassin."

Fendina laughed out loud. "Hire and pay an assassin with what? I still have no idea what is in those chests…and other than those chests, I have absolutely no property whatsoever."

Several other questions, answers, inquiries and suppositions were asked, answered and voiced without changing anything. The final conclusion was that it had to be a very professional assassin. The investigation would have to go somewhere else, to find the individual responsible for the crime.

Krezdon and Haneenda had to send word to the other Sector Commandants and the Council Representatives. A new Supreme Commandant would have to be appointed as soon as possible.

3

For three years, the assassination remained unsolved. In that time there were quite a few changes in the city political arena.

The Governor, Angtozo Beremotz, died in his sleep. Almost a year after Jeltiynul had been killed. He was replaced by Eyoral Fandatoy. Less than a month later, she died in a fall down a flight of stairs. Premterol Jydo was appointed the new Governor, and promptly committed suicide. Xuzo Poroby was then appointed and was still the Governor.

Haneenda Torsydo was appointed Supreme City Commandant. Three months later, she died from a stroke. Sector Two Commandant, Sholloh then took over the office. He along with Thesha Telyil died in a fire. Much to his amazement, Krezdon was then promoted to the position.

Each time a new Governor or Supreme Commandant was appointed, someone had to take their place. Each time a death occurred the same thing. Three years after the assassination of Jeltiynul, there were only two people who held the same position they had had at the time of the homicide.

Krezdon looked at the roll call: Governor Xuzo Poroby. Council members: Sector One, Daznak Slytiloran, Sector Two, Poltrist Guyot, Sector Three, Hebtezz Nosso, Sector Four, Ahach Keez, Sector Five, Pamema Broofon, Sector Six, Tansiki Jorsydo, Sector Seven, Biyaba Jop, Supreme City Commandant, Krezdon Chashchy, Sector

Commandants: Sector One, Takariy Jebshon, Sector Two Piromin Dezelba, Sector Three, Chash Ea, Sector Four, Sintiyna Azareemon, Sector Five Deshdeena Byharton, Sector Six, Belziyd Pebodom, Sector Seven Goroben Hebedissor.

Pamema Broofon and Goroben Hebedissor were the only ones who were still holding the same office they had had at the time of the murder.

Krezdon was going over the paperwork that had accumulated since the assassination. Everything was at an absolute standstill. Not one credible lead that could be used for solving the crime. He was losing a lot of faith in the Wizards who were trying to solve it through their divination.

"Excuse me, Lord Chashchy."

Krezdon looked up a bit startled. Standing at the door was the woman who had replaced him as Sector Four Commandant: Sintiyna Azareemon. She made him nervous, because she was much more intelligent than he. She was at least ten years older than he was, but still looked like a teenager. She kept her light brown hair pulled back tightly. This helped add to her youthful appearance. She was short, petite and had a figure that did not show signs of having given birth to six children.

"Yes, Lady Azareemon, What can I do for you?"

"Ihavethereportfromthecensus. Wouldyouliketotakealookatit?
He smiled. "Of course. Let's kill a little of the monotony, looking it over."

She dropped the report on his desk and waited patiently while he looked it over.

He snickered when he came to a certain part of the report.

"What is so funny about a census?"

"Three years ago, I brought this report to the late Lord Hremborn. He made a comment about the percentages of a person. Look at that figure: We can now hire 4.8 new people into the constabulary, and 5.4 into the city guard. How do you get .8 of a constable and .4 of a guard? Just how do you divide an individual up?"

"You can't. You just have to decide whether you want 4 or 5 new constables, and whether you want 5 or 6 new guards."

"Yes, but it still seems like only yesterday that tomorrow will be exactly three years, since the assassination."

"A lot has happened since then, and yet no one has been able to come up with anything to solve the crime."

He shook his head sadly. "Nothing."

She perked up a little. "Well, I understand that not everything is sad news. I understand that your wife is now pregnant." She snickered slightly. "Married only three months, and already you are adding to the population."

"How did you know that? She informed me of it, just last night."

Sintiyna simply smiled, then turned and left his office.

'Women!' he thought. They read minds or something like that. A telepathic grapevine that enshrouds the entire city.

Another knock on the door interrupted his thoughts. He looked up and saw the Sector Seven Commandant, Goroben Hebedissor and Sector Seven Representative Biyaba Jop.

Goroben was a very dark-skinned and very tall man. He normally was very calm and always helped calm others in any bad situation, but he did not seem calm himself right now.

Biyaba was just two years older than Krezdon. She had long, thick blonde hair, which she had probably not cut since she was born. She was always a stickler for detail and very organized.

Today both of them seemed very worried.

"Excuse us, Milord, but we have a crisis to report to you," said Goroben.

Krezdon closed his eyes. "Oh no! Not another assassination - please!"

"No, Milord, much worse."

He looked at Goroben incredulously. "What could possibly happen in the waterfront area that would be worse than an assassination?"

They entered and Goroben started the report, before he even took a seat. "It seems, Milord, that we have been inundated with a rather large, and somewhat crippled, group of merchant vessels."

"Oh? When did this happen?"

"Two days ago, these ships came limping in to the harbor, after going through a very nasty storm at sea."

"Storm!" Biyaba butted in. "It was a tempest that puts all

previous storms to shame."

"Yes, My Lady," said Goroben. "But, the important issue is that they are here." He turned back to Krezdon. "Anyway, they arrived two days ago, and they told us of this horrible storm, that they had gone through, and they arrived here - the first port they could find, since the storm."

"The first port they could find? What kind of pilots did they have on these ships?"

"They tell me that by some freak coincidence, not one officer, on any of the ships, survived. All washed overboard or died at their post."

"So they are a group of ships, without any leadership. If that is the case, how did they get here?"

"There are among them, quite a few very experienced crewmen. They were able to pull together, and head in the direction of the greatest land mass that they could see - from whatever crows nests were still there. Ours was the first port that they found."

Again Biyaba broke in: "Tell them *our* problem, not theirs!"

"Yes, My lady, in time, first he must understand *their* problem before he can understand *ours*."

Krezdon felt a little insulted, but tried to hide it. "Just get on with it."

"Yes, Milord. According to what they tell me, these ships were just purchased from the great shipyards in Lower Oosam. What paperwork survived the storm shows that fact. They started out from Lower Oosam with a total of forty of the giant merchant ships. The storm hurt them badly. Thirty-two ships arrived here; the other eight - only the god of the sea knows what happened to them. After the storm cleared, they were able to get this ragtag bunch together, and sail them, as best they could."

"I don't understand why you're making such a big fuss about this storm. Ships have been lost at sea before - what is so extraordinary about this one?"

Goroben glanced over at Biyaba. "Well, Milord, these ships came from Lower Oosam. Are you aware of the different types of ships, and where they come from?"

"No, when I was a constable on the waterfront, I just dealt with drunken sailors, not the ships. I have never had any dealings with naval matters - military or civilian."

"Oh, well, the Lower Oosam shipyards are most famous for their expert work. They build the largest, sturdiest ships of any kind, anywhere. For a storm to have sunk or destroyed eight of them, and shattered the others in this manner…no other ships, made in any other lands, could have possibly survived."

"So that is *their* problem - what is *ours*?"

"Several. We do not have the proper ship repair facilities here. With what little help we can give them, three of the ships should be able to set sail, in about four days. The problem there is that they have no officers or pilots and we have no officers or pilots that we can spare."

"Three! What about the other twenty-nine?"

"I have inspected all of the ships, Milord. One of them, I

have condemned. I have made out a full report for the government of Tabrow, so they shouldn't have any questions about it."

"Tabrow?"

"Yes, Milord, that is where they were headed - Tabrow."

"Why should they have questions?"

"The process of condemning a ship, requires that a full report is given, before it is towed out to sea and burned, until it sinks. I assure you, Milord, the ship is quite finished. All four masts were torn right out of the heart of the ship, taking the main deck and a large portion of the next deck with them. It was a pure miracle the crew on board, not only survived, but kept that wreckage afloat and got it into the harbor."

"How did they get it in here without sails?"

"The damaged ships were tied together, using what little sails they had left on the ships that still had masts. Anyway, there are two ships - that if taken back to Lower Oosam, maybe the shipwrights there will be able to repair them."

"That still leaves twenty-six," said Krezdon grimly.

"Yes. That leaves twenty-six, badly damaged, but not irreparable ships. If we try to repair them, here, just enough to make them seaworthy, we will completely eradicate all of *our* supplies, for several months to come. With the supplies we have here, we could *possibly* repair…maybe five more."

"That still leaves a lot of junk floating around our harbor."

"Yes, My Lord, twenty-one ships…and their crews."

Krezdon nearly gagged.

"The ships were purchased by the government of Tabrow, for their economic growth and trade. There was no cargo on any of the ships - only crew. The voyage home, was to be a time of training for the new crewmembers. They started at Lower Oosam, with over one hundred men and officers per ship."

Krezdon's shoulders sagged. "That's over 4000 people total!"

"Yes. They started with 4000 plus. They crawled into our harbor with 1977 survivors. We can mourn and lament with them over their deceased shipmates...but we still have 1977 living, shipwrecked men in our city. 1977 men where, according to international maritime law, we are responsible for the billeting, medical and feeding of all of them."

Goroben and Biyaba now both sat silently, while Krezdon digested the information. He took several minutes trying to comprehend the magnitude of the situation. He looked up at Goroben. "If this happened, two days ago; why are you just getting the information to me now? Why not two days ago?"

"It took this long, just to get it all together."

"You could have given me some kind of preliminary..." He waved his hands in the air helplessly "...something, when they first got here!" He started rubbing his forehead. "Have you informed the Governor?"

"We have sent runners, to call an emergency council meeting, and have not been able to locate the Governor, as yet."

The emergency meeting had been a total disaster. Sixteen people all yelling, and nobody listening. The only thing that was agreed on was that the whole mess was going to cost a fortune.

Messengers were going to be dispatched to inform the King, all surrounding communities, as well as the governments of Lower Oosam and Tabrow. The main problem was the amount of time it was going to take. The local runners could be back in two or three days. Getting the runner back from the King in the capitol city would take almost twenty days. Getting the information to Tabrow would take at least three months, one way. Getting help from Lower Oosam was improbable. If they did get any help from Lower Oosam, it was also three months, one way.

If they could get help from some of the local communities, it would be some help. Not much - but at this time, any help would be very welcome.

4

The ride home was not exactly comfortable for Krezdon. One of the roads was badly in need of repair. Every bump was magnified through the entire carriage and only increased the pain in his skull splitting headache. When the ride was mercifully over, he walked very slowly and painfully into the house.

He was met at the door by one of his slaves, Zisdesta. She was about twelve and not quite physically mature. She had short dark brown hair and her big brown eyes were full of tears.

He stopped and looked up. "What's wrong with you?"

"Groyshon is dead, master," she said flatly.

'I am going to have to control my temper,' he thought. Ever since his promotion to Supreme Commandant, he was becoming more irritable and easy to anger. This was the third slave he had whipped to death. Groyshon had spilled some fruit juice, this morning, and Krezdon had beaten the slave unconscious.

He walked into the dining room. Temela, his wife, was sitting at the table. She was a very petite woman, with long blonde hair that covered her entire back. She looked very upset.

He mustered a little kindness before opening his mouth. "What is wrong with you? Are you mourning Groyshon as well?"

"It's not Groyshon, I'm thinking about. I'm mad about Meenema."

He felt his dander rising a little. "What did she do?" His head started hurting even more.

"It's not what she did, it's what you did."

"What? I haven't whipped her. I haven't had any reason too."

"I found out that I'm not the only one here, who is pregnant."

"She's…uh…pregnant? What makes you think I did it? What about Bertiyr or Pyrsko…or Groyshon?"

She slammed her fists on the table. "They are all eunuchs."

He sighed. Meenema was a beautiful girl. Radiant blonde hair, and green eyes. She had reached maturity at an early age, and filled out nicely. He had spent a small fortune on her. He thought about every inch of her magnificent body. He *had* gone through several nights of ecstasy with her. 'If she is pregnant, it has to be mine,' he thought. "There are times that you don't feel like doing anything and I have needs." 'Maybe that will help…not much,' he thought, 'but maybe it will work.' It didn't.

She stood up and screamed at him. "I am your wife! I am the one you married. Yes, my parents made the agreement with you, but I raised no objections. Why would you need *anything* from her?"

He started thinking about how Kamezee Hremborn had talked about Fendina. Now he was hearing the same thing from his own wife. There should be a difference. Jeltiynul had completely ignored his wife. The master-slave relationship there, had been homosexual. Krezdon was having a heterosexual relationship.

He looked deep into Temela's eyes. It was not anger he saw, it was pain. Pain from mental agony. The issue was not who or what he was having sex with. The issue was that he was having sex with someone else other than the woman that had gone through the marriage vows with him.

He took hold of her hands. "Temela, I promise you, by all the gods, that I will never touch anyone except you. You are my wife, and I treated you badly, by doing what I did. It will never happen again."

"Are you going to sell her?"

He sighed. "No. The child is mine. The child will be raised, in this house, as a free individual. Reason one: The child is mine. Reason two: It will remind me to keep my hands off other women. Reason three: If I cannot keep my hands off her or any other slave girl…with them in the house, I will not be out chasing some diseased whore on the streets. Reason four: We should have female slaves here to take care of your needs."

"Reason three, sounds like you don't plan on keeping your promise."

"Reason three, is there because, there might be some time, when you push me away, and tell me to take my urge out on her."

She gave him a disgusted look. "I'll think about it."

While they ate their dinner, they discussed several things: Replacing the dead slave, disposing of the dead slave, he should control his temper so they did not have to replace any dead slaves, names for the babies, tomorrow is the third anniversary of the unsolved assassination of Jeltiynul and other non-essential subjects. He did not want to worry her about the financial catastrophe that was going to hit the city.

He went to bed that night thinking. Deep in thought about the assassination. Total frustration in the investigation. They had used every form of questioning - magic or normal. He had watched all of the different magic being used at the crime scene. Every effort had been totally futile. The only clue from the divination was that it had been someone close…but who? How? Why?

One thing that had hurt the investigation was the disappearance of the ex-slave Fendina. After a few questions, he had gone to the bedroom, removed the three chests, from under the bed, took his freedom document from the lawyer and vanished.

Several of the investigators had gone back to the idea of the slave assisting an assassin. Others had tried to accuse the oldest son. Others tried to blame the irate widow. No proof of any of it.

Tomorrow is another day. Right now, we have to work on our biggest problem. 1977 foreign, shipwrecked sailors and 32 crippled ships. Yes, right now that is definitely our main dilemma. Who knows how big a problem it will be before it finally gets resolved?

5

Krezdon was awakened in a startling manner. Temela was screaming her head off. He sat up trying to find out what was wrong. His investigation was cut short, in the form of a large fist, full force, right between the eyes.

He was awakened again. This time, it was a bucket of water being poured over him. Before the cobwebs cleared out of his head, he was jerked to his feet, and went through a wave of nauseating and agonizing pain.

As the fog slowly cleared, the horror of reality was almost too much to take. He was still in his bedroom. Temela was nowhere to be seen, or heard. Three strange men were checking manacles that had been placed on his wrists. He also noticed that it was extremely difficult trying to breathe through his nose.

"Who are you? What is the…?"

He was cut off by a smack on the back of his head. "Shut your face, slave!" The man spoke with a heavy accent. He was tall and lanky. His hair was dark brown and stringy. His beard was in the same ratty condition. He was wearing, what looked like some kind of light brown outfit. It resembled a uniform, and had a naval emblem on it. He gave a very contemptuous smile that showed even more in his dark eyes. He was well tanned and make Krezdon wonder if he was from one of the damaged ships.

The other two men in the room were wearing the same type of

outfits. One of them was short and looked almost emaciated. He, like the first man was deeply tanned and had very unkempt dark hair and beard. His smug smile showed two rows of very rotten teeth.

The Last one seemed to be the one in charge. He was very dark skinned and enormous. Krezdon had never seen a man that tall, or as heavily muscled as the monstrosity that was barking orders at the other two. He was speaking in a language that Krezdon could not even begin to identify.

Krezdon made a few more attempts, trying to communicate and find out what was going on. Each time, he was stopped by another hard swat to the back of his head.

The big man walked up to Krezdon slowly. The smile on his face looked anything but friendly. The voice did not seem to match with the body. It seemed too high pitched - but when you are as big as this man was, no one criticized you…in your presence. "Hey little man, if you want to keep your face, keep it shut." The big man turned and headed for the door. A simple wave of his big hand, and Krezdon found himself, being dragged out of the room, down the stairs and out of the house.

As he was being dragged through the house, his confusion was multiplied. There was absolutely no signs that the house had been ransacked. There was also no sign of his slaves or wife.

The front door showed no signs of any damage. One of the slaves must have opened it for these brigands. He made a mental note to rip the hide off all of them, until he found out which one had allowed them in. Then he looked back at the leader. If no one had opened the door, that monster could have probably shattered the door, with very little trouble.

When they dragged him out the front door, they made him stand up. One of his slaves, Prysko, was trampling the flower garden and having a wonderful time doing it. He stopped for a moment and to watch the humiliation that Krezdon was going through. He gave Krezdon a vulgar gesture and went back to trampling the garden.

The giant gave a grunt and waved for the unhappy procession to continue.

Krezdon saw that the sun was just above the horizon. Exactly three years ago, today, he had been awakened, to be told of an assassination. Now, he had been rudely awakened to another nightmare, far worse than the other. He had no idea how this had happened, but he was sure that rescue of some type was going to come at any moment.

They pushed him forward. At first he thought of just standing there. Then he remembered, being dragged down here had not been a very pleasant experience. He had not been able to gain his feet inside and now there were several painful bruises all over his body. His hands were numb from the manacles and there was no way to stretch the kinks out of his shoulders, as long as his arms were chained behind him. Obediently walking along with them seemed to be the best option.

They exited the front gate. He had been thinking of what audacity these people had. They were going to parade the Supreme Commandant, down the street, manacled, and in his nightshirt. Once he got through the gate, he began seeing a bigger picture of what was going on. There were people from at least nine different prominent families, already in the street. They were shackled in the same manner that he was. Women on one side of the street, men on the other and all of them wearing nothing but nightshirts. Everyone was being kept in line by several brown suited men. Any sound made by any of the prisoners was quickly stopped with a whip or a hard slap across the face.

He finally saw Temela. She had been taken a short way up the street. He could see the pleading in her eyes. There was no way to comfort her. Not at this time. 'Later,' he thought. Vengeance and punishment would come later - tenfold.

Several more of his neighbors were brought out - in the same manner. The looks on their faces showed either shock or fear...or both.

The slaves of each family started coming out into the street. They were wearing some of the finest outfits that their masters owned. They were having a grand time. Bertiyr was dressed in one of Krezdon's finest suits. Prysko had chosen an outfit that was more conservative and far more comfortable. Meenema and Zisdesta were wearing some of Temela's finest dresses, hats and shoes.

Krezdon heard a shout from one of the brown-suits. He looked where the man was pointing. Two large wagons, each drawn by a team of big work equines, was slowly advancing. The first wagon had a team of six equines and was open. The other had a team of four and was completely enclosed.

A man jumped off the first wagon. He ran up to where all the people were being held. He, like all the other captors was wearing that same brown uniform. From what country though? As a Sector

Commandant, he had been given a large binder that showed the military uniforms from all of the sovereign nations…everywhere. These were totally unfamiliar.

The new man on the scene did a quick survey of the situation. "Excuse me," he shouted. "All of you former slaves, we need your assistance."

Krezdon was about to raise a protest, but checked himself quickly. He had been back-handed enough for one day. Right now, the best thing to do, is observe and find out: Who, what, when, where, how and why. Analyze it and then see what he could do about some major retribution.

The new man, on the scene, looked a little neater than the other uniformed men. He also looked extremely tired. Again he hollered for everyone's attention. "Please stay with your former masters. We must get an accurate inventory of them and your assistance is desperately needed, to speed up the process."

Several protests were started by the prisoners and were all cut short by hard slaps.

'Inventoried?' Krezdon was appalled. 'What are they going to do, count us like so many cattle? Who do they think they are fooling with?'

The one doing the talking turned to the women. "Are any of you with child? If you are, take one step forward."

No one moved.

He continued: "If you are pregnant and you do not tell us now, it could go very badly for you, later on."

With her teeth clenched, Temela stepped forward. Three other women stepped forward as well.

"Very good," he said. "If, however, you are not pregnant, and you tell us, now, that you are…well, I will make arrangements. We will get ten or fifteen volunteers, who will service you nightly, until we are sure that you are."

Two of the women stepped back. The third looked at the speaker, terrified. Temela stood her ground.

He walked up to the scared one. "What's the matter? The answer to the question is either yes or no."

"I'm…uh…not…I'm not sure."

"You're not sure of what?"

"My husband and I…uh…we…well, I might be…but, I'm not sure."

He shouted something in that foreign tongue, to one of the men on the second wagon. The man jumped off and ran up to the officer (?). They had a short conversation, after which the new one started digging in a large satchel on his side. He pulled out a long piece of green ribbon. The officer tied the ribbon, loosely, around her neck.

The officer went to Temela. "That one wasn't sure - are you?"

She nodded.

"You don't look like you are."

"I've only been married for three months," she spat.

He snickered, said something to the new man. This time a red piece of ribbon was brought out of the satchel. He tied the red one around Temela's neck. The man with the satchel then took both marked women to the rear wagon.

Meanwhile, some more of the brown suits were pulling long lengths of chain out of the first wagon. They started heading the male prisoners over to the rear of the wagon. There was another brown suit there with a maul, an anvil and a large box of connecting links. They started putting manacles on the ankles of each man and then connecting all the men together.

Krezdon was in total anguish. He had no clue who these people were and the "hope for rescue," seemed even less of a possibility than a few moments before. He was the Supreme Military Commandant of the city. He and the military part of the council, were the ones that they would be depending on to plan a swift and decisive counter-attack. The only thing that he could think of that might work as any form of a counter-attack, would make him fish bait.

After the men were connected in one long string, they were force marched towards the waterfront. The piece of chain, between his legs, was slightly longer than a hand span. This made walking very difficult, especially at the pace they were being pushed too. In order to move at that pace, everyone had to do an awkward hopping move. At first someone ended up falling. The individual that was unfortunate enough to fall, was quickly and brutally punished. This was a strong motivation for them to unify there steps as best as possible.

Waterfront! Naval uniforms! Thirty-two ships with almost 2000 men aboard! The thoughts slammed into his mind like being hit with a club. $1 + 1 = 2$. A diversion. They faked a story about a storm. They damaged the ships. They suckered an entire city, into welcoming them in, with open arms.

A message had been dispatched to the government of Tabrow, to inform them of the disaster. It would be, at a minimum, 84 days for the message get to Tabrow, and for someone to return. Three days those men had been able to scout out the city, finding all the weaknesses, and seeing the schedule of the city guards. This was arranged too well...too precise. This was the execution of a plan that had been in the making for a long time. But who? The uniforms were not recognizable. Their language was unfamiliar. Was the ultimate destination of the convoy just a clever ruse? There was no real way to tell where they were from or where they were going...until we get there.

The mental revelation distracted him from the hopping march, he lost rhythm and ended up flat on his face. The usual results happened. The men if front of him had not seen him falling and as soon as the chain behind them went taut - down they went. The men behind him saw it and were able to stop. One of the overseers was there, before he could even struggle to his knees. He did his best to keep from screaming, but the nightshirt was virtually no protection whatsoever from the stinging lash.

He decided that the best thing to do was quit thinking. Just concentrate on that ridiculous hopping rhythm, to avoid any more whippings. He also wanted to avoid that painful fall. With his hands behind his back, there was no way to catch yourself or brace for the fall.

Try to concentrate on something, for a long time. Your mind tends to wander. He had not had a chance to even get a glass of water, or do his morning constitutionals. His stomach was complaining and his bladder was being stretched to the limit. His throat was parched. He wondered for a moment if it was his imagination, but it sounded like there were several men in the string who were panting in rhythm to the run.

They were called to a halt. They had come to a place where another human chain of men was being linked together.

Krezdon tried to moisten his mouth. All he got was a huge mass of phlegm that was more disgusting than relieving. He noticed that several other men had tried to do the same and were now spitting on the ground.

He also noticed that the string of women, from his area, were nowhere in sight. He wondered if they had had a harder time getting the rhythm, or if they had been taken by a different route.

A few of the men in Krezdon's line had tried to get a little rest during the stop. The guards would not allow it. Each one that tried to sit was quickly reminded to get up - by the whip.

Now that he had a moment, he started a mental file: Home invaded, stripped of dignity, paraded in the street in our night clothing, manacled, treatment like common slaves, physical abuse, no nourishment, no rest…oh, are they going to pay for this. I will have fun ruining them, physically and mentally.

"Isn't this a fun day?"

The voice sounded familiar and was mocking. It also came with a hard slap on Krezdon's back that sent him pitching forward.

"Yes, just a lovely day!"

Krezdon struggled to see who the heckler was. "Prysko! What is this? Stop this nonsense, right now, or I'll flay the skin off your back."

"You'll do what? You will be lucky, if you survive the day, DOG!"

"How dare you…" raged Krezdon.

Prysko slapped him, before anything else could be said, and grabbed hold of his ears. He started *liberally* spitting in Krezdon's face. Between each mouthful of spit that was being hawked up he would say: "How dare I? Just watch!"

Now Krezdon was pleading: "What's going on?"

Prysko laughed in a sinister way. "Changing of the guard."

The last gift that Prysko left before ending his amusement, was a hard punch in Krezdon's bladder. Since there had been no chance of the morning use of the chamber pot, he had had no chance of relieving himself. Now he had no choice.

A new gruff voice broke in on Prysko's fun: "Hey, get him up!"

"Why?" Asked Prysko. "Let him get himself up."

"You knocked him down, you pick him up. If he is laying down, he is getting rest. He gets no rest."

Prysko grudgingly obeyed. He grabbed Krezdon by the left arm and hair and jerked him up. Now that he was standing, he was no longer laying in a growing puddle of urine - now it was running down his legs. When the urine hit his ankles, he let out a squawk from the new pain. The manacles had rubbed his ankles raw and the urine was not comforting. Another thing to add to the revenge file.

Krezdon could only stand there, putting up with the pain and make any attempt he could to get the spittle out of his eyes. With his hands numbed and firmly held behind his back, it took quite a while to clear his vision. After finally clearing his eyes, he noticed the man in front of him, on the line. The shackles on the ankles and wrists had bloodied the man. Krezdon wondered if he looked the same: Blood on the feet, as well as dribbling down his backside, from the wrists... and a very large yellow stain.

He heard the clanking of chains. He looked back in the direction the noise was coming from. The women's string was just getting there. The women were all exhausted and dirty. The dirt on the front of their nightgowns, showed that they had all taken some nasty falls. Several had bloody chins and noses, showing that they had landed on their faces rather than their chests.

Then he noticed that the new string of men was being added to his string - in the rear. He groaned. This new group had not taken any of the hop steps yet, and so did not know the rhythm. He knew that they would be taking quite a few more spills, before they got to the waterfront.

As the last connection was being made in the men's line, the women were called to a halt. The entire line collapsed as one, and the whips started making their horrid sounds as the women were coaxed to get back up.

The slaves that had accompanied the group, were laughing and jeering at their imprisoned masters, which helped add to the misery.

The guard gave the command for the men's line to start again. Back to the agonizing rhythm.

After going some ways without anyone falling behind him, he saw a man, about ten ahead of him, collapse. He saw all the men in front, pitch forward as their ankle chains suddenly stopped. He stopped and waited for them to get the man up. He did not get up. They beat him severely with the whips and he showed no reaction. One of the guards came up and kicked the victim several times. When he got no reaction, the guard pulled out a small axe and after three chops, picked the man's head up and put it to the side. He then chopped the man's feet off and pulled the chains away from the corpse. Two brown suits pulled the corpse off to the side and the line was again given the command to move.

They had three more stops where more men were added to their string. By the time they arrived at the waterfront, Krezdon estimated that the string was at least 250 men and boys. As they were taken through the market area of the waterfront, an inventory was taken on all the men. As each man arrived at the main desk (?)...command post (?) or whatever it was, he was identified, tagged, separated from the line and taken to who knows where. Each one seemed to be taken somewhere different. How they were being divided up, or why he could not figure out and was not even going to guess until he arrived at the desk.

As he moved closer to the desk, he heard what was going on. The man at the desk would ask who the person is and the former slaves would give up all the information willingly. The man would then look through a large set of blue binders. Krezdon nearly gagged. The timing had been perfect. The blue binders were an alphabetical listing of everyone in the city. The new census had just been completed and they had it all. Name, age, sex, occupation and…how many slaves they owned. All that information had been painstakingly listed with great accuracy. Here it was being used against them.

Each individual, after being found in the books, was sent to a numbered stall. The ex-slaves were cooperating thoroughly with the conquerors. Krezdon figured that they had no clue as to how they were being used. *These people are using them. As soon as they have everything they want, these people will be putting those fools right back into slavery. The only difference will be who their new masters is.*

When Krezdon finally arrived at the desk, it was well into the afternoon. He was exhausted, hungry, dizzy and weak. The man behind the desk, looked extremely tired as well, but it was doubtful that he was hungry.

"Name?"

Prysko merrily ratted. "This is the Supreme City Commandant, Lord Krezdon Chashchy."

"Yeah, but right now, he's not even Commandant, of his own bowels," added Bertiyr.

The man smiled. "Really? Well, here we have one of the biggies. As soon as the chain is cut, take him to stall 9."

Bertiyr looked very happy. "What happens there?"

"There is a man there, who will brief you."

Another brown suit, reached down and pulled the connecting link. Krezdon was now independent of the string, and he was led by two of his former slaves, to stall 9. They were not polite or slow.

On arrival at stall 9, another brown suit was there who again took Krezdon's name. He checked it off a list that was on his table. He saw his name and the names of all the male council members. Three other names were checked off.

The guard removed the shackles. Krezdon accepted the removal of the agonizing objects as stoically as possible - with his mouth shut. He did his best not to acknowledge the removal. His arms fell limp at his sides. He did a quick mental inventory. He could feel nothing from the elbows down. He was sure of his ankles - they were throbbing.

He was then dumped in a room. It was somewhat dark and he had to wait for his eyes to adjust. There was a small window that had been barred. The window opened up to an alley, which explained the lack of light.

The three other men in the room came into focus. Belziyd Pebodom, Sector Commandant Six, sat there staring off into space in a total stupor. Goroben Hebedissor, Sector Commandant Seven, gave Krezdon a halfhearted nod of greeting. Ahach Keez, Council Representative Sector Four, was staring at Krezdon with a face full of hate.

"This is all your fault," growled Ahach. "We get overrun by a pack of hoodlums and I see no resistance to it at all. What were you doing? What were you thinking? Why...?"

"Shut up, you idiot!" Goroben growled at him. "None of us saw this coming until we were helplessly shackled."

"Crying about it, and fighting among ourselves, isn't going to help matters at all," said Krezdon.

Ahach looked around in disgust. "I can't feel my hands."

"Don't worry about that," said Goroben. "The feeling will come back soon enough - too soon, in fact."

"What do you mean?"

"I've got the feeling back in my hands now, and I wish…I didn't. There was already enough pain from the knees down."

Krezdon tried to change the subject away from pain: "Who was here first?"

"I was," said Goroben. "Belziyd was thrown in here, just after dawn. Ahach, maybe twenty minutes before you arrived."

"How long have you been here?"

Goroben snorted. "All flaming night. After that chaotic meeting, last night, I went directly home. They were waiting just inside my front door."

"I'm so hungry," cried Ahach.

"Don't worry," Goroben said sarcastically. "They'll feed you soon enough…unfortunately."

Krezdon did not like the sound of that. "What do you mean? What are they feeding us?"

"From what I can make of it…cold fish guts laced with raw sewage."

A few moments later, they did bring in food. What Goroben

had described *was* the easiest way to describe the slop that Krezdon found in the bowl.

Ahach put his bowl off to the side and again gave a hateful look at Krezdon. "You're not going to eat that garbage, are you?"

"It's rather hard to think on an empty stomach," said Krezdon flatly.

"It's also difficult to think, when you're vomiting!"

Krezdon ignored the comment and choked the gooey mess down.

A few moments later, Hebtezz Nosso, Council Representative, Sector Three, came flying into the room. Directly behind him, cam Takariy Jebshom, Sector Commandant, Sector One, and Daznak Siytiloran, Council Representative, Sector One.

"Welcome to the royal suite," said Goroben flatly.

Takariy looked around a little confused. "Shall we call the meeting to order?" He glanced around a little more. "No. I see we do not have the minimum 60%, in attendance yet."

Ahach was enraged. "How can you be so stupidly apathetic? We are in trouble and you sit there making witless jokes."

"What would you have me do? Celebrate or pee on myself?"

"Stop the bickering! We have a crisis and it's our job to overcome these situations." Krezdon wanted to knock a few heads around, but he did not know if his hands could take the punishment. "I suggest we all do some heavy thinking, for a while. See if you can come up with some sensible or feasible solution. Before we voice any

· of them, let's wait until the rest of the council is here."

Hertz shook his head. "Why wait? Why not make some suggestions now?"

"Because if we come up with something, now, and all here agree on it, we will have to repeat it, once someone else shows up. That someone might have a good argument against it, or a better solution. We wait!"

Xuzo Poroby, City Governor, was the next to show up. After being informed of what was known, he sat and joined in the silent wait.

Piromin Dezelba, Sector Commandant, Sector Two, and Poltrist Guyot, Council Representative, Sector Two, both showed up well after dark. The only way they could be recognized was by voice.

"Now that we are all here, let's see what we can figure out," said Krezdon.

"We are *not* all here," said Ahach. "There are still six, who are not here."

"Didn't you see the list out there? None of the women were on it. They have been taken elsewhere," said Hebtezz.

Ahach continued with his ranting: "We do not have a quorum. We must have at least 60%, or nothing we say can be implemented."

"You are unbelievable," said Takariy. "So somebody just peed in the wine. Rather than punish the guilty party, you would have us just sit there, complaining about the taste. May the makers preserve us from your gargantuan stupidity?"

Krezdon was ready to strangle Ahach. "Ahach, you are helping the invaders! You are helping them accomplish their mission. They have put the women somewhere else. We know this, and knowing the intelligence of those women, they are fully aware of the same thing. We have to make a decision, if we do not have all the members here - tough! Whatever our decision is, we are forced to make it without the women. By the way, you say we don't have 60%? 60% of 16 is 9.6. We have 10 here - so we do have your flaming quorum. Can we please stop griping about insignificant numbers and try to accomplish something positive?"

"No, we don't!" shouted Ahach. "Belziyd has been sitting there, in a stupor, ever since he got here: We only have 9."

There was a collective groan.

Goroben spoke up: "For your information, Belziyd has shown himself to be mentally disabled. This means that until we have a full meeting, to choose a replacement, his position is vacant, and now there are only 15 on the council. 60% of 15 is 9. As you said, we have 9."

Before Ahach could come up with another inane protest, Xuzo gave his input: "The women are probably doing what we should be doing. They are thinking of a way to rescue us. We should be thinking of a way to rescue them, and the entire city. If you don't shut up, we will be discussing a bunch of silly procedures, while the entire city is being rescued, by someone else. Won't we look silly, if the city is rescued and we are still bitching about numbers and procedures? Something else for you to consider: You are a Sector Council Representative. I am the governor. My rank is superior to yours. My word and command is superior - during peace time. This city is under attack. That means 'an act of war.' During war time, Lord Krezdon, is the Supreme Commandant, and the Sector Commandants, are his seconds. We the Council Representatives are now secondary to them. During war, there is no vote. The Supreme Commandant's word is law. That means that your precious parliamentary procedures, have been pitched to the side, until the war is over."

Ahach looked around desperately. "But...no...we..."

Before he could continue, Piromin broke in: "Ahach, if you don't shut up, the next time those guards open the door, what they will find is 8 council members, 1 dummy and 1 corpse."

After a few more hours of bickering, they all passed out from exhaustion. They only agreed on one thing: Ahach - SHUT UP!

Morning came all too soon. They were fed some more of that fishy smelling slop.

They each inventoried what was left of their bodies. Wrists and ankles, rubbed raw. The soles of their feet were covered with open and running blisters. Their chests were bruised and battered to the point that lifting the arms caused even more pain. Strength - gone. If they had decided to make any attempt to escape, or fight back, they might have collectively taken down one guard…if the guard happened to be alone….deaf…blind…mentally deficient…or crippled…or asleep…or dead already. The painful dance from their homes, had drained them physically. They were now desperately hanging on to what little dignity they might have left.

They had no way of telling time. They could only go by the dim light coming through the window, and when they were fed. Other than that, they were totally ignored.

For two days nothing happened. Their aches did not subside at all. The only sound they heard was an occasional hammering of metal on metal - more chains being forged, or more people being chained together in one of those strings. The only things they could smell was their own excrement, fish and a smell of something burning. The smoke had a very pungent odor that hung in the air.

The third morning, Krezdon was awakened, by a kick in the ribs. He could not think or see straight. He heard a belligerent remark from Goroben that was followed by a loud slap. His emotions became very mixed, when he realized that his wrists were shackled again. The pain from the other day's abuse, was still so intense, he had not noticed the new agony, until he heard the rattle and felt the weight of the chains.

Several guards were in the room. The majority of them were checking on Belziyd. The man had not moved, since being dumped there. He had not eaten. He was sitting in his own excrement and seemed to be totally oblivious the flies that were all over him. Two of the guards took hold of his arms and dragged him out.

Krezdon felt himself being picked up. They pulled him along with the others, out of the room. Even though it was very late in the day, the light was blinding. His eyes cleared, just in time to see Belziyd being thrown, head first, into the middle of a large fire. His legs kicked a few times and then went still.

There were several other fires going on around the waterfront. Shops, taverns, tables in the market place and two of the piers. The smoke in the area was extremely thick, but not so bad that he could see the wind blowing it all inland.

Krezdon was dragged with all the others out on the only dock that was not burning. At the end of the dock, there were two longboats. Each of the councilmen were dumped into the boats - five in one, four in the other.

The brown suits were discussing something, but Krezdon was unable to understand it. They seemed to be waiting for something, but he could not figure out what.

The only sounds that could be heard, now was the crackling of the fires. He felt bitter anger as he saw one of the other docks collapse into the water. Occasionally he heard some other structure collapse behind the wall of smoke. Each time, he added the occurrence to his file of vengeance. It might take a long time, but vengeance was going to be accomplished against these people…maybe.

There were three men still on the pier. They were sitting on some barrels, carrying on a casual conversation, pointing back towards the city. The smoke seemed to be getting thicker, and the pier that Krezdon and the others had just walked the length of, was burning at the other end.

There was a shout. No one was sure where it had come from. All the guards were standing and looking back at the flaming city. Then, a group of men came out of the smoke on the pier. They were holding rags to their faces. They were wearing the uniforms of the city guard. Piromin was sitting next to Krezdon and the two men looked at each other in shock. They each seemed to be silently asking the other a certain question about traitors.

Krezdon looked back up at the approaching men. They stopped as soon as they got to the end of the pier, and started breathing the fresh air. The smoke had caused them all kinds of grief as they had walked through it and they were now blowing their noses, wiping tears out of their eyes, coughing and spitting. As each one finally recovered, he started stripping the city guard uniform off, revealing that all too familiar brown suit. They laughed and joked with the men who were in the longboats.

The new arrivals started climbing into the longboats. The three men who had been on the pier already were now breaking open the barrels that they had been sitting on. They pushed the barrels over and a thick, dark brown liquid oozed out of each one. One man ran to the nearest flames and lit a torch. He came running back to the longboats. The others finished shedding the city guard uniforms and threw them on top of the brown sludge.

Everyone got into the longboats and they shoved off. Krezdon looked out to sea for the first time. The only ship left in the harbor, was one of those massive Oosam cargo ships. This was the first time he had ever seen one of them and he finally realized just how big they were. He thought of how the stories, he had heard, did not do the giant ships any justice. No story could have possibly prepared him for actually looking at one. He could not understand how something that big could float.

The boat stopped about half way to the big ship. One of the guards picked up a longbow. He took an arrow and put the tip in the flame of the torch. He then aimed the arrow at the pier that they had just departed from and let fly. The arrow was hit by the wind and flew off to the left. Several of the other guards laughed and snickered. He gave them a dirty look, took another arrow, lit the tip and took careful aim. This one landed true, in that dark liquid from the barrels, and huge flames immediately shot up and seemed to engulf the entire pier.

Krezdon lowered his head and tried not to cry. He looked away from the city to the sea. He saw Goroben sitting there with a mixture of shock and anger on his face. If his jaw had been clenched any tighter, he would have shattered his teeth. The veins were standing out on his temples and neck. Krezdon decided that this was not the time to ask what the problem was. He watched as Goroben lowered his head and just sat there brooding.

When they got to the ship, each one of the Malantroi City

Councilmen was fitted with a halter, and each one hauled up on the ship as if they were cargo. As Krezdon was raised up, he was able to get a better view of the city. Nothing as far as the eye could see, but smoldering, blackened remains. Nothing. Their city and everything in it was gone. They had lost their freedom and had nothing to go back too, if they did escape. He, like all the other councilmen, just hung his head in silent agony. The city of Malantroi was officially dead.

Once he was lowered to the deck, he was immediately dragged away by two of the brown suits, hauled down into a dark cargo hold and dumped. He could do nothing but sit there and feel sorry for himself as he grieved over the lost city.

8

Krezdon's daze ended when someone slapped him. He looked up into the face of another one of men wearing that accursed brown suit.

"Hey, Stupid! You want somting eat? Or maybe you want slow death by starve, eh?"

Sitting next to Krezdon, was another bowl, of the foul smelling fish muck. He grudgingly picked it up and started eating. As usual the goo assaulted his taste buds, and hit his stomach like a great war hammer.

The guard snickered and then walked away to slap someone else.

Krezdon looked around in the semi-darkness. He was a little surprised by what he saw. According to what he knew about slave ships, the holds were usually a nightmare of overcrowding, stench and death. There were a total of twenty men in this part of the hold. Each one had plenty of room to stretch out. They were not cramped at all. The smell told him that it was definitely a brand new ship. He and the other men, were the first cargo.

After the guard had finished smacking and insulting everyone with the swill, he left. They all watched him climb the ladder and then pull it up behind him.

Goroben looked at Krezdon and spoke quietly: "These wretches had us figured out proper. They planned too well.

"All right," said Krezdon. "You have some little secret for us? What is it?"

"They duped us. They had everything planned so perfectly. Just days before the completion of the census, they bring a supposedly crippled fleet into our harbor."

Piromin was listening in. "What do you mean supposedly?"

Goroben sighed. "I inspected the ships. I looked at the one that was the most damaged, first. I told them to take it out to open sea and burn it. They towed it out to sea, and that was the last I saw of it... until now."

"Maybe they repaired it," said Daznak.

"Impossible! All four masts were gone. A major part of the main deck was gone as well. It would have taken at least five months to repair it. They could not have possibly done it in five days."

"They didn't repair it," said a strange voice.

Goroben looked toward the sound of the voice. "Who are you and what do you mean?"

"I am Borip Deesh, and I said; they didn't repair it. It was never damaged. They disguised it...with magic."

"Impossible! I inspected this ship. I walked right through the mast if that's the case. I sat right down on the top of the stump, of one of the masts."

"It was an illusion. You saw what they wanted you to see. You saw what you expected to see. As they led you around the ship, the illusions did most of the leading."

Takariy broke in: "So, how do you know, so much about magic?"

"Because I am a wizard."

"So am I," said another voice.

Ahach had to get his thoughts in, "and who are you?"

"Hold it," said Krezdon. "Before we start going crazy, with a bunch of strange voices, let us do some introductions."

The nine councilmen introduced themselves. Then the others: Zenzorodan Kytaw, Borip Deesh, Nytombul Prayhith, and Nal Koropeff - all wizards. Paratroy Keldigin, Zusto Bengeftra, Chach Tsoolsa, Morhabo Ferrif and Jayoor Trastooss - all professional slavers. Berrum and Teliyum Parda - slave auctioneers.

Daznak spoke up: "If you gentlemen are slavers - what are you doing in here?"

"These men are independents," said Zusto. "They are not going according to the rules."

"Rules!" screamed Ahach. "What kind of rules do slavers have?"

"We do have rules, and a guild," said Morhabo. "You must be a member of the guild, otherwise the guild will hunt *you* down. There are certain places that are not raided, for slaves. Your city is one of those places, because we can usually dock there for supplies."

"How are these rules going to help us?" asked Daznak.

"There are about 800 different locations, where you can sell slaves," said Paratroy. "Of those, only five could handle slaves, in this volume. I know, and am known at all five. When we get there, I will set us free, because of my membership and we will punish the renegades."

"Aye, and punish them good," said Jayoor.

"How will this help the rest of the citizenry, of Malantroi?" asked Daznak.

"I have never heard of a raid, on this scale," said Chach. "It will put a glut on the market, and we should be able to get the majority of your people back. There is no way we can get everyone out."

All of the slavers agreed with the last statement.

"You wizards," said Goroben. "How were you duped or captured? How was it possible for all this magic, to be done, and you didn't attempt to stop it?"

"That wretched half-breed," said Zenzorodan. "I have never seen anyone, so powerful in my life."

"He made some kind of charm," said Nal. "It is like nothing I have ever seen or heard of. They are seven pointed stars. I have used five and eight pointed stars in spells and charms, but never seven. That half-breed has found a way to turn it into a symbol of power, and has cut off most of our spell casting abilities."

"What do you mean - half-breed?" asked Daznak. "I mean a man is a man. How could any man be a partial of something else?"

"Half-Elfin," said Nal flatly. "There are over 100 different types of Elfin races throughout the world. There are none that are indigenous to our part of the country. There are some races that are more common than humans, in some countries. This one is the issue of Heyyah and an Elf mating."

"How can you be so certain, that he's a half-breed?" asked Ahach.

"I have drawings and descriptions of each different type," said Nal. "Some are very similar, but I know enough to tell the differences between each one. This halfling is similar to the Kalash, but enough difference is there, to show that he is not a full blooded anything."

Krezdon listened to the conversation as it went around the different areas. He started analyzing the situation as best as he could. These people had duped the entire city into welcoming the invasion force with open arms. They arrived two days in advance of the attack, which gave them plenty of time to distribute their troops all over the city. They had a powerful wizard with them, who had been more than capable of out-spell casting the local wizards. They had pounced on their hapless victims, the very evening, of the day the victims had supplied a list of the entire citizenry. They knew the most efficient means of destroying your ability to fight back.

Questions: After all this planning and prisoner taking, would their people be so foolish as to take all their newly acquired slaves, to a place where the captured slavers could simply take back and take over? All this careful and precise planning, could they have possibly, stupidly overlooked something like the slavers guild? Was there just one wizard, or were there several more, hidden somewhere around an unknown corner?

What happened to the priests? There were temples devoted to different gods in the city. The priests depended on the citizenry, for the devotions. They would not have just stood by, and watched the citizens being stolen, right under their noses…would they? A temple without worshipers is broke. What stopped the priests from stopping this raid? Had these invaders figured out a way to trap and/or defy the holy representatives of the gods?

Was it just the 1977 sailors? He could not remember the exact figure, but there had been over 31,000 citizens, according to the census. Better than 15:1 against the invaders. Then he remembered the city slaves. That count had been almost 60,000. The slaves had allied with the attackers and that alone was almost 2:1 in favor of the invaders.

What happened to Temela?

What happened to the women of the council?

What happened to the women…of the entire city?

9

Krezdon woke up. They had been out to sea for… (?). He had lost count. Did it matter? Eventually they would get to their destination.

He had a few more questions added to his list. The guards would come in and make sure everything was clean - twice a day. According to the captive slavers, that was unusual. Normally they would clean, their holds, once every three days. These people were going to a lot of trouble, in order to insure the health of all the people in the hold. Why?

The food had changed. They were fed larger portions that consisted of fresh meat, vegetables, some fruit and bread. Had their captors run out of swill…or was it possible that they had started to believe the words of the captured slavers? Each time the guards had brought food, and done the cleanups, Zusto had done his best to sway the guards. The answer had in all cases been a laugh or a slap. But, was he getting something accomplished, or were they to be kept healthy, for a better price on the auction block?

Another point, the slavers had brought up: On a long voyage, in a crowded hold, you starve the slaves. You make them clean up, all the excrement, with their bare hands and make them haul the dead out. This would aid weakening them and in breaking their spirit. Here, they *were* uncomfortable, but not crowded. They were well fed, the conditions were kept sanitary and morale was very high. What was the point of having a slave, that still had the capability, mentally or physically to fight back?

The main hatch above them came open. Every one of them groaned or squawked and covered their eyes. A ladder was lowered, and one of the guards came down.

"Arright! You people stink," he said. "We try to keep dis place clean, but you muss be clean as well. I, open your chains, you climb up de ladder and you clean your butts."

The guard walked over to the corner at the far end, from Krezdon. As the manacles around the ankles were unlocked on that man, another guard came down the ladder, holding a club. The first man released was Jayoor.

"You go to de ladder, now," the guard said. "A man up dere, show you what you do."

Jayoor walked slowly to the ladder. He was still wearing the manacles on his wrists. He stopped at the ladder, and held his hands up to the second guard. "Do these stay on?"

The guard jabbed Jayoor in the ribs with the club. "Up de ladder, dog. Go! Now!"

Jayoor made the climb, somewhat unsteady. He was favoring his newly bruised, right side. When he got to the top, the guard then started to release the next man.

Goroben was chained next to Krezdon. "Very clever," he whispered. "One at a time. That way, we have no chance of overpowering them, down here."

"Mm-hm. Might as well just lay back and be comfortable, until they get to us."

They did continue with this procedure. Only one prisoner was "loose" in the hold at one time. The guard went down the line, on the other side. Krezdon was almost impatient, waiting for his turn. He did everything he could to hide his anxiety. The guard finished the other side, then went to Goroben. Goroben's stride was not the usual confident swagger that he normally had. He stumbled a little on the way to the ladder and had a little difficulty, going up.

The guard finally released Krezdon. He grunted in pain as he stood up. His feet were still tender from the painful dance through the streets of the city. The rungs of the ladder did not make his feet feel much better. When he reached the hatch opening, the light was even more blinding. He tried to let his eyes adjust, but was roughly pulled up by hands that he could barely see through his squinting eyes. The smell was something completely different. The salt air of the sea was a jolt - an incredibly refreshing jolt. It made him realize just how stale the air had become in the hold.

He was shoved into a line behind Goroben. In the bright light, he could not really see what was going on, so he decided to just look down, until his eyes were totally adjusted and be patient.

When Goroben reached the head of the line, two guards ripped his nightshirt off of him. He was then directed to another line. It was now Krezdon's turn to be stripped naked. They tore his filthy nightshirt off and threw it overboard. He was then given a small rag, and directed to one of five water tubs. The water was clean and fresh. He started cleaning himself with a feeling that came close to ecstasy.

After a few minutes of bathing, he glanced around. The guards did not seem to care what the prisoners were doing. He was appalled at their lackadaisical attitude. Are they that confident of their total control?

After the washing each prisoner was given a loincloth. Not much, but it did help a little in the modesty area.

He finally got a good look at the men he had been talking too all this time. The problem was, he did not know which voice went with which face. No time like the present to remedy that situation.

The wizards were easy to pick out. For one thing, they were shackled in a different manner. The chains on everyone else were the normal dull gray steel, and simply connected the two wristlocks together. The chains on the wizards were a bright silver, and had smaller links. There was a third chain on them that was connected to a collar. All three chains were linked in the middle by a wafer thin piece of metal, that had a seven pointed star etched in it. They could not break the bonds, and anyone else who touched the chains, got a brain scattering jolt, that left the victim incapacitated for several moments. The four men were continually spouting their frustration over the strange symbol. They had never seen it used under magical circumstances, and how it was stopping their powers was baffling.

As far as trying to solve any problems, the two auctioneers were completely worthless. The only talent they had was to "talk up" the price, and nothing else.

Krezdon decided to pick the minds of the slavers. The five men were sitting next to the starboard rail, eyeballing the situation.

Paratroy Keldigin was not a tall man, but he was built like a gorilla. He had about as much body hair as an ape as well. He had a gravelly voice that sounded like he was straining to talk. His confidence was growing daily, concerning revenge against these silly amateurs. "They have no idea as to what they are doing, or how to do it," he said. "They could have broken us, so easily. Their methods at the start were very good. They dished out major punishment for minor infraction. They demanded absolute obedience, and listened to no complaints. They used pain and exhaustion, very effectively, but did not follow through. They have not accentuated their hold on us though. They treat us too nicely."

Zusto Bengeftra was a small, wiry man with an enormous nose. The way his eyes darted around, along with his big hawk nose, made him look like a big rat. "I agree. They haven't pushed their advantage. They could have broken most of us completely. Now, they'll have to start all over, again, before they can gain any type of control over us. The only thing, that I can compliment them on, is the organization that went before the raid."

Chach Tsoolsa was a black man, who normally kept his head shaved. He said it made him look more vicious, and kept his slaves in line. The time spent in the hold had allowed his hair a chance to grow a little. He was lean but muscular. "These people are a disgrace to the profession. I did not like the idea of joining the guild until now. This kind of thing has to be stopped. When you grab people to sell as slaves, you do not grab people that you sell too, or fellow slavers. You grab peasants. They are easier to break and control. They do less complaining about the situation and they accept their fate completely."

Morhabo Ferrif had a look about him that made you want to go somewhere else. It was difficult to look at those piercing blue eyes. He could win a staring contest with a statue. His face was a roadmap of scars. You could not be sure how many arguments he had been in, or how many he had lost. There were several scars lining their way through his patchy brown hair. "This food they are giving us, it makes me wonder what is going on. I don't remember having food this good, even as captain of my ship. After twelve years on a ship, it just doesn't make sense, that they could have fruit and vegetables, that fresh, after sixteen days on the open sea. They are pampering us - why?"

Jayoor Trastooss had the face of a little boy. It was difficult to believe that anyone with a face that innocent looking, could be a slaver. He had thick blonde hair, bright brown eyes, and a very pale complexion. He had a high pitched, nasally voice, that no one liked listening too. "Interesting set up. If I had had a ship like this, I could have quadrupled my profits. That hold that we have been placed in - I could put 80 or 90 in that hold alone. Look around here. There are six hatches that open up here on the main deck. Just those holds alone could hold over 500 slaves. Who knows how many in the lower decks? I swear, by the gods, when we reach our destination and the guild confiscates these ships, I am going to claim one, for my trade."

The slavers had been taken in another way. During the time the raiders had been in port, they had stopped in Malantroi for supplies. They were on their way home, with a fresh load of slaves. The slavers had been taken by surprise, and thrown into their own holds as their cargo was released. Later they had been moved to this ship. They had no idea what had happened to their ships or crews.

Krezdon listened to each one and finally broke in: "Do you see any chance of overpowering these thugs and then taking the ship?"

Paratroy laughed. "What for? These fools are taking us to a port, where we will be set free, and then placed in total control. Why push things? They will be handing us their heads on golden platters, soon enough."

Krezdon walked away, feeling like he needed another bath. He was beginning to not like them, especially Jaysoor. He spotted Goroben and decided to pick that man's brain. As he approached Goroben, he noticed Piromin and Takariy heading in the same direction.

They got together and glanced around at their captors for a few moments. Krezdon spoke up first: "What do you make of the situation?"

"I don't know," said Goroben. "The confidence of these people is getting on my nerves. They are allowing us total freedom on the main deck, right now. They are so sure that we can't do anything."

"Total freedom," scoffed Piromin. "Look around. They have at least fifteen men carrying whips or clubs that are watching us. They had us completely duped in the city. Why would anything change now?"

"Duped!" Goroben grunted. "They had us right where they wanted us, and now they're rubbing our noses in it. Like I said before, this is the ship that I condemned. Now I see it - intact! Look off to the port side here. Those ships that are in the convoy…they're numbered. I remember the numbers of the ships that I said were no longer seaworthy. The two in the front showed major damage in Malantroi…now they, like this one, are completely intact." He shook his head in frustration.

"I talked to the wizards," said Takariy. "The only way, I could stop them from whining about those wretched little charms, was to belt one of them. They said that there is no real reason for the guards to make much effort, as long as that half-breed is around."

Krezdon followed Takariy's gaze. So! Here was this awesome, all powerful wizard. He was a little shorter than an average man. He was wearing a pair of extremely baggy brown pants that went just below the knees. His soiled white shirt was just as baggy, and was presently open in the front. On his feet there was a pair of very ragged sandals. His dark brown hair hung down below his shoulder blades. His mustache and beard were not long, and had not been groomed, with much care. His fair complexion, had somehow (maybe by magic) avoided the sunburn that was showing on the faces of the rest of the crew. He was slightly overweight. Krezdon had heard many things about Elves, but until now had never seen one. If not for the incredibly long, high ears, this Elf would look like your normal run-of-the-mill, slob. The ear lobes went slightly lower, than what would be normal. The top of them, went back slightly and then went straight up to tapering points that were above the top of his head.

Piromin grunted. "What is so overwhelming, about him?"

"He might not look like much, but he sure shaded me," said Goroben. "He shut those wizards off and he made the entire fleet look like scrap lumber."

"So he threw a little dirt in the stew," said Takariy. "Right now, you're whispering as if he could hear us."

At that moment, the Elf looked directly at them, and smiled.

Piromin and Takariy both gasped. Goroben rolled his eyes in exasperation.

Krezdon could do nothing but look away in disgust. "Well…

crap!"

Takariy cleared his throat. "Let's change the subject," he said nervously.

"Now it makes a little more sense," said Goroben. "There are only two guards, watching us. If that...breed, is watching all of us, out here at the same time..."

"This is really getting me nervous," said Piromin. "We see more and more arrogance. They are showing off, their absolute control over this situation. They have absolutely no fear of us at all. They have fresh food, even after all this time. They are allowing us total freedom on the main deck. Either they are complete idiots - which I doubt - or they have a very nasty surprise waiting for us, at the end of this voyage."

They had a short discussion that included a lot of nervous stammering and very few points being made. They kept on glancing up at the half-breed. He had folded his arms and still had that smug smile on his face.

After four hours of relative freedom, they were herded back down in the hold. They were all still a little confused over the lengthy vacation on deck.

After everyone was back in their place and chained down, Ahach started complaining: "Those rotten bastards! Now, I see why they kept us up there, all that time."

Several whats and whys were thrown at him.

"They kept us up there practically naked," he wailed. "Just long enough to get sunburned - all over."

Krezdon turned to Goroben and whispered: "Why can't he keep that big mouth of his shut? Suddenly, I am very uncomfortable."

The response was an angry grunt.

10

The trip lasted several more days. No one was counting any more.

"We've arrived," said Zusto.

"How can you tell," asked Ahach. "We can't see anything, outside."

"I can tell, by the sounds. The side of the ship just scraped against something - probably a pier. The anchor has been dropped. I hear birds. There is a lot of activity up on deck."

"Your ears are fantastic, my friend," said Paratroy. "Soon, we will turn the tables, on these ridiculous fools. I, will enjoy it - immensely."

Chach gave an evil sounding laugh.

They all covered their eyes, in anticipation of the hatch being opened. They had all become used to the scraping noise that preceded the opening.

The glaring light did not happen. Krezdon heard the hatch being opened...but no light. He pulled his arm away from his eyes. Through the open hatch, he saw a small portion of one of the masts, and stars. Lots of stars, filled what little sky he could see. He breathed a sigh of relief.

The ladder came down. A guard came down, carrying a lit torch. He looked around, until he saw the flame reflecting off of the special chains, the wizards were wearing. He smiled, as he headed to them and started pulling the ankle chains.

Krezdon could see two men looking down through the open hatch. One of them hollered something at the guard in the hold.

The guard stopped what he was doing, and gave a disgusted sigh. He looked up at the opening and hollered back: "You know, I can't understand that lingo. Now, what do you want?"

The men up top laughed. "I said: Which group is this?"

"What? You've got the list. This is main hold two. Check your listings."

There was some unintelligible conversation between the two dark forms, and then they disappeared.

The guard finally got the first one of the wizards unlocked. "All right, insect - up the ladder!"

Borip got up scowling, and headed for the ladder. He climbed up slowly. As soon as he reached the top, an arm appeared and yanked him out of sight. Everyone heard him yelp and expected to hear a body hit the deck above them. The thump never occurred.

Krezdon felt a little uneasy. He did not feel half the anxiety that the three remaining wizards did.

The guard had now released Nal. The wizard made an audible gulp. He cleared his throat, and glanced around, as if he was begging for help.

"Well, what are you waiting for? There ain't no lackey, for you here. Move it!"

Nal got up, eyeing the guard. He side stepped to the ladder. He sighed and headed up. As he neared the top, he looked around the foreboding hatch.

The guard growled and headed up the ladder. He moved the torch near Nal's bare feet. Nal yelped, and scurried up a few more rungs. Another yelp came from his throat, as the arm came out, grabbed hair, and Nal vanished through the hatch.

Zenzorodan went next. Nytombul last. The results at the top of the ladder was the same for both of them.

The guard headed up the ladder, without releasing anyone else. He pulled the ladder up and closed the hatch.

"Here we go with the wretched mind games, again," said Xuzo.

"They do have some strange ways," laughed Jaysoor.

"Well, if they're not going to pull us out yet, I'm going to get some sleep," said Takariy.

Ahach started in on his complaining. "Why don't they let us out of here? They took those wizards, why not us?"

"They *know* who we are. Those bastards are going to try something else," said Xuzo. "Maybe slip us in one at a time, and hope that none of the auctioneers, here will notice us, for who we are. Believe me: I will not be kept silent."

"We will win in the end, I assure you," said Chach.

11

They were awakened, when the hatch was opened. The sun was up and again they were blinded by the light. There were several curses thrown at the one who opened the hatch. Krezdon heard Goroben make a rather nasty remark about the man's lineage.

This time there were five guards, in the hold, before they started releasing people. They were, in no way, polite about shoving the prisoners in the direction of the ladder. Ahach went first (complaining all the way), then Goroben. Takariy and Krezdon were released next.

Krezdon climbed the ladder, slowly. His feet were still very sensitive and the light was causing a waterfall in his eyes. He had to feel his way up the ladder. He reached up for the next rung, and instead, felt himself being pulled out of the hold, by several rough hands. He was dragged to...another part of the deck. After they let go of him, he rubbed the tears out of his eyes. He finally got to where his vision was coming back into focus.

The ship was docked at the very end of a very long pier. On both sides, he could see several dozen Oosam merchant ships docked at this and other long piers.

The half-breed was sitting on the rail near the gangplank. He no longer looked like a slob. His hair and beard had been groomed. He was wearing black pants that were stuffed inside a pair of shiny, tight fitting, knee high boots. His shirt was bright red silk that was open at the collar. He had a cape that seemed to have no clasp holding it in place. The cape was black on the outside with red silk inner lining. A large red translucent stone hung from a gold chain, around his neck.

"Look at the weaponry, on that breed," said Goroben.

Krezdon looked him up and down. "What of it? A sword hanging on his left side, a dagger on the right, and some kind of large dirk, strapped to his right boot...so what?"

"The one on his leg has a chain on it. The chain goes from the hilt to the scabbard, as if he doesn't want it to escape."

"Maybe it's some kind of thing to keep thieves from stealing it."

"Either that, or he does not want to use it."

"When you have a Long sword, at your side, which is easier to reach, why worry about that silly thing?"

"Why wear it?"

"Why not? It looks rather valuable."

Goroben shrugged.

The others were all on deck now. The auctioneer brothers, were the last ones to come up.

Paratroy finished rubbing the tears out of his eyes, and was looking around with a mixture of fear, confusion and shock on his face. He looked the entire harbor over and all he could say was: "Uh oh."

Ahach gave him a startled look. "Uh oh? Uh oh, what? Don't

give me an uh oh! I don't want to hear uh oh. What's the problem?"

Paratroy just shook his head. "I don't recognize this place. I have no idea where we are at all."

"I don't either," said Morhabo.

"Look at the flag, on that ship, in front of us." said Chach. "We're in Lower Oosam."

Jayoor was still rubbing his eyes. At the mention of the country, he stopped. "What?! Are these people crazy? Slavery is totally illegal here."

"No, I don't think, they're crazy," said Zusto. "I think we may be in big trouble. If they all docked at the same place…they have a *very* good reason."

Ahach fainted.

Krezdon looked at the half-breed. The Elf had that smug smile on his face, again.

One of the guards cracked a whip. "All right! Move it, you animals!"

They started marching towards the gangplank. Krezdon looked at the Elf again. The smile was still there, but his eyes…it looked as if there was some hidden sorrow behind those steel blue eyes. The Elf turned, went down the gangplank and headed up the pier to the city.

The sixteen men followed. Confused, worried, disillusioned, frightened, angry, numb and close to panic. Each man going through his own feeling. They could smell the sea, a fish market and the new wood of the piers. Several different types of birds flew around, singing all types of nature's songs. There was also the incessant sound of clinking chains, holding their wrists together.

The city did not have the look of some of the other places that Krezdon had been. The stone buildings were clean, the wooden ones did not have any warped or loose boards on them and the pier itself, had either been built or completely repaired, within the past few months. The signs on the stores showed no wear or age of any type.

Krezdon could hardly wait to pick Goroben's brain. Goroben was the Sector Commandant at the waterfront, back in Malantroi. He had a very analytical mind. He was more experienced at virtually everything. Krezdon had been using Goroben as a primary advisor and confidant. Sometimes it was more like a crutch.

Biyaba Jop was the Council Representative from the waterfront. She had been appointed, when her husband Grathgo had died. She was very knowledgeable as well, but he had no idea where she, or any of the women from Malantroi had been taken.

They were led off the pier, straight to a blacksmith. The smithy was ready. Iron collars were lined up on a table. Sixteen iron collars. There were rings on opposite sides of the collars. A chain, about nine spans long was attached to each ring, as they were once more, put in a line. Krezdon could not help, noticing how proficient the smithy was at attaching the collars, and chains. He also noticed the big smile on the fat smithy's face. After getting collared, they were lined up again and herded down the street.

People walked by on either side, ignoring them completely, as they continued down the street. Krezdon kept on watching his main confidant. Goroben was just as tired, but still alert enough to be looking around, noticing everything.

There was a strong desire, to block out everything. He knew that if he did, then he would be giving up all hope. He had to form his own mental defenses against it. He had to keep hoping. The humiliation and helplessness kept adding. It was no longer a game of physical pain. These people were playing a cruel mental game. He had to persevere. There was not much more that they could do…was there?

They were taken to a large brick building. The guards had a short conversation with two others, standing at a side entrance, and they were taken inside. They proceeded down a hallway that was well lit with torches. They turned into a large room and the first thing Krezdon saw was Bertiyr.

Bertiyr was still wearing the dress uniform. It did not appear to be damaged. He must have had it cleaned, while wearing other of Krezdon's wardrobe. Bertiyr walked slowly towards Krezdon. "Well, it's about time that you got here."

Before Krezdon could even think of an answer, a voice off the side interrupted. "Is this, the last group?"

"Yes sir, all ships are cleared," said a second voice.

Krezdon looked over at the man, standing behind a desk. It was the only piece of furniture in the room. His, had been the first voice. He looked around the room at different people as he spoke: "Would you people, please identify, this rabble?"

Bertiyr and several other people, all started speaking at once.

"One at a time!" the man bellowed.

They were herded up to the desk, and each one of the council, was identified. No one identified the slavers. As each one was named, he was then taken from the line and headed off through another door.

Krezdon was still adding things to his file. Bertiyr was going to pay dearly for this. He now found himself being led down a hallway, like an animal. There was a length of chain, connected to his collar. The guard was holding one end like a leash. He had a torch in the other hand.

They started down a flight of stairs. He was not certain how far he had gone, when he started counting the steps. He stopped counting at 150. He knew exactly where he was being taken. They passed four landings on the way down and stopped at the fifth. The stairs still continued down. The guard let him through a small passageway, to where another guard was standing at an open door. He was taken in, and hooked to a ring in the wall. Goroben, Daznak and Piromin were already here, hooked to the wall.

The guards left the room. The door was closed and now the only light they could see was a faint glimmer at the bottom of the door. The door was locked and the light receded until the darkness was absolute.

Krezdon listened for any activity, outside the door. After hearing nothing but the men in the cell breathing, he spoke up: "All right, Goroben, out with it. You've been surveying everything around you, ever since we left the ship. What have you seen?"

"It's over," said Goroben flatly. "We are going to disappear. Even if King Suntram does mount some kind of counter offensive, we could vanish, without a trace. The slavers were wrong. We have all been taken prisoner, and our captors plan to keep it that way."

"We can't just disappear," said Daznak angrily. "If this city is taken, no door would be left unopened. Someone would eventually find us."

Goroben let out a long sigh. "A long time ago, I saw some men setting up for a battle. They built a temporary wall. Some clever architect, put wedges at certain points in the wall. If the enemy got too close, all they had to do was yank those wedges out and the wall would collapse on the attackers, obliterating a great number of their forces. I saw wedges like that in the wall, just below the third landing. All they need to do is hook a strong chain, to the ring in the wedge. Yank out all of the wedges and they would cave in and bury, the entire lower portion of this structure. A bit of well placed dirt, before the enemy gets to that level and no one, except the ones who pulled the wedges, would know. We would all die here in an unmarked crypt."

Piromin interjected. "What do you smell here? Take a good whiff. Nothing but dirt. This structure is brand new. I have had the pleasure of taking a few prisoners into cells that were deeper than this one, back in the capitol city…before I moved to Malantroi. They reeked of human droppings and sweat. This cell and the entire level smells like…newly turned dirt. The door when it closed - it didn't creak. That door and the frame around it are brand new. No one has ever occupied this cell before."

12

They had no idea how much time had passed, since they had been imprisoned. They kept track of time, by counting the times they were fed. They were all usually ravenous by the time the tasteless mush arrived. Each time they were blinded by the torch, and could only hug the bowl close to them and wait until the torch was gone, before eating.

"I wonder what they are planning to do with us," said Goroben. "They brought us here for a reason…what though? Why? We have had no trial, we have been given no information. Usually, a conquering force will give some information to their prisoners…even if it is just to irk them."

"They have fed us 23 times," said Daznak. "They have to have something in mind…but what? It serves no purpose to keep us in here, without something to…rub our noses in."

"You can bet, what little you have left, they do have some purpose for keeping us alive," said Piromin. "Just exactly what it is, I can hardly wait, to find out."

"You may not want to know," said Krezdon.

They were removed shortly after their 37th meal. The guards came in, unhooked them from the wall, and off they went.

Krezdon knew he had to keep his mind busy, in order to fight them. 'Don't allow them to break you,' he thought. Countless times, he had contemplated that thought. 'I will not be broken. They have taken my freedom, but I will not let them take my mind.'

As he was led out, he decided to count all of the steps. That would give him an idea of how deep they were underground. He was taken out to the landing...and they went down. They passed two more landings, on the way down, and then through a long passageway. At times the passage sloped up, sometimes it was level and sometimes a downward slope. It twisted, sometimes sharp turns, others were long easy turns. He could not help wondering what kind of raving lunatic had designed this underground passage. There seemed to be no side passages at all.

They came to the bottom of a circular staircase. Up they went. He started counting. Up and up and up. 150 steps, he heard someone behind him wheezing. 250 steps, he was wheezing. 320 steps, his breathing was getting really ragged. His mouth was completely dry. He realized that he was counting out loud, and the time it took to say the number, he had taken at least two or three steps...or was it four? He was forced to move this concentration on making each next step. He was beyond 400, but had no real idea how far over that figure he was.

A sudden thought hit him: This staircase had no landings or passageways off to the side. It was nothing but one horribly long staircase. It would only lead to one place. The only purpose behind it, was to cause the complete exhaustion of people like him. He had been sitting in that cell for at least a month. His muscles had been wasting away. They were breaking him physically, through this torture. That was the reason for the passageway and the torture of this staircase.

The men who were leading him probably went up this staircase daily and were not suffering at all. They had probably had a good drink of water, before starting this arduous trek.

After an eternity, or two or three lifetimes, and several waves of dizziness, they finally reached the top. A level area with a door, opposite the top of the stairs. Krezdon looked at his three companions. Goroben and Piromin seemed to have come through with some of their dignity intact. Daznak, who was younger than the other two looked almost dead. Krezdon did not know how he himself looked, but he was not really eager about getting near a mirror.

Then another painful misery. The door was opened and it was a bright sunny day. He had grown used to the flickering torches, but was definitely not prepared for this. He was dragged through the door. He had his eyes clinched so tight, that he was getting a headache.

He heard a lot of voices around him. He felt a breeze on his entire body. He smelled fish, fruit, vegetables and tanned leather. They were being dragged through an open market place.

As he walked along, there were times he felt cobblestones under his feet, other times there was wooden planking, sometimes just dirt and finally stone.

Occasionally he would attempt to open his eyes momentarily, in order to get used to the bright light. He could not focus on anything through the tears. Each time he opened his eyes, however, he was able to keep them open longer each time.

He was led into a very large room. He heard footsteps and the rattling of chains, echoing off the walls.

He could hear raspy and ragged breathing all around him. It seemed that there were a great many people being brought into this room.

They put a new set of shackles on his wrists and ankles. 'This is stupid,' he thought. 'What kind of idiot, changes your shackles?'

Then he saw why. These new shackles could be hooked together with a pole. They could force you into any position they wanted, depending on how long the pole was and where they put it. He was forced to his knees. He was not allowed to stand or sit. He had to stay there with his full weight on his knees...on cold stone.

He was still having trouble focusing. He had to depend more on hearing, rather than seeing. For the most part he had to be content with just kneeling there and feeling miserable. He could hear, that others were being chained up, in the same manner that he was. Many others.

After what seemed another eternity, he noticed that the light was not as bright as it had been before. He dared to open his eyes, keep them open and look around.

The room was not large, it was massive. He could not even estimate, how many others were chained up in this room. Rows and rows of mostly men. There was a clear aisle in the middle of the room. It seemed to be hundreds of prisoners, chained up in neat rows on either side of the aisle, all facing the aisle. At one end of the aisle was a set of double doors. At the other end, there was a long table and what looked like a forge that would be found in a blacksmiths shop. Several long iron or steel rods were leaning up against the side of the forge.

'Wonderful,' thought Krezdon. 'Now after all that, they are going to torture us. What do they hope to find out from us? They already knew the best time to strike….what more could they not know about us?'

He looked around and noticed that there were very few guards, still in the room. With all the prisoners chained up, they did not need very many. He looked at the pole that was hooked to his shackles. The bottom had been placed in a hole in the floor - the top was connected to a huge overhead grid. The grid work covered the entire room, except for the aisle. Everyone was kept in their place by the pole and the grid.

The people in the room were all in different states of undress. Most of them had "fouled," themselves. He looked down at his loincloth. It was not in much better condition than any of the others in the room.

Some of the people were crying, some whimpering, some just staring off into space and others, like Krezdon, he was just trying to maintain some kind of dignity and sanity.

The doors came open. Several guards came in, with huge steaming cauldrons, and carts with hundreds of bowls on them. They started going down the lines handing out bowls of…something. He wondered if he would be able to eat something hot - or warm, after all this time. When they got to him, he tried, again, to be as stoic as possible. He took the bowl and started slowly sipping. It did not seem to have any aroma…or taste. He had a hard time, trying to conjure up enough spit in his mouth. The fact that the slop, was a liquid helped immensely. It hit his stomach like a sledge hammer.

The evening dragged on.

13

Morning arrived. Krezdon had no feeling in his arms. He did have an abnormal amount of agony in his knees though.

The tormenters, had used the rods to place each person in a position where they could not get up off of their knees, nor could they sit. The pain was working in the favor of the captors.

His eyes were still a little sensitive to light, but he was getting some tolerance back, especially if he squinted a lot.

Several guards entered. They started removing the people, row by row. Krezdon noticed that no one was resisting the guards in any way. He doubted if they were capable of any resistance. He doubted if he could either.

His turn finally came. He was unshackled and virtually dragged out of the room. He was taken down a long hallway, to a small room. They ripped the loincloth off of him and dumped him into a large tub of water.

A large guard with several teeth missing stood over him. "Clean your nasty self off. Do a good job of it, or I will clean you myself." He held up a large stiff bristled brush and shook it for accentuation.

Krezdon worked some feeling back into his arms, and scrubbed himself off. The hardest part to clean was his extremely sore knees. He found that his hair was a nightmare of tangles, knots and vermin. He also found more facial hair than he would have ever worn before. The guards seemed to be in no hurry, so he made sure that the bath was thorough. As each layer of crud came off, he began to feel human again.

After the bath, they gave him another bowl of the odorless, tasteless slop. It did not hit his stomach as hard this morning.

They put the shackles back on and led him off to another destination...naked. Once again, they had allowed him a small particle of dignity, only to knock him down again.

He was taken to a private cell. The only thing in this tiny room, which resembled furniture was a small chamber pot. He could not stand up without hitting the ceiling. The room was too short for him to lay down flat, even if he went corner to corner.

He heard people moving about in the corridor. There was very little noise other than that.

He felt helpless. Hope for successful retribution against these people was draining away. He had no idea what they wanted. He had no one to plan with, against them. Hundreds of questions that, so far, he could only guess at. Here in this box, he had no one to talk to, or with. No friends, to help or hinder. All he had was frustration, irritation, anger and scabs on his knees.

He heard doors being unlocked and gruff voices ordering people out of their cells.

Krezdon's turn finally came up and he obeyed. He cooperated more from curiosity, then from being broken. What is the point behind all this? What do they want? So far, no one had asked anything. He was the Supreme City Commandant. There had to be some kind of intelligence data that he held in his head, that could cause some kind of misery back home. They did not seem to care.

He was being dragged off somewhere else now. Some other destination for some unknown purpose. He noticed that the people who had been imprisoned here, were now being dragged off in different directions. All of the people now were naked. All of them had large nasty scabs on their knees. The looks on their faces was mostly despondency and exhaustion. A few showed signs of anger, anguish or shock.

He thought he recognized some of them, but he could not be sure. The looks on their faces seemed to distort their features.

He along with many others were hauled into another massive room. This one did not have the grid work above them. Instead, there were hundreds of chains hanging from the ceiling.

In the middle of the room, there was one of those furnaces that you would see in a blacksmith's shop. There were two men stoking the fire in it. It had to be very hot, because they were sweating profusely and each one had to walk away for a moment, to get a drink of water from a small barrel.

Everywhere he looked, the words of that had been said in the dungeon came back to him: "This place is brand new." No musty smells from long use. The floors were smooth and even. No signs of wear. The manacles and all the chains were new - no rust. Was it possible that a city this size, could all be so new?

He was taken to a spot in the room, where the manacles on his wrist were attached to one of the chains from the ceiling. He stared up at the chains wondering how long he would be here. Being attached to these ceiling chains, gave you no chance to sit or even kneel. As long as these chains were attached to you - you stand.

This room was like the other one with the grid. There was a central aisle and everyone was chained to the ceiling, facing the aisle. This one was different in that, for the first time since he had arrived, he saw women from Malantroi. The women were on one side of the aisle, men on the other and not one stitch of clothing on any of them. Some of them made feeble attempts at modesty, but in this position it was very difficult.

As he looked around, he was stunned by what he saw. He recognized virtually everyone hanging from the chains in this room. All of the council was here. The Governor, Sector Representatives and Sector Commandants. All of them except for Belziyd Pebodom, the one who had been thrown in the fire. All the members of the city elite and very possibly their family members.

He searched the faces frantically, looking for Temela. He finally spied her. She was sitting on a stone bench, on the back wall. She and two other women, who were further along in their pregnancy than she was. She looked pale and thin...and defeated. He desperately wanted to go to her and comfort her, but he knew that it was impossible.

He felt himself slipping into the same pit of lethargy. 'NO!' he thought. 'I must and will fight back. They will not break me. They have abused me, but I will have the final victory. I will remain strong...I hope.

There were still a lot of unoccupied chains. He could do nothing, but wait and watch, while they filled the other places in the room. Eventually, someone would get around to telling them something…even if it was something that the people of Malantroi did not want to hear.

He noticed that they were now bringing in a lot of people that he did not recognize. These people were being treated even worse than what Krezdon had suffered. These people had gags in their mouths. Instead of their wrist manacles being attached to the ceiling chains, these people were being attached to the ceiling with iron collars. Then he saw one of them he did recognize - the rat-faced slaver from the voyage. There was no mistaking those big bulgy eyes and that nose.

More people were hung up behind him. He was losing interest in looking at faces and trying to recognize them. His stomach was growling too much to concentrate on people.

He was surprised by silence. The chain rattling had ceased. He looked around and could not see any of the ceiling chains that was unoccupied. He also noticed that the guards seemed a little anxious.

Three men walked into the room. The guards that were in the room snapped to attention. He could not tell any difference in the uniforms of these three, and all the others. They were better groomed, but there were no other marks to distinguish them as superior in rank.

Several men came walking in. These men were dressed in very fine clothing. Several of them were carrying large blue binders. Krezdon cursed silently and clenched his teeth. The binders were the city census reports. The careful meticulous paperwork that had been done annually for over 300 years, was still going to be used against them.

The men continued on, ignoring all of the hanging people. They moved off to Krezdon's right and seated themselves behind some tables. They opened the binders and sat quietly.

Krezdon shook his head. More waiting. More not knowing what is going on. They just torture us like a cat with a mouse.

A new sound brought everyone's attention back to the main entrance. Four bare-chested men were moving a small stone table of some kind into the room. Two others were carrying what looked like a part of a framework for a building. There were large pieces of wood that formed an X, and four boards that connected them at the points.

Another man came in pushing some kind of covered cart. They moved all of their paraphernalia to the center of the room, near the furnace. The framework was placed next to the stone table. The cart was opened and two men pulled some wooden mallets, and some small rods out of it. The rods were about an arms length, and looked as if they were made of some kind of porcelain. Once they were set up, they just stood there...waiting.

Krezdon could hear another group, walking slowly through the rows, behind him. He was not sure who they were, and was afraid to look. He heard them make several trips back and forth before they finally got to his row.

The half-breed was the first one Krezdon saw. The Elf even more groomed since the last time Krezdon had seen him. He was dressed exactly the same as before in the black and red silks, along with the same weaponry. He looked totally disinterested in what was going on.

Then Krezdon got a little bit of a shock. Three Elfin women came into his line of vision. These three women had the exact same Elfin characteristics as the male, except for the beard. He noticed that their ears were virtually identical to the male. For one Elf to have ears like that, was a sign of being a half-breed. For four Elves to have the same characteristic, meant they were not of mixed blood. This was a specific race of Elves, but Krezdon had no idea which one. Only the Kalash were supposed to have the extremely tall ears.

The three women were dressed almost identically to the man. They all had black pants, black boots and black cape. The shirts were different: One woman wore a blue shirt and had blue lining on her cape, the second had a yellow shirt with yellow lining and the third had a green shirt with green lining to the cape. They all had that same strange, oversized hilt on some kind of dirk, strapped to their right legs. The hilt on each one was chained to the scabbard that it was in. Then he noticed that each one had a stone on a golden chain around their necks. The stones were the same colors as their shirts.

All four Elves seemed to be wandering among the chained people with no apparent interest in anything.

Then came another entourage. There were eight rather large men, who were tall and muscular. They appeared to be bodyguards for the last man in this group. This man was slightly taller than the half-breed (?). He had dark brown hair, and a very carefully manicured beard. He had a whimsical smile on his face as he looked at the faces of the prisoners. He was wearing some kind of small crown that was barely more than a ring around his head. His clothing was rather drab. Dull black boots, baggy gray pants, and a gray shirt. There was a sword hanging on his left hip, but judging from the jewels on the hilt, and scabbard, it was more or less ornamental.

Krezdon could not help staring. The man in the gray outfit looked very familiar. He had definitely seen this man before...but where and when?

The group continued down the line. When they arrived where Krezdon was standing, the man in gray stopped, looked Krezdon directly in the eyes, and his little smile turned into a huge grin. He snickered and walked on.

'He recognized *me*, thought Krezdon. 'I know, that I have seen him somewhere before, but…I cannot remember who he is.'

The prince or king or whatever he was, stopped in front of Goroben as well. Krezdon could not see the expression on the face of the gray man, but he did see a look of shock and confusion on Goroben's face. Now Goroben was looking around, confused, as if he were trying to remember where he had seen this man before.

To make matters worse, the man in gray stopped in front of Governor Poroby as well. Xuzo's reaction was identical to Goroben.

Krezdon started really digging into his memory now. 'This man recognized me, Goroben and Xuzo. He did not recognize the other men from the council. What do the three of us have in common that the others don't?' He started running over the history of each individual on the council. 'What was the common denominator?' He thought of each council member, when they were voted into their position, and what they had done since then.

'That's it. It's not what they have done since being on the council, but when they were placed in their position. Goroben had been the Sector Seven Commandant for over 15 years. Xuzo had been the Council Representative, Sector Three for 10 years before being placed in the Governor's seat. I have been a member for just over 4 years. No one else has been on the council, longer than any of us…

except the women. There were six women on the council. Who has been here the longest? Three of them were Representatives, three of them were Sector Commandants.'

He looked over where the women were. He was trying to remember when each one was posted to their position. Pamema Broofon was the only woman that had been on the council, longer than he had.

'The group has not inspected the women yet. I'll watch when he gets to Pamema. If his reaction to her is the same, then that will be the proof I need for…what?'

Something before all the others were elected to the council, between three and four years ago. There had been so many things happen, so many people he had come in contact with…

He watched the group as they finished the inspection of the men. They walked casually and silently across the room to the women, and continued the monotonous tour of the prisoners.

When they got to where Pamema was standing, all doubt was removed. The man in gray and Pamema recognized each other. Her memory was better than Krezdon's, because as soon as she got over her initial shock, she nearly shouted: "Fendina!"

All he could do was stand there and think about that murder: 'Must I be haunted to my grave by the people involved in that fruitless investigation?'

Before Krezdon could think of anything else, he and everybody else were put in a state of shock and reality by what they saw. Fendina's expression changed instantly to anger at the mention of the name. He made some kind of signal to one of his bodyguards. The man walked up to Pamema and made a nearly successful attempt at ramming his fist completely through her head. The blow was so violent, that as her head snapped back, her feet came completely off the floor and then she hung limp.

Fendina looked at the Elf, nonchalantly. "Wake her up, will you?"

The Elf sighed. The red stone at his throat sparkled, and Pamema came back to consciousness. Almost half of the left side of her face was already swollen, and starting to turn different colors.

"My name is *not* that heinous sound," he shouted. "I am Prince Zebyuro Progerom." (Prince?). "I am a Prince of Oosam. From now on, anyone of you who calls me anything other than: Prince Zebyuro, Your Majesty or Master, will be severely punished. Is that clearly understood?"

The statement left a definite mark on everyone in the room.

Now there were several more questions running through Krezdon's head. Where does he come up with the idea of calling himself a Prince? Could there have been that much wealth, in those three chests? What else is there, that we do not know about…Zebyuro? What did he mean by the term - Master?

Fendina, or Zebyuro, or whatever his name is, calmed himself, and continued the inspection. The smile was gone. He was moving faster, and paying less attention to the victims hanging from the ceiling. He went to a large ornate chair located behind the tables, and sat down. The bodyguards formed a semicircle behind him.

The Elf nonchalantly walked to the center of the room. He picked up one of the small rods on the stone table, and inspected it. He gave some quiet instructions to the men around the table. They cleared the other rods off the table and placed them in a storage box. He looked back at Zebyuro, and raised his eyebrows in a questioning manner.

"Well, Soolchakan," said Zebyuro, "let it begin."

Soolchakan turned toward the men. He glanced around briefly, then pointed.

Krezdon was not sure who the Elf was pointing at, but was sure he would find out soon. Two of the men, that had brought the equipment into the room, headed in the direction the Elf was pointing. Krezdon heard some chains rattling behind him. Somebody growled a protest, and was then dragged by the two men, to the center of the room.

"You fools don't know who you are messing with," shouted the prisoner. "I'll have all of you on the block! I may even buy you myself, and really put you in your place…!"

The red stone on the Elf's neck sparkled again, and the shouting stopped. The prisoner made some desperate attempts at opening his mouth, but was unable to do so.

The guards were attempting to chain the struggling prisoner to the framework, and not having very much luck.

Once again, that wretched little red rock sparkled to life. This time however, it did not just do a quick twinkling and then go out. It flared to an almost blinding point, bathing the entire room in crimson.

The glare died down and the only "red" glow left, was a strange aura that surrounded the prisoner. He stood frozen inside the shimmering cocoon. He offered no resistance as the guards chained him, spread eagle on their rack. As soon as he was locked in place, the glow vanished. The prisoner looked around, somewhat dazed. When he realized where he was, his expression changed to raw hatred as he glared at Soolchakan.

Prince Zebyuro spoke up: "You are Torson Nohorok. You are a professional slaver. You will tell us the names of all your associates, your raids, your home port, your safe havens, your crewmembers and anything else dealing with your illegal and immoral activities."

Torson glared back at the Prince. "As soon as I have you in chains, I'll piss in your face. Every time I have a bowel movement, I will make you clean my ass with your tongue!"

Zebyuro looked at Soolchakan: "Proceed," he said calmly.

The stone table was moved in front of Torson. They positioned it so that it was touching his legs. Soolchakan's stone flared up, and the short legs on the table grew. It stopped growing as soon as the table top was level with Torson's groin.

Zebyuro looked at the ceiling: "Are you going to give us the required information, voluntarily?"

"I am going to enjoy having you as a slave," growled Torson.

"Continue!"

One of the guards took the porcelain rod from Soolchakan. He grabbed Torson's penis and shoved the rod up into it. Torson's face became a grimace of pain and hate. His attempt to fight the pain was successful, only in the fact that he did not scream.

"This is your last chance," said Zebyuro flatly. "Give us the required information, or suffer the consequences."

Torson grunted a few times, breathing hard. He mustered what little control he had left and said: "You are going to beg, for me to kill you. I will show you no mercy…"

Zebyuro sighed in exasperation and signaled.

Two of the big men picked up the wooden mallets. There was a collective gasp, and several screams, the loudest, of course, being Torson's, as they started the grisly demolition of his genitals.

Several of the hanging people fainted, many others vomited. There were those who winced from sympathetic pain, while others just stared in horror.

After a few dozen solid hits from the mallets, they stopped pounding. In that short time Torson had screamed himself hoarse. His weak screams continued for a few moments and died off to sobs.

The Elfin woman, dressed in the blue shirt stood up. She walked to the side of the room where the women were. The blue stone at her throat glowed and all of the women who had fainted were aroused. All those who were vomiting, stopped and looked around surprised.

The Elfin woman, dressed in yellow, did the same for the men's side of the room.

The woman in green, sat down at a table, and inked a quill, getting ready to start writing. The other two women joined her at the table and got quills ready as well.

Once again the red stone glowed. Torson was again cocooned in a red aura. The room became quiet. The only sound that could be heard was the hoarse sobs coming from Torson. Soolchakan, bowed his head, folded his arms and the glow in his stone faded.

One of the guards watched as the glow around Torson faded as well. As soon as it was gone, the guard placed the mallet in front of Torson on the table.

The guard leaned close to the prisoner. "Who are your associates?"

Torson did nothing but continue sobbing.

The guard glanced at Soolchakan. The Elf nodded, slightly.

The guard looked back at Torson. "What is your home port?"

Again he looked at Soolchakan and waited for a nod.

"What is your safe havens?"

This time it took a little longer time before the Elf nodded.

"Who are your crewmembers and where can we find them?"

The elf shook his head several time. Each time he shook his head, this question was asked again.

Krezdon noticed that as each question was asked, the three Elfin women were writing furiously on their papers. What could they possibly be writing about? The prisoner was not saying anything. What could be so important to them that they had to be writing something down now?

The answer to his questions came from a conversation behind

him. He looked back and saw the wizards from the city, all chained side by side. They were all staring dull-eyed in the direction of the torture. They would move their gaze (?) back and forth from the victim, to Soolchakan, to the three Elfin women.

"I think he is…reading that man's mind," said Nal.

"Yes," said Zenzorodan. "He *is* reading the man's mind…but how is he transmitting at the same time to the women?"

"He isn't," said Nytombul. "The women are reading his mind, and writing it down."

"But…you can't do that," said Nal. "You cannot possibly concentrate on mental reading, and scribble all that stuff down at the same time."

"I thought that you said that you couldn't do any magic," growled Krezdon.

"We can't do any major spells. Cantrips on the other hand, are very simplistic and they do not seem to be blocked," said Nal. "I think that they are allowing us to do the Cantrips so that we know just how powerful these four are."

"You're not paying attention to the aura," said Borip. "Look at the aura. The aura from the victim, to the Elf has a silvery shimmer to it. The aura from him to the women…it's different. It's not silvery, it's…white?"

"You're right," said Nal. "What kind of Elves are these? That white glow…means that it is an inborn trait. They are not using magic, as we know it. They are using racial capabilities."

Nytombul's gaze changed from the dull look to shock. "It

can't be," he whispered. "No…they're supposed to be…extinct."

Nal looked at Nytombul. "What are you babbling about?"

"I have studied the histories…what I can find, about all the Elfin races. There were, in fact, three races of Elves who were tall-eared: The Kalash, the Teltermak and the Owlam. The Kalash are around today and they travel about quite a bit. The Teltermak and the Owlam, were supposedly all killed off centuries ago. They were hunted down and killed because they had all kinds of inborn, racial magical skills that made them extremely dangerous."

Nal grunted slightly. "How can you be sure that these are not Kalash?"

"Because Kalash do not have any magical, racial capabilities. They are deadly in combat with swords, and second to none in archery…but they do not have any natural magical abilities. The Teltermak and the Owlam did…or do…depending on which race these four are."

"They're Owlam," whispered Borip. "The stones. I remember hearing of the stones. Those stones at their throats. That was a legend, in regards to the Owlam. Those old paintings from centuries ago, show tall-eared Elfin people. The paintings that were supposed to be Teltermak, all had hair that was anything from white to straw colored. These Elves have dark brown hair. They *are* Owlam!"

"No wonder we were undone, so easily," muttered Nal.

Krezdon felt a little sick. He was looking at living legends. A race of Elves that had been so dangerous that they had been hunted down, in a search and destroy system. *They* had allowed everyone to think that they were all dead, but in fact had just hidden. What was so important to them, that they came out of hiding? The issue of slavery? Was that the only reason they were here? He looked around the room helplessly. There were slavers, politicians and wizards hanging from the chains. He had no idea how many other occupations were here. He figured that he would find out in due time…maybe the hard way.

Soolchakan opened his eyes. He looked up at the Prince and shook his head.

"Remove the garbage," said Zebyuro.

While two of the guards removed Torson from the rack, two others were collecting the next victim. This one was even less enthusiastic about the rack than Torson had been. Three other guards had to help drag the new victim to the rack. Again they were aided by a glow from the red stone.

Krezdon recognized the next victim. Paratroy Keldigin, one of the slavers that had been in the hold, on the trip from Malantroi to…wherever here is.

The same questions were asked and the same results occurred. This time Krezdon was a little less in shock - at first. When the first victim had been dragged away, Krezdon had been too horrified to look. This time he saw the results of the rod and mallets. Now he lost what little there was in his stomach. The redesigning of the man's genitals had turned everything in his crotch to a stringy mass of bloody pieces of meat hanging between the man's legs.

A third victim was dragged to the center of the room. This one did not have any courage whatsoever. Before he reached the rack, he was sobbing and blabbering the information that had been asked for.

The three women were writing as fast as they could.

Soolchakan shouted at the blubbering prisoner. Everyone, including Zebyuro had to cover their ears: "One fact at a time, idiot! We need to get the information down correctly. As fast as you are going, all we're getting is gibberish." A deep thundering bass voice that reverberated from wall to wall, and left your ears ringing.

Krezdon still had hope of retribution. He tried to memorize as many things about the Elf that he could. He wanted to make sure that he remembered every little detail about this individual…just in case. He would definitely remember that voice. His ears hurt for at least three days after that shout.

The two guards took this prisoner to the table where the three women sat. They knocked him to his knees as soon as he got there. The one in blue asked the questions, while the other two continued writing.

After they finished with him, he was taken away, with his body, but not his dignity intact.

The next man who was brought up, was just like the first two. He allowed himself to be permanently maimed, rather than freely give the information. Krezdon wondered if they had any idea that the inquisitors were getting their information, telepathically.

The torture went on for quite some time. 57 men had been brought forward. 18 had given up the information and 39 had been mutilated.

All the other people hanging from the chains had nothing left in their stomachs, and somehow, each time someone fainted, a red, blue, yellow or green glow woke them up again.

Then they started on the women.

The first one they took up, had a savage look in her eyes. She was totally defiant. Why not, she did not have a penis that could be...rearranged. Krezdon almost found himself in a morbid state of curiosity, wondering what they were going to do to her. He did not have to wait very long.

The fire that had been in the furnace was still being stoked up. Now some of the guards were putting on large gauntlets and pulling red hot irons, and knives, out of the fire. As she was questioned, pieces of her skin were either burned or cut off. She tried desperately to keep up her taunting defiance, but was quickly losing the battle, each time another piece of skin, was thrown into a bucket. Then she lost her fingers and toes. Then she lost her breasts, ears, nose and a large portion of each hip.

Zebyuro looked at her whimsically. "Do you want to talk now?"

She shook her head violently. She tried to fight through the pain. After a little more of losing flesh, they stopped burning her. A guard held her chin up and started asking the questions. Again, Soolchakan, stood there with his head down and arms folded. Again, the women were quickly writing as each question was asked.

Zebyuro watched the women as they wrote. When all three stopped and Soolchakan looked up. He sat back and smiled. "I think that this one will be perfect for cleaning out the sewers."

"She's too tall," said Soolchakan flatly.

Zebyuro snickered. "And…?"

The woman in blue, got up from the table and walked up to Soolchakan. The two of them placed their stones together. The glow from the united stones turned purple. A purple beam came from them and hit the tortured woman. The chains fell off of her, and she fell to the floor in a moaning heap. She started screaming in agony, as what was left of her body, started changing shape. Her legs shortened to very short stubs. Her arms lengthened considerably.

"Let's see," said Soolchakan. "We need to do some adjustments on her back. Once that is done, she will fit through the sewage tunnels with no problems at all."

There were several loud popping noises and she arched her back each time a sound was heard.

Zebyuro again taunted her. "I take it, woman…that you are not going to talk at all?"

She again shook her head violently.

"Well, she does not want to use her tongue, wisely…I think that she has no need for it at all."

Another purple beam came from the stones. The woman gagged a couple of times and her tongue fell out of her mouth.

"Take that thing out on a leash," said Zebyuro.

They had obviously been prepared for this situation as well. A man in one of those familiar brown suits came in, with a leash and collar. He placed it around her neck and dragged her out. The strange croaking sounds that came out of her mouth haunted Krezdon for some time after that.

He noticed that there was a long pause as Zebyuro allowed the full effect of the spectacle to sink in. It was working. Several women were hyperventilating from panic. Others had to be re-revived several times in a matter of seconds, by that irritating red glow from the Elf's stone.

Zebyuro stood up and shouted triumphantly: "Bring on the next one!"

Soolchakan pointed. Krezdon could not see who was being pointed at specifically, but the whole room heard her ear splitting scream.

Two guards started dragging the blubbering, panic-stricken woman to the center of the room. Soolchakan gave a signal to them, and they hauled her over to the Elfin women.

This one took quite some time for the full questioning to be over with. Partially because she answered each question at least three times.

Krezdon shook his head. He realized what they were doing. First, select one that will probably not crack, under pressure or torture. Give that one the full gruesome treatment, for the best effect. Then get the ones that will crack the easiest.

The inquisitions had, so far, been limited to the slavers, and slave auctioneers. What did they have in mind for the rest of the people? Krezdon worried about that question for some time, while they questioned 12 more women.

By the time they had finished questioning the slavers and slave auctioneers, it was past sundown. There was no more feeling in any part of Krezdon's arms. His shoulders were pretty much out of it, as well. All the feeling was the pain in his feet, and the mental torture going on in his mind from the macabre scene that had taken place in front of him.

A group of brown suitors walked in with several large cauldrons and bowls, on large carts. They started going through the rows, giving a bowl of some kind of white glop to each prisoner. The chains seemed to lengthen and all of the people, that were hanging, were now allowed to sink to the floor.

When Krezdon got his, he was not sure that he could eat anything, after what he had witnessed. The smell of burned flesh, still hung heavily in the air.

He looked over at Temela. He noticed that the bowls that were handed to the pregnant women, had steam coming out of them. The women were blowing on it to cool it down. They were also sipping it slowly. All the other people in the room, were gulping down the contents of their bowls.

He grunted. Apparently they want the newborn babies to be healthy enough for…whatever.

He saw at least two dozen brown suits enter the room. They took all of the intelligence paperwork from that the Elfin women. They also carried the tables out.

Much to the relief of all the other prisoners in the room, the torture equipment was also removed. Other than the prisoners, the only people left in the room were Zebyuro, his bodyguards and the four Elves.

As soon as all the noises of moving equipment had subsided, all eyes went to Zebyuro. The Prince stood, clasped his hands behind his back and started a slow, nonchalant walk towards Soolchakan. The whimsical smile was back on his face. He stopped when he reached the Elf. He whispered something to Soolchakan, who merely shrugged and folded his arms.

He looked slowly around the room. Then started: "Good evening, ladies and gentlemen. Tonight is the end of a very expensive undertaking that was three years, in the planning and execution. We did a slave raid on your city. A very successful raid. We freed 59,641 people that you…pieces of garbage, had in bondage. We captured 33 slave ships that had another 7,192 illegally enslaved people. Then there was your slave auction building that had another 351 people that we have now given back their dignity and freedom.

We have now enslaved you. You, who dared to call yourselves, the masters and owners of other people.

In your city, there were 31,745 free citizens. We captured every one of them. Unfortunately, only 30,061 made it this far…alive. Before we took you in the raid, every citizen, age 20 or older, had at least one slave. In the case of your aristocrats, even some of your younger children had a slave. There were two cases where a four-year-old child owned a slave. How utterly moronic. Someone was so foolish, as to put the decision of life or death, over another living being, in the hands of a four-year-old child.

Your port city was a safe haven, for all slaver ships, going from anywhere to anywhere. We caught 33 in port. We were hoping for at least 20. 33 was a tremendous thrill. We did not take all the captains, first mates and navigators alive, but we did get the majority of them here.

One thing that was really disgusting about this safe haven bit, was how they paid their docking and re-supply fees. They did not pay with money, they paid with…" He rolled his eyes in disgust. "…merchandise!"

He looked around and sighed. "I know from your city census, that you had 59,641 people in slavery, inside your city limits. Do you know how many people were enslaved in your entire country? Does anyone here know? 59,641 in your city - 59,732 in your entire country. Does that tell you something? In your entire country, outside your city jurisdiction, there were only 91 slaves. Over 99% of all slaves abused and misused by one city."

"Excuse me…uh…your Majesty."

Krezdon looked over to the voice, a little stunned. It was Governor Xuzo, who had spoken up. 'Maybe I should have spoken up,' he thought. 'This was an attack and thus a military endeavor. No, just listen, find out from his bragging and be ready to act.'

"Who…oh…the illustrious Governor of Malantroi. Of course, you are not a Governor anymore, are you?" He laughed menacingly. "What do you want, *slave*?"

Krezdon could tell that Xuzo was angry. He also knew that Xuzo was a careful diplomat, (just like any boot-licking bureaucrat), who was good at controlling his temper…in front of strangers…or royalty.

"What of retribution…Your Majesty? A raid of this size, on a major port city, is bound to force our King to strike back, with full force against you."

Zebyuro looked at Xuzo, mocking awe. "Your…King? His most Royal Majesty, Suntram Ryana? He will not lift a finger to assist you." He started walking around with a triumphant air about him. "Two days before we struck, we sent an Ambassador to King Suntram. He was fully informed of everything we were going to do. If he wants to be isolated from the rest of the world, he will strike back. If he wants to break off all alliances, even with two of his cousins, and a sister, who are themselves, monarchs, he will strike back. If he wants to save his own self-righteous buttocks…he will do nothing."

"What are you talking about? King Suntram, cannot let this mockery of justice go unpunished."

"It was a mockery of justice, allowing your city to exist! The safe haven, and home, of not just slave merchants, but assassins as well."

Xuzo stood there with his mouth hanging open in shock. He shook his head to get both oars back in the water. "No…that…uh… that coven was destroyed! Lord Krezdon, exposed that coven, several years ago. Yes, we have slave merchants. Slavery is legal in many countries. But…assassins? There is no way that we could have possibly allowed another assassin's coven back into Malantroi."

Zebyuro gave him a menacing smile. "Do you think for one moment, that I would possibly make a charge like that, without proof? If I could not prove it, King Suntram would have already taken the steps, to declare war, and this city would be under siege, right now!"

"What…what proof? It…uh…please…I…uh."

"24 years ago, the Queen of Oosam died in a mysterious manner. Queen Senseea, heavy with child at the time, left her bedchamber, without the escort of her ladies, or nurses or midwife. She fell down a flight of stairs. During the tragic fall, she suffered two unexplainable injuries. The first one was the fact that her skull was crushed. According to the physicians, in order for there to be that much damage, to the skull, it would have required a suicidal dive, head first, down the stairs. There were pieces of her brain, skull and skin on the very top step. In a normal fall, she should have completely missed that particular one. The physicians also said that the…" He cleared his throat. "…indention in her head, was the wrong shape, for that type of injury."

"So it was a freak occurrence that caused…"

"SILENCE!" Zebyuro glared at Xuzo. "I am not finished, idiot! I have barely begun."

"I beg your pardon, your Majesty."

"As well you should. Anyway, the only way she could have suffered that massive an injury, would be a fall over a balcony, landing head first on some kind of circular railing. That would have also broken her neck. Her neck was intact."

He cleared his throat. "The other injury was a large puncture, directly into her womb. That puncture, *any* puncture of that nature, is impossible during a roll down a flight of stairs. It had to have been done, with a large pointed weapon."

Zebyuro walked up and got right in Xuzo's face. "The head wound killed the Queen; the puncture killed the child. Absolutely a murder…but no murderer ever found. No motive could be found either."

He backed away, walked around a little and sniffed. "King Tooron, needed an heir. He had to get married again. By some miracle, a Duchess from Eang named Amrona Telshawin was available... immediately. She was there, she was willing, and she was ready to become the new Queen, console the King in his grief and start on a new heir, *now*. Two months later, they were married, and she quickly became pregnant. She bore two children for King Tooron: One son, one daughter."

He stopped again and closed his eyes. "A little less than 11 years later, the King was found with a dagger, rammed into his forehead. The Queen, the Prince and the Princess...vanished. No clues. No leads. No reason why. Not a trace. One dead, three disappeared. Why? How? Those people who are supposed to do that divination and see what happened said that it was all somehow blocked...magically or...the gods ignored it."

He fiddled with one of the rings on his fingers. "24 years ago, slavers had raided the shores of Lower Oosam. In a six day period, 31 villages were swept clean of over 13,000 people. As a result of these raids, King Tooron, with firm resolve, put forth an edict, for the complete eradication of slavers and slavery. 2 days later Queen Senseea is dead. 63 days later King Tooron is married to Queen Amrona, who spends the next 11 years, using every method she can think of, to stop the King from enacting that edict. 3 days after he orders the Oosam military to make the destruction of slavery *the* top priority, the King is dead...and his edict dies with him."

He looked as if he were fighting back tears. "No one knows who killed the King. No one knows who kidnapped the rest of the royal family…until now."

He looked back in the general direction of the men. "Amrona Telshawin, which, by the way, is not her real name, was and still is a professional assassin. She is possibly a slaver as well. She was hired by the slavers, to stop King Tooron from carrying out his edict. Stop him by persuasion or extortion if possible. If that didn't work…kill him. Kill him and destroy his entire family line."

He looked up at the ceiling and then his gaze went towards the women. "She, being a sound believer in profiteering on healthy slave flesh, rather than killing the children, she sold the anti-slave King's children…into slavery. She sold the two children - her own children…into slavery, in her real home: Malantroi."

His gaze went back and forth, over all the women. "During her lifetime, she has used a lot of money and influence, to pay wizards, for the spells that keep her young and beautiful. This way no one would know her on sight, because they would be searching for someone… much older."

He started walking among the women. "Her mistake there was that she only stayed youthful. She did not have them alter her appearance, enough to not be recognized…by her own son…in Malantroi."

He had been walking slowly through the lines of the women. Now he stopped in front of a woman in the third row. He did not move for several moments. The woman refused to meet his gaze.

"The woman who murdered my father…the woman who sold me and my sister into slavery."

He gave a signal. Two of his bodyguards went up to the woman, unhooked her and dragged her to the center of the room.

She was definitely different than the other women, or the men for that matter. There was no fear in her eyes. Instead there was nothing but glaring hatred. Her jaws were clenched tightly in defiance. The same defiance and hatred Krezdon had seen on the faces of most of the slavers.

Zebyuro looked around. "Do you want some proof? Do you want to have absolute proof? I am not just spouting idle words. I will show you, what your King Suntram already knows. I will show you why your King will do nothing."

He looked at Xuzo and then Krezdon. "It became necessary to imprison the entire city, in order to find out, exactly how many citizens were involved in the assassin's coven."

He looked back at his mother. "This woman assassinated a King, and possibly the Queen. No monarch, anywhere in the world, would stand by your King Suntram, if it got out that he stopped me from doing the noble thing. I am destroying a coven that was responsible for killing a King, a Queen and unborn Prince or Princess. Now, you will see…absolute proof."

One of the guards left the room.

'This is crazy,' thought Krezdon. 'The only way they could prove it, is with one of those wretched little stink boxes.'

While Krezdon was pondering, the bodyguard returned, escorting an elderly man…who was carrying one of those rancid little truth boxes.

While the old man started the necessary preparations on the truth box, Zebyuro started orating again. "Some of you may not recognize this woman. She was a recluse most of the time, but she did show herself, occasionally, among the upper class. You may know her as: Lady Aboreema Keldigin."

Krezdon nearly collapsed. Keldigin! Could it be possible? Is she related to the slaver Paratroy Keldigin? He had not even considered it until now, but $1+1=2$.

Zebyuro continued: "She is the sister, of one of the slavers, we talked with, earlier. I don't know if her brother is part of the coven, but we intend to find out."

He smacked her in the back of her head. She ended up flat on the floor. She tried to get up, and was very rudely stopped. "Stay on your hands and knees," growled Zebyuro. "*That* is the perfect position for you."

The old man had the truth box ready. Krezdon was grateful for the size of the room. For once he would see the foul smelling thing in operation, without having to choke on the fumes.

Aboreema looked at the box and then faced the floor. She made some kind of strange squawk and then spit out a rather large portion of her tongue.

Zebyuro sighed and shook his head. "Soolchakan, can you do something to remedy her stupidity?"

Soolchakan picked up the tongue. Aboreema made an attempt at backing away. Soolchakan looked up at the Elfin women. "Bonarain, can you give me a little help?"

The Elf in blue, grasped the stone at her throat. It started glowing blue and blue beams shot out of Bonarain's eyes, at Aboreema. Aboreema froze in place.

Soolchakan looked up at the women again. "Kiyalee?"

The woman in yellow came up behind Aboreema. She placed her hands on either side of Aboreema's face. Kiyalee's stone glowed yellow. The glow went to her hands and Aboreema opened her mouth.

Soolchakan looked up at the last Elfin woman. "Chyning? This may be a little tricky…" He shrugged.

Chyning came over and knelt in front of Aboreema. Soolchakan knelt next to Chyning. He placed the tongue, back in Aboreema's mouth. Both Chyning and Soolchakan then held two fingers in Aboreema's mouth. Soolchakan's stone glowed red, and Chyning's stone glowed green. They sat there for several moments like this and then both got up. Kiyalee took her hands away from Aboreema's mouth and then all four of the Elfin stones stopped glowing.

Aboreema looked up at the Elves with sheer hatred in her eyes.

"We have cast a little spell on you," said Chyning. "With this spell, you will not be able to pull that stunt again."

Zebyuro walked up next to Soolchakan. "She might not be too cooperative in answering questions."

Soolchakan scoffed. "What do you suggest, Majesty?"

"Some simple persuasion…some kind of physical agony…if she refuses to answer."

"No problem," said Soolchakan, as he glanced at each one of

his Elfin colleagues.

"Very good." Zebyuro glared at Aboreema. "Are you a member of an assassin's coven?"

She turned her face away from him. For a moment nothing happened. Everyone in the room was expecting one of the stones to start sparkling. Instead, Bonarain made a few strange gestures. Aboreema arched her back and gagged. Her body shuddered several times until she let out a long moan. She made several desperate attempts at fighting the pain. Finally she collapsed on the floor sobbing and giving up a weak: "Yes."

Zebyuro chuckled. "Now, that wasn't so difficult, was it? Let's try another question: How many other assassins are...were... there in Malantroi?"

"None," she said in a small voice.

Zebyuro's head snapped to look at the truth box. The smoke remained a bright blue. He opened his mouth to say something, but checked himself. He cleared his throat and regained his composure. "So, you were the only representative of your coven, in Malantroi?"

She fought hard to not say anything. Both Bonarain and Kiyalee were now making gestures. Aboreema started writhing on the floor. The two Elf women stopped their movements, and Aboreema lay there panting. "No!"

"Where are they?"

She clenched her fists and tried to cover her face. All three Elfin women started doing identical gestures. Aboreema screamed in agony. "They are...on their way...to...Blasinigen...for a meeting."

"When did they leave?"

"Four days…before….your raid."

Zebyuro cursed. He looked at his bodyguards. "Homborik! Send a dispatch to…uh…whoever the King of Paselter is. Tell him… or her…of this gathering. Unfortunately, by now, the meeting could be over."

One of the bodyguards saluted and departed.

Zebyuro looked back at Aboreema. "Did you murder, Queen Senseea?"

She smiled. She clenched her teeth to fight the pain. The gestures made by the Elfin women became more animated. Aboreema screamed over and over. She was again, writhing on the floor, clutching at her stomach. She tried not to answer, but finally said "yes," several times.

Zebyuro snickered. "You are only making it harder on yourself. The truth will eventually come out."

She glared up at him panting. "I should have killed you too," she spat.

"Temper, temper," he snickered again. "Idle threats will get you nothing. Now, did you act alone, or was there some assistance?"

She gasped. She made an attempt at fighting the pain again and took a swipe at the truth box. Soolchakan made a quick gesture. Her hand shot back so fast that she slapped herself in the face and bloodied her nose. She did her best to stifle several screams, but once again ended up writhing on the floor, sobbing and shouting something in a foreign language.

"I speak Eangese, as well," said Soolchakan. He turned to Zebyuro. "She said that there were two accomplices."

"Really?" Zebyuro smiled. "Were either one of them in your coven, in Malantroi?"

She started crying. "One of them is dead." She tried to keep from speaking again, but could not keep fighting. She shouted something else in another foreign language.

"My, my, my, we are well versed in other tongues, aren't we?" Soolchakan shook his head. "That language isn't spoken anywhere, except for a few small villages in northern Tuvalow. She said that the other one has been condemned to life at the Turgon wall...for attempting to steal the crown jewels, in Agrosha."

Zebyuro was not prepared for the last statement. He let out a loud guffaw that turned into a giggling binge. He made several attempts to stop laughing, but kept going for several moments. He finally laughed himself out, wiped tears from his eyes and said: "Well, we should find out who..."

"We'll find out later," said Soolchakan. "There can't be too many prisoners at the Turgon wall, who have tried to steal royal possessions. Plus, she said that he was sentenced to life. He's not going anywhere."

"You're right, my friend. We don't want to get off the subject." He glared down at Aboreema again. "Let us continue with the death of King Tooron. Were you involved in that assassination, as well?"

"Of course, you idiot!"

"Keep that up and you might change my mind, about your

punishment. Now, how many helped you with that crime?"

"No one! I enjoyed doing that one, all by myself."

"That figures. Who helped you, in kidnapping my sister and myself?"

"My brother."

Zebyuro looked around at all the people still hanging. "There you are, you vermin. Your city was the refuge for an individual who assassinated *and* kidnapped members of a royal family. King Suntram would be a fool, to give you any assistance at all."

Goroben broke his silence. "Your Majesty, you have the confession you wanted. I can understand, the arrest of this assassin and her coven, but how can you possibly use that as justification for keeping the rest of the Malantroi populace in bondage? I can understand King Suntram's cooperation concerning the assassination, but not the enslavement of the rest of the city. Surely he would have to make some kind of retributive strike, for the sake of the innocents."

Zebyuro smiled. "I promised, King Suntram, that we would not attack any other city, town, village or farm. I informed him that of the people who were enslaved in Malantroi, some 80% of them were originally citizens of Oosam. I also informed him, that I could muster some 60% of the Oosam navy, whose sole purpose would be a complete naval blockade of your entire coastline. I have promises, from several other countries: Promises that they will assist in this blockade. Enough ships to form a military wall around your country. This would cause an economic catastrophe in a very short time."

He smiled and walked up to Goroben. "I had ten years, to

observe the city, and make plans. Then three years to set up the execution of the plan. I also have the assistance of four of the most powerful wizards in the world."

"Yes, your Majesty, you have planned and executed well. No flaws that I can see...so far. What I wonder about is...how you justify keeping us as slaves, in a country, where slavery is illegal."

"A simple definition. You will be treated as slaves. You will be called slaves. On paper...*on paper*, it will be called prosecution and punishment of criminals, for numerous crimes, against Oosam and humanity."

Soolchakan spoke up. "The trials have already taken place. You have all been found guilty, of a variety of charges. You have all been sentenced to life."

"Yes," said Zebyuro. "We are going to give you the privilege and ecstasy, of the life - and death - you gave to so many other victims. Now, it is our turn. Now, we are in charge. You are now the servants. You will now enjoy the life of absolute obedience. You will obey the slightest whim of your...owner, keeper...absolute master. It will not matter, how sick, how depressed, how tired or whatever. You must obey without question or delay. Imagine the joy of capital punishment... for the smallest of errors or delays. Imagine the exultation, when your master decides to flog you, for no reason at all...at least no reason that you know of."

A man off to the side screamed at Zebyuro. "You can't do this!"

Krezdon looked for the origin of the scream. 'Oh yes, Ahach Keez. Wouldn't you know, he'd be the one to say that?'

Ahach continued: "You have no right to do this to anyone of us. We are the government and nobility of the city of Malantroi. I can understand your enslavement of the peasants and riffraff...but not..."

"I was the Crowned Prince of Upper and Lower Oosam, when I was kidnapped and subjugated into slavery. My sister was the Crowned Princess Sanyee. You do not seem to be indignant about that. You are merely a Council Representative. Are you saying that your appointed rank, is higher than my birthright? If your wretched city can enslave me, why am I forbidden from enslaving you?"

"It...it's...not right," whimpered Ahach.

Zebyuro looked back at his bodyguards. "Let's show this slave, just exactly what is right."

Two big men marched to where Ahach was chained. They released the ceiling chains and dragged him to the center of the room. His whining protests were ignored. One of the bodyguards slammed Ahach to the floor, while the other produced a whip.

"You cannot do this," whined Ahach. "I am a..."

His words were cut off by the whip. Instead of protesting, Ahach was now screaming. Somewhere after the 20th stripe, Ahach passed out.

Zebyuro looked at Soolchakan. "Wake him," he said flatly.

The familiar sparkle from the red stone, and Ahach was awake. The beating continued. Each time Ahach passed out, Soolchakan used that magic in that stone, to reawaken Ahach. Each time the red sparkle lasted a little longer and got a little brighter. The light turned to an unwavering glow. The whip wailed it's morbid song about a dozen more times, before Ahach again lay silent. The glow went out.

Zebyuro looked down at the bloody mess. "Why don't you arouse him again?"

Soolchakan shrugged his shoulders. "I am not a god."

Zebyuro looked around at the desperate, shocked, woeful and panicked faces. "Does anyone else have a desire to question my rights or authority?"

The silence was broken only by a few quiet sobs and sniffling.

"Back to the business at hand," said Zebyuro merrily. "First, however, take that piece of buzzard bait, and dump it over the east wall."

The bodyguard that had wielded the whip, took hold of one of Ahach's ankles and dragged the body out of the room, leaving a trail of blood as he went.

Zebyuro smiled at Aboreema. She swallowed hard. "Lady Aboreema Keldigin. The first ten years of my life were good. For that, I will not sentence you to death."

Her eyes became wide with fear, in anticipation of what might come next. Her jaw started quivering a little.

Zebyuro's smile seemed to get bigger. "Soolchakan, what are your capabilities, as far as controlling her future actions?"

"That depends entirely on what you want. Certain people have strong wills, others have immunities that occur, either through intestinal fortitude, fear, stubbornness…or divine intervention."

"Can you make it…in some way…permanent or exceedingly

difficult for anyone to remove her...penalty?"

"That's the easy part."

"Excellent! What shall we do now? We should execute her for two murders, and two kidnappings, but that is too kind...too merciful. I think about the next ten years of my life, and I find I cannot be merciful. I cannot be lenient. I cannot allow a professional assassin to run free, or be with others, while she still has the mental capacity for murder. We must change her mind."

Soolchakan stood there for a moment with a pained look on his face.

"Are you ready?"

"A few moments, Your Majesty," said Soolchakan.

Soolchakan walked slowly towards Aboreema. She tried to crawl away. A quick sparkle from the stone, and she froze in place. He stood over the petrified woman. He closed his eyes and folded his arms. The three Elfin women joined him, encircling Aboreema.

Bonarain looked at Zebyuro. "You want us to alter her thinking process. You want her to be punished, know she is being punished, know why she is being punished and not be able to do anything about it." She sighed. "Is there anything else?"

"I may have to think of it as we go along. You sound as if it may be difficult, if not impossible," said Zebyuro.

"Give us a few moments," said Bonarain.

All four Elves took the gold chains from around their necks. They held the stones over Aboreema's head. The stones pulled themselves to each other and became one. They formed a small globe that started glowing. All four stones lost their original color, and the globe started shimmering with a golden light. The glow became so bright that it was painful to watch. It seemed to pulsate and make a humming sound. The bright light faded to something less painful to look at. The four Elves, themselves started to shimmer with light.

A voice came out of the circle of elves: **"What is it you want?"** No one could tell which one of the four had asked the question.

Zebyuro was rubbing tears out of his eyes. He cleared his throat. "She needs to lose the desire to kill."

"That cannot be changed."

"I want her to *not* be able to kill."

The shining coming from the elves started pulsating again. It seemed to jump from one to another in the circle, in a random manner. The strange voice spoke up: **"Henceforth, if she has a desire to kill, or hurt, it will cause her grievous pain. If she tries to hire a killer, or talk anyone into killing or causing pain, she will suffer agonizing pain."**

A beam came out of the globe and encircled Aboreema. She squealed in pain.

"Let's see," said Zebyuro. "She gave birth twice, that I know of. She did not love those children. She does not deserve to be the mother of any others."

"Complete sterilization." This time a dark bolt of electricity came out of the globe. She let out a long mournful moan.

"She has had her appearance magically adjusted."

"**That is a fact**."

"Can you make it permanent?"

"**It is already most of the way there. A minor adjustment will make it permanent**." Another beam from the globe and she gasped.

"She likes using her body, to accomplish her job. Look at her - she needs to be more attractive."

"**She does not need any more vanity**."

"No. A body that will turn men's heads. Her appearance must give men, almost incontrollable lust."

"**We have seen women with beguiling physical traits. We have found that the more physically attractive a woman is, the less humble she is, and the more demanding she is. Help us with this - as we are not sure exactly what you want**."

Zebyuro gave a slight grunt. "All right. Make her a little more top heavy."

All four Elves suddenly had a confused look on their faces. Multicolored beams went from one to another. Then, Aboreema's head started swelling.

"No, no, no," shouted Zebyuro. "I meant her breasts! Make her breasts larger. Larger but not too ostentatious."

Her head went back to normal, and her breasts started enlarging.

"Well, let's see." Zebyuro had a shocked look on his face as he watched. "…Uh…that's…incredible…the…uh…STOP…uh… wow." He looked away and cleared his throat.

"**What else?**"

"Uh…well, take a little off the waist and put it on the hips."

After this adjustment was done, the bodyguards seemed to be losing a little of their composure. There were also several of the male prisoners who were getting aroused at the spectacle. Some turned their heads and tried to hide their exposed genitals. There was a lot of biting of lips, clearing of throats and some staring at the ceiling. Others just let it happen as they gawked at her.

"**Is that what you had in mind?**"

"Uh…that'll work." Zebyuro cleared his throat nervously. "Uh…did you add something…uh…something more than just physical stuff?"

"**We assumed that you wanted a certain amount of physical allure in the equation. You did say 'something that would turn, men's heads'.**"

"Turn heads, yes! This will make them throw their necks out of joint."

"**Do you want us to lower the appeal?**"

"NO! No, no, no, no, no. That's perfect."

"**Anything else?**"

"Yes. Her attitude must match the desire that men will have for her. She must respond, in a way that they will…appreciate."

The voice sounded confused: "**She is already conceited.**"

"No! Make *her* have an uncontrollable desire for men."

"**That is going to take a major adjustment.**" Multi-colored beams came out of all four Elves, directed at Aboreema. Her facial expressions changed several times during the ordeal. A few beams of light shot out of the circle, flew around in a random manner and disappeared. Beams of light came out of the globe, their hands, their eyes and foreheads. "**Anything else?**"

Zebyuro looked momentarily startled. He had been dazzled by the light show that was going on. "Uh…how far does her desire go?"

"**All that a man has to do, is touch her, and she will do everything possible to please him. She will not let any man go away, disappointed.**"

"Touch her? Where?"

"**Anywhere.**"

"Good! She should also have no modesty whatsoever."

"**That's already done. What you have now is a totally immodest, nymphomaniac.**"

"The final touch: She should be totally immune to any and all of those nasty social diseases. We don't want her causing an epidemic."

Her entire body started glowing. When the glow faded, she looked like she was totally exhausted. "**Done.**"

"Oh, by the way, will she enjoy it?"

"**No. She will suffer physically if she does not go through with it. She will not feel anything good for or about herself. She**

will appear enthusiastic, but will not really enjoy it."

"Excellent! Now, my dear mother, who sold me and my sister Sanyee into slavery, will now be a love slave, for the entire palace garrison." He turned to his bodyguards. He looked for the one that had the most lust in his eyes. "Tharkon, take that woman to the barracks and introduce her to her new home."

The shimmering lights all faded from the Elves. The stones fell away from each other and went back to their original shapes. All four Elves looked a little worn out. They stepped back from Aboreema and she collapsed in place. She struggled to get up. She glared at Soolchakan and his colleagues.

The bodyguard in question smiled sheepishly. "Your Majesty... uh, you heard..."

"Don't worry! If you have to give her a full tour - do it."

"Tharkon's sheepish smile turned to a shameless grin. He almost ran to where she was laying. She looked as if she was getting ready to say something insulting and/or obscene. Tharkon touched he shoulder and she gasped. She tried to shrink away from his touch, with a look of horror on her face. She looked down at the floor stunned. She tried to crawl away, but then turned back, and got very personal with him and looked as if she was going to do something sexual, right here and now. He reached down, picked her up and carried her out of the room.

"Good-bye, dear mother, and have fun in your new job." Zebyuro stood there with a huge smug smile on his face.

As Tharkon carried her out of the room, a new group of ten

bodyguards came in. They all gave Aboreema a fast glance as they passed by. The bodyguards that were still in the room, all looked at Zebyuro with their eyebrows raised.

Zebyuro looked at the new shift. "Ah, the changing of the guards. Right on time. You gentlemen, who have been on duty, can now go…and indulge yourselves. You gentlemen, who are just coming on duty, will find out later, what has just happened."

Soolchakan glanced around the room at all the other prisoners. "Do you have anything else in mind, for any of these other people?"

"Why?"

"If you don't need us anymore, we have other things that we need to get done."

"No, that will be all, for now, and thank you very much."

As the Elves left, Zebyuro once again turned his attention to the other prisoners hanging in the room. "The auctions to sell all of the other citizens of Malantroi have already been done. That is why you people…the elite, have had to wait so long. The auctions to sell all of you, to your masters, will start tomorrow. Tomorrow, you will begin a life…or lack thereof as the garbage that you are. He headed for the door with his fresh shift of bodyguards. Just before getting to the door, he turned back: "Have a wonderful day, all of you." He left the room chuckling.

Krezdon heard the wizards talking behind him.

"That is them," said Borip. "They are Owlam. All of what I have heard: The stones, the swords, the immense power. Those four *are* the ones from those legends. I…thought they were a myth. What we have seen in front of us today, are *the* four most powerful wizards to ever walk this planet."

"I would love to be able to just sit there and listen to them talk of history," said Nal. "It is rumored, that they are older than the Turgon Wall."

"We were captured by an invading army," said Zenzorodan. "Those four: Soolchakan, his wives, Bonarain, Kiyalee and Chyning, could have taken our entire city, by themselves. We never had a chance."

"It doesn't make sense though," said Nytombul. "What do they hope to gain from this venture? What I have heard of the rare species of Elves...they usually do not get mixed up in the affairs of others. They stay to themselves. Why are they involved in this?"

Krezdon shook his head. 'What difference does it make.' he thought. 'They got involved, here we are, and we're doomed to life as slaves.'

14

The next day gave Krezdon the full taste of bitter defeat. He was hauled up on to a platform, naked. He heard people shouting bids. He heard an auctioneer taking the bids. He did not hear the final bid. He was taken away, with an iron collar around his neck, being dragged on the end of a leash.

He was taken to a fish market. Here he was shown what would be the rest of his life. Here are fish. The fish are to be prepared for the market. Cut, skin, gut and clean the fish. Many fish are cleaned one way. There are certain special ones that are cleaned a different way. Some are dangerous, if they are still alive. Some are dangerous, even if they are dead. Some have poison glands that have to be carefully removed, otherwise, you contaminate the whole thing. Others have certain internal organs that have to be kept for physicians and wizards.

It did not matter to Krezdon. All of the fish stink.

In the morning, you cut, gut and clean the night catch. In the evening, you cut, gut and clean the day catch. All those fish.

He pretended that each of the fish was his master: Trovoson Nykochosk. That way, when he brought the cleaver down to decapitate the fish, it was one clean swift cut. Do the same with the tail. The first few days, he had made several mistakes, because he had never done anything like this in Malantroi. There were numerous scars on his back, because of those mistakes.

The main point that Zebyuro had tried to put across, was

what it was like to be a slave. Living through the daily horror, that the smallest mistake was answered with massive retribution. Fine! Lesson learned. Now you have to learn it over and over again, each day.

Back in Malantroi, he had been able to celebrate the High Holy Days, the holidays and take a few days off, here and there. Here, he had no idea what day, month or year it was. Even on a holiday, people still had to eat. That meant, there was no break as far as preparing the fish was concerned.

There were nine other men in this fish factory. Krezdon and seven others had been here since the auction. He did not know where the ninth man came from...or when. Two died after some time. They had been replaced during the past... (?) how ever long it had been.

The only time, that any of them had been taken away from the monotony, of massacring fish, was when the master had taken them off somewhere for breeding. He tried to remember how many times he had been dragged off for the mating business. He had been taken to the same place each time. No matter how tired he was, he had been ordered to perform. Sometimes, it had been difficult, but with that whip hanging over you, you found a way.

One of the things he wondered about was: Why did they have to do it in such a cold manner? He had no idea who the woman or women, he had mated with were. Each time, the woman had been on her hands and knees. Most of her body had been hidden under a large dark cloth. The only part of her body that was exposed, was the part necessary for breeding. From what he could guess, she did not know who she was being bred with either.

Fish chopping, eating, sleeping and occasional forced sex. No change in any of this doldrums for however long he had been here.

He might have been able to tell how many years he had been here, if the seasons would change. In Malantroi, there were four seasons. Here, the weather was either raining and hot, cloudy and hot or clear and hot.

He had no idea who was still around. He had heard nothing about anyone on the council, or their families…or his family, for that matter. He had not seen a single one of them since the auction.

15

Krezdon woke up to the shock of being drenched with water. He looked up at Trovoson in complete confusion. This had never happened before. Normally he was awakened with a club, a kick or a lash.

"The Prince has ordered your presence, today," growled Trovoson. "Get your filthy butt up and get it cleaned. Don't want you stinking up the palace."

The normal routine was broken. It was usually get up relieve yourself, do what you could to work the kinks out of your muscles, eat…some…unrecognizable slop, then go chop fish.

He was flabbergasted. 'A Bath? Go to the Palace? Why? What new torture has the Prince come up with now?'

Something was definitely going on, but he had given up hope, a long time ago.

He was led to a real bathtub. Normally, he would clean himself, using cold water out of a rain barrel. This was clean water, and it was slightly warm. He wished he could have time to enjoy it, but he better not push his luck.

He finished cleaning, and got up to drip dry. He swallowed hard. The memories flooded back. During the trip, they had played some cruel mental games. They would give something and then take away, then give and take again. They gave a little and took a lot. What are they going to take today?

He wiped the moisture off his body, and tried not to think about the misfortunes.

"Hurry up, fool," shouted Trovoson. "We haven't got all day."

Krezdon went to the door, expecting to be hooked up to the leash. Instead, Trovoson threw some clothing at him.

"Put that on, fool!"

Now, he was completely perplexed. Clothing? Trovoson was not as angry as he usually was. Impatient, yes, but not angry. Why?

Trovoson saw Krezdon's puzzlement. "Do you plan on keeping the Prince waiting all day?"

"Uh, no master, I…no."

He put the clothing on. After all this time, wearing nothing but a loincloth, the clothing felt strange and itchy. Yes, he knew something was coming, and he would probably not like it.

After putting the shirt and trousers on, Trovoson handed him a pair of sandals. He looked at them dumbfounded. He was not sure what to do with them, until Trovoson slapped him in the face with one of the sandals.

After getting completely ready, he was surprised when he realized that the clothing fit very well. The sandals chafed his feet a little, but they were the correct size as well. This was getting interesting, as well as frightening.

Krezdon walked to the front door. Trovoson was waiting there with a brush. He threw the brush to Krezdon.

"Here, make yourself presentable."

Krezdon took the brush and walked up to a mirror, near the door. Something else new - he had not looked at his reflection in a mirror since… He looked helplessly at the hollow-eyed, skinny apparition staring back at him from the mirror. "Oh, gods, what is that?"

"That's you, stupid. Now brush that mop and duster."

Easier said than done. He had to work on several dozen snarls, tangles and knots, throughout his hair and beard. The painful quest for a neat appearance was finally over. He sighed, put the brush down and presented himself, to his master.

"Oh well, it'll have to do. Let's go."

As Trovoson headed out the door, Krezdon was again surprised by the fact that there was no leash. He looked at the leash hanging on the wall. He had never been able to go anywhere, without that leash. Trovoson had never forgotten the leash before. He shook his head and followed.

Trovoson was walking ahead in a hurry. Krezdon had to really move in order to keep up. He spent most of his time at the chopping table, so walking was not that familiar anymore. He followed, obedient, bewildered, scared and intrigued.

As they walked to the Palace, he noticed several other odd things going on. They passed the familiar fish market, but there was no activity going on there. No selling or buying, only other people, dressed the same as Krezdon: Brown shirt, brown pants, sandals and the iron collar. They were all being led, by someone…without any leashes. All of them were headed to the Palace.

He could not even think in complete sentences now. His hands were sweating profusely.

They arrived at the outer gate. There were several lines of people. It was easy telling the difference between the masters and the slaves: The iron collars. The owners were reporting in and departing. The slaves were being led inside the gates. Once inside, they were being separated and led in different directions.

Once again he was trying to find a conclusion to the mystery but felt that it would be better to just see what happened as it happened. Probably the same however, they are going to give something and then take away even more.

Trovoson finally reached the table and reported in. He talked quietly with one of the Palace Guards.

The guard checked something in a large book, snickered and nodded. He motioned to another guard, who came up to the first one. They talked quietly in each other's ears and then the new guard motioned to Krezdon. "You! Come here. Let's go."

Krezdon looked at Trovoson who pointed to the guard and said: "Move it!"

There was a large lump in his throat. He readied himself and followed. One step at a time, no matter what kind of pit he stepped in, or how shaky his legs.

He was led into a large room that looked hideously familiar. He looked up at the ceiling. No chains or rings to hook them too. Well, they had had plenty of time to remove the wretched things.

There was furniture though. Several long tables with bench

seats. The guard led him to the end of the central table and told him to sit down.

There was a haggard looking, white haired man with dark skin, sitting across from him. The man sat there placidly with a sad look on his face. Krezdon, on the other hand, was a nervous wreck. He was drenched with perspiration, his hands were shaking, he was having trouble breathing and he still had an elephantine lump in his throat. He did not know whether to throw up, dirty his pants, chew on the table or spit.

He looked closer at the old man. The man who was staring down at the table top, seemed oddly familiar. Krezdon searched his memory for a few moments until it hit him: "Goroben," he whispered.

The old eyes looked up slowly. They were still clear as they had always been. His brow furrowed slightly and then he smiled. "Krezdon," he said softly. "It's been a long time."

"What do you think is going on here?"

"I don't know. I am too old to be frightened by anything, anymore. They've done their worst and I'm still alive. I'm probably alive, due to the fact that my master did everything he could to kill me, and I'm just too stubborn to give him the pleasure."

Goroben's tranquility was contagious. Even though Krezdon knew that Goroben was nearly twice as old, he seemed the same: Hard-headed.

They conversed for a while. Not much to talk about: Krezdon chopping fish and Goroben working as a stable hand, and how long have we been here - I have no idea - what happens now - who knows

- wish I knew what was going on here - we'll find out soon enough.

They heard footsteps. A guard came in leading a pregnant woman. She looked tired…and she looked familiar.

Goroben smiled again. "Ah yes, our Sector 6 Representative, Tansiki."

She looked up puzzled. She glanced back and forth at the two men. Then she smiled and nodded.

During the next hour, several other people were brought in. Maniki, wife of Hebtezz Nosso, Sector 3 Representative. Tethtorm, husband of Sintiyna Azareemon, Sector 4 Commandant. Nem, wife of Daznak Siytiloran, Sector 1 Representative. Sestenya, wife of Gorvernor Xuzo Poroby. Trenya, wife of Ahach Keez, Sector 4 Representative. Desdeena Byharton, Sector 5 Commandant. Shashy, wife of Piromin Dezelba, Sector 2 Commandant. Pemema Broofon, Sector 5 Representative. Nayna, Goroben's wife.

When Nayna sat down next to her husband, they had a very tearful reunion. The others in the room were all now suffering from the anxiety about their own spouse. Trenya had been there, when her husband, Ahach had been beaten to death. Krezdon also remembered the cold-blooded death of Belziyd Pebodom. He wondered if Belziyd's wife Steesha was still around.

More people came in. Daninya, wife of Takariy Jebshon, Sector 1 Commandant. Krev, husband of Tansiki Chondok (a very nervous reunion, due to her pregnancy). Daznak Siytiloran, Council 1 Representative (again a husband meeting his pregnant wife Nem). Kavondo, husband of Deshdeena Byharton, Sector 5 Commandant (another husband greeting a pregnant wife).

Krezdon did not give up hope on Temela. She was 15 when the raid had imprisoned them all. She had been pregnant then…probably now as well, seeing as how virtually all of the other women were in the family way. He figured, that if they had been here 10 years (which was entirely possible), that would mean that she was still only 25. The sadistic wretches had probably planned it this way.

Temela finally walked in. She was exhausted and well into the later stages of pregnancy. She stopped at the first table and leaned on it, to catch her breath. She looked around the room at the others present. When she met Krezdon's gaze, she bit her lip and lowered her eyes. She made a feeble attempt at covering her swollen stomach, with her hands.

The guard, who was being very patient with her, said something to her. She glanced up at him and then started the trip across the room, towards Krezdon.

There were several thoughts going through his mind as she approached. What would be the best thing to say? He was not exactly sure.

He could hear her sniffling as she came closer. She had kept her eyes on the floor the entire time. One hand, she kept on her back, the other she used to wipe her tears away.

He stood up to help her get seated. Not once did she look up, or say anything. After making sure she was as comfortable as possible, he sat down next to her, put his arms around her shoulders and hugged her close. He put his mouth near her ear and whispered: "It's not your fault. I still love you."

Her sobs became more audible. Her body jerked from the

crying. She did her best to hug him back. She still did not look up.

"I wonder," said Nayna. "Could this be another one of their heartless little games?"

Several comments of agreement came from different people.

"They were so cruel, when they raided Malantroi. The cruelty continued on the voyage, and came to a head here, during those bloody interrogations. None of us have seen each other in a long time. It is nice to finally see my husband again. Will I ever get to see him again?"

Krezdon felt Temela hug tighter. He did the same.

He looked around. He had not heard Temela's escort depart. He did hear the sound of footsteps again…a group, marching in unison. All eyes went to the entrance. The last statement was burning in their minds. The entourage entered, Prince Zebyuro and ten bodyguards.

Everyone in the room had been well conditioned, over the past few years. They all started to drop to their knees.

"Never mind that," said Zebyuro. "Get up, get up! We can dispense with that formality here…for the moment." They continued marching to the end of the main table, where Krezdon was sitting. Two of the guards came up with a large chair, from somewhere, placed it at the end of the table and Zebyuro enthroned himself. The guards formed their semi-circle behind him. "Ah Ladies and Gentlemen," Zebyuro said cheerfully. "Interesting times, wouldn't you say?"

Another group of people entered the room. In this time, there were still the ten bodyguards. The difference with this group was the five women. One woman walking along slowly, in the middle of the procession who was dressed in a rather elegant manner and had a large jeweled tiara adorning her head. She had a sad look on her face and kept her eyes down as she walked along. The other four women were not dressed quite as chic as the one with the tiara. They all kept their eyes on the lead woman and stayed behind her.

"Ah, my dear sister, the Princess Sanyee," said Zebyuro. "Welcome to this momentous occasion."

She looked away as if embarrassed.

Zebyuro turned back to his captive audience. "You must forgive my sister. She has become a bit of a...recluse...since being freed from...you people and your criminal ways. I am hoping that one day...she will fully recover...the joy I saw in her when she was a child."

His words were met with silence.

Another chair was brought up and Sanyee sat down next to her brother and continued staring at the floor with a somber expression on her face.

Zebyuro looked around smiling. "I know at least one of the questions, going through your minds: Why are we here? We are here for a report. A pleasant report."

Now Krezdon was really suspicious, or confused, or suspiciously confused.

"Before any questions are voiced, I will try to answer most of them. It is now exactly seven years since you were sold into slavery. During that time, we have built a vast mountain of paperwork, devoted entirely to you people. This consists of weekly reports on every one of you by your masters. This has been a very time consuming and expensive undertaking…and you are *not* worth it."

Krezdon looked at some of the other people. He, like they, did not like the sound of the last remark.

"The time has come," continued Zebyuro merrily, "to put an end to this waste of money. The time has come - we set you free."

Krezdon's mind went blank. The only thing he could think of was to keep holding on to Temela.

"Just in case you were wondering, we never had any intention of keeping you all here as slaves for life."

"Excuse me, your Majesty," said Goroben, "if you had planned to release us after a set amount of time, why didn't you tell us this, seven years ago?"

"Simple! If we had told you, then you would have acted like any other prisoner, being punished for a crime. You would have been counting the days, until your release. The punishment would have served no purpose. Your specific punishment, was designed to show you the total hopelessness and helplessness of slavery. A criminal, with a set sentence, has hope: The release date. A slave has no hope. A criminal acts differently as the end of their incarceration draws near, while a slave acts the same, until they drop dead."

"You sentenced us to seven years," said Xuzo, "without us knowing it was just seven years, yet there were those who have been killed."

"Yes, there were originally 31,074 people in Malantroi, when we attacked. 30,061 lived long enough to make it here. Today, the count of the survivors is 20,769. 10,305 of your friends and family died, so that you may learn the complete horror of slavery."

Pamema stood up and nearly screamed at Zebyuro: "What are you talking about, you beast? You say over 10,000 people died to teach us a lesson? What lesson did the 10,000 dead ones learn?"

Zebyuro stared at her menacingly. "The 10,000, *are* the lesson," he said flatly. "If you people had not practiced slavery, none of this would have ever happened."

Another long silent pause.

Goroben cleared his throat. "You say that you are going to free us…"

"We *have* freed you."

"…Uh, yes, thank you for the correction. So now, we are free. What do we do? None of us have any money, none of us have any possessions. The skills that you were (ahem) kind enough to teach us, I don't think any one of us wants to continue with that. We are free to do what?"

Zebyuro chuckled. "We will take you back to Malantroi, where you can take up, where you left off, seven years ago."

Krezdon usually let Goroben ask the questions (why not, he was much better at it, but this one…). "Take up *what*? You burned the city, you burned the piers, ransacked our homes…it will take years to get any form of normal back."

Zebyuro sat quietly waiting for the tirade to end. He looked at Goroben with a smile. "You were the one who inspected a certain… crippled fleet of ships, were you not?"

Goroben looked up at the ceiling and simply nodded.

"You saw several severely damaged ships. I believe that you said, one of them had suffered, 'fatal damage'."

Another nod.

"You found out, after the city had been taken, that all that damage, was a massive illusion."

Another nod.

Zebyuro looked back at Krezdon. "We arranged it, so that you on the council, were the last ones to leave. Before you left, you witnessed an even greater illusion. All of them, compliments of the mysterious Owlam Elves. The piers, the city, like the ships, were never damaged. The city itself, is intact. We did not do any damage to any buildings or their interior. We did rearrange a few things, but nothing that cannot be undone in a few hours or days."

"But I saw, my…uh…ex-slaves wearing some of my clothing," said Krezdon weakly.

"Well, they had to wear something!" Zebyuro rolled his eyes. "As to all your possessions, you talk about having nothing. You are correct - here. Here you have only the clothing on your backs. In Malantroi, most of your possessions are still there. We - meaning myself and King Suntram - did not allow any widespread looting or ransacking."

"But there were things stolen," said Deshdeena.

Zebyuro raised his eyebrows and put one hand to his mouth. Then lowered his hand. "Stolen? No! Stolen - that is a bad word for it. The correct term would be compensation to the people that you

404

kept as slaves. If we had not allowed them a few liberties, they would have arrived here, totally destitute. Consider it. It is only fair. They were compensated, in the same manner that you are requesting and/or demanding it."

"Speaking of material possessions and wealth," said Krezdon, "how was it possible, that those three chests, that you inherited, could have contained enough wealth for all this?"

Zebyuro looked bewildered for a moment. "Three chests? Oh! That's right! There were three chests. Well, one of those chests, never left Malantroi. It's at the bottom of the harbor. That particular chest was full of nothing but...cosmetics. That stupid monster, actually thought that I would want to remain a homosexual. No, all the wealth that I received was in two chests."

"And all this was purchased with the..."

"No, no, no. I used that money to gain passage on a ship to Eang. I was looking for help - magical help. I knew, like everyone else, that the legendary wizard, Wyhoshton, lives there. I found him." He sighed. "The bastard owns slaves. No way to expect help from him."

Zebyuro shook his head and sighed again. "I wandered through Eang and Paselter and other countries on that continent. In a small town in Tabrow, I came across Soolchakan. There was a man, beating a young boy. The boy was a slave. Soolchakan used his magic to convince the man, to free the boy. Soolchakan and I had a long discussion after that. He agrees with me completely on the subject of slavery."

Zebyuro stopped and signaled to his bodyguards. One of them

came up with a goblet and handed it to the Prince. After taking a sip, he continued: "Soolchakan claimed that he was tired of doing the job by himself. He was getting so little done. He welcomed any assistance in destroying slavery. It was his magic that built this palace. His magic built almost half of this city. The vast majority of the gold in my treasury, was supplied by him."

He took another drink from the goblet, looked up and shook his head. He had a look of total awe in his eyes. "I've seen his vaults. He has nine vaults, larger than this palace. All of them...packed with... immeasurable wealth. He is willing to devote every speck of gold and silver he has to the complete annihilation of slavery."

Zebyuro looked in a sinister way around at all the faces. "No. All that wealth did not come from those chests. It came from the hearts of millions of souls, who despise slavery. I am simply a catalyst, for the correct use of it."

More silence from the audience. The lessons of the past seven years were sinking in. No one could think of a valid argument for stopping the anti-slavers, or how they spent their money.

Zebyuro again broke the silence. "You know, going back to the subject of inheritance and that monster Hremborn, what did you finally come up with, concerning his murder?"

Krezdon snorted in disgust. "It was never solved. The fact that you discovered that assassin's coven in Malantroi, leads me, now, to believe that maybe *they* were responsible."

The Prince chuckled. "I'm glad to see that no one else suffered...for what *I* did." He gave them a big grin.

Krezdon and Goroben were joined by others in a startled: "What?"

"I did it," said Zebyuro merrily.

"Wait a minute," said Krezdon. "You proved that you didn't do it. The truth box...it never...how did...but...the smoke stayed blue. How?"

"With the truth."

Krezdon looked at Goroben. For the first time that he could think of, he saw Goroben totally stunned.

"You directed a question at me: Did you kill Hremborn? Did I say yes, or no? No, I didn't. What I did was mislead you with another truth. I told you that, the sow - Lady Hremborn - had promised to kill me, after her husband died. She said that after the monster died, she would whip me daily – one lash day for every day - the monster took me to his bed, rather than her."

Zebyuro stopped momentarily to see if there would be a reaction. He saw none. He scoffed and continued: "For a free man, a sentence like that is devastating. To a slave - Consider: What did I have to look forward to? As long as he was alive, a nightly bout of being sexually abused. As soon as he died...well no more sexual abuse, but agonizing physical abuse. I figured with what she promised, I would not live, for more than...oh twenty to twenty-five days. Agonizing, painful and slow, but I had no life to look forward to. Why not just get it over with? I had nothing left to lose."

"But the will," said Krezdon angrily. "What about that? The will stated that, at the moment of his death, you were to be set free."

"I did *not* know about the will. That was just as big a surprise to me, as it was to you. Don't you remember, what I said? I told you that if I had known about that clause, in the will, Hremborn would have been dead, before the ink was dry. I never lied. I just did not answer your question, and I never lied. That is how I beat that smelly little box. I told you a truth that you were not expecting and you reacted, as a free man, not a slave, and put the puzzle together in a different way than what had really happened."

Zebyuro held the goblet up for a refill. "I have often heard that no matter how well a plan is set up, ahead of time, it never comes out exactly as planned, due to unforeseen circumstances. This was a case, where the 'unknown,' turned out to be positive…for me."

"If you did not care what happened to you," said Goroben, "why did you, even try, to mislead the investigation?"

"A challenge…having fun. Keep you people in a dither, for as long as I could make it last. A slave does not have very much to look forward to, in any circumstance. So, it was a personal challenge, just to see how long I could get away with it."

He took another long drink from the goblet. He readjusted himself in the chair. "There was another reason as well. If you could prove that I killed Hremborn, there was a possibility that I could have been sentenced to prison or death or even the Turgon wall. After a certain amount of time in prison, I could have been given back to that sow and she would have carried out her morbid promise. Die now or later, it didn't matter. What did matter, was that I no longer had to put up with any more of his molestations. That was a choice I made and had decided to live - or die - with the consequences. Either way it did not matter. What mattered, was that I was not going to be molested by that *thing*, again."

"You were still able to fool the truth box," said Krezdon. "You said, that he was still alive, when you left. How could that have possibly been the truth? How could he have been killed after you left, without someone else doing it?"

"You remember, I said I needed magical help, to do this. To set up this city and the raid on yours. I learned that lesson, from setting up his death. There was another time, before, when I had been sent to the harbor, to get one of those Melsoosta fish. The normal procedure was to meet the fishing boats, as they docked, at sunrise, in order to get the best fish. After purchasing the fish, you have to buy certain spices, for the proper preparation of the fish. The spice merchants usually did not open, till later. So, I had time to kill at the market prior to returning to my cage. One morning, there happened to be an individual, who was selling certain strange items. Some of them were quite useful. Some of them were only interesting. One of the items was this peculiar black string. It burns...so, so fast. You could take a piece as long as your finger, and a piece that is twice your height. Put a flame to both at the same time, and both would burn instantly. In less time than it takes to wink your eye. It burned so fast and completely, that it did not scorch anything it was touching, nor did it leave any ash residue. The only thing left, after it burned, was a weird smell."

"A weird smell," said Krezdon cautiously. "It smells like something has burned, but it doesn't smell like anything else that has or is burning."

"Exactly! Unfortunately, the smell lingers for quite a while."

"So, that is what I smelled, in his bedroom."

"Of course. Anyway, I tied one end to the ring on that odd knife, ran it through one of the rings in the ceiling - you know, one of those rings for holding up a mosquito net. The other end was tied to the dresser. I placed a time candle on the dresser, a short time before I left. The knife was suspended over his head. When the flame of the time candle hit the string - poof - the string is gone and the knife falls. The weight of the knife is what drove it through his head and killed him. He *was* alive, when I left. I did not lie about that. He did die after I left, when the flame on the time candle burned the string."

Goroben looked puzzled. "How could you be sure, he wouldn't move, or wake up, prior to the string burning?"

"I had *ten years*, to study that monster's habits. He rarely moved, when he was asleep. He was always the last, in the house, to wake up. I had no doubt, of where the target would be. As I said, when I left, he was alive. That was the truth."

Goroben shook his head. "What of the possibility, of someone else going in there, prior to the candle burning down? How could you be sure that no one would...?"

"Normal procedures, habits and punishment. The sow had several slaves. Their job was to get up around sunrise, and start breakfast. They were not to awaken any member of the family, until breakfast was on the table. The one time, that rule was broken, Hremborn whipped the offending slave to death. There was no reason to break the routine - unless one of the girls *wanted* to die."

Krezdon felt disgusted. Use your own habits against you, in the most despicable way. Observe any and all habits and exploit them.

"I'm curious about something," said Tansiki. "Why are you letting us go? Owning slaves, shows how much wealth and power you have."

Several people gasped.

"You sound as if you want to remain a slave," said Zebyuro incredulously. "Why?"

"No, I don't want to remain a slave. I am just a little puzzled about your motivation for freeing us. I understand the lesson you wanted to teach us, but there has to be more."

"You're right. For one thing, slaves, like equines, are expensive to keep healthy. Unlike equines though, slaves are capable of rebellion. The master has just as much to fear, as the slave. Another reason, is that, when you have slaves doing all of the work, you tend to get fat and lazy. You depend, too much on the work that they do. You forget how to do, for yourself. Another reason, you have a tendency to become abnormally cruel. You have something there that you can kick, slap, maim, torture or kill. Something that you can take out your anger and frustrations on, no matter how diabolical your method. You lose all inhibitions about killing another person. This could lead to killing someone who is free. Killing a slave is not a crime - killing someone who is free is murder. Is that enough motivation for you?"

Tansiki bit her lip and bowed her head.

Daninya spoke up. "What about these poor women, and the children? Ever since we arrived here, a lot of the younger women have stayed pregnant. Not once did the woman know, who got her pregnant. Not once did the men know who they were getting pregnant. If you send us back to Malantroi, do all these bastard children go back

411

with us? How will we know which child goes with which family?"

The Prince smiled. "We are not totally heartless. As I said before: We kept very careful records on all of you. Not once, was there an illegitimate or adulterous mating."

For the first time, Temela looked up. Her eyes and nose were puffy and red. Her cheeks were covered with tearstains. She tried to say something, but was so overwhelmed, she was unable to speak. She lost all control and buried her face against Krezdon's neck, laughing and crying.

Krezdon himself felt a great relief. He felt himself having to fight back the tears as he held her close. She no longer felt shame and neither did he. He was going back home...with a family...of... (?) "Uh...Temela." He gently pushed her away, so he could see her face. "Temela?"

"What?"

"How many children, do we have?"

Her expression changed from joy to confusion. She thought for a moment and swallowed.

"How many?"

She placed his hand on her swollen abdomen. She looked up at him and gave him a weak smile. "This is number nine...I think."

Krezdon pulled her close again. He was losing the battle with his emotions. She was pregnant when they got here, and now he was going to meet his full family. He *was* a father.

"Oh, fine," said Deninya. "There were married couples having children. What about the people who were not married, who had children?"

Zebyuro shrugged. "So we arranged a few...thousand marriages," he said nonchalantly. "We did everything we could to keep them as consistent as possible. I'm sure that, due to certain circumstances, the parents of those in question, will probably agree. If they don't...tough!"

"Not that I'm for or against them," said Goroben, "but, what about the slavers? Are they going to be freed as well?"

Zebyuro snorted. "Silly fools! The life that they *joyfully* forced on so many people, they could not stand, for themselves. We obtained an enormous amount of information from the interrogations. We were able to incarcerate over 3,000 slavers, from that information. We also took their families. In many cases, those families had been slavers for at least 15 generations. The chain had to be broken. Not just the iron chains that bound people in slavery, but the family chains, that kept slavery going."

Zebyuro shook his head and looked around as if he were awe struck. "Within the first year of incarceration, 90% of them committed suicide, or rotted away from depression. The other 10% were dead by the end of the second year. But, no, we could not have let them go, the life they forced on others, they could not stand for themselves. One of the main answers to your question: No, we would *never* have let *them* go."

Xuzo spoke up: "Did you allow them to reproduce, while in prison?"

"No! One of the first things we did with them, was total

sterilization. Male, female, young, old...all were denied any capability of making more generations of slavers."

"My children," said Temela, "when do I get to see my children? I know I have given birth to eight other children, but I don't know how many are boys or girls."

"After we dine," Zebyuro said calmly. "Right now, there are 450 people, going through the records. They are triple checking all the records. We are going to absolutely confirm, that we are matching the correct children, to their natural parents."

Krezdon was feeling somewhat angry. "Why all this mass production of children?"

"An entire new generation, that will be raised hating slavery. It is all a question of slavery: Why should it be allowed to exist? Why shouldn't we destroy the concept of slavery? We who were slaves, wish to convey to everyone, the true nature of it. We who were treated inhumanely, can afford the choice of how we treat others. Slavery must be abolished...globally.

"I'm curious about...something," said Goroben.

Zebyuro raised his eyebrows as he looked at Goroben. "Yes, what is that?"

"You kept...moving us from place to place...when we first got here. We spent...so many days...just sitting in a dungeon cell...or... just sitting. Why were we...just sitting and waiting?"

Zebyuro nodded. "The difference between the peasant and the elite. The peasants were easy to break. They were taken to the auctions, that we set up and they were sold and taken to their...place of incarceration. The elite…it takes a little while to convince you that no one is coming to rescue you. No one is going to pull you out of the nightmare. Doing a lot of sitting and thinking about your grievous situation helps in breaking you. Having you witness the torture of the slavers while you were publicly stripped of everything, including your modesty…finally broke you. Then you were all ready to be sold and accept your fate."

17

Krezdon looked back over the stern of the ship. They had lost sight of land, two days ago. He kept turning things over in his mind. The raid, the torture of the slavers, the imprisonment, the surprise release...and a shockingly large family. He hated the people of the city of Semoron, but...they probably hated him for the same reason. He had to admit, a lot of respect for them as well.

The baby in his arms stirred. He rocked...what's his name, a little. This was the youngest of his children. He had to run through the roll call of the children again: Tantaya, a girl, about 6 ½. Nansa, a girl, just over 5 ½. Rondynon, a boy, nearly 5. Debdem, a girl, just over 4. Revlorm, a boy, almost 3 ½. Tylorok, a boy, about 2 ½. Lylee, a girl, just over 1 ½. Vontol, that's his name. Almost 8 months old. And a 9th one that was nearly here.

It had been a nervous reunion with the children. Temela had baptized every one of them, with her tears. She had made several attempts at holding all of them simultaneously. Due to her advanced pregnancy, the overwhelming number of children and her emotional state, she had worked herself into complete exhaustion.

There was little doubt, concerning the parentage of these children. All of them had Krezdon's eyes and pinched jaw. They all had Temela's small upturned nose. If Krezdon had had any question about the validity of the records, kept by the people of Semoron, nature had supplied undeniable proof.

Vontol's mind was asleep, but his kidneys were not. Krezdon sighed in disgust. Time to see if there was a dry diaper anywhere on board. Between Krezdon's herd and all the others on board (all of them under the age of 7), there were some 80 or so children on the ship. The toddlers and babies seemed to have a conspiracy of keeping every available diaper, saturated.

Krezdon walked down the stairs (?) to the main deck (?). He could not understand why the ship's crew had such strange names for ships parts. Each mast had a different name, each sail had a different name, each deck had a different name, they called the floors, decks, and they called the windows, portholes and a thousand other terms that he could not comprehend. He would not be surprised if they had a different silly name, for each one of the steps he had just descended.

On the main deck, Tantaya and four other girls were relating some story to Goroben and his wife Nayna, with wide-eyed expressions and sweeping gestures. The two adults were listening with large smiles on their faces.

Krezdon headed to the room where Temela was taking care of three of the youngest of the herd. Maybe she knows where some dry linen is located. He found her sitting on the bed, trying to comfort Debdem and Tylorok. The two youngsters had been seasick from the moment they had boarded. Lylee was sitting on the floor, giving all of her attention to a large piece of wood.

"He's done it again," said Krezdon.

"Done what…oh."

"Is there any more dry clothing for the babies?"

She giggled. "Sure, they gave us plenty."

"Don't get up, just tell me where it is, I'll take care of it."

Temela continued the struggle to get up. Her large stomach and the rocking of the ship were giving her quite a challenge. "I think he has something to say to you."

"Huh…who?" He turned around. Goroben was standing at the door, the smile still on his face. "You're sure a quiet one!"

Goroben chuckled. "Your wife is very perceptive. I do need to talk to you."

Temela took Vontol in her arms. "Before you go, remember, I have seven years to make up. Eight children and not a single kiss for it."

Krezdon smiled, he squeezed her lightly and planted one on her lips, as best he could, considering the awkward position they were in.

"Maybe I shouldn't be watching," said Goroben.

Temela broke off and said: "Don't worry, the way I am right now, not much more could possibly happen." She gave Krezdon another quick peck. "Now, go, discuss your state affairs."

Krezdon gave her a playful swat on the rump, then left with Goroben. They walked quietly along the hallway (?), out onto the main deck and over to the left (port?) railing.

"I was wondering when this conversation was going to come up," said Krezdon sadly.

"It's not really what you think."

"Then what?"

"In a short time, we will be back in Malantroi. We will have a tremendous amount of work to do."

"Which, in all probability, includes voting on a new Supreme Commandant."

"Why?"

"I didn't exactly do the best job in the world. My job was to stop something like this from happening."

"It was *all* of our jobs."

"So, what you are saying, then, is that we will all have to have a new council, entirely."

"Yes, the council is there, to stop this sort of thing from occurring. We thought, we had every single contingency covered. Our watch towers were facing every direction, except the one that was used to kick our sanctimonious teeth in. Ten years ago, if someone had told me, that an ex-slave, was going to attack and completely imprison the entire city, and not lose a single one of his soldiers…" He spread his arms and shook his head. "…what idiot, could possibly believe that?"

"It happened," shouted Krezdon! "We failed! We should have seen…"

"Will you shut up and listen! Quit thinking so negatively. Think about the things that sunk our ships as a whole."

Goroben huffed. "First of all, the source. A Prince, who for the first ten years of his life, was educated in all sorts of things, including gathering intelligence data, and exploiting the weaknesses of their enemies. He had ten years to do just that."

Goroben looked over at some of the children playing and then turned back to Krezdon. "Where was he held as a slave? Was it in the stable of equine breeder, like me, or a fisherman like you? No! He was a slave, in the very bed of *THE* Supreme Commandant. He could not have possibly been placed in a better position to gather valuable intelligence information."

He slammed his fist onto the railing. "He murdered his master, and had the ability to out think the investigating team, because they saw him as nothing but a slave. He confused them with other truths and they accepted it, because he was telling the truth and who would suspect a slave of that kind of guile?"

Krezdon leaned on the rail.

"Granted, it was dumb luck, that he ran into this…uh…what's his name…Soolchakan. They met, and we were then helpless in another aspect, because of the magical abilities of those four Elves. I talked to Borip and Nal: Two of the most powerful wizards, dwelling in Malantroi. According to them, those Elves were displaying abilities that made them and all other wizards, look like incompetent fools."

Goroben leaned on the rail as well. "When the attack was executed, they had us all concentrating on that diversionary tactic. We were worried about a bunch of shipwrecked sailors. They, in fact, turned out to be a sort of expeditionary force, heading the invasion."

Krezdon interjected: "Prior to the invasion, they had shredded our integrity, in half the countries, throughout the world, diplomatically. We became a pack of abnormalities, that no one would even consider assisting."

"Right! We had an assassin's coven in our midst, that he could prove, had a Monarch assassin and kidnapper of royalty in it."

"And we can go on, but what has that got to do with our suitability as city leaders?"

"The law. We, the entire city, were taken in one big scoop. Who are we supposed to blame? Who are we supposed to fire? According to the law, if anyone holds their position on the council for more than 5 years, nothing short of a royal edict, or death, can oust you."

"So that leaves you and Pamema."

"No. That leaves all of us that survived the imprisonment."

"Huh?"

"There was no council meeting in the past seven years. There was no vote to push any of us out of our position. The Prince did not give us any message, from King Suntram, which says any of us have been dismissed, fired, defrocked or sentenced to death. Until the King, officially notifies us, that we have been dismissed from office, we are still the Council of Malantroi."

Krezdon had to mull that one over for a few moments. "What are the odds, that we will be notified, that we've been dismissed, when we arrive?"

"Heavily against us, if we do not have a plan, when we arrive."

"So, we get together, with what we have and start working on it."

"Right. The only ones who can call a meeting, other than at the regularly scheduled times, are either the ranking member, or the one with the most longevity. I have the longevity, you have the rank. The other four surviving members of the council, are on board this ship."

"Let's get to work."

18

The first order of business was the abolishment of slavery, for the city of Malantroi. This included that their ports would no longer be a safe haven for slavers.

They realized, that they were 10 members short of a full council, so they had to work on that one as well. They came up with 6 from the surviving spouses of the old council. The other 4 would have to be voted on, once things calmed down a little from the exodus back to Malantroi.

One large consideration, that they discussed: A great number of their problems, could have been avoided, if they had never practiced or allowed slavery in their city to begin with.

When they arrived back in Malantroi, Krezdon just shook his head. The piers were all intact and every part of the city, that he could see, looked intact as well. All of the smoke and charred remains that he had seen, *had* all been an illusion. Once they got off of the ship, he would probably see a lot of dust and numerous things that were falling apart from neglect. Yes, they had a lot of work ahead of them.

Goroben and Xuzo, were standing next to Krezdon, as they looked over the city.

"A very welcome sight," said Xuzo.

"No matter how dusty, or neglected," said Krezdon?

Goroben leaned over the railing, and pointed: "Who is that?"

Someone was walking out on the pier. They had been told, that the members of the council, would be the first ones brought back. They could clearly see someone coming out on the pier to meet them.

"Maybe, he's an emissary from the King," said Xuzo.

"Maybe," agreed Goroben.

"No! It's not," said Krezdon. "It's that wretched Elf."

Xuzo growled angrily. "Haven't we had enough? What is he here for? Are we going to be reminded of what we went through back there? Maybe he's here just to gloat."

"It doesn't matter why he's here," said Goroben. "Don't forget - we were told, by several sources, that we don't stand a chance against him."

"Wait a minute," said Xuzo. "Back in Oosam, we saw only one man and three women. I think I see at least three men, on the pier, now, and a few more along the beach."

"Let's wait, until we dock," said Krezdon. "Let's wait and find out what they have to say, before we speculate ourselves into a frenzy."

As the ship approached the pier, the three councilmen, realized that they did not recognize any of the greeting party.

When the crewmen on the ship, threw lines to the men on the pier, the Elves did not touch the lines. They made gestures with their hands and the lines tied up to the pier by themselves, to secure the ship. They then made more gestures and the gangplank went into place by itself.

Krezdon cleared his throat. "Does anyone really want to get into a shouting or pugilistic match, with any of these guys?"

Xuzo grunted.

"I don't think, that any of *us* would like the outcome," said Goroben.

Xuzo looked at Krezdon. "Well…is this a military or a civilian situation?"

"Let's try to keep it civil," said Krezdon.

Xuzo nodded. He headed down the gangplank, with Krezdon following.

The closer they got to the Elves, the more convinced Krezdon was, that none of these, were the ones they encountered back in Oosam. Obviously, there were other Owlam. Krezdon wondered if they were as powerful as the quartet from Oosam.

One of the Elves met them at the bottom of the gangplank.

"Welcome home, gentlemen," he said with a friendly smile and outstretched arms. "My name is Bikaropin of the Fourth. I, and several of my relatives, have been watching over the city, making sure that it was still here, when you got back."

Xuzo smiled back at him. "Thank you, for…watching the city. Has there been any…mischief?"

Bikaropin shrugged slightly. "Unfortunately, there were some who tried to take advantage of the situation. We have detained them. If you wish to incarcerate them or reap some other kind of punishment, we will supply you with all the evidence we have on each one."

Xuzo looked back at Krezdon, then back to the Elf. "Again, thank you. We will have to have a discussion, among ourselves, to determine what to do about the thugs."

"Yes, of course. It is my understanding, that you have several women, who are in the latter part of pregnancy. We have some coaches, waiting for you and them, in order to make it easier for all."

Xuzo smiled. "I'm sure that the ladies will appreciate that. One thing I am wondering, though…are you here, just to greet us, or are you, now, some kind of keepers, or watchers?"

Bikaropin snickered. "No. We have no plans of staying. Once all of your city guards and constables have arrived, we will be on our way. The only reason we will stay, will be to give evidence, for any trials on the looters that we captured."

Xuzo laughed. "Yes, I suppose that we will need witnesses."

Bikaropin gave a slight bow. "Now, if everyone will depart the ship, your transportation awaits you, at the end of the pier."

The people all came down the gangplank, looking at the city. Some had a look of relief, some were crying and some - like Temela - just wanted to get home and relax.

Three female Elves, helped Krezdon and Temela, keep their herd of children together. The three introduced themselves as Dawuni of the Fifth, Chenny of the Seventh, and Metmiti of the Thirteenth.

After getting all of the children into the coach, Krezdon could not help his curiosity. He looked at the three and asked: "Fifth, Seventh and Thirteenth…what?"

Dawuni giggled. "I am of the fifth generation after Soolchakan, Bonarain, Kiyalee and Chyning. Chenny is seventh generation and Metmiti is thirteen generation from the four."

He was not sure whether he wanted to know more or not.

Temela whispered to Metmiti: "That woman over there...why is she glaring at us like that?"

Metmiti whispered back: "That is Nadiwi of the Second. She is the reason why, Soolchakan is so anti-slavery. I don't know when, and they won't tell us, but when Soolchakan and Bonarain were young, Nadiwi was stolen by slavers and held in bondage, for some time. When Soolchakan and Bonarain found her, they did horrible things to the people who held her as a slave and the ones who enslaved her. If it were up to Nadiwi, all of you would still be imprisoned."

Temela swallowed hard and just looked down, with a rather worried look on her face.

On the way to their old home, Krezdon pointed out different things to the older children. They looked around wide-eyed with wonder at this new home.

They arrived at the house. Temela sat there in tears as she looked around. Prysko had been successful in demolishing the entire garden. None of the bushes or plants were anywhere to be seen. The entire area was overgrown with weeds.

After getting everyone out of the coach, Krezdon let them all inside. There were sufficient rooms, for all of the children, but there were not enough beds for them. Now, he was making mental notes, on what he needed for his family.

Chenny walked over to the fireplace, threw several pieces of wood in, made a strange gesture and a rather large fire flared up. "We'll have something for all of you to eat, very shortly," she said in a very charming manner.

Krezdon almost felt like he had a headache coming on. He wondered if the entire Owlam clan were wizards. If they were, then it was no wonder they were able to create such a massive illusion of destruction.

Metmiti came up to Krezdon. "What do you want done...with this?" She held up the whip, that Krezdon had used to beat several slaves to death.

He took the whip and looked at it with disgust. He heard some of his children crying. He looked over, where they were. The four oldest were looking at him with terror in their eyes.

"I didn't do anything wrong," wailed Tantaya.

"I be a good girl," cried Nansa.

Rondynon and Debdem tried to hide in a corner crying.

"That's right," said Krezdon. "None of you have done anything wrong. Here." He held the whip out to Tantaya. "Why don't you be a good girl and put this nasty thing in the fire?"

All four children now looked at him confused. Tantaya slowly walked up to him, looking at the whip. She looked up at him fearfully. She held out a shaking hand and took the whip. She slowly walked over to the fire, looking back several times for assurance from her father. Each time, he motioned for her to continue. She stared at the flames for a few moments and then tossed the whip in. She was joined by the other three as they watched the whip being engulfed by the flames.

Krezdon came up behind them, knelt down, put his arms out and pulled all four of them together in one big hug. "We will never have one of those vile things, in this house again."

All four children looked back at him, through tears of joy.

"I'm going to check on your mother now," he said as he let go of them. He walked in and found Temela nursing Vontol.

"Krezdon, dear," she said.

"Yes."

"I don't want to sound too demanding, especially since we just got back." She sighed. "But, could we please refrain from having any more children for a few years?"

Krezdon started laughing. He walked over to her and kissed her on the forehead. "I quite agree."

"Thank you."

"Right now, I'm wondering, what we are going to do, after these three leave."

"Do about what?"

"What are we going to do about meals? I mean who is going to prepare the meals around here?"

She looked up at him slack jawed.

He looked back, confused. "What?"

"What? WHAT!? What do you think, I have been doing for the last seven years...other than having babies?"

"I don't know...you never told me."

She looked startled for a moment. "I didn't?"

"No."

She grimaced. "Well, for the last seven years, the only time I left a kitchen, was...for breeding purposes, or giving birth. Well, they also had me wet-nursing, other children."

"So now, you can cook!"

"Yup! What can you do?"

His shoulders sagged. "Gut fish."

"Well, that might come in handy, seeing as how, we're going to spend the next 18 or 19 years, preparing large meals, for a large family."

"Yup! We are going to do it ourselves. No slaves. We might have to hire...some servants. I don't know, right now, how to do that."

"I'm sure, we'll figure something out."

"Yes. Like he said back there: It all comes down to the question of slavery...should it be allowed to exist? Well...I say no. It is so one-sided. It is so vicious and cruel. It's not really a question anymore...it's a proclamation of intent. No one really needs it. I for one...will do everything I can...to make sure that it never happens in this city again."

MYSTERIOUS WAYS

On a cold late March morning in New York City, a solitary man carrying a briefcase walks up onto one of the elevated platforms to wait for the subway. He walks along the platform to a place where he is comfortable in waiting for the train to make it's appearance. He is dressed in a long black overcoat, black pants and shoes, with a dark furry hat on his head. He looks down at the snow on the platform, which is quickly turning to slush. The temperature had crept above 40 degrees which is mercifully melting a lot of the snow. He looks around, for a good place to put the case down without getting it wet. The only place appears to be one of the unoccupied benches. He places it on a bench and stretches.

Another person comes up onto the platform. A young woman comes up and notices the man. She is young and a little on the skinny side. She has on red boots and a matching red overcoat. She has a red knit cap on with her long black hair cascading down below her shoulder blades. She glances back and forth nervously with large brown eyes that show a little fear in them. Her facial features show her Italian ancestry. She appears to be worried about being alone on the platform with a strange man. She stays near the stairs for safety.

The man sees her and notices her anxiety and pulls a section of newspaper out of his pocket and starts working on a crossword puzzle. When she sees that the man is not interested in her she relaxes a little. She walks towards the benches, looking for any possible dry spot to sit down.

Suddenly she sees something between two of the benches. She screams and her fear of a stranger is overwhelmed by her phobia. She runs across the platform to the man and makes a flying leap, straddling his left shoulder.

He is momentarily staggered by her move and fights to stay on his feet. He finally steadies himself and stands there in shock for a few moments. He checks his balance and then looks up at the terrified young lady.

"There's a snake over there," she says frantically.

He clears his throat and calmly looks where she is pointing. "A snake?"

"Yes," she cries. "There's a snake over there."

He stands there with his eyes closed for a few moments trying to assess the situation. With her still up on his left shoulder, he makes the awkward walk over to the benches. He looks down between the benches and rolls his eyes. "That, young lady, is a cable."

"What? Are you sure?"

He clears his throat again. "Yes. It is definitely a cable. If you will take a close look at it, you will see that it is braided. That is steel cords braided together. No snake looks like that."

She looks at it closely and then laughs nervously.

"Another thing, young lady, if it were a snake, considering what the temperature has been lately, the snake would be either frozen to death or at best - hibernating. Plus, I personally, don't know of any snakes that exist here in New York City...unless they're in a rather warm aquarium in a pet store or the zoo...or at someone's home."

Again she laughs nervously. "Sorry. I just wasn't thinking." She gulps hard. "It looked like a snake from a glance."

He walks closer to a bench and squats down a little. "Madam, you may now dismount, please."

As she starts to remove herself from the perch, both people let out a squawk of pain and surprise.

He appears to be in total shock. "What is jabbing me in the shoulder…in several places?"

She has an anguished look on her face. "I have some piercings… down there."

He initially looks confused. Then a reality hits him. He closes his eyes. "You have body piercing…in your…oh dear."

"Yes," she said with a pained look on her face.

"Uh…I hope you don't mind my asking…but, how many piercings do you have? I mean I feel like I am being jabbed in more than one place."

Through her grimace she says: "Eight. Four on each side."

He looks away from her with his eyes closed. "No comment," he said flatly.

She looks down at him. "What do I do?"

He shook his head. "Either you reach down…there and get those… things…out, or I have to reach up and…get them…out."

"Don't you dare touch my…" She looked off to the side with pain and extreme embarrassment on her face. "I'll get them."

He shook his head again. He lightly scratched the center of his forehead with his right middle finger. "Whenever you're ready, be my guest."

"Why don't you take your coat off?"

"Good idea."

He unbuttons it and attempts to start sliding out. Once again, both of them let out a pained squawk. He pulls the coat back to it's original position with a pained look on his face and she is breathing rapidly, in and out, through her teeth.

"That's not going to work," he said.

She sighed and reached down in her crotch and started fumbling around. He looked off to the side trying to be as laissez-faire about it as he could. After a few moments, she let out a frustrated sigh. "I can't do it. Your head is in the way."

"Well is there someone you know that can help? Your mother or..."

"No! Not my mother. I don't want her to know... Maybe one of my sisters could help."

"Okay, fine. Where do we find one of these sisters?"

She looked around helplessly. "Well, one of them lives a short distance from here. We'll have to get to her place."

He shook his head. "Fine. Give me some directions and off we'll go." He leaned down awkwardly, picked up his briefcase and headed for the exit.

As he was going down the stairs, a young couple was coming

up. When the couple saw the two - in their odd situation - they stopped and stared nervously at the pair coming down the stairs.

"I lost a bet," said the man in black flatly.

The gaze of the two went up to the woman perched on his shoulder.

"She did too," he added.

He headed down the stairs, gave the couple a friendly smile and nod, and continued on.

The couple watched the odd pair descending, then looked at each other, shrugged and headed up the stairs.

He was wondering if he should hide rather than have everybody he passed see the two of them this way. The "lost bet" seemed to be working rather well with anyone they saw in avoiding all kinds of embarrassing questions.

After walking five exhausting blocks she finally identified the building where her sister lived. "Okay," he said. "Which apartment does she live in?"

"She lives in number 504."

He looked up. "The fifth floor? Please tell me that there's an elevator."

She grimaced. "No, there isn't," she said meekly.

He hung his head and groaned.

Getting through the door was a little challenging. He could not really lean or squat down without losing his balance. She had to lean down over his head in order to accomplish this task. By the time he finally climbed to the fifth floor, he was panting heavily and staggering, more than walking.

After some semblance of catching his breath, he asked: "Do you think your sister is in?"

"I don't know. She slid a key behind the knocker, so if she isn't in, we can still get in."

'Oh joy,' he thought sarcastically.

After knocking several times and receiving no answer, he checked the door knocker. It slid to the side a little and he saw part of the key being exposed. He pulled the key out and unlocked the door. "Are you sure that your sister will be alright with this?"

"Whether she is or isn't, I don't have much of a choice."

He cleared his throat, sighed and entered. Again, she had to lean over his head in order to get through the entrance.

He walked through a hallway to a living room. "It's awfully cold in here."

"She can't afford to keep the heat on all the time. She only turns it on when she's here."

"So, no point in taking my coat off is there…even if I could?"

She glanced around with a pained look on her face. "No."

"So, where do I…" He cleared his throat "…attempt to sit down?"

"The couch will have to do."

He sat down and she tried to take the weight off his shoulder, by standing on the couch in a squatting position. Her legs got very tired very quickly this way. They moved to an overstuffed armchair. Here he could slouch a little to the left and she could kneel on the arm of the chair. While this was still not the most comfortable position available, it was attainable with minimum effort for both.

…And they waited.

She made a few more attempts at reaching the piercings. No matter what she tried she could not get past his head and coat and her underwear and dress. Several times she started whimpering as a result of the frustration she was going through.

Just before 11am they heard someone messing with the knocker. They then heard someone unlocking the door. The door opened and they heard someone walking in. In came - not the sister - but a man. He was somewhat tall with a mop of light brown hair that covered his ears, his forehead and most of his eyebrows. He had small brown eyes and huge lips. He was wearing tan knee-high snow boots, blue jeans and a military parka that had obviously seen better days. The man came in humming and walking very casually. He stopped short when he saw the two of them in their ridiculous position.

"Angelica? What…? Who…?" He had a heavy New York accent.

The two of them looked up and she grimaced. The "lost bet" thing would not work here.

"Hello, Rudy," she said with a pained look on her face.

"What's going on here? You're…dressed so it ain't sex, but…

that don't look very comfortable."

"Look, this is complicated," said Angelica. "Do you know where Luciana is?"

"Complicated?" Rudy raised his eyebrows. "I can hardly wait." He looked down at the strange man. "And you are?"

"Just call me 'Saddle'," said the stranger with blunt sarcasm.

"Okay, Saddle it is. Is your explanation complicated?"

"She landed on my shoulder and the piercings, between her legs, got caught in my coat. Does that take out some of the complications?"

Rudy did several double takes looking from Saddle to Angelica. He laughed a little and then looked at Angelica. "You pierced your...?" He turned away laughing out loud.

Angelica pounded her fist on the top of Saddle's head several times. "Why did you tell him that? Now everyone is going to know."

"Considering what has happened, he was going to find out anyway. Are you telling me that you got those piercings and you wanted to keep them a secret?"

"He's going to tell everybody and people will start thinking all kinds of things about me."

"You've got piercings in your...crotch," he said calmly. "What are they supposed to think?"

Rudy finally was able to get a little control over himself. He looked at Angelica. "You got piercings in your hoo-hoo and now their caught in his coat. Oh man, this is rich. So, what do you need your sister for?"

She clenched her teeth and eyes. "I need someone to reach in between my legs and get them out of his coat, so I can get off of him."

Rudy giggled again. "I'll get them out for you."

"Don't even think about it, you pervert," she growled as she held up a fist.

He giggled again. "You pierced your goodies - several times - and I'm the pervert. Oh that's really rich. I haven't pierced anything."

Angelica huffed. "Do you know where Luciana is?"

"Nope." He went into another bout of giggling.

Saddle was getting a little frustrated himself. "Do you have any idea who might know where Luciana is?"

Rudy snickered. "I could call Bob or Tony, but I can't guarantee anything."

"Don't call my brothers," Angelica pleaded. "I need someone to find Luciana."

"Well, I don't know where she is. I do know where Tony is right now. Maybe he knows where Lucy is."

Angelica moaned in agony.

Saddle just sighed. He did not seem very happy about the situation either.

Rudy snickered again and picked up the phone. After punching the number in he looked over the odd pair again and shook his head and turned away as he started laughing again.

Saddle groaned. "I hope that that is sweat soaking through the coat and onto my shoulder."

Angelica let out a pained moan. "I'm pretty sure that it is."

Rudy stood looking at the pair with a huge grin on his face. He jerked suddenly and started talking on the phone: "Hey Deedee, can you get Tony to come to the phone? Tell him it's a family emergency…No, I'm not joking…It's not like death and dismemberment, but someone needs to talk to him…Thanks." He looked back at the couple again, then looked away giggling. "Hey, Tony, what's up…Yeah, I called you…Well your sister Angie is in a bit of a predicament…What?… No, no, no, no, no, no, I didn't have nuttin' to do wit it…I came over here to Lucy's place and I found Angie…No, I don't think the cord is long enough to reach her. Look, what I'm calling about is the fact that she needs Lucy…What?…No, she needs Lucy to come over here and help her…No, no, no, no, it's more of a female problem…No, I'm not jokin' man!…Whatever…If you don't believe me then come on over…Yeah…See yah!" He hung up the phone.

Angelica let out a hoarse wheeze. "What!? Is Tony coming here?"

Rudy giggled a little bit more. "I guess I didn't sound too convincing. He wants to come over here and find out for himself…as to what's going on."

"Oh, great!" said Angelica.

"Oh, by the way," said Rudy. "He threatened me - as if he thinks that I did something, so he's bringing Bobby with him."

"No!" shouted Angelica.   Saddle let out a grunt of pain as she shifted her weight. She had a rather pained look on her face as well. She shifted back to where she had been before in an attempt to ease the pain. "Why didn't you tell him that Bobby didn't have to come with him?"

"Hey," said Rudy, "I'm not worried. As soon as they see that I had nuttin' to do with this mess…I'm okay." He sat down, looked at the couple again and started giggling again.

Saddle looked up at Angelica. "Tony and Bobby?"

"My brothers," she said in an anguished voice.

"Why do you think that they'd be coming over here from what he said over the phone?"

"They might think that Rudy did something to me. My brothers don't really like Rudy that much, but Luciana does."

Rudy took off his parka and showed that the only shirt he had on was a tank-top undershirt that would be better off as a dust rag (or it might just be one).

They waited for several minutes in silence. The only thing that could be heard was Rudy's non-stop giggling.

They heard someone messing with the knocker, the key being inserted, the door coming open and two men walking in. The two men are completely different as far as their bodies are concerned. Their facial features show that they are related to each other as well as the girl mounted on Saddle's shoulder. The first one in is just under six feet tall and is bundled up, all in denim, with the exception of a black knit cap. The second one is well over six feet and heavily muscled. He is wearing black snow boots, blue jeans and a plaid winter coat. The two men come to a halt and have a totally dumbfounded look on their faces when they see Saddle and Angelica.

Rudy looks up at the two and starts laughing even harder.

The smaller man speaks up: "What the…? I mean…what are you two doing?" His accent is not nearly as pronounced as Rudy's but it is definitely New York.

Rudy controlled his laughing a little. "I told you that you…"

"Shaddap!" shouted Angelica. "Look Tony, I need Luciana… or Sophia, I don't care which, but I need their help."

Tony is now even more confused. "For what?!"

"They're stuck together," said Rudy through his chuckles.

Tony shakes his head and with his arms splayed out a little: "WHAT?"

Rudy gains a little control over himself. "They are stuck together because of some body piercings."

The larger man speaks up. "Body piercings?" He looks at Saddle. "Dude! What are you doing piercing your shoulder?" He has a virtual New York *street* accent.

With that, Rudy is on the floor, laughing uncontrollably in total hysteria and Angelica is almost in tears.

Tony looks at the larger man. "Bobby, what did I tell you?"

Bobby looks a little confused. "Bout whut?"

"If you can't say something righteous or intelligent - shaddap!"

Bobby looks a little guilty. "Oh," he said in a small voice.

"But he said that that guy had some piercing."

Tony looks at Saddle. "Is that what he meant? You pierced your shoulder?"

Saddle sniffed slightly and cleared his throat. "No," he said in an informative way. "He simply said: Piercings. He did not say who had the piercings. But, to clear things up - I did not have any part of my body pierced...until she jumped up on my shoulder."

"But, but..." Bobby came in. "The only part of Angie that's touching you is..." Reality mixed with horror came across his face. "Oh, Angie...

You...you don't mean...?"

"I think she did," said Tony with a look of disgust. "What's Momma gonna say? Does she know about this? ...and Poppa...ho boy, he's gonna hit the roof."

"You don't have to tell them," said Angelica through clenched teeth. "Just find Luciana or Sophia. I need either one - or both - to help me."

"Help what?" said Tony helplessly.

"Get us unstuck," said Saddle in a churlish manner.

Tony looked at Saddle a little disgusted. "Hey, you stay out of this - you're not part of this."

Saddle looked at Tony absolutely flabbergasted. "I think I am, whether I like it or not. I'm the one who is stuck on the bottom."

Tony tried to say something with an angry look on his face. He took in a breath and froze. His expression changed to confusion and contemplation. He let his lungs empty slowly and then licked his lips. He shrugged helplessly. "Whatever."

By now Rudy has slowed considerably in his laughing. He is holding his sides in pain. Each time he lets out a little chuckle it is followed by a small moan of agony and he puts his hands on his side. He has tears streaming down both cheeks. He walks, hunched over into another room. He is heard blowing his nose and then the flush of a toilet. He comes out of the bathroom, still holding his sides, trying to take short controlled breaths.

Tony stands there, still a little confused. "So, why do you need Lucy or Sophie?"

Angelica looks up helplessly with her eyes closed. "I can't reach around this guy's head, in order to get to the rings, to get them out of me or his coat. I need them to get the things out, so I can get unstuck from this guy." She looks at Tony. "Okay!?"

Bobby perks up with a smile. "Why don't we just take a knife and cut the guys coat?"

Tony slaps Bobby in the chest with the back of his hand. He stands there glaring at Bobby with clenched teeth.

Bobby lowers his head. "I'm shuttin' up," he said despondently.

Tony shakes his head looking at Bobby. "I cannot believe that you and I come from the same gene pool."

Angelica looks around. "So, does anybody know where either Lucy or Sophie are?"

"Sophia is at her job," said Bobby

"No, it's lunch time. She's probably gone to that greasy little diner that she likes," said Tony. "I don't know the number to that diner."

"Yeah, but she got a job," said Bobby.

Tony looked at the ceiling. "So?"

"Well since she got that job, she got uppity and got one of those cell phones," said Bobby.

"I don't know the number," huffed Tony.

"I do," said Bobby.

Tony froze for a moment. He looked at Bobby confused. "You know something useful?"

"I know her cell number."

Tony looks up at the roof baring his teeth. "Then call her!"

Bobby looked at Tony somewhat confused for a moment. He shrugged, went to the phone and started punching in the number.

"Sometimes he amazes me," said Tony. He looked at Angelica completely baffled. "He just…sometimes he…well you know."

"Yeah," said Angelica dryly.

Bobby stared off at nothing then finally: "Hey Sophie, this is Bobby

…Hunh?…You gave me your cell number…Of course I remembered it…I called you din't I?…What? Oh, do you know where Lucy is?… Angie, she got a problem…"

Tony grabbed the phone. "Sorry, Sophia, this is Tony. Angelica got herself...a bit of a...crisis and she needs some help...No, I can't help her, it's a." He cleared his throat. "...female problem...No, I don't want to talk about it over the phone...We are at Luciana's apartment right now and...Look, could you come over here or find Luciana and get her to come over here?...No! I'm not gonna talk about it over the phone...Luciana is where?...You got the number?... No, I don't have the number off the top of my head...I don't know if I ever knew the number to St. Mark's Cathedral...Wait, if she's there, then she's farther away then you are...Look, Angie needs some help and...No, I'm not gonna talk about it over the phone...Do you want me telling your problems over the phone?...Please, come over here and help Angie or get Luciana. PLEASE!"

"I know the number to St. Mark's," said Bobby.

Tony stared at Bobby. "Half the time, you can't even find your own apartment - but phone numbers you always remember." Tony shook his head and then stared at Bobby in disbelief. "What goes on between those ears?"

Bobby took the phone back and hung it up. He picked it up and started punching in numbers again. Before he could do anything else Tony took the phone from him again.

"Hello, is this St. Mark's?...Yeah, this is Antonio Carlucci. Is my sister Luciana there? I need to talk to her...Yes, you could say that it is important - to Angelica...Please, let me talk to Luciana." He lowered his head and shook his fist. He took several deep breaths and waited. "What?

...Yeah, Lucy! Hey, we need you to come back to your apartment for something…Yes, it's important…No, I don't want to tell you over the phone…No, Angie needs you…*real* bad…Look, she's having a certain female crisis…No, she don't want me to talk about it over the phone…Please!…I know you're doing something important, but what's Poppa always saying? Huh? Family comes first…Thank you!" He hung up the phone and growled. He looked at Angelica. "Okay, one or both of them is coming. Don't ask me when they're gonna get here, I don't know."

"I hope it's soon," said Saddle desperately.

Bobby looked at Saddle angrily. "What? You got some kind of problem? You in a hurry to get somewhere?"

Saddle looked despondently at Bobby. "No, nothing major. I have a young woman 'stuck' on my shoulder and I need to go to the bathroom - badly."

"So what's stopping you from going to the bathroom?"

Saddle closed his eyes and made a strange sound in his throat. "I had a hard enough time, coming up those stairs…with her… enthroned on my shoulder. I can't even figure out the logistics of trying to relieve myself while balancing her up there. If I were to lose my balance and fall…I don't even want to think about that."

Bobby looked threatening. "Yeah? Well, you hurt my sister and I'll…"

Both Angelica and Tony shouted together. "Bobby, shaddap!"

Bobby looked at both of them confused for a moment. He got a look of frustration on his face. He huffed took off his coat and sat down on the couch next to Rudy and started pouting.

Saddle looked off to the side. "Do we have any idea how soon either of the sisters will get here? "

Tony growled. "Whoever gets here, gets here when she gets here."

"Well that really narrows it down," said Saddle flatly. He put his knees together and grimaced in pain.

"I gotta ask," said Tony. "How…did you…why…did you… are you…up on his shoulder?"

Angelica groaned. "I walked up onto the platform. I thought I saw a snake. I ran to the only human on the platform for help."

Tony looked up with his arms spread out as if asking some heavenly being for help. "Snake?!" He shook his head. "In New York City? In March? A snake?"

"Angie is scared of snakes," said Bobby in an informative way.

Tony looked at Bobby with his mouth wide open "No kidding? How did you figure that one out?"

"Ever since you scared her when she was little, with that rubber snake, she's always…"

"I know!" shouted Tony. "I was being sarcastic." He looked back at Angelica. "What made you think that there was a snake…in New York…on an el…in March?"

Angelica hung her head. "It looked like a snake," she said sadly.

Tony went through a few hand gestures and facial expressions trying to think of something to say. Finally all he did was look down and say: "Unbelievable."

They hear the key in the door. They hear the door open. In walks a rather short woman. She is bundled up in a black leather coat that has a fur lined hood. She has black snow boots that go all the way up under the coat. She looks around the room to see who is here and what is going on. When she sees Angelica and Saddle, her face freezes in a dumb looking stare. She looks at Tony. "What is this?" She - like her siblings - has a strong New York accent.

Tony smiles. "Hello Sophia. That is the crisis. The two of them are stuck together."

"Stuck…? How…? What…?"

"Body piercings," said Bobby.

Sophia looks at Saddle horrified. "What kind of an idiot are you? Who pierces their shoulders?"

Saddle rolls his eyes and lets out a grunt in disbelief.

"He didn't pierce anything," said Bobby.

Sophia looked at Bobby confused. "Well that would mean that Angie…" She opens her eyes wide in shock. "Holy freak show! Angie, you didn't…I mean…" She furrowed her brows in concern. "Did you?"

With her eyes closed and a pained look on her face, Angelica simply nodded.

"You pierced your…you…uh…down there…your…*body*?"

"That's what happened," said Saddle in a merrily sarcastic

way.

Sophia took off her coat, revealing a light grey business outfit. She tossed the coat over the back of the couch. "So why don't you pull the silly things out and unstick yourself?"

Saddle started up: "She can't…"

Sophia immediately snapped at Saddle. "I'm not talking to you! I'm talking to my sister!"

Saddle looked off to his right a little exasperated.

"I can't reach them. Everything is in the way. I need help getting them out."

Sophia looked around the room, realizing that she was the only other female in the room. "You don't mean me…do you?"

Rudy started laughing again.

"I think she does," said Bobby. "Especially since Lucy ain't here."

Tony smacked Bobby in the back of the head. "She ain't no dummy, DUMMY! She knows that."

Sophia looked a little sick. "But how…? I mean why…can't you reach…whatever those things are?"

Angelica looked and sounded as if she were going to cry. "I can't reach around his head and my dress and my underwear."

"Well tell him to get his fat head out of the way."

Saddle gave Sophia a dull stare.

"It's not that easy," moaned Angelica. "I've tried. I just can't see what I'm doing and..." Her voice trailed off and her face turned red.

Sophia put her hands up against her head. She shook her head a little with her eyes closed and her mouth open. She threw her hands down to her sides. "How do you put the silly things in? Do you use a...?" She suddenly got a strange look of horror on her face. "...a mirror?"

Rudy started laughing even harder. Tony started giggling. Angelica turned even redder. Saddle tried to get his head away from her and moaned painfully as he did it.

Sophia continued with a look of total disgust on her face. "What do you do? Do you sit there on the bathroom counter, spread out to the mirror and...? What do you do?"

Angelica sat there with her fists and teeth clenched up against her chest. "I put a mirror on a stool and I stand over the chair as I put them in." She looked at Sophia angrily. "Are you happy now?"

Now Bobby joined the other two men in the laughter that got louder and uncontrollable.

Sophia put her right hand up to her forehead and closed her eyes. "Holy freak show!"

"Please," pleaded Angelica. "Can you help me?"

With her head arched slightly forward and a bit of a scowl on her face, Sophia started slowly walking towards the couple with her arms clenched tightly to the side of her body. She came up to the right side of Saddle and looked up at Angelica with her teeth bared. "Oh, you are gonna owe me!" She shook her head. "Oh yeah, big sister, you are gonna *really* owe me on this one."

Angelica whimpered a little.

Saddle sniffed and scratched his nose. He looked down and sighed.

Sophia slowly walked over to the "couple". She reached up and lifted Angelica's dress. She started to reach for the panties and looked back at the couch where the three men were seated. The trio had stopped laughing and were looking, with huge grins, at what was transpiring.

"What are you lookin' at ya perverts?" Sophia glared at all three. "Get out there in the hallway. This ain't no two-bit peep show."

"But you might need some help," said Bobby.

Tony slapped Bobby in the back of the head. With his teeth clenched, he angrily grabbed both Bobby and Rudy by the hair on the back of their heads. "Come on! Let her do what she has to do without no audience." He dragged both men out into the hallway, where all of a sudden the laughter started up again - very loud laughter from all three.

Angelica looked up and shook her head. She had a pained look on her face. A tear trickled down her right cheek.

Sophia took hold of the waistband of Angelica's panties and pulled them down a little. She stopped and looked at Saddle. "Get your fat head out of the way," she snapped.

Saddle tried to duck his head down by his right shoulder even further. "I'm doing everything I can to stay out of the way," he said calmly.

"Yeah right," she said impatiently. "You're probably enjoying this in some perverted way."

He let a small growl escape from his throat.

"And don't you dare, be staring at my breasts," she scolded.

He raised his head and glared at her. "I swear to you, by all that is holy, I am not enjoying this situation in any way, shape or form. Nor, do I have any reason to stare at your breasts."

She glared back at him. "For some reason, I can't believe you. You seem to have a very dishonest face. Now, keep your fat head out of the way, so I can see what I'm doing."

He closed his eyes and lowered his head as far down as he could.

She pulled the panties down further. She peered in looking for the piercings. "I can't see a thing." She huffed a couple of times in frustration as she was attempting to ascertain anything that could be done. She looked up. "Hey Angie, can you raise up a little?"

Angelica tried to lift herself a little. "I can't! I'm up as far as I can get," she moaned.

Sophia huffed again. "Hey you, Saddle, try hunching down a little."

As Saddle tried to cooperate, Angelica yelped in pain.

"Don't do that," Angelica pleaded. "Don't do that, you're stretching me out of shape."

Sophia let out a growl of frustration. "I need some room to see what I'm doing and see what's…in there. If you two don't separate a little bit, then I can't see anything."

Saddle looked up at Sophia. "Why don't you try going in from behind?"

Sophia opened her mouth to protest and then stopped herself. She stared off to the side in contemplation. She shrugged. "That might just work. Then, at least, I don't have to worry about your fat head being in the way." She sniffed and then walked around behind Angelica. With a disgusted look on her face she peered down at Angelica's derriere. She looked toward heaven and crossed herself. She sighed, reached down and raised Angelica's dress. She then pulled the panties down while grimacing. She peered carefully into the "area" of importance. "All I can see is your butt," she said dejectedly. She sighed. "Someone is gonna have to shine a flashlight up there in order for me to see what's where."

Angelica moaned in frustration.

Saddle just sighed.

"We may have to wait until Lucy gets here…or maybe call Mamma," said Sophia.

Angelica looked at Sophia with terror in her eyes. "Don't you dare call Mamma! She'll kill me!"

Sophia snapped the waistband against Angelica's rear end. "Well then that leaves Lucy. We'll have to wait till she gets here…if she is coming that is."

Both Angelica and Saddle moaned.

Sophia headed for the hallway. "Hey Tony, did you call Luciana?"

Tony wiped some tears from his eyes as he was snickering. "Uh, yeah! I called her as well. I don't know when she's gonna be here."

"Well, I hope it's soon, because I can't do this alone."

All three men went into a new spasm of laughter.

At that moment the door comes open. Another woman walks in. She looks like a slightly taller version of Sophia. She sheds a large blue coat revealing a white silk formal dress. She looks at the three laughing men with a totally perplexed and somewhat suspicious expression. "Okay," she snapped. "So what's so important that you gotta get me back here? I get here and you jokers are laughing your heads off. If this is one of your stupid jokes…I swear Tony, I will kick you where it hurts you the most."

"Hey Lucy baby," said Rudy merrily. "How ya doin'?"

"Don't 'baby' me, you jerk. I love you, but this had better not be some joke." She like the rest of her family had a strong New York accent. She walks over to the thermostat on the wall. "It's cold in here." She adjusts the dial and immediately the heater kicks in.

Tony points towards the living room while still giggling in an uncontrollable manner.

"I'm not going anywhere until you three knuckleheads stop laughing and tell me what's going on. And what are you doing here anyway? Why ain't any of you at St. Mark's today?"

Rudy gets his laughing down to a controlled chuckle. "Why?

What's going on at St. Mark's…today?"

Luciana's jaw dropped. She smacked Rudy on the top of his head. "We were supposed to be welcoming the new priest to St. Mark's today."

All three men stop laughing and look at her more seriously.

Tony looked at her puzzled. "What's wrong with the old one, Father Jenkins?"

Luciana snarled at Tony. "Just that. Old! Father Jenkins is eighty-five years old."

The three men look at each other even more puzzled.

Rudy shrugged his shoulders. "So?"

"Haven't any of you three clowns been to mass lately? Huh? Don't you remember what happened two weeks ago?"

Tony gives her a sheepish smile. "Uh…no."

She held her hands up with her mouth open and looked heavenward. "Two weeks ago, Father Jinx was giving his sermon. He stopped. Everybody thought that he was pausing for affect. But he doesn't start up again. Then we hear snoring. Everyone thought that it was that Polish butcher who always sits in the third row. You know the guy who is always falling asleep. Even his wife thought that it was him. She punches him in the side and then we all realize that it's not the butcher, but Father Jenkins who has fallen asleep - right in the middle of his own sermon. Now, finally some of those Bishops realize that Father Jenkins needs to retire."

"Okay," said Rudy. "What's that got to do with today? Why

should we be at St. Mark's today?"

With her fists clenched at her side she puts her face right up to Rudy and practically screams at him. "To welcome the new Priest!" She stands there breathing hard for a few moments while all three of the men glance back and forth at each other with guilty looks on their faces.

Tony chuckles nervously. "Well, did you have a nice time welcoming him?"

Her shoulders dropped. She looks at Tony sideways. "He never showed up. There's about fifteen people looking all over the place for him. They had him check into some hotel for the night and he was supposed to come in early this morning. We were gonna have a welcoming ceremony and give him the grand tour, but…well we don't know where he is."

Bobby looked around at the others. "Well can't Father Jinx carry on for a few more weeks?"

Luciana smacked Bobby on his forehead. "He's not just old, he's getting senile."

Rudy looked a little worried. "Are you sure?"

Luciana took in a deep breath and then let it out slowly. "Yes, I am sure. We are all sure. We are sure because, Father Jenkins now thinks that Moses was the father of Abraham *and* King David."

"That don't sound right," said Bobby.

All three, Luciana, Tony and Rudy looked at Bobby aghast. They all looked up and crossed themselves.

Even though she was at least five inches shorter then Tony, Luciana stuck her face as close to his as she could. "Now, what is so all fired important - and you cannot discuss it over the phone - that I have to come here and possibly miss meeting the new Priest?"

Tony just pointed towards the living room.

She gave Rudy an evil glance. "If you two have cooked up some prank…"

Rudy put his hands up. "I swear to you baby, this is no trick. We are not trying to pull anything on you. What happened here - none of us three had anything to do wit it."

Luciana started slowly walking towards the living room. She kept her eyes on the three men looking for some "telling" smirk or smile. She turned her gaze towards the living room and stopped in her tracks when she saw Sophia standing there with her hands on her hips. With a puzzled look she said: "Do you know what's going on?"

Sophia beckoned Luciana with her right index finger and then pointed into the living room. Now Luciana's curiosity (and suspicion) was really growing.

With a frown on her face Luciana marched forward. "If you people are playing some joke on me, I swear that heads will…" She stopped and stared stupidly at the strange couple in her favorite overstuffed chair. When she finally was able to re-engage her brain, she looked around at some of the other people in the apartment and then back at the couple. "What are you two doing?"

"They're stuck together," said Sophia informatively.

Luciana looked at Sophia baffled. She opened her mouth

trying to think of something to say. "What? Stuck? How...do you get stuck...?" She looked at Angelica and then Saddle. "Stuck?"

"There are some body piercings," said Sophia.

Now Luciana looked horrified. "Body piercings?" She looked at the ridiculous positioning of the two. She looked at Saddle. "What kind of a perverted moron are you? Body piercings in your shoulder?"

Saddle covered his eyes with his right hand. "In...credible," he said helplessly.

The three men in the hallway went into a new wave of uncontrollable laughter.

Luciana looked at the men dismayed. "What is so stinkin' funny?"

Sophia tapped Luciana on the shoulder. "It's not the man who has the piercings. It's our big sister who has the piercings."

Luciana looked at Sophia and then the couple totally astounded. She looked again helplessly at the three men laughing in the hallway. She looked back at the couple and a now had total disgust on her face. "Oh! Oh! Oh! You...my big sister...you...Oh! You pierced your... Oh!" She was flapping her arms up and down and spinning around as she vented. "How could you...Oh! Oh! That's...Oh! What were you thinking?" She covered her face with her hands for a few moments. She then let her arms drop by her side. She continued staring at the couple totally bewildered. A form of cogitation came across her face and then she looked at Sophia. "So, what am I supposed to do?"

Sophia licked her lips and then raised her eyebrows. She gave Luciana as sweet a smile that she could muster and said: "It seems that because of the position that she is in, she can't get to the piercings and get them unstuck. She needs our help to separate the two of them."

Luciana looked totally revolted now. She glared at Angelica. "You want me to stick my hands up in your...you want me to...ARE YOU CRAZY?"

"She can't do it herself. She needs our help," said Sophia flatly.

"I think I may throw up," said Luciana.

"Please," wailed Angelica. "Please help me. I got no one else to turn to."

Luciana shook her head. "What did you say to Father Jenkins in confession? I mean...you defiled your body. What kind of penance did he give you for this?"

"I lied to him," said Angelica angrily. "I told him that I had one piercing...somewhere else. He...well he made me do some penance and...that was it. I didn't tell him that there were eight of them...or where."

"You lied in confession? Do you have any idea how serious that is?" Sophia and Luciana were both looking at Angelica in horror.

Angelica was getting impatient. "Will you please stop trying to evaluate and get us unstuck?"

Luciana looked at Sophia. "Why didn't you...unstick them?"

"I tried," said Sophia with her eyes closed. "There is a problem. It can't be done alone."

"Uh...why not?"

"We need a flashlight, and more than two hands."

"I think I'm gonna be sick."

"Yeah, well save it for later. Let's get this dirty work out of the way and then you can be sick."

"You said that we need a flashlight?"

"Yeah, there isn't enough light…to see up between…"

"You mean, up between her… I think I'm gonna be sick."

"You got a flashlight?"

"Yeah, in my bedroom, in the nightstand on the right side of the bed."

"I'll get the flashlight and you can see what I saw while I get the light."

"I think I'm gonna be sick."

"You can be sick later, go take a look."

"So, how do we get his head out of the way?"

Sophia sighed. "We go in from behind."

"I think I'm gonna be sick."

"Go take a look," growled Sophia.

Luciana walked behind Angelica. She closed her eyes and crossed herself. She lifted up Angelica's dress and took hold of the waistband of the panties. She pulled them down and took a look. "I know I'm gonna be sick." She sighed. She let go of Angelica's clothing and held her hands up. "I can't do this. I can't put my hands up...I can't do this."

Angelica sighed. "Don't you have some rubber gloves?"

"How'd you know about that box of rubber gloves?"

"You told me about it when you had that yeast infec..."

"SHADDAP! You don't have to tell the whole world about that."

Angelica was sitting there with her teeth clenched. "Do you still have the rubber gloves?"

Luciana sighed. "Yeah. I'll go get em."

Luciana passed Sophia coming the other way out of the bedroom.

"Where you goin?" said Sophia.

"To get some rubber gloves," said Luciana despondently.

Sophia's jaw dropped for a moment. She stood there thinking and then quietly said: "Good idea."

Luciana came back out with a box of latex gloves. She pulled two out and started putting them on. Sophia pulled out a pair and began donning them as well. They both split the fingers of the gloves with their fingernails.

"Oh no," said Sophia. "Am I gonna have to cut my nails in order to do this? I ain't cutting my nails for this."

Angelica moaned.

Saddle cleared his throat. "Don't pull the gloves completely down on your fingers. Pull them on just enough to where you can work. Then put another pair of gloves on top of that. Does that help?"

Both women looked at each other thoughtfully. They shrugged simultaneously and then started the double-gloving. After the glove preparations the stared at each other for a moment.

"So," said Luciana. "Who is gonna hold the flashlight?"

"I'll tell you what," said Sophia. "You do the ones on your side and I'll do the ones on my side."

Luciana looked up helplessly. Her shoulders sagged. She crossed herself again and sniffed. "Okay. Let's...do this."

Sophia got ready with the flashlight. Luciana crossed herself again, she pulled the dress up. Sophia pulled the panties down and shined the light in the "appropriate" area. They saw that the rings were open with one end stuck in Angelica and the other end stuck in Saddle's coat.

"This is disgusting," said Luciana. She heard some giggling off in the hallway. She dropped the dress back down. "Get outta here you perverts! We don't need an audience."

The three men retreated back into the hallway with more gales of laughter.

Luciana grunted. She lifted the dress back up and sighed. She made an attempt at dislodging the first ring. "It ain't working," she huffed. "We need a fifth hand. I can't hold the dress up and get the ring out."

"Why don't you tape the dress up?" said Saddle.

Dara J. Carr

"Stay outta this," huffed Sophia.

Then both women looked at each other somewhat slack-jawed.

"That's a good idea," said Luciana.

"Uh, yeah, I guess it is," said Sophia. "Uh…thanks for the suggestion."

"You are more than welcome," said Saddle in a calm manner.

Luciana went back into her bedroom. She came back with a tape dispenser. She tore off a strip and while making the attempt at taping the dress up, the tape stuck to the latex gloves and tore them. Luciana growled in frustration, tore the gloves off, taped the dress up and then put another set of double-gloves on.

As Luciana looked closely into the "area", a loud pop is heard as she smacks Angelica's bare bottom. Angelica lets out a surprised yelp. "If you ever do something like this again," said Luciana, "I swear, you're on your own."

While they were working, Angelica went through a few mental and physical gyrations as she turned at least fifteen different shades of red. She was also looking towards the hallway to make sure that the men were not trying to sneak another peak at what was going on.

The first one was brought out. Luciana stared at it in horror. "Two inch hoops? You got eight, two inch hoops in your…panties? No wonder they went all the way through his coat."

Angelica hung her head and groaned.

"Excuse me, Angie," said Saddle. "You're digging your fingernails into my scalp."

470

Angelica pulled her hands away from his head and gasped. "Sorry," she said in a small voice.

The two workers both gave sounds of frustration and disgust as they extracted more of the hoops.

"What's the matter?" asked Angelica. "Why haven't you got all of them?"

"Those two front ones," said Sophia. "We can't reach them from back here. We're gonna have to go in from the front on those."

Angelica sighed.

"Don't worry," said Saddle. "I'll do everything I can to keep my fat head out of the way."

"Well you keep looking down," said Angelica. "Don't you look at me."

Saddle sighed. "Well, if I happen to see something that I have never seen before, then I won't know what it is and it really shouldn't bother you or me."

Angelica grunted in disgust. "Get something to cover his eyes."

Luciana quickly went into the bedroom and came back out with a pillowcase. She put it around Saddle's head and taped it into place. Then they went through the task of taping the dress up and pulling the last two rings out.

Once the final ring was out, Angelica grunted and groaned as she dismounted from Saddle.

"I desperately need to go to the bathroom," said Saddle.

"Where is it, please?"

"I gotta go too," said Angelica. "I gotta go real bad."

"Ladies first," said Saddle dejectedly. He then groaned in pain, pulled his knees together and started rocking back and forth a little.

Luciana and Sophia helped Angelica into the bathroom which was right off of the living room and then came back out.

"Okay, you bums can come back in here," shouted Luciana.

Saddle heard her relieving herself and looked back at the opening in shock. He looked around the room. "Don't you have a door for your bathroom?"

Luciana put her hands on her hips and looked at Bobby. "I used to," she said while giving Bobby an accusing look. "Somebody had a temper tantrum. Over what, I don't know. But he still hasn't fixed it."

All the people in the room looked at Bobby who flushed and chuckled nervously.

Sophia looked at Saddle. "There was one day when…"

Saddle held up his hands. "That's quite all right! I don't really think I need to know. It's something in your family and not my business."

When the "noise" from the bathroom ended, Sophia looked towards the bathroom. After several moments of awkward silence she speaks up: "Are you okay, in there?"

"My legs are cramped," cried Angelica in anguish. "I need

some help."

"Please hurry," begged Saddle as he rubs his, now free, left shoulder.

Luciana huffed as she headed into the bathroom. "What is that? What are you doing? Oh good grief! Get a pad."

"You tore something open," moaned Angelica.

"Well whose fault is that? If you hadn't done…that…thing on your…thingy, then this would have never happened. Here, here's a pad. Put it on. Hurry up, so that guy doesn't do his business out there. Okay, now get your panties back on. Good, let's go."

Luciana helped Angelica out of the bathroom and Saddle made a beeline into the bathroom.

While the people in the room heard the sound of urination and a loud contented sigh coming out of the bathroom, they all looked around wondering just exactly what to say. Any form of admonishment aimed at Angelica could not possibly punish her as much as she was mentally kicking herself right now.

But of course, egos will get in the way.

"I still can't believe that you did something that stupid," huffed Luciana.

"Yeah, that was really, really stupid," said Sophia.

"Oh, you got a lot of room to talk," shouted Angelica.

Both Luciana and Sophia looked around with their arms spread wide.

Luciana spoke up first: "Like, for instance…what?"

"You and Rudy," scolded Angelica. "You two are having sex and you're not married."

Luciana's looked wide eyed in shock at Angelica. "How did you know…?" She looked at Rudy. "You big-mouthed vulgarian. You been bragging about it."

"No, I haven't." said Rudy in surprise. "I ain't said nothing."

Luciana was heading towards Rudy, ready for full physical combat. "Then, how could she possibly know?"

"You got a key on your front door," shouted Sophia. "Angie and me come in one day. We saw your clothes scattered all along the hallway. We come into the living room and the two of you was doing it right here on the living room floor. If you don't want people to come walking in on you, you shouldn't leave the key out there."

Tony headed towards Rudy, in a rage, with his fists ready. "You been humpin' my sister?"

"Who are you to criticize? You're doing the Bocatelli twins - both of them," shouted Rudy.

Sophia stood there in shock. "Both of them?"

"Yeah," said Rudy. "Both of them - at the same time."

Tony was momentarily stunned. "How'd you know that?"

"Because I heard them talking at Mancuso's diner." said Rudy. "The two of them are hoping, that one of these days, you make up your mind which one you like better, so's the other one can go find a man of her own."

Angelica looked accusingly at Tony. "So, what did you tell Father Jinx in confession? Did you tell him how you're poking two different women - neither of which you are married to?"

"Are you crazy? I didn't tell him I was in bed with them. I'd be doing penance from now until I'm an old man."

Sophia sat down on the couch and giggled a little.

Tony looked at Sophia with anger in his eyes. "Oh yeah, laugh it up, like you're so innocent."

Sophia stood up angrily put her fists on her hips and waved her head back and forth as she scolded back: "I ain't jumpin' in bed with nobody, so what have I got to be ashamed of?"

With a deadpan look on his face Tony came back: "How many times have I had to drag your drunk butt home, hold your hair behind your head while you puked up all that rotgut whiskey and then put your passed out carcass in bed? You're only nineteen years old and you're already nearly as bad a drunk as that Irish family that owns that bar you go into. Now, did you confess about your *underage* drinking?"

With a pained look on her face, Sophia sat down on the couch and pulled her knees up to her chest. "No," she said timidly.

"You drink too," said Bobby to Tony.

"I'm legally old enough," shouted Tony. "Plus, I never got so hammered, that I needed someone to take me home."

Bobby scoffed. "Sex fiends and drunks, all of you."

"Well you ain't so perfect," shouted Luciana. "You're just a big, stupid bully. How many times you been arrested for assault?

Huh?"

"Well they ain't put me in jail for it!"

"No," said Angelica. "Because you got the brains of a five-year-old and so you keep getting off because of diminished capacity. You won't listen to any of us, when you get mad. You ain't had no reason to hit any of those people, other then you lose your temper over nuthin', and then we gotta go and explain it to people, how dumb you are. Did you ever confess to Father Jenkins, as to why you attacked those people?"

"No way! Father Jinx would have made me go apologize to all those cruds, what I busted their heads. I don't apologize to nobody."

"All right! Enough!" Luciana shouted. "Look, let's stop chewing on each other and maybe try to help find out where this new Priest is."

Sophia looked up at Luciana. "Why is it so important to you that you gotta be part of the welcoming committee? You ain't no bigwig in the church."

"Look, ever since I accidentally started that fire, where they had to replace five of the pews, I been on Father Jinx bad list. Okay, so I'm gonna do a little brown-nosing with the new Priest and maybe I can get outta the dog house."

Bobby looked confused. "How'd you start a fire in the pews?"

"She was tryin' to learn how to smoke cigarettes," snickered Tony. "...and somehow sprayed *way* too much lighter fluid, all over the place, while tryin' to fill up her lighter. When she flicked the lighter - *Poof*!"

"But it was the confession booth that burned up," said Bobby.

"That's where it started." Tony chuckled. "She didn't tell nobody, until the confessional *and* some of the pews was gloriously in flames."

"It was an accident, and it was ten years ago. I was only thirteen at the time. I been doing penance ever since." pleaded Luciana. "Now, I'm trying to get in a good start with this new Priest. He doesn't know about the fire and I'm hoping that Father Jinx don't tell him."

Tony growled. "You keep saying: New Priest, new Priest, new Priest - what's the guy's name?"

Luciana stuck out her lower lip and looked down pouting. "I can't pronounce it."

A chorus of "Huh?" was aimed at Luciana.

She walked over to her coat, pulled a pamphlet out of the pocket and handed it to Tony. "Nobody seems to know how to pronounce his last name. We was all hoping that when he got there, he would introduce himself and then we'd know."

Tony took the pamphlet, with an air of superiority. He looked down his nose as he scanned the pamphlet. "Hokay, let's see…usher in a new era…Father Jenkins is ready to retire…so we welcome this new Priest… who graduated from Notre Dame." He gave a shrug and nod of approval. "…his name is…Father Raymond…" Tony stopped cold and looked totally baffled. He cleared his throat nervously. He opened and closed his eyes, several times. He held the paper out at arm's length. His lips moved several times as if he were trying to say something. Then turned his head sideways, while still looking at the

Dara J. Carr

pamphlet. He turned the pamphlet upside down. He now had a look of total loss on his face. "Gee, I don't know." He shook his head again. "Has anybody got any kind of guess?"

Angelica scoffed at Tony. "Well genius - why don't you try it?"

Tony looked a little guilty, then nervous. He raised his eyebrows as he again looked at the pamphlet. He shrugged. "Make a civic? Mass a cavick? ...Uh, Messy cave in?"

"Lemme see that thing," said Rudy. He grabbed the pamphlet and stared with a blank expression for several moments.

"So..." said Tony, "...Mr. Know-it-all - how would you pronounce that?"

Rudy slowly turned his gaze to Tony. "Wrong," he said helplessly.

Sophie grabbed the pamphlet. "Let's see - M, A, C, E, C, E, V, I, C. Her face changed to confusion. "Holy Crap! Why can't people have normal names? This looks like he's some jerk from Lithuania or Romania or Bulgaria. These eastern European names are so crazy."

From the bathroom they all heard: "The first syllable is Muh - rhymes with duh. The second syllable is Seh - rhymes with Yeah. The third syllable is suh - rhymes, again, with duh. The fourth syllable is Vick - rhymes with sick. The emphasis is on the second syllable: muh - SEH - suh - vick."

Tony looked around the room somewhat confused. Then with an air of superiority, he said: "So, what makes you the expert, on this name?"

Out of the bathroom came Saddle, drying his hands on a cloth. Minus his coat and now showing that he was wearing "the Roman Collar". "I think that I should be able to pronounce my own name: Father Raymond Macecevic, at your service." With that he gave a slight, polite bow.

Everyone in the room sank to their knees with looks of anguish and terror on their faces, crossing themselves as they went down.

Father Raymond looked around at the worried faces around him with a huge friendly smile. "Well, well, well. What have we here? Arsonist, bully, fornicators, alcoholics and one who defiles her body. All of them joined together by those three magic words: Don't tell Mom!" He clasped his hands behind his back. "The Lord works in mysterious ways, his wonders to behold. I was wondering when she jumped on my shoulder, this morning, where was the Lord leading me? My, my, my. Don't we have a situation?"

"You're not gonna tell anybody," said Tony helplessly. "I mean if we say that this is under the 'Sacrament of Reconciliation,'…I mean, you can't tell anybody."

"No," said Father Raymond, with a big smile. "…but…you are."

There is a loud chorus: "WHAT!?"

Father Raymond clears his throat. "Since you are claiming this as part of the 'Sacrament of Reconciliation,' that means that I have to declare what your penance will be."

Now there is a loud chorus of groans.

"Where do I start? Let's see…Bobby! Yes, you are going to

have to go to all the people 'what heads you busted,' and definitely apologize."

Bobby looked at him horrified. "All of them?"

"Oh, yes, all of them."

"But...but...but...I don't remember all of who they is."

"The cops can give you all forty-two names," said Tony glumly.

Father Raymond looked at Bobby in shock. "FORTY-TWO?"

Bobby shrunk down closer to the floor grimacing. "I lose my temper a lot."

Father Raymond crossed himself. "You are also going to be enrolled in an anger management class.   Tony, you should help him, you seem to be able to control his rage."

Tony's shoulders dropped and he had a helpless look on his face. "Do you know how long that's gonna take?"

"Long enough, where you should be able to make some kind of decision about those sisters. Which one you're going to marry and which one you're going to stay away from - permanently! Plus, in the meantime, you don't touch either one of them, until you are married. Then of course, you never touch the other one again - no matter what."

Tony closed his eyes and then looked off to the side looking as if he had some horrible taste in his mouth.

"You also need to repair a certain door in your sister's home."

Bobby grunted a sort of consent.

"Oh, by the way - are those twin sisters part of my parish?"

"Yeah," said Sophia.

"Good, I'll have a little talk with them, as well."

Tony was kneeling already. Now his forehead was on the floor as well as he groaned in misery.

Father Raymond pursed his lips in thought. "I will need to find out from Father Jinx - or your parents - what the penance was that you were given for burning down the confessional...and the pews." He looked at Luciana smiling. "Then of course, there is your acts of fornication. We'll have to come up with something new for that."

Rudy tried to make himself small and slink away.

"No, I'm not forgetting you...Rudy. Are you part of my parish as well?"

Rudy looked up disgusted and nodded.

"Well, we are going to have a few discussions about your penance as well."

Rudy looked down at the floor and growled as he shook his head.

Father Raymond licked his lips. "Underage drinking?"

Sophia cringed and ducked her head down with her hands on the back of her head.

"Do the people who serve you...know that you are only 19 years old?"

"No," she said meekly.

"Well, you're going to tell them."

Now Sophia's forehead was on the floor.

"And, of course you are going to STOP consuming alcoholic beverages."

Sophia whimpered again.

"And of course, let's not forget the one, who started this ball rolling. Angelica." He shook his head. "The name means: *Little angel.* That doesn't sound like someone who exposed herself, in order to defile her own body."

Angelica whimpered. "I wasn't going to show them to anybody and I didn't expose myself."

"You had to expose yourself in order for those piercings to be done. Don't tell me that it was done in the dark...or by some blind person. Someone had to be able to see what and where the holes were going to be poked." In a flat commanding voice Father Raymond told her: "Lose the rings, let your body heal and don't ever do anything like that again." He let all of what he had said sink in for a few moments, while the rest of the room was whimpering and gnashing their teeth. "Now, I'm going to have to think of what other penance you should be doing."

Another combined chorus of: "There's more?"

"I am also hearing about fabrications and half-truths being told IN the confessional. This is the Sacrament of Reconciliation! It is to be taken seriously. Obviously you are NOT taking it seriously. So, yes, there will be more penance, so that you will realize the gravity of the situation."

"Just a little more," said Luciana in a small voice. "I mean…"

Father Raymond was indignant. "Little!?"

"Okay, a couple of things," said Angelica helplessly.

Again Father Raymond looked indignant. "Couple!?"

"Let me guess," said Rudy. "The mind boggles."

Father Raymond gave an evil chuckle. "*You* are getting warm."

Again a chorus of groans.

"Yes," said Father Raymond. "I see that I am going to have an interesting time with this family. What started out in a mysterious fashion has turned into a very informative day. Isn't the Lord God… just wonderfully mysterious in his ways?"

www.ingramcontent.com/pod-product-compliance
Lightning Source LLC
Chambersburg PA
CBHW060756030726
47503CB00002B/268